To GWR, for everything

the love wars

L. Alison Heller

NEW AMERICAN LIBRARY

New American Library
Published by the Penguin Group
Penguin Group (USA) Inc., 375 Hudson Street,
New York, New York 10014, USA

USA | Canada | UK | Ireland | Australia | New Zealand | India | South Africa | China
Penguin Books Ltd., Registered Offices: 80 Strand, London WC2R 0RL, England
For more information about the Penguin Group visit penguin.com.

First published by New American Library,
a division of Penguin Group (USA) Inc.

First Printing, May 2013

 REGISTERED TRADEMARK—MARCA REGISTRADA

LIBRARY OF CONGRESS CATALOGING-IN-PUBLICATION DATA:
Heller, L. Alison.
The love wars/L. Alison Heller.
p. cm.
ISBN 978-0-451-41623-0
1. Women lawyers—Fiction.   2. Mother and child—Fiction.
3. Manhattan (New York, N.Y.)—Fiction.   I. Title.
PS3608.E453L68 2013
813'.6—dc23   2012028342

Printed in the United States of America
10 9 8 7 6 5 4 3 2 1

Set in Walbaum MT STD
Designed by Alissa Amell

acknowledgments

Thank you to the wonderful Elisabeth Weed for believing in me and for being wise and fun in equal measure. And also to Dana Murphy and Stephanie Sun.

The excellent Kerry Donovan—working with you is so darn enjoyable that I feel like I'm getting away with something. (And I suppose I am because of how much better you've made this.) Thank you so much for working your magic in such a collaborative, affirming way. Thanks also to everyone at New American Library: Kara Welsh, Michele Alpern, Anthony Ramondo and Jesse Feldman.

To my smart early readers for their on-the-money comments: Alice Peck, Diane Simon, Jacqueline Newman.

For friendship, sustenance, letting me use your home as an office, lending an ear, sound advice, lovingly caring for my kids or otherwise helping me accomplish this dream (and, in some cases, all of the above): Alejandra Lara, Joanna and Kevin Constantino, Lori Dyan, Anne Joyce, Suzanne Myers, Michele Brown, Donna Karlin, Conrad Tree, Sabrina Eliasoph and Laura Dave. (Also, to One Girl Cookies DUMBO for great coffee, and an incredibly inviting writing space with too many treats.)

To my colleagues and clients from the matrimonial world, past and present, for friendship, humor, humanity and teaching me so much about law, life and New York.

Thanks to my family: the amazing Grandma Kay and the memory of Grandpa Lester. The generous and sharp Edith Roberts.

Samantha Heller, the best sister/reader known to woman, for being so supportive in all matters generally and this book specifically. Also, big hugs to the Heller-Bhattacharyya clan—Raj, Kannon and Dashiell—for your open-door policy with what I'm sure will remain the nicest and most convenient writing nook I've ever had the pleasure of using.

The fiercely loving Sue Ann Heller, my constant sounding board on this novel and all else. Your faith in me is a gift, as is your ability to help me digest life. And to Charles Heller—one of the most eloquent writers (and thinkers) I've ever known—we miss you every day.

And, of course, to Zoe, Gigi and Glen. Z&G, you're the magic in my life and I'm beyond grateful for you both. (Note, though: when I open my computer, I'm not trying to get you to play with me. Truly.) To Glen, thank you for all: your support, pride, solidity, laser-sharp smarts and for always, always being the funniest person I know. Even when it's the hour of savages at the Cheesecake Factory, you can still crack me up about it. And that's saying something.

Promises and pie crust are made to be broken.

—Jonathan Swift

the love wars

An opened three-pack of pastel-colored sticky notes triggers the fight in the kitchen. Our brawling, which has already swept through several rooms of the house, focuses on the small things: loose wedding photos; extra toilet paper rolls; the ordinary ceramic soap dish bought in happier times. Never mind that I've never set eyes on any of the stuff we're fighting about, or that I'm not actually part of this couple (or any other, for that matter). I'm here solely for the battle, to guard against, as my boss Lillian delicately put it, any *"hell hath no fury* burning and slashing shit."

Now, though, we've taken a sharp veer into the surreal. The kitchen—gleaming white marble countertops and floor tiles, six-burner stove, massive central island—should be the set for some celebrity chef concocting culinary masterpieces. Instead, it's where Stewart Billings is desperately trying to smuggle sticky notes into a garbage bag filled with his "personal items," those things he's allowed to take when he's booted out of this six-story town house (Central Park adjacent) later this afternoon, pursuant to the terms of the prenuptial agreement he signed seven years ago. The rest of us, two lawyers and his soon-to-be ex-wife, Liesel, watch him with various degrees of disbelief.

"Stewart. Sticky notes down," Liesel says, walking forward with her palm extended.

"But I bought them," he says, wiping his nose with his sleeve. "I remember doing it. I was deciding between these and—"

"Stewart, please. Have you ever really *bought* anything?" She presses her fingers against her palm, opening and closing them like a fourth-grade teacher commandeering a contraband video game.

I try to catch the eye of Erika, the other lawyer, but she is suddenly typing feverishly on her BlackBerry, wholly consumed.

Stewart blinks at me, fixing his features in a puppy dog pout. We've been at this for several hours, long enough that he's pegged me as the softy. Not that I have any real competition in this group.

Before I can respond, Liesel cuts in. "Megan is my lawyer, Stewart."

"Molly." I offer my third reminder of the day. "My name is Molly."

"Whatever. She's here to protect me from you, you idiot." She waves a hand at me. "Tell him."

I pause, trying to come up with a politic response for Liesel.

"Hello?" Liesel snaps her fingers in my direction. "Speak. Tell him you're here to protect me."

"I'm here to make sure the move goes smoothly." I am mortified at the squeak in my voice. "Why don't you split the sticky pads, maybe each take one and a half?"

Liesel snorts. "Thanks, Pollyanna, for that crackerjack legal analysis. Stewart, I'm warning you. Put them down."

Stewart, displaying a bravery I have not yet seen this morning, defies her, clutching the sticky pads with one hand and continuing to root around the drawer with the other.

I walk over to Erika and lower my voice. "Maybe one of us should run out to get another packet of notepads? It might help move things along."

Stewart, hearing me, drops the notes on the counter. "It's not about the sticky pads. It's the principle of this whole thing." His voice descends from a wail into a forlorn whimper. "The principle of this whole, incredibly fucked-up thing."

Oh Lord. Is he crying? Without thinking, I grab a tissue from my pocket and offer it to him. Luckily, Liesel misses my lapse into empathy; she's too busy staring at Stewart with frosty disdain. "Which incredibly fucked-up thing?" She flashes a harsh smile. "That you slept with your trainer? Or that your gravy train's ending?"

Unsurprisingly, Stewart does not look soothed.

When his sniffles become impossible to ignore, Erika finally looks up from her BlackBerry. "Stewart." She frowns, taking his arm and leading him out of the kitchen. "Let's go calm down."

Liesel stalks over to the kitchen island, flicks the sticky notes in the open drawer and slams it shut. "I'm going upstairs." She throws the words over her shoulder, not bothering to look at me.

"But what about the rest of—"

Still walking away from me, she cuts me off. "I'll be in the cat room. Don't follow me; strangers upset them."

The cat room? I don't even get a chance to ask before Liesel exits the room and heads upstairs, her feet pounding a percussive BOOM on each step.

part one

down the rabbit hole

My descent down the rabbit hole into Bacon Payne's matrimonial department began at approximately eleven in the morning two months before moving day at the Billings house. I had finished packing up the last crumbs from my desk in the corporate group (stapler, ficus, opened box of Thin Mints) and, Bankers Box carefully balanced on my forearms, took the elevator to the firm's thirty-seventh floor.

When the doors opened, Kim, the matrimonial department's secretary, was pacing back and forth, clutching a stack of files. I had seen her before; she was one of the smokers that huddled outside the firm's service entrance, the group that Kevin, my former office mate, had dubbed "the Dementors." The nickname was spot-on: the smokers clustered outside, miserably sucking down their cigarettes and creating a cloud of perpetual smoke, regardless of weather, time of day or, presumably, their workloads.

Although she had obviously been waiting for my arrival, Kim barely glanced at me as she shoved the files into my box, squashing my ficus in the process. "Getfamiliar.AnyquestionsaskLiz," she said, her back already to me as she led me down a hallway and nodded into an office.

I peered into the empty office. "Is this—," I started to ask, but Kim was already halfway down the hall.

My name, Molly Grant, was on the nameplate, so it probably was my office, I reasoned, and the one next door that read ELIZABETH SHER must be Liz's. I glanced in to see a woman talking into one of those goofy headsets that always made me think of telephone operators in old movies.

"I know, Bob, I know," she said, her hands waving as though he were in the room, "but that still doesn't get to our issues with the holidays. Mmmm-hmmm. Yup. No, so what if she's Jewish?" She shook her head emphatically, and her blond corkscrews bobbed along. "They celebrated Christmas with the kids *every single year.* It's a family tradition. No, no, no—let me finish— Ruby should be able to continue the family traditions too."

A few minutes later, Liz, apparently having resolved Ruby's holiday plans, buzzed my intercom. "Molly," she said, her shout floating through our common wall a beat ahead of her muffled voice on my speakerphone. "I'm finishing up some calls, but lunch when I'm done?"

"Okay," I yelled in the direction of her office.

"Hi, Bill. Liz Sher," I heard her say, her voice now sharp with purpose. "Listen, if you're going to spend that much money on hookers, please use cash, not your credit card. It's just bad planning."

I suppressed a smile. If Bill and Ruby were reliable indicators of our clientele, I would not be bored.

When I graduated from law school, I thought corporate law sounded perfect: arm's-length, sophisticated business transactions on behalf of anonymous institutions. It would be, Dean Laylor advised me, the best antidote to what he referred to as "that unfortunate clinic incident."

And there was nowhere better to bury myself in the paperwork generated by sterile financial transactions than the corporate group of the Manhattan headquarters of Bacon, Buckley, Worthington & Payne, LLP.

Home of five hundred impeccably credentialed lawyers, Bacon Payne's client list included behemoth global financial institutions, cutting-edge technology companies chockablock with newly minted millionaires, and the rulers of several obscenely wealthy foreign nations. Bacon Payne's plush Park Avenue offices boasted an art gallery, complete with an original Miró, a state-of-the-art gym and a dining room (not cafeteria, mind you). Year after year, its attorneys received the highest compensation in Manhattan.

The day after I received my offer, Tara Parker, my law school's director of career services, who clipped around the halls like a championship mall-walker, tracked me down in the library. She leaned her blond-cropped head close to mine and said in a stage whisper, "Well, this is it, honey. Your life is about to start."

I met the gaze of her fiercely mascaraed eyes and felt her words in my soul. This must be what I had been working so hard for all of my life.

Right before she walked away, she patted my arm. "Have you seen their Miró?"

I shook my head.

She rolled her eyes. "Exquisite."

Five months and twenty-nine days after starting, I recognized that I'd made a mistake. I had just spent an all-nighter summarizing the contents of thirty-six Bankers Boxes filled with mind-numbing financials related to the sale of a German poultry feed company. When I finally presented my memo to a partner named Doug King, he yelled at me for twenty minutes for the unforgivable crime of spelling "document" as "dicament" on page 4.

I stood stone-faced through his diatribe—even nodding occasionally to affirm a few insults of which Doug King seemed especially proud—but immediately afterward I ducked into a secluded internal stairwell and burst into tears. My big problem wasn't just that Doug King (who I later learned was nicknamed

Douche King) had called me "lazy," "stupid" and "the face of Bacon Payne's lowered hiring standards." Nor was it that I was exhausted enough to hallucinate tiny brown floating bugs around my peripheral vision. It was that I didn't give a flying fig about any of the work I had done since starting at the firm.

At that point, it might have made sense to look for another job, but I dug in my heels. I had to stay. Not for the salary, although Bacon Payne paid more than any other firm, but for what some starry-eyed associate had dubbed the "Payne-ment." Every Bacon Payne associate who came in as a first-year and made it to his or her fifth anniversary in good standing was given a whopper of a lump-sum bonus, equal to one entire year in salary.

The second I heard about the Payne-ment, I did some quick calculations—all Bacon Payne associates did at some point—and realized that if I was diligent about paying off my student loans the first five years, I could easily knock off the rest with the bonus. Five years after law school, I could be free to do whatever I wanted.

To be honest, my fantasy was only planned up to the part where I lassoed the American Dream for the Grant Family by paying off my parents' home equity line of credit, a loan they'd taken out nine years before to finance my college tuition. I was fuzzy on the details, but with the three of us debt free, I was sure the rest would fall into place and I hung tight, sloughing through three interminably boring years. Until I realized that there was a better way to wait out my sentence at Bacon Payne.

I'd been on the elevator after yet another all-nighter, desperately wanting a shower—it was one of those sticky July days and I felt incredibly smelly and greasy-haired. Factsination!—the news and information service that was helpfully displayed 24-7 on monitors on our elevators—made me yearn for the days of Muzak. The word of the day, the screen informed me, was *paroxysm*, as in *Mr. Smith had a paroxysm of rage when he saw all the work still on his desk.*

I stopped myself from flipping off the screen as the doors opened on the thirty-seventh floor. A female attorney stepped in, looking so crisp: showered, clean and downright elegant.

"I still can't believe that," she said to her companion, an older woman in a proper pink suit whom I took to be a client. "He claimed ignorance to every question: how much he made, what his credit bills totaled, the purchase price of the ski house. I've never taken a deposition like that."

"I told you he was slimy and evasive," said the client. "Will this hurt us?"

"Not at all, Joyce." Crisp lawyer's voice rang with confidence as she looked sternly at the client, her voice ringing with confidence. "We're right where we want to be."

I was stunned. My own days were filled with nebulous orders barked down a chain of command from partner to senior associate to midlevel associate to me. It was like the childhood game of telephone with the punch line being that billions of dollars were at stake. Meanwhile, this lawyer, this clean and well-groomed junior associate who looked not much older than I, had been advising actual human beings and taking depositions—something I'd only seen on television.

I had always sort of thought of the matrimonial group with a touch of distaste, like distant relatives whom you had to invite to Christmas dinner, but inevitably got a little too drunk and messed up the Heritage Village arrangement. But maybe I had gotten it all wrong. Maybe it was the place to be, the most exciting department at Bacon Payne.

Lillian Starling led the group and her name was constantly in the gossip magazines because of her high-profile cases. I was thrilled each time I spotted one of her rich and famous clients in person. We all were: every so often, one of the other associates would rush down the hall, stick his head in one of our offices and whisper, for example, when the star of that TV show *Night Wings* was there, "Dana Carter, in reception on thirty-three, *now*." This year alone, I had pretended to nonchalantly walk by the reception area to see a Brazilian pop star (great skin), a two-time Oscar winner (much shorter in person than in his films) and one of New York's senators (flagrant nose-picker), all waiting for Lillian Starling.

So, I embarked on "Operation Transfer" (Kevin, a firm believer in nicknames, also deserved naming credit for that one). I hounded Lionel Baird, the corporate group's assigning partner, for work involving the matrimonial group. He had looked a little concerned, as though he was missing something—most corporate associates were not eager to do divorce work, which at Bacon Payne had all the cachet of ambulance chasing—but a few weeks later, he knocked on my door with an assignment: Rick Roth had retained Lillian Starling for his divorce. One of Mr. Roth's big problems was his wife's claims that Rick's company, Little Miss Fancy—a girls' clothing company based, Lionel had said, on the "puked-up tutu aesthetic"—was marital property. Lillian, in order to understand the worth of Little Miss Fancy, needed a corporate associate to cull through the company's financial records.

I culled. And after I spent an entire month of eighteen-hour days sorting and organizing and sorting some more, one of Lillian's associates, a first-year named Denise, quit, and I was invited to take her spot.

I had to reassure Lionel Baird that no, I had not been hit on the head, nor was I under duress; I did genuinely want to transfer to the matrimonial group and yes, it would mean the world to me if he could advise Dominic Pizaro, the head of corporate, to sign off on the move. (Dominic himself would not have an opinion about this; to Dominic, junior associates were as indistinguishable as one ridged potato chip from the rest of its bag mates—just another snack that might break on its way to being eaten.)

And so, I felt a warped joy upon hearing Liz reprimand her client about his escort fees: it meant I was finally on the right track.

A few hours later, I sat at one of the booths in the Bacon Payne dining room with Liz and Rachel Stanton, another matrimonial associate.

"So tell us," said Rachel, sinking in the seat across from me. "How it went down."

I summarized my role on the Little Miss Fancy assignment and Liz swallowed a forkful of penne. "You must have done one heck of a job with that due diligence."

"I also sort of made a personal appeal to Lillian about how much I wanted to be in this group."

Early one evening during my third week of work on the Roth case, I was bracing myself to open yet another one of the forty boxes, wondering whether my daily headaches indicated the return of my caffeine addiction when Lillian Starling breezed in.

"This is Little Miss Fancy?" Her sharp brown eyes darted around the room, taking in the stacks of boxes and barely glancing at me. I jumped up from my chair with astonishing torque considering the cushy depth of the leather seat.

This was the closest I had been to Lillian. I towered over her even with the lift that her voluminous brown hair gave her—the side effect of the extra inches offered by her hair was a dwarfing of her face, which looked disproportionately tiny, like a Monchhichi doll. And that hair! Expertly layered and blown out, it had every shade of brown I could imagine: highlights of caramel, copper, ash brown, chocolate, chestnut, fawn and russet. I could tell that had I read *Vogue* with the zeal that I reserved for *People*, I would have been able to quickly identify the designers responsible for her expensive nubby black and oatmeal suit and and heels.

"Hi, Ms. Starling. I'm Molly Grant, the corporate associate assigned to the case. Can I help you find anything?"

"Yes, we have a financial statement due to the court this week and we need some of the tax returns and registers. . . ." Her back was to me and she started impatiently lifting the lids off the boxes without looking at their contents, "Oh, God. Is this in any kind of order at all?"

"Here, let me show you." I quickly lifted two of the boxes, plunked them down on the table and handed her a manila folder from the side of one. "Copies of the tax returns and financial reports from the years prior to and immediately after the marriage, as well as the date of commencement of the action. And this memo summarizes all of the numbers. The backup documentation is in here."

Lillian glanced at the folder, her face impassive. And right then, at that exact moment, my parents called, the conference room's ordinary soundtrack—layers of sterile HVAC system white noise—suddenly pierced by the loud and twangy string chords that kick off Lynyrd Skynyrd's "Sweet Home Alabama." Lillian's head jerked up from the memo. I intoned seven *I'm sorry*s in a meditative chant and rushed to turn off the phone, honestly believing in that moment that getting a personal call at seven o'clock at night indicated severe perversions in my character.

Lillian gave a shave of a nod—dipping her eyelids, not her chin—but it was, I knew, a miniature stamp of approval. "I like that song," she said distractedly, and I could not determine which had won her over: my snap to attention or my taste in Southern rock.

Her eyes returned to the memo and she said, "Helpful," confirming it by opening the flap on her Birkin bag and sliding in the document. Emboldened, I started talking. "Actually, Ms. Starling, I've sorted almost everything, so let me know if you need anything else. Also, I just wanted to say—thanks for the opportunity. This is really interesting work and I'm actually a big fan of yours. I would love to work on more matrimonial cases with you if you ever need me." The words had poured out in an obvious and desperate attempt to force a connection between us.

At the memory of this, I smiled sheepishly across the table at Liz and Rachel. "Did I say appeal? To be honest, it was a flat-out genuflect."

"Now I get it." Liz grinned and pointed at me with her fork. "You're the perfect hire. You fed her ego, plus she gets to stick it to corporate."

"What, like an East Coast/West Coast thing? The gang warfare of Bacon Payne?"

Rachel laughed. "More like a one-sided inferiority complex thing. You know how corporate deals are constantly paraded in front of hires, clients, summer associates? Well, Lillian hates being a little fish in a big pond. A chance to steal an associate from corporate is vindication."

I thought of Kevin's words from earlier that morning. "I can't believe you're actually going to become a divorce lawyer," he had said as I gently placed my ill-fated ficus in the Bankers Box. "Have you no ambition?"

"Plus the timing was right because Denise had just given notice," I said. "Why did she leave, by the way?"

Rachel dropped her head, suddenly focused on locating the remaining chickpeas in her salad, and Liz squinted and twisted her mouth. "She and Lillian had some differences. Lillian didn't really think she was"—she paused, searching for the right word—"committed to the practice and the clients."

"Any advice for how I can appear committed?" Even as I asked, I wasn't really concerned. I had already proven myself, literally doubling my workload as a sign of my interest.

"Just be available to her," said Liz. "You'll figure it out."

"I'm still trying to figure it out," Rachel half laughed. "Hey," she said to a woman approaching our table.

It was the lawyer from the elevator; my memory had not exaggerated her crispness. She was one of those glossy and elegant women native to Manhattan but rare in a law firm: shiny chestnut-colored hair, clear blemish-free skin, groomed eyebrows and nails. Her body was narrow and lean without being bony and I was sure all her clothing looked perfectly put together, with no wrinkles, sweater pills or pet hair to be found.

Women like her had been making me feel rumpled and sweaty since I had moved to New York, like they had the answer to some question I didn't even know how to ask. Usually these insecurities were subterranean, of the low-grade, nagging variety, but that day in the elevator, seeing her had pushed them center stage, under a spotlight.

I looked down at my nails—they were shapeless but clean. I probably wasn't sweating, given that there wasn't a partner in sight and, as always, all thirteen floors of Bacon Payne were set to a freezing sixty-eight degrees.

"Uh-oh. Are you scaring the new kid?" Crisp lawyer glided into the booth and smiled at me. "Don't get caught up in any of this drama. But definitely let us know if you have any questions along the way. I'm Hope," she said, extending her hand.

"Hi. Molly."

Liz raised one eyebrow and sipped at the straw of her soda. "And that's your advice? So too-cool-for-school. Hey, listen. I need to brainstorm with you guys about the Landing case. Did you get my e-mail? How much support would you offer if the husband has made one million eight for the last two years but is on track for two million three this year? The wife has a medical degree but quit to raise the kids—"

"Which really means supervise the nanny." Hope directed this to me.

"Hey, there's a lot of coordination involved in supervising a nanny," Rachel said, and they all nodded seriously for a minute before bursting into laughter.

"Anyway," said Liz, "the kids are ten and thirteen. . . ."

And then they were off, heatedly discussing alimony scenarios for the rest of lunch as I tried to follow along.

I was back in my office, reading a support motion, marveling at the numerous expenses required to maintain the Husband's bonsai garden, when my phone rang.

"Hi." I picked up on the first ring.

"Molly," my dad whispered. "We just wanted to say good luck."

"Thanks." I lowered my voice to match his. "Are you whispering because you're finally going to tell me where you buried the gold?"

There was a pause that I correctly interpreted as my mom pulling the phone away from him.

"Sorry if we're interrupting, but we waited until lunchtime so we wouldn't get you in trouble by calling." No dramatic whispering from her; her voice was standard "business brisk," as it always was when she was at their shop.

"I won't get in trouble for talking on the phone, Mom. Lawyers are supposed to talk on the phone."

"So, how's day one?"

"Great." From years of receiving that same answer to this question, my parents thought Bacon Payne was the Best! Place! To Work! Ever! Such were the implicit terms of our family arrangement: my parents had gone above and beyond to provide me with opportunity beyond their means, and in exchange, I did not squander, eschew or complain (to them) about same opportunity. Today, though, I felt a little more honest than I usually did.

"Can't wait to hear about it. Oh, honey, I have to go. There's a scramble with the register tape."

"Can't the cashier fix it?"

"Frank's on the register today." She said this as though it meant something to me.

"What's wrong with Frank?"

"Nothing. It's just his second day. Here, talk to your father. Oh, wait, no, he's disappeared. Frank?" She raised her voice thirty decibels. "Don't touch that. No, just. No, Frank, just leave it alone. I'm coming. Oh, wait—"

"I'll call tonight." As I replaced the receiver, my intercom buzzed, making me jump.

"EverettBunchwantstoseeyou.Hisoffice." Click.

I had forgotten to ask Liz, Rachel and Hope about the other members of the group. Everett was a relatively recent partner in the matrimonial group and when I had researched him online, all I found was a note in the Cornell Law alumni magazine from several years ago about how Everett Bunch, New York alumnus, "was working and playing hard in the Big Apple," and a PDF document from some time ago listing him as one of the members of a dangerous-sounding organization called "the Lawyers Basketball Pub Madness League."

I peeked into his office. He was on the phone, facing away from me and reclining in his chair, giving me a perfect view of his peach-fuzz crew cut that showed the exact breadth between each of his hair follicles. At my tentative knock, Everett did not turn around but waved his hand in a vague gesture that I assumed was an invitation to enter, so I did, perching on one of the black leather chairs opposite his desk in standard associate pose: pitched forward in my seat, legs crossed, legal pad poised on lap.

From what I could tell from his side of the conversation, Everett was reminiscing about some evening, the highlights of which involved a "smoking" waitress named Eileen and an overindulgence of Absolut Vodka. The exhaustion of those topics eventually led to a work discussion, allowing me to conclude that I was not, despite my suspicions, bearing witness to a conversation about new pledge brothers.

"So, dude, did you do the enhanced earnings analysis yet?" Everett said, still turned away from me. "Okay, so what's the thumbnail sketch on the practice? Uh-huh. Yep." He scribbled something on a piece of paper next to his phone. "Oh, she's going to be pissed." After several more minutes of lengthy good-byes and promises to "catch you later," he hung up and looked at me.

"Do you know who Noah Wasserman is?"

I racked my brain, the anxiety rising. Was he a partner at the firm? A huge client? Who was Noah Wasserman? Who?

"No," I said slowly, after it became clear that Everett was not going to volunteer the answer.

He narrowed his eyes until they were two little slits behind his glasses. "He is a forensic accountant. One of the best. He has valued assets of several clients for us. Learn his name if you want to work in this department."

"Okay."

"Another thing you should know if you want to work here is how things work. I am a partner." He raised his eyebrows. "It's your job to impress me. Not the other way around. You should have introduced yourself."

Was he kidding? I felt my cheeks flush. "I'm so sorry. I really didn't mean to offend you. I just started and I have been unpacking and trying to figure things out. . . ." I trailed off, uncertain.

He stared me down for several seconds before responding. "We expect a lot of our associates here. Lillian and I both like things done a certain way. So, what cases have you been put on?"

Still stunned, I managed to recall the names of a few of the files on my desk.

He nodded. "Okay. Nothing big-league. I'll probably have

something for you to do within the next week, so look out for my call." He picked up his phone receiver. "You can go now."

I started to limp back to my office, but then I remembered that there was one more lawyer in the matrimonial group, Henry Something—still an associate, but senior enough that I didn't want to risk having another conversation like the one I just had. I circled the hallways on the thirty-seventh floor until I found his nameplate, HENRY BENNETT.

He was at his desk, head down, poring over financial statements.

I knocked gently on his doorframe. He gave no sign of having heard me, so I knocked again a little louder. Nothing. I took a few small steps into his office. "Hi, Henry. I just wanted to introduce myself. I'm Molly Grant."

"Okay." He didn't look up.

Was he already pissed? I spoke a little louder. "I just started today. I'm really looking forward to working with you."

Nothing. How much ass-kissing did this guy need? "It's an honor."

He looked up from his documents. "It's an honor?"

I nodded uncertainly. "Yes, I'm really happy to be here."

"An honor?"

"Yes."

"Thank you," he said in a genuine tone of voice. "Thank you for interrupting my workday with that proclamation." He was straight-faced, but his eyes betrayed utter ridicule. "Will you be sharing such meaningful sentiments on a daily basis, or just when you're moved to do so?"

I did not answer, just slowly backed out of his office, hell-bent on retreating to mine.

the value of hard work

I surreptitiously check my BlackBerry. Two new messages; one is from an anxious client. A wave of stress makes my stomach clench. I pick nervously at the bent cardboard corner of my legal pad.

I try to remember the elements of false imprisonment from Criminal Law and wonder whether I have enough for a successful claim against Everett, who is lounged in his chair, making small talk on an interminable phone call with someone named Jim.

Twenty minutes ago, when Everett started the call—which has nothing to do with any of the mindless assignments he has pelted me with—I tried tiptoeing out of the office. He had put the call on hold and motioned to the chair, telling me to "sit down, Molly, and wait until I'm done."

"Oh, I'll come back as soon as you're done. I have to—"

"Sit down. I'll be off soon."

But of course he wasn't.

I am certain Everett doesn't like me, so it never ceases to amaze me how much time he makes us spend together. Now that I am starting to get more substantive work, this togetherness is torture. Every hour I spend with Everett translates into an hour that I will have to stay late at the office, catching up on actual, billable work.

From my peripheral vision, I see someone stick a head in the doorway. It's Kim. "Lilliannow."

Everett jumps to his feet. "Hey, man, Jim, gotta run, talk soon." He slams down the receiver, rummages through the piles of paper on his desk to find a notepad and races out of the door, stopping only to turn back to me. "I'll find you after."

"Okay," I say, silently debating whether I should hide from him in the library or an empty conference room. Before I can decide, Kim nods at me.

"Sheshouldcometoo."

Curious, I follow Everett and Kim next door to Lillian's office, which anchors the southwest corner of the floor and is the size of two partners' offices combined. There are huge windows, with city views, and despite its grandeur, Lillian has prioritized the room's comfort. "Make my guests feel cradled," I have imagined her directing, pinning the interior decorator's gaze with the sharpness of her own. And, like everyone else in Lillian's life, the decorator had complied. It is a place where clients can, over a cup of hot tea, be lulled into telling their deepest secrets.

Two silver floor lamps with ecru lampshades emit a cozy yellow glow. A plush ivory throw rug cuddles the industrial gray carpet that covers the rest of the law firm. The walls have tasteful prints with safe illustrations of pretty, nonthreatening things found in nature: beaches and mountains, flowers and leaves. Opposite Lillian's big desk are two guest chairs with garnet-colored seats and backs, and behind them is a beige suede couch with deep cushions and a garnet chenille throw blanket. Hope occasionally naps there while pulling all-nighters and swears by its comfort.

Lillian sits at her desk peering over chic circular glasses at some papers. She looks up when we come in and pushes her glasses to the top of her head, where they teeter precariously on her expertly blown-out hair.

"Molly." She nods to the chair and I sit. "Are you free for lunch after I finish up with Everett?"

"Of course."

Lillian turns to Everett, unsmiling. "Bruce at the Bar Group called. He didn't get the materials."

Everett turns red. "I thought we had until the sixteenth. Your talk's not until the twenty-third, right?"

"Well, he needs them now, Everett. Now."

He stands uncertainly.

She waves her hands toward the door. "Go. Do it. All the materials, six copies and the outline."

Everett scurries out of the room and Lillian rolls her eyes at me. "Why do boys always need so much direction?" She grabs a fancy-looking olive green bag and a winter white jacket from the coatrack by her door. "I was thinking the Modern."

"Okay, great. Let me just get my things."

I had been to the Modern my first year for a summer associate event called "Wine, Dine and Refine" that involved a multi-course tasting menu, several rounds of a delicious drink that mixed Pimm's and apricot liqueur and a tipsy, loopy private tour around the museum and sculpture garden. I round the corner toward my office wondering whether they still have the house-cured salmon on the menu. It had been delicious, delicate and velvety and—

I walk right into a mass of French blue cotton, my head smacking against someone's arm. I step back. It's Henry Bennett, the world's most unfriendly associate.

We do that thing where we face each other and, like idiots, step in the same direction and then, trying to remedy that, step in unison in the other direction. Even though the hallway is more than wide enough for us to go around each other, we can't seem to get unstuck from blocking each other's path.

I smile. "Care to dance?"

He stops and folds his arms over his chest. "Maybe master walking before you take on dance?"

"I was just joking."

He nods, unsmiling. "Funny."

"Sorry," I try again, although he probably doesn't deserve the effort. "I have a lunch with Lillian—my first."

"Ooooooh." He raises his shoulders and claps his hands, as though I've told him that I'm going to skip to the American Girl store over lunch and pick out a new doll best friend. "By all means, after you. I had no idea you were on such important business. Godspeed."

He's jealous. Lillian doesn't seem to have the same level of camaraderie with Henry that she does with Liz, Hope and Rachel. I don't blame her; his personality doesn't exactly encourage interaction.

At the restaurant, Lillian hands her unopened menu to the server and orders a microgreen salad, dressing on the side, and an iced tea. I mimic her order, reluctant to rock the boat by taking the time to review the menu. So much for the salmon.

Lillian looks at me. "Just a salad? That must be why you're a toothpick."

"Oh, please, Lillian, just look at yourself."

She beams at me, reveling in our thinness.

I am slim, but normally so—I have two lanky parents and, at least before starting at the firm, got regular exercise—not much of a mystery there. When I first started at Bacon Payne, though, I was stunned at the number of women who, upon initially meeting, felt it appropriate to remark on my size instead of, say, inquiring politely how I was finding the city, or asking what made me go into corporate law. A few even went a step further and, having established that I was on the skinny side, asked in effect how I had done it. By the end of the first month, I was tempted to tell them my secret was McDonald's with a colonic chaser each morning, followed by a public recitation of the poem "Jabberwocky," just to see if it would elicit a knowing smile. "Ah, the Egg McCarroll Method," they'd agree.

Instead, I eventually started pointing out how ridiculous it was for someone with the build of a greyhound to be making such a fuss about my frame. Based on the pleased responses, I knew I had stumbled onto the right reaction.

"So, tell me, how is everything so far?" Lillian asks.

"Everything's great. And everyone's so help—"

Her phone rings and she holds up her index finger as she presses it to her cheek.

"Lillian Starling. Oh, yes, hello. Tell her I'll call her back after three." She taps the end call button with a flourish. "Sorry. Where were we?"

"I was say—"

"Oh, great bag, Molly."

"This? Thanks." I look at my red tote. I am pretty sure roughly ninety percent of the female associates at Bacon Payne, as well as thousands of office workers everywhere, own a similar bag. It has handy internal pockets but isn't winning any design innovation awards.

"You know Theora Fredericks gave me a rouge Hermès leather tote bag that looks pretty similar to that. She was my first big client."

I had bought my bag at a boutique on Columbus Avenue during my first year, after reading about the store in a *New York* magazine blurb. I had circled the shelves for several weeks, initially fleeing whenever the pixie-haired salesclerk interrupted my browsing to offer guidance. Eventually, though, I convinced myself that I *needed* a bag from this store—a real New York boutique—to legitimize my big-city experience. The least expensive one in the shop was four hundred dollars, which still seemed outrageous, but it was red, instead of black, which made me feel bold. Splash of color aside, Pixie Hair was disappointed.

"Nice for the office," she had said with a shrug, as though offering consolation. The bag is a far cry from Hermès.

"You represented her?" Theora Fredericks recently passed away, but she had been one-half of the power couple that owned the boutique chain of Fredericks Hotels. Theora and her husband had divorced and reconciled decades ago, but all the newspapers were dragging out the story again as part of her obituary.

"I did. I had a nice little practice before, lots of bankers and professionals, but that was my first case where the whole city was watching to see what happened."

"How did you get the case?"

"I had represented her oldest friend from childhood and done a great job, so she referred Theora to me."

Our salads arrive and Lillian pours a dollop of dressing on hers.

"Was it stressful?"

"It was terrifying, but I loved every minute of it. And after my name got in the papers, the phones started ringing off the hook."

"Wow, what a break."

Lillian fixes her sharp dark eyes on me. "Oh, no, Molly. I know you know the value of hard work, so don't tell me you really think that. I busted my ass for that moment." She pours the rest of the dressing on the salad and swishes it around with her fork. "It's like everything in this world. The winning formula is singular focus and wanting it more than anything. Period."

She continues, "I'd done a lot to prepare for Theora Fredericks. I put myself through City College and New York Law School. I slaved away at Myers Greenspan and then when it merged with Bacon Payne, I billed twenty-four hundred hours a year so that I wouldn't be pushed to the curb like the other associates I came in with. I treated every single client like the most important one, so that when one of them knew a Theora Fredericks, I was right there, the natural choice."

I nod and do some quick math in my head. Billing twenty-four hundred hours translates into billing well over forty hours a week, which means working an estimated sixty or seventy hours per week, fifty-two weeks a year. Not much time left over to spend with family members. I know from office gossip that Lillian has a grown daughter whom she never mentions and three divorces under her belt. Husband number four is a Columbia biology professor named Roger Fields, whom I had met briefly one evening when he came to pick her up for an event. Tall and lanky, he has flaky skin and an absentminded, laconic manner that contrasts with Lillian's intense energy. Purportedly, he is the world's leading expert on elongated insects. I can easily imagine him contentedly spending his days with praying mantises and grasshoppers.

"And we all have to have each other's backs. No one understands what it takes to make it except those of us going through it." Lillian grabs a roll from the middle of the table, tears off a bite-sized piece and dabs it in the sterling silver bowl to soak up the remains of the dressing. "This dressing is delicious. Don't you think? I taste—a cheese? Parmesan? Pecorino? Can you tell?"

I dab a piece of lettuce in the dressing and put it in my mouth thoughtfully.

Lillian grabs my arm. "Molly, I'm so glad you're on my team. You're going to fit right in, I can tell."

a forced chance meeting

Two months after starting in the matrimonial group, I've taken my first Saturday out of the office. After sleeping in, I meet my best friend, Duck (née Caroline Duckworth), and her husband, Holt, at a Chinatown restaurant that's equally inconvenient to their home in Brooklyn and my Hell's Kitchen apartment.

"I can't help it. It looks so bad but it tastes so good," Holt says, reaching for the gelatinous pumpkin custard. He successfully spears a rectangular piece with his chopsticks, bringing the quivering mass up to his mouth and chomping off half.

"So, Molly," Duck says, "our Aspen trip is definitely on. We rented a house."

"A sick house." Holt's mouth is full of food. "You should come out."

"Thanks, but no way I can take time off now."

"Not now. In February. Who goes to Aspen in November?"

I let out a low whistle. "You rented a whole house in prime ski season? How much does *that* cost?"

Holt, a bond trader at Goldman Sachs, does his best impression of a discreet smile. "A fair amount. But it'll be totally worth it."

"Is Duck planning on skiing?" I laugh. "Because it might be worth it just to see that show."

When Duck and I met during freshman orientation at college, she was probably the thirtieth person that asked where I was from. She was definitely the first who hugged me after I told her, though. "Oh, me too, me too, fellow Tar Heel," she had said, "and between you and me, it makes me a little nervous to be surrounded by all of these Yankees."

Of course Duck, whose daddy was a banker in Charlotte, was from what I thought of as the Real South, where they actually used terms like Yankee. In Duck's North Carolina, the girls were butter blond, giggly and befrocked; the guys were tall and broad, with perfectly broken-in baseball caps. There were debutante parties, gently twanged *y'all*s, large stately homes, beach houses and sweeping magnolia trees. My North Carolina was much less frilly: vacations working at Cheddar and Better, the kitchen shop that my parents own; uniforms of jeans, sweats and hoodies; drives into Chapel Hill to hang out at a record shop or on the UNC campus; and sneaking into Cat's Cradle to hear an under-the-radar hipster band.

But there was something comforting about our common roots when compared to the East Coast kids at our tiny college in western Massachusetts who knew nothing about hush puppies, real barbecue or the art of superficial courtesy.

Duck smiles. "The beauty of Aspen is that you don't need to ski. There's plenty to buy there."

"You said you'd take a lesson." Holt points his chopstick at her.

"I said I *admire* people who take lessons," says Duck.

As they discuss the finer points of ski instruction, I look at the table next to us. Six couples are enjoying a rowdy meal, all of them in their late twenties or early thirties. Before the others had joined them, one couple—she with short red hair and dangly earrings and he with an eggplant-colored shirt—was alone at the table, sipping tea and arguing intensely. As I waited for Duck and Holt to arrive, I'd caught snippets of their fight, which, based on how many times I heard the terms "shopping addiction" and "cheapskate assholery," was about finances.

When their friends arrived, Eggplant and Dangly Earrings both pasted smiles on their faces, but now midway through the meal, Dangly Earrings is turned away from Eggplant, and although Eggplant's hand rests on the back of her chair, his fingers curl up defensively, warding against contact with her shoulder. I feel a twinge in the pit of my stomach for them, as though I know exactly where they're headed. Even though I'm new to this work, there's something about dissecting broken marriages every day that alters your perspective.

As their whole group noisily files out of the place, Duck looks at me and back at them. "You checking out her boots? Gorgeous, right?"

I sigh. "I was actually wondering if being a divorce lawyer has already curdled my romanticism."

"What romanticism?" Duck snorts. "When was the last time you even had a crush on anyone?"

Duck's question is hanging in the air, but I'm focused on a large group that's filing into the restaurant's entrance, milling around the long entry hall as they wait for their table. I scan the group the way I usually do, only this time, he's there. He's actually freaking there. Caleb Frank. The timing is straight out of a romantic comedy, although Caleb would be a disaster as a leading man. He'd probably be seducing the key grip when he was supposed to be rushing to the airport to stop the female lead from moving to Chicago.

It's not a complete coincidence to spot Caleb here, though. I did innocently recommend this restaurant to Duck and Holt after Caleb tweeted last year that it was one of his "faves." And it is my fourth visit to the place since reading the tweet.

Caleb and I were over in college. And that was that. Well, there was a handful of meaningless times in the years following graduation, yes, but those were minor little aftershocks. One recent night, though, alone at my desk at Bacon Payne, I had idly typed his name into a search engine. Jackpot! Pages and pages popped up, detailing all the fantastic things that Caleb Frank had been up to in the past four years while I had been stuck in document-review hell. It was pure masochism, a one hundred percent guarantee of feeling crappy, so of course, I kept at it, becoming increasingly obsessed. Which is why I haven't shared this with Duck. She will point out to me twenty different reasons why my interest in Caleb is unfounded. And she will be right.

Now that I see him, I realize this and I want to disappear. My expression must betray my distress, because Holt freezes mid-bite and Duck's head starts swiveling around like a drunken top. "What?" she says.

"Don't look over there." I speak without moving my mouth, as though we're hiking and I've just spotted a bear on the trail. "It's him."

"Him?" Duck, of course, does not realize that in my world the generic pronoun refers to Caleb Frank; she probably thinks I'm having Joan of Arc–style visions.

"Caleb Frank."

Duck and I exchange nervous looks. Should we leave? Hide under the table? Strike a fabulously casual pose? Our eyes are still locked when Caleb saunters over to the table. "Good to see you two are still inseparable."

Unfortunately, Caleb looks even better in the flesh than he does on the Web. Since I've known him, some secret ingredient has mixed with the golden brown waves, the half smirk, the chicken pox scar on his temple, elevating him from appealing to irresistible.

"Hi, Caleb." I somehow manage to sound casual.

"Mol-lee Grant." He dips his head in greeting. "How long has it been?"

I pause as if the question has stumped me. "Years, I guess." *Four years and one month. The Lodge, homecoming weekend, two years after we graduated. Well, really I just saw your back because you were in that alcove, right outside of the men's room, pressed up against that freshman with long brown hair. Ah, memories.*

"Yeah," he says. "I think I heard something about you guys being in New York."

We nod in agreement, having established that we are all, certainly, in New York.

He reaches over me and extends his hand to Holt. "Caleb Frank. I went to college with this comedy team."

Duck and I, on cue, look at each other drolly, eyes innocently wide, and Holt chuckles. "I'm married to this one." He points to Duck. "Nice to meet you."

"So, what are you all up to?"

"Oh, just trying to keep up in the big city—," I say at the same time Duck says, "Molly's a super hotshot lawyer at Bacon Payne."

He smiles and nods slowly. "Nice," he says as I am struck by how boring that sounds.

"Yeah. How about you?" I decide to play dumb and pretend I don't know about his founding of a joystick company, Da Styck, Inc., with a business school buddy; the sale of that company for an eight-figure price tag; his subsequent purchase of three homes (Manhattan, Sun Valley and the Hamptons); his amateur triathlon competitions (a phase that seemed to have petered out two years ago after a mediocre finish in the South Maui race); and, of course, his on-again, off-again relationship with Anastasia Peppercorn, party girl and heir to the Peppercorn Vodka fortune.

What's funny is that when we ended things back in college, I nursed my wounds telling myself that I, obedient overachiever, was on the way up, while he, who could rarely roll out of bed in time for class, was headed nowhere, even if he didn't realize it yet. The fact that he has turned into a master of the universe disrupts my adopted narrative more than a little.

He smiles at me. "You know, just trying to keep up in the big city." I smile back, despite myself.

He looks over at his table. Although I see three hipster grunge guys and two willowy blondes in all black, Anastasia, with her trademark shock of pink hair, is not among them. "Well, I best get back to my table, but it was great to see you guys." He's looking right at me as he says it.

I smile and nod, pressing my suddenly sweaty palms against my legs to dry them.

"Hopefully we'll see each other around soon." He squeezes my shoulder, gives a little wink, and then he's gone, swaggering back to the hipster/model table.

And just like that, I feel a jolt of adrenaline. I'm sure it's relief. I saw him. I finally saw him, and my dignity is intact. I didn't start sobbing, jump into his surprised arms or pelt him with dumplings. Maybe this is the closure I needed.

"So, what were we talking about? Aspen?" I direct my question to Holt because I can tell even without looking at her that Duck now wears the anxious expression of the hiker who spotted the bear.

Holt launches into a long description of the Aspen house and I pretend to pay attention, but out of the corner of my eye, I'm watching Caleb.

all is right with the world

It is a little before nine o'clock in the morning, and I am reading my e-mail at my desk, even though I just checked my BlackBerry fewer than five minutes ago in the elevator on the way up to thirty-seven. Frantic e-mail checking is the tic of every Bacon Payne lawyer.

Kim buzzes me on the intercom. "LucyFowleronWades." I press hold and rummage around on my desk until I find the Wades file. Last week, Lillian had told me to read up on the case—an instruction that I knew meant she was passing the baton of responsibility to me. "Yes," she had added when I read the name on the folder and looked up, my mouth agape. "Wades as in that Wades."

I skim quickly. Our client is Kira, thirty-eight, married to Jonathan, thirty-nine. Neither Jonathan nor Kira work, aside from parenting their twins along with three full-time nannies. They live off Jonathan's substantial trust fund and Kira's considerable inheritance; his great-great-great-grandfather Clarkson Wades made a fortune in banking, and her mother was an oil heiress turned fashion designer.

Lucy launches right into it. "Listen, we have some real problems about Thanksgiving. I'm following up on my letter. Jonathan needs some time with the twins. His parents do a whole big thing."

I scan the correspondence file. "Yeah, but isn't their thing in their house in Rhode Island? That's almost a three-hour drive."

"So? What's the problem?"

"The problem is that he hasn't ever been alone with them. A three-hour drive isn't exactly easing in." I delicately decline from parroting Kira's accusation in the file that Jonathan is an alcoholic who cannot be alone with the twins.

Long pause. "Will you hold while I call Judge Brown? We're not going to be able to work this out ourselves and Thanksgiving is too soon to do papers."

Brown's court clerk tells us that Brown will hear our arguments over the phone at two thirty and I run straight into Liz's office. This will be my first time talking to a judge.

Liz frowns. "The holiday tug-of-war is always tough—they're always like judgment calls, not legal arguments. It's all nuance. I think Brown usually errs on the side of allowing liberal visitation, though. It might be worth it to cave and try to stipulate before the call. Have you asked Hope?"

Hope defers to Rachel, who has been before Brown recently, and the four of us camp out in Rachel's office, talking in circles.

"Well, what if Brown gets pissed and then gives him the whole weekend just to punish her?"

"But she has to fight against it! What would Molly tell the client otherwise?"

"Maybe there's some alternative that she can offer, like some time on another day?"

Rachel takes off her horn-rimmed glasses and cleans them on her shirt. "We're not helping. You should really go ask Henry."

I make a face.

"He's really smart," says Rachel, almost apologetically.

I take a deep breath before knocking on his door. He is at his desk as usual, typing furiously.

"Henry? I need your input and it's somewhat time sensitive."

"Wait," he says, and I sit down across from him. "Okay, talk." He keeps his eyes on his computer screen.

I tell him about the morning's events and he listens. "Is the husband really an alcoholic?"

"All I know is that Kira, our client, keeps talking about it, but there's no proof of it. No DUIs, no arrests, no rehabs."

"Bring me the file."

I comply. He reviews the attorney notes and correspondence. "What does Kira say?"

"I haven't called her yet."

He rolls his eyes. "Okay. Here's what you need to do. Call Kira and see if you can get real anecdotes about the substance abuse. Obviously there's no time to get an affidavit before the call, but you should offer to get one for the court. Have her give you dates, details, et cetera. Assuming she can, Brown will respond to that. The strength of Kira's position is that if something were to happen to the twins, it's on Brown and he doesn't want that responsibility. You should also prepare Kira that she has to offer him some reasonable time over the weekend. Maybe she could drive them out to Rhode Island for a few hours on Friday or the nannies could supervise during his visitation? Figure it out."

"What if her examples are weak?"

He sighs. "Well, then you should probably stipulate that he take the kids rather than risk pissing off Brown. Use your judgment." Henry turns to his computer and starts typing again, not acknowledging my rushed thanks.

I call Kira and get an earful. Of course she has examples. Jesus, that's all she has been trying to tell Lillian since hiring her. Well, for starters, how about last weekend when he was supposed to spend time with the twins but came over three hours late and then passed out drunk on the couch while the twins and the confused nanny made pretend cupcakes around his slack body? And then there was the week before when he had shown up at their apartment all jittery, high on something, wanting to take the twins to the Coney Island Aquarium in his new car, which turned out to be a rented Mini Cooper with no car seats. Will that be enough? And Lillian said that Kira had to make sure that he saw the twins or she would look like a bad mom, but what about two weeks ago when Jonathan went five days without calling or checking in? Just disappeared! And, oh, you should see his apartment. She swears she is not making this up—there was broken glass on the floor from a wine bottle. Broken glass, just lying there!

By the end of our call, I not only feel comfortable with the arguments that I will make; I also believe in my heart that the Wades twins will have a much safer Thanksgiving without being chauffeured by Jonathan.

When two thirty rolls around, my rehearsed arguments are strong enough to cause Judge Brown to strongly advise that Jonathan stay in New York if he wants to see the twins on Thanksgiving. I hang up the phone, triumphant.

I strut down the hall to thank Henry. He's on the phone and won't catch my eye as I loiter in his doorway, so I head to Rachel's office to report on my triumph. I am recounting Lucy Fowler's impotent arguments when Everett interrupts us.

"Molly, a word."

I follow him into an empty secretary carrel across the hall. "Listen, Molly. We need you to work this weekend."

I helped Everett last weekend. Meaning that I waited two hours for Everett to show up and then held his hand as he tried to properly organize documents for Lillian. This entailed my changing the letter tabs to number tabs in three copies of five-hundred-page binders and then, on Everett's whim, changing them back again.

"Everett, I'm already working this weekend on several of Lillian's cases."

"Well, fine, but I'm prepping Lillian for trial next week and I need you to get me organized."

"I'm sorry. I can't."

Silence.

Give me enough silence after an appeal for help, and I will agree to almost anything, just to end the awkwardness. It's how I wound up as a moot court judge in law school. And Public Interest Foundation bake sale coordinator.

But not this time. I bite my inner lip.

Everett's face starts to get red. "You are the junior associate. Your job, your only job, is to help the partners, whenever, wherever. If you want to work nine to five, go get a job at a freaking Burger King, but here, being available on the weekends is your responsibility. I can't believe I have to tell you this."

"Everett, I work on the weekends all the time. Just last weekend I—"

He moves his face an inch from mine. I can see the acne scars on his cheeks and a mole on his cheekbone that's sprouting a hair. "No, Molly. You don't get to pick and choose when you're available. This is Bacon Payne. Where the fuck do you think you work? You won't last another month here with this attitude." He stalks away.

"Are you okay?" Henry stands in the doorway of his office, his tone almost kind.

My shock at Everett's ire is compounded by Henry's having started a conversation with me. "I guess so. I just don't see why I should still have to help him. I mean, I have my own cases now. I'm sort of drowning in real work."

"Trust me, he's not even worth getting this defensive for. And he'll give you some space after that conversation."

"Okay."

"So, were you coming to see me?"

"What?"

"Before? You looked in when I was on the phone."

"Oh, right, yes. Your advice was super helpful with Brown. We had to argue it and their request for Thanksgiving was denied, so thanks."

"Don't take it too personally. It could just as easily have gone the other way."

"Of course." I try to sound like I'm not insulted, shrugging nonchalantly before turning to head back to my office.

I've come remarkably close to a moment of professional confidence, but thanks to Henry and Everett, I'm back to feeling like a hapless idiot associate. All is right with the world.

in which i get it

A week later, I am back in my office when Duck calls. "Guess who called me?"

"Prince Albert in a can."

"Dork, did you really just reference Prince Albert? Okay, 'Who?' I'll tell you who—Caleb Frank."

My stomach flips and while I want to know if he asked about me, instead I say, "Really? Why?"

"Well, he didn't specifically mention you, although he did say that it was good to see us and we should all hang out."

"Sounds very breezy."

"I know, right? No, the thing is, he wants to hire me to design his new office space—a whole suite of offices by the High Line. Gut renovation."

"Wow."

"No way I'm doing it, but isn't it funny?"

"Why wouldn't you do it?"

"Oh, come on, Mols. It'd be weird."

"Because of me? That was five years ago. Plus, isn't this sort of a big deal? The chance to do an Internet millionaire's splashy offices?"

Long pause. "Yeah."

She's dying to do it. And maybe actually hearing about Caleb more frequently will provide me with some perspective, like immersion therapy. "You have my blessing, really. I'll call later, okay?"

"I'll think about it."

I look at my watch: two minutes until my meeting with Lillian. Time enough. I turn to my computer and type in "An." My screen helpfully offers up the remainder of the phrase: "-astasia Peppercorn." I spend a lot of time with this machine, and it knows me well.

There's one new picture from two weeks ago on some society photographer's Web site. Caleb and Anastasia have their cheeks pressed against each other as though they're at one of those amusement park photo booths, her pink hair mingling with his blond curls. He's gazing at her; she's pouting straight at the camera. Lovely.

I click out of the screen, grab my notepad and walk down the hall to Lillian's office. She's summoned me to sit in on a consultation with a potential client. Usually, clients are nervous before a first meeting with Lillian—the point at which a divorce morphs from the theoretical to the actual—but nine times out of ten, once they get talking about how they want things to end up, they can't stop. Lillian nods supportively as the bankers with stay-at-home wives, out of work for eight years while raising the kids, assume they'll be exempt from paying alimony; she gently hands tissues to the jilted and stunned, who believe that because it was not *their* choice to end the marriage, they should walk away with a bonus prize, like say maybe both homes and the securities accounts; she furrows her brow in empathetic outrage when the moms insist they must get final decision-making authority for the children because of their husband's long-held belief in homeopathy or Catholicism or just plain negligible common sense.

I know, as they sit in her office and claim them, that none of these clients will wind up with any of these awards, and while Lillian doesn't explicitly promise anything, she is, as she's explained to me, selling hope along with the heartbreak. An initial consult is a beautiful thing, she told me after the first one I observed; it's probably the *only* place in divorce law where there are no unful-filled expectations yet; once a divorce becomes real, that's all it is—a series of unfulfilled expectations, the most fundamental, of course, being the unfulfilled expectation of until death do us part.

I relax in one of Lillian's cozy garnet guest chairs. Increas-ingly, when I'm here, I've felt Lillian's office using its powers to lull me. I remind myself that I am there for an assignment, not a coffee-and-gossip session, and listen to her phone call.

"I know, Ethan. Oh, that's too bad," she says, making delicate pen marks on a pad of paper. "Well, why did you let it get that high? If they're not paying, just stop the work. Yes, just like that. I do all the time." She laughs. "Oh, good. See you both then."

"Ethan Crosby?" I ask.

She nods. "I called him to find out about Fern Walker, the woman we're scheduled to meet with. He represented her in her divorce." She taps her fingernails distractedly on the desk, a manual ellipsis that explains why her burgundy nail polish is a little chipped at the tips.

"Oh, I didn't realize it was postjudgment."

"Her divorce was about two years ago. This one doesn't smell good. The ex is Robert Walker. Do you know who that is?"

I do.

As a first-year corporate associate, I had volunteered to assist in a closing on behalf of the Aristotle Foundation, an education nonprofit. I had thought the assignment would be understaffed, but when I walked into the conference room, twenty people, three of them partners, were fluttering around as though prepar-ing for a presidential visit.

I had walked over to Holly, a second-year, the next junior per-son in the room. "What's going on?"

Frantically stacking papers, Holly had lowered her voice. "Robert Walker is expected to show up. This morning."

I lowered my voice too. "Who's Robert Walker?"

"You know Options Communications?"

"The cable company? Of course. I'm not a moron."

Holly looked uncertain. "Walker's the CEO. He's a first-time donor to Aristotle, and it's a big haul—a shitload of complex assets, probably to get his girlfriend on the board or something. Anyway, the firm has been trying to get Options' business for years, so everyone's going nuts at the thought of an audience with him." She pushed a stack of papers toward me. "Here, help me sort."

The fevered activity continued for the next hour, peaking when Robert Walker phoned in, about forty minutes after he had been expected to appear.

Doug King, the most senior partner in the room, punched the phone's speaker, clasped his hands together and leaned forward, grinning madly. "Mr. Walker, what an honor."

"What. The. Fuck."

Doug King leaned farther forward, his face contorting a little bit. "Mr. Walker? Hello? This is Doug King, senior corporate partner at Bacon Payne. We're preparing everything for the transfer. Such a generous donation—"

"What. The. Fuck. Stop calling my office, you morons. Does no good deed go fucking unpunished?"

"Mr. Walker, there must be some misunderstanding. We expected you here—"

"Well, obviously, asshole. Can't I just give a fucking gift? You idiots need me there to wipe your ass too? You can't just messenger papers to my office like anyone who actually gets shit done in this town?"

It was more than a little satisfying to see Doug King turn white, pick up the phone and murmur apologies like a schoolboy, but the flip side was that anyone capable of inspiring such behavior in Doug King was one scary guy.

I opt against sharing that story with Lillian.

"He's the CEO of Options Communications." She nods, letting the gravity of this sink in.

"Oh. Have they become clients?"

"Not yet, but I can think of sixteen partners who will shit a brick if we go after him. And on top of that, Ethan says this consult, the ex-wife, is a mess." She frowns. "I hate wasting my time." She looks at me.

"If it would help, I could do it for you?"

I don't for a second think that Lillian Starling will seriously want me to substitute for her in a consult. She has practiced for over thirty years and bills at nine hundred dollars an hour. A monkey can tell the difference between us; certainly a client in distress who had waited weeks for an appointment will not be pleased.

Apparently, that is exactly what Lillian wants. "Molly, you just get it. I love having someone who gets it. You sure you're comfortable with this? It's not too much for you? You have the list of attorneys that we refer to?"

She doesn't wait for a response. "Kim will give it to you. Also, have her set up a conference room so you're not meeting in your office. That would be embarrassing even for this Walker woman. What will you tell her?" She stops herself, cocks her head and extends both palms in a gesture that makes me think of Don Corleone—equal parts proud and possessive. "You'll figure it out, I know."

She picks up her phone and starts dialing, my cue to leave. "Oh, Molly—"

I turn, hoping for one last pearl of wisdom.

"I forgot to tell you. I'm having a night for us, just my girls. We'll have drinks before the firm holiday party on the seventeenth."

I'm not sure who her girls are, but I'm glad to be one of them.

6

---

fern walker

I had anticipated an hour of hostility and blame, and I wouldn't
have thought any less of Fern Walker if that's what she had
delivered. Fern is extremely gracious about the bait and switch,
though. She understands, she understands. Lillian must be so
busy. This must happen all the time (never, that I know of, actually). And she has been through a divorce, so she knows that associates are very much the muscle of the operation. She is just so
grateful that I can take the time to listen to her. Yes, Fern Walker
seems downright lovely, no easy feat for anyone consulting with
a divorce attorney, let alone someone who spent years with that
tyrant I heard on the phone.

I watch her as she fidgets with the string of a lemon-ginger
tea bag, steeping in her mug. She has delicate features and the
kind of proportional tiny figure that men love. Her hair, shoulder
length and prematurely gray, hangs over her dark eyes in sharply
pointed bangs.

Fern could probably be very attractive if she spent one-quarter
of the time on her appearance that the rest of our clients do. Now,
though, she looks like it's all too much—her delicate features have
been colonized by her bone-tired expression and puffy eyes; her
hair is tangled into a half-completed ponytail. The two plastic
drugstore bags that she's schlepped into the meeting evoke what I
think of as subway New York, the city in which real people live

and get the stuffing beaten out of them by attempting the basic acts of daily life: getting their laundry done, going to the post office, commuting. And though her appearance is downright disheveled by Bacon Payne client standards, I have a sense of déjà vu. "You look familiar. Do you mind if I ask where you're from?"

She nods, as though this is a perfectly reasonable way to begin. "Pittsburgh. You?"

"North Carolina."

There's a moment of silence during which Fern stares into space. I lean forward. "Why don't you just start by telling me why you're here?" I tell myself this is a fine start, professionally appropriate, even as I sense that Fern is too distracted to realize that I don't have a clue what I'm doing.

"Bob and I got divorced two years ago. We have two kids. Anna is six and Connor is three. I'm here about them."

"How long were you married for?"

"Nine years."

"Was it a messy divorce?"

"It was pretty simple actually. We had a prenup." She smiles weakly. "I mean Bob Walker without a prenup—would never happen. So everything was pretty set—I made a copy of the agreement for you." She reaches into her canvas tote bag, pulls out a yellow file folder and hands me a neatly clipped stack of papers from the top of the pile. "The thing is, I wasn't myself at the time."

"What do you mean?"

"I was still sort of shell-shocked and not coping all that well when we finalized things. After Connor was born, I had postpartum depression for a little over a year."

"That sounds rough."

"I spent a lot of time in bed, unable to handle any of the things I used to do."

"Like what?"

"Being organized and on top of things is—well, used to

be—my thing. Before Connor, I was in charge of running the house, you know? Bob used to call me CEO of Home, Inc."

"How romantic." I say it without thinking, but before I can apologize, Fern's lips purse in the ghost of a smile.

"It really was a full-time job, with everything Bob has going on: signing up Anna for classes, buying her clothing, furnishing the houses, interviewing the babysitters, planning the meals, doing school applications for Anna, the charity work, all of that.

"But after Connor was born, I was in such bad shape that I just sort of stopped. I mean, not just the house stuff. I stopped doing anything: brushing my hair, teeth, you get the picture. And Bob tried to understand for the first few months, but when it dragged on, he just sort of stepped in and started dealing with all of it himself. He's very driven, very successful, as you know. I mean, it's obvious, I guess. And he doesn't deal well with sickness or weakness. I think because of his father. He drank, and Bob, well, he always thought it was disgusting how his dad would check out and disappear for weeks, and then he saw me doing the same thing."

"That seems unfair."

She shrugs, as if to say, what's the difference?

"Were you officially diagnosed?"

"Oh, yeah. I saw several doctors—my OB referred me to a psychologist and a psychiatrist. I also tried acupuncture, took progestin, which is supposed to be a more natural therapy. I was breast-feeding, so at first I didn't want to take anything. Then we tried the more gentle meds that wouldn't be passed through my milk. Finally, after a while, I just stopped breast-feeding so I could take the strong stuff. That worked, but it was a slow process."

"And by then the marriage was over?"

"Exactly. After Connor turned one, I started to see the light at the end of the tunnel, but it was too late for Bob. I don't think he's ever really got over the image of me as this crazy, needy person." She wraps the string around her tea bag and squeezes out the excess water. "And I was pretty bad. I guess I understand why he left.

"The one thing is, and the reason I'm here, I was supposed to have a lot of time with the kids. I moved out of the apartment after the divorce—it was in the prenup that I would—and the kids stayed there, which just made sense given my mental state. The agreement says that Bob has primary custody in terms of decision making but that when I can handle it and when things are appropriate, we'll go to a fifty-fifty schedule. That sort of never happened. We've been divorced for a year and a half and I've seen them less and less."

As she flips open the agreement, I examine her again. God, who does she remind me of? This is going to drive me crazy.

She opens to a tabbed page. With a ridged fingernail, she points to a custody provision that echoes what she said. There's a minimum schedule that she'll see the kids no less than twice a week and one weekend day every other week. It's a far cry from a fifty-fifty schedule.

"How much less? What's the last time you saw them?"

She looks at her hands. "Two months ago. I had asked to see them for a Saturday. Bob said yes. Sometimes he says yes, sometimes he says no. I planned a great day: the Natural History Museum because Connor likes dinosaurs, or at least he used to, lunch at the burger place and then a movie. Bob called and said they were too scared to go with me for the whole day, but I could take them to a movie. I met them outside the movie theater, and they didn't even hug me." Her eyes water as she recounts her children's reaction. "They were with their nanny the whole time. She sat next to Connor at the theater and unzipped his coat because he didn't want me to do it. They told me that they weren't allowed to have popcorn because it's a choking hazard. Can you imagine what that's like? Your own children telling you what they're allowed to eat? And then after the movie, they asked their nanny if they could please go home now. She made them thank me for the 'nice movie.' Like I'm a stranger. They don't call me Mommy or even Mom anymore—they stopped that last year."

"Did you see them much before that?"

"We haven't had much time together this year, just a handful of visits: some dinners, a lunch and some trips to a bookstore or toy shop, always with their nanny."

"Any phone calls?"

"I've called every day. I've walked by their schools a few times to try and see them, but it hasn't worked, which is probably for the best because I might've caused a scene."

"You're prepared to sue for custody?" I'm not trying to challenge her, but I am worried, whether she can handle the fight.

Fern returns her attention to her tea bag string, wrapping it around her finger twice like it will serve as a reminder of something. "I have this hope," she says, her voice breaking, "that if I start strong, really stand up for the rights that I have, once he knows that I'm serious and that I'm well enough to be trusted, we can settle out of court, respectfully, without pulling the kids between us. And then, in twenty or thirty years, he and I will be laughing about all of this stuff and maybe share a dance at their weddings."

I nod, not because I think this is plausible, but because her eyes, still on the tea bag, light up as they envision what I recognize as a fantasy—Robert Walker will pulverize her into mincemeat the first chance he gets. "Fern, I hate to bring this up, but Lillian's fees are very expensive. A custody battle like this, it will take hundreds of thousands of dollars."

"Of course."

"You should definitely ask that Robert pay for counsel fees, but there's no guarantee that you'll get them. Any lawyer at this level is going to ask for the money up front."

"It's not a problem."

"Oh, good. Did you get enough in the divorce settlement?"

"Um, a little under a million. I put most of it in the apartment, but about two hundred thousand dollars is in a retirement account."

I have no idea what Robert Walker is worth, but my guess is that to him a million dollars is chump change, just enough to cover landscaping of the manicured shrubbery around the infinity pool.

"So, nothing liquid? How would you pay counsel fees?"

"Oh, I've looked into it. I can break into my retirement and take out a home equity loan on the apartment. And I have a steady job managing the office of my friend Brian's flower shop, Petal and Stem."

"I know that place. And that provides you with enough income to finance legal fees?"

"Not really."

I must have winced because she quickly adds, "If it comes to it, I could always borrow from some friends too."

I sigh and rake my fingers through my hair, gathering it into a ponytail as I think. If Fern takes on this fight, she'll have nothing left to live on.

"Don't worry about the money. I will come up with it, I promise. I've never been late with paying a bill and I'm not going to start now." She blinks quickly as if to stop from crying and stares at the wall for what seems like a minute. Then she touches my sleeve. "Please. I need help."

I stammer something about needing to talk to Lillian before taking the case and I rattle off some names of other attorneys she should contact, but I know as soon as I hear it.

It's the exact same plea. The exact same wounded, desperate look in her eyes.

I can feel a pressure in my chest—a heart squeeze—as I realize that I haven't met Fern Walker before. She, or rather the wounded desperate look in her eyes, just reminds me of Karen Block.

And this time, I know better than to make any promises.

a textbook case of parental alienation

I met Karen the summer before my third year of law school, while volunteering at my law school's AIDS clinic. I was really excited about the work—no making outlines from pages of lecture notes, no cramming, no test taking, just assisting on some cases under the careful eye of a supervising instructor. There was only a handful of clients and they needed help with simple but necessary paperwork—things like disability payments and the occasional employment discrimination issue.

One afternoon, I went down to the offices at the scheduled time to assist Dorothy Golds, my professor, with an intake meeting for the upcoming semester. I had done a couple before, no big deal.

A young woman was standing just inside the doorway, shifting her weight from side to side.

"Are you here for the clinic?"

She nodded, head down, her long brown bangs momentarily obscuring her eyes.

There was no sign of Dorothy, so I introduced myself and escorted her to the interview room.

"Name?"

"Karen Block."

"Age and birth date?"

"I'm twenty-three. Um, born April twenty-fifth."

"And when were you diagnosed?"

"Diagnosed?"

"Yes, HIV positive or AIDS. When? It doesn't really matter. I just need the date."

"Um, not. I mean, I don't. I don't have HIV. That's not why I'm here."

"But this is an AIDS clinic. All of our clients have—"

"Listen, I don't have AIDS—"

"But if you don't—"

"Listen, shut up about freaking AIDS, all right? My husband is going to kill me."

She'd gotten married three years ago. They had a volatile relationship, she'd said, and occasionally their arguments got physical. Last week, Tim found out she'd been cheating on him. It wasn't a big thing—she had just hooked up with an ex-boyfriend a few times. He hadn't hit her, hadn't yelled, just looked her dead in the eye and told her he was going to kill her. And she believed him. She had been staying at her sister's apartment, but he knew where she worked; he knew her friends; he could find her. And he would. She knew it.

Yes, she had gone to the cops. But she had no bruises, no evidence that he would follow through. They couldn't help her. She thought maybe she needed a protection order or whatever they were called, not that it would help, but at least it would be something. Or just someone in her corner. Someone who could tell her what to do, where to run, how to hide, get a judge involved. She'd called a lawyer but they wanted one thousand dollars up front and she didn't have that. She worked at the university— laundering the towels and uniforms of the university athletic teams—and her friend from work had told her to come here, to the law school.

I told her to wait right there. Dorothy was leaning against the receptionist desk, flipping through mail. When I burst out with the story, she sighed, blinking her eyes with great effort—*not this tired scenario again*. With an air of resignation, she reached over to the file cabinet and grabbed a few papers stacked on the top, her button-down shirt coming untucked from her pants in the process. She stuffed the shirt ends back in sloppily with one hand as she led me into the interview room.

Karen sat, staring down at her cutoff jeans, as Dorothy thrust the list at her and explained, no, very sorry, we can't get involved in criminal or domestic violence matters. No, that's not what we do here. One of the organizations on this list should offer assistance or shelter or whatever you need. Yes, really, that's all we can do.

Karen ignored the list, waved it away actually, and walked slowly to the door. I wished her good luck, in the same benign tone I would if someone had bought an ice cream maker at my parents' store. But it was enough to make her turn and grab my arm.

"Please," she said, not breaking eye contact for what seemed like minutes. I had never seen a look like that before—dark, haunted and broken. "Please. I really need help."

"Try calling one of the people on the list." My voice was still in salesperson mode as I pulled my arm away from Karen's grasp, replacing it with the list of referrals. "I promise. It's what they do."

Karen accepted the list and resignedly folded it into quarters, the expression on her face shifting from a clear, focused terror to a closed-off blankness, like a computer monitor succumbing to a virus by blipping out into fathomless black.

Still, I was satisfied. All I wanted out of the moment was for everyone to play her part without a scene: Dorothy and I as the do-gooders, politely disseminating helpful information; Karen as the grateful recipient of our largesse, taking the list with an appreciative smile and going on her way.

After Fern leaves, I take a moment to collect myself. Then I surprise myself by going straight into Henry's office.

He looks up and raises his eyebrows without smiling. "Molly. Again. What now?"

I turn around to leave. "Never mind."

"No, no. Come on in. Sorry to be abrupt."

"Okay." I plop down in his guest chair. "Well, this one is truly over my head." I recap my conversation with Fern. I don't think that I can adequately convey her desperation, but by the end of my narration, his face, normally affectless, is grave.

"Shit. That sounds like textbook parental alienation."

"I was wondering." Alienation is when one parent pits a child against the other parent, force-feeding her horrible stories, and basically brainwashing the child against her father or mother. The courts consider it a type of child abuse. "Does she have a case?"

"Assuming she's telling you the truth, yes. He could lose custody. Courts have been pretty clear on it."

"What's involved with proving a case?"

"A lot. It's somewhat evident from the kids' behavior, but you'll need a forensic expert. And, of course, it's really expensive and very involved. I'll get you some names of files to pull that will give you a good idea of where to start." He rolls his chair in front of the computer screen, starts typing and then stops. "Hey. Wait a second. Why did you have a consult alone? You're like an infant, experience-wise."

"Yeah. That's the other thing. Lillian told me to get rid of the case because of Robert Walker. But don't you think when she hears the story—"

"Oh no. Stop right there. To Lillian, sending you into the consult is tantamount to tossing the case in the trash."

"Well, thanks."

"I just mean that if Lillian wants the case even a little, you can be sure she'll take the consult and establish a relationship from the get-go." He looks at me. "Don't bring this up with Lillian. Kamikaze mission."

"Okay, I won't. It's heartbreaking, though."

"It sounds bad. What did you tell her?"

"I gave her a list of referrals."

"Well, that's all you can do. If she calls, you have to refer her elsewhere or"—he slices his finger across his throat—"professional suicide."

the girls and the twirls

As it turns out, Lillian's "girls" are Liz, Rachel and Hope, the group with which I already spend most of my waking hours. We've never hung out at the bar at the Four Seasons, though. I love the Four Seasons. The extra-large windows are covered by dramatic curtains made of thousands of tiny pewter-colored beads that ripple like water. There's a pool in the center of the room, and delicate trees placed around the borders of the dining room, decorated to sync with the season outside. It's exactly what you imagine a fancy New York restaurant to be when you're growing up in North Carolina.

After Lillian ordered a car—so we wouldn't have to walk the three blocks from the office—we rode over and commandeered a table at the bar. It feels clubby and rich, with warm wooden walls and a dramatic stalactite chandelier dominating the ceiling.

As Lillian orders a round of Kir royales, I lean over to Rachel. "Where's Hope?"

She glances quickly at Lillian and whispers back, "Client drama. She'll be late."

"So, Lillian, how did the Linden four-way meeting go today?" Liz asks. Liz has an astonishing memory for Lillian's schedule.

Lillian sips her drink. "Oh, it was fine. Suzie Linden kept her mouth shut, thank God. That woman is so annoying—she's so concerned about holding on to her vacation home that she's not focusing on anything else. It drives me crazy: 'the Vermont house, the Vermont house.'" She pitches her voice even higher, presumably to imitate Suzie. I wonder if Suzie is a helium addict.

Lillian looks at Rachel. "I told her to call you tomorrow to discuss it. We have to get her to realize she can't afford the upkeep on the Vermont house and the Tribeca loft without dipping into the mutual fund that she'll need for retirement, okay?"

Rachel nods. "I'll work on her tomorrow."

Lillian continues. "And Greg Hertslitz is a schmuck. That guy lawyers by brute force. I mean, Suzie is a stupid nag, but she's nervous. And he came on like a tornado. Did I ever tell you guys about the time Greg and I got into a screaming match in the lobby of the First Department Appellate Division?" She tells a story that sounds familiar, except that when I had heard it before, maybe the screaming match was between Lillian and Bonnie Werther in the rotunda at Sixty Centre Street. Or maybe it was in the library with Colonel Mustard. The Kir royales are clearly starting to have an effect.

"All right. Enough work chat." She turns to Rachel. "Where did you get those shoes? And your nail polish is cute. Hey, did you see what Svetlana did with my nails?" Lillian holds up her French manicure and wiggles her fingers. "We all have to go to her again."

"Oh, is that the light pink on top of that glossy nude again? I love that combination. It looks great," says Rachel.

Lillian beams thanks and turns to the rest of us. "So how's everyone? Give me the update. Liz. What's going on with you? How's Adam?"

Liz has been living with Adam, an accountant, for the past three years. She barely sees him during the week, but their relationship appears stable and boring nonetheless. Lots of Chinese takeout and recorded television shows.

"Fine. Everything's good. He's working hard."

"Is he coming tonight?"

"No, he has to work late." Liz pouts but I know it's an act. Earlier, she had told me that after his third Bacon Payne holiday party, Adam had sworn off attending any more.

Lillian nods. "Rachel? Did you and your mother make up?"

Rachel sighs. "Yes. I promised that I wouldn't be late to Thanksgiving next year and she promised not to log in to my Facebook account as me. And I changed my password so she can't even if she wants to. Balance is restored . . . for now."

"Let's talk about men! Any dating news?"

Rachel shakes her head and pumps her fists. "JDate reject!"

I laugh. Rachel and I have commiserated about the hopelessness of being single in the city and working around the clock.

Lillian tilts her glass toward me. "And Molly?" She squints her eyes. "I bet you're a heartbreaker."

I shake my head vigorously. "No broken hearts in my wake."

Lillian leans toward me. "Oh, come on. What's your most recent romantic conquest? Dish! We're all family here."

Out of the corner of my eye, I see Hope rushing toward the table. I say a silent prayer of thanks to be out of the hot seat as we all turn toward her.

"Sorry I'm late." Hope's eyes dart toward Lillian. "I finished the draft of the Statement of Proposed Disposition. We can submit it tomorrow."

Lillian barely makes eye contact. "So glad you could join us." I think she's sneering.

Hope stands uncomfortably for a moment. Liz secures a chair from another table and pushes it next to hers, squeezing Hope's shoulder. Hope looks at her gratefully, gives a half smile and sits down. I've never seen Hope so uncomfortable in her own skin.

Lillian peers at her phone. "Oh. I missed a call from Roger. We're supposed to meet in the lobby now and go over to the Palace together. Anyone who wants to come in our car, let's go."

Rachel gets up and runs to catch up to Lillian, laughing as

she says something that I can't hear. Liz and Hope stay at the table, Hope whispering and gesturing, Liz listening and nodding. Neither of them looks at me, so I walk down the stairs and catch up with Lillian, Roger and Rachel.

Every year, Bacon Payne holds its Christmas Gala at one of the grand New York hotels. This year, one of the ballrooms at the New York Palace has been taken over by the party-hungry lawyers of Bacon Payne.

The room is extremely dark, but after a few minutes, my eyes adjust enough to see the outline of a buffet in one corner of the room. People are lined up waiting for what I imagine is the usual ballroom fare—slightly soggy chicken Marsala, overcooked new potatoes and rice pilaf.

The gala is never about the food, though. The bar, the *axis mundi* of all Bacon Payne events, commands the opposite corner, already crowded even though it's still early. In a third corner of the room, a DJ in an all-white suit and dancing enthusiastically blares ABBA's "Dancing Queen."

The whole event is a dangerous trap: there's a river of alcohol and music with great beats. You have to participate, but if you indulge too much, you will be the star of your very own Bacon Payne legend and the whole firm will snicker about your foibles until the following summer, when some tanked summer associate will do something to take away your title.

Last year, Anthony Cooper, a young tax partner, did the worm on the dance floor for thirty minutes, after which he puked on the head of the litigation department, after which he passed out. And don't get me started on the dirty-dancing older lawyers, usually married, who feel no compunction about grinding on female employees decades younger than they are. The wisest strategy is to lie low and blend in.

I am still feeling the effects of my Kir royales. Lillian and

Roger have disappeared to schmooze and Hope and Liz are no-where to be found. Rachel pulls my arm. "Let's go to the bar," she shouts, pointing exaggeratedly to it, in case I have missed her meaning.

I order a whiskey sour and Rachel and I clutch green and red cocktail napkins, sip our cocktails and scan the dark room. The DJ has worked up to "Brick House" and more people are dancing.

"Who's that with Henry?" He's ushering an attractive woman toward the buffet, his hand on the small of her back.

Rachel shakes her head, indicating she didn't hear me, and pushes her ear toward my mouth.

I repeat the question and gesture toward them.

She looks and nods. I miss a lot of what she says but hear "Julie."

"What department is she in?"

Rachel laughs, shakes her head and shouts directly in my ear, "JULIE. Henry's GIRLFRIEND."

I give her a surprised look, which Rachel correctly interprets as a request for more information.

"Glamour job. Something at a gallery."

Henry has a girlfriend? It's hard to picture. I try to imagine them brushing their teeth together. "Julie, you forgot to floss," he'd say with an eye roll, pushing the container in front of her and stalking out of the bathroom.

And how on earth does Henry act when deciding how to spend a Sunday off? "Sure, let's see that Bruce Willis movie with all the other idiots," I can imagine him saying in an expressionless mono-tone, absorbed in his BlackBerry. "And then wait on a long line for overrated brunch. You go right ahead. Yep. Right behind you."

Poor Julie. Well, on the plus side for her, she probably gets to leave work at five o'clock and do things like exercise, go out dur-ing the week and have standard mani/pedi appointments. I watch as they navigate the buffet. She doesn't look bored and miserable. She's clutching his shirt and whispering something to him. He laughs in response.

Rachel grabs me and shouts in my ear, pointing wildly to the left. "Oh my God—Kim's doing the robot. Let's go."

"I'll meet you." I see Kevin, my former office mate from the corporate group, across the room, animatedly telling a story to a group of corporate associates, and make my way there. We hug as though we haven't since each other in months, even though we still keep close tabs on each other. Soon after switching departments, I realized that Kevin somehow possessed a rock-solid understanding of the politics in the matrimonial group.

"So, is Everett Butt-Munch still giving you a hard time?" I haven't seen Everett yet tonight and look around to make sure he isn't in earshot. No, he's far across the room, deep in conversation with Liam, one of the paralegals. Poor Liam.

"You were right—Lillian keeps him on a pretty tight leash."

Now we both look around, to make sure she's not in earshot. Kevin nods with his chin. "There she is, by the door."

Lillian is talking to Dominic Pizaro, listening intently. They are both miniature—probably about five feet two—but because of the angle at which she's leaning forward toward him, she appears shorter. Whatever he's saying must be funny because Lillian keeps laughing and touching his arm.

Roger stands behind her holding two drinks and staring into space. Poor Roger.

"Ah, good ol' kiss up, piss down," says Kevin.

"She's not that bad," I say. "She just took us all out for drinks."

"Whatever," he says.

"No, seriously. She's actually good to work for." I lower my voice. "Between you and me, I'm kind of thinking that this is where I could be for a while."

He looks at me in mock shock. "No more five-year plan?"

I shake my head. "Nope, I'm thinking long-term."

He shakes his head. "I guess that make sense—all the people drama. You like that stuff. Hey—guess how much I billed last month? Really, it's insane."

About twenty Motown hits later, the DJ has worked up to eighties pop and is bopping his head to "Take on Me." I have checked my inhibitions and am dancing with Rachel, Kevin and some assorted corporate associates.

The DJ starts playing KC and the Sunshine Band and cranks up the volume so I can barely hear anything else; more people crowd the dance floor. I haven't noticed any overt displays of inappropriateness so far. Someone must have slipped the DJ some cash to create the perfect environment for the birth of this year's legend. Who could resist KC and the Sunshine Band? Way to up the ante, Mr. DJ.

Obviously a little wasted, Rachel and Kevin start bumping hips.

I turn to Rachel. "I used to go dancing all the time, but now it's only at weddings. I miss dancing!"

"What?" She smiles and leans closer.

I lean in to repeat my brilliant observation.

As Kevin shimmies over to me, the DJ puts on some Kool and the Gang. I've been to enough of these things to recognize that this means the party will end soon.

I've had a genuinely good time tonight—a first for a Bacon Payne party. What's even more notable, I realize, is that for the past—I don't even know how long—I've actually been in a good mood. I bathe in the great-feeling combination of alcohol and good cheer and feel myself grinning as Kevin twirls me around.

Finally, finally, finally. My life feels like it's falling into place: I like what I do. I feel competent, useful. I can't believe how simple it all was: going to the matrimonial group is the best move I've made.

elf and other tearjerkers

For the first time since graduating law school, I have managed
to escape Bacon Payne for four full days to spend the holidays
with my family. Of course, my parents, the exhausted owners of
Cheddar and Better—Hillsborough's premier kitchen supply and
specialty foods shop!—expend so much energy hawking the fantasy of a picture-perfect Christmas dinner for their customers
that they have no interest in trying to achieve one themselves.
Tomorrow will be as it is every year: the Grant family, clad in
pajamas, periodically shuffling from the couch to the table to
grab a handful of gourmet caramel butter-crunch popcorn or
spread some duck pâté on an artisanal rosemary focaccia crisp.
Our dining room already looks like the lobby at the annual con-
vention for gift basket treats—delegates from the vacuum-sealed
meat category clustered in conversations with boxed pears and
chocolate-dipped shortbreads.

I scope the offerings. There's some maple-honey ham in a
clear bag that I know my mom will try to crown tomorrow's "en-
trée," so I bypass it and grab a tin of pimento cheese straws. I pop
off the top, grab the remote and settle in on the couch.

I am exhausted, having spent the day at the store. Ostensibly
I was there playing the part of stock girl, unpacking boxes in the
back room with the goal of shelving the last-minute gift items—
single-serve French presses, prewrapped boxes of chocolate

caramels—that we were trying to push out the door before the holidays.

I was slicing packing tape with a paring knife when my dad pushed against the swinging door. A tower of boxes stacked too close stopped him from opening the door all the way, so he stuck his mouth and nose through the sliver of space.

"Hey," he said, talking loudly, as though into a cave. "You there? Come to the floor for a sec."

So I had stopped unpacking, shifting the boxes to create a small path, and followed him out to where a woman with blond waves pulled back in a sloppy bun was waiting, a Cheddar and Better tote bag stuffed with paper-wrapped deli items slung over her shoulder.

"Here"—my dad put his arm around my shoulder as I wiped my dusty hands on my jeans—"she is."

"Hi." I smiled politely.

"Your dad is so proud of you," said the woman, glancing at my father. Indeed, his eyes, a green so sharp that the color is visible behind his glasses, reflected this. She continued. "I hear all about your achievements, so I had to meet you in person. And Bacon Payne! The big leagues, huh? I've gotta go prepare." She rolled her eyes. "It's a whopper of a meal tonight—but so, so great to meet you." She nodded at my dad. "Just one cup of milk? You sure?"

"No more," my dad said, nodding. "You'll be fine."

"Nice to meet you too. Merry Christmas," I called after her, turning to my dad. "And that was?"

"Gertie Manning," he said, as though it explained every-thing. "She's a professor at the law school, so naturally, we talk about you."

"Naturally," I said.

As it turned out, Professor Manning was just the first through the receiving line. My dad pulled me out of the storage room six times—approximately once every hour, to meet all the customers shopping on Christmas Eve who had—to his knowledge—ever been, known or needed a lawyer.

The message was as subtle as the Parkers' annual Christmas lights glowing into my parent's front room from across the street every year, casting enough yellow and green and red to make the walls seem like they've been painted: the life I'm living, the things I've achieved, they're not just for me. I'm keeping the dream alive for all of us.

I'm flipping through channels and licking cheese dust off my fingers when my dad finally comes in the front door. He steps out of his hiking boots and lugs four canvas totes with the green Cheddar and Better logo emblazoned on the front to the dining room table.

"You brought more?" I say.

He nods. "Mostly extras from the gift baskets, heavily Christmas-themed." He grabs a pretty bag of peppermint-stick chocolate, tied with a red ribbon. "You want?"

"I love those things."

He tosses it to me, shrugs out of his coat and then collapses in the brown leather recliner next to the couch. "Mom asleep?"

"Yeah. Worn-out from all the cooking."

We grin at each other. "How did the heritage turkey drama turn out?" When my mom and I left, he had been dealing with a last-minute shortage: two fewer turkeys delivered than customers in need.

"The backup farm in Tennessee covered one, and I gave Mrs. Baxter some Cornish game hens and a ham on the house. I think it gave me an ulcer, though." He shakes his head. "I'm so glad you're not in this business."

"I promise you, Dad. My business is not so different." I imagine presenting one of my clients with a comped Cornish game hen. *Roast this with butter and garlic, and I swear you'll forget all about that pesky restraining order against you!*

He rakes his hands through his light brown hair. "Trust me. Law school? A profession? Smartest thing you could've done."

"All right, Dad," I say, to end the conversation. I don't want him getting teary-eyed about the Bacon Payne benefits package again.

He reaches behind his glasses to rub his eyes and blinks at the TV. "What are we watching?"

"Not sure." I look at the screen for a few seconds. "Oh, *Teen Mom*."

He snorts. "What?"

"It's about teenagers who get pregnant."

"You're kidding me." He shifts uncomfortably.

"Hey, you and Mom could've starred on it," I say, lifting my eyebrows with mock excitement.

"Yeah, that would have made for great TV."

"You know," I continue to goad him, "isn't it weird, when Mom was my age, she had an eleven-year-old? Can you imagine me with an eleven-year-old?"

He shudders. "I would kill you if you got pregnant."

"Dad! Are you kidding? I'm twenty-nine. Most people are of the opinion that it's acceptable and safe to procreate by then."

He stops and stares, his green eyes boring into mine in a way that reminds me of being sixteen and having to tell him that I crashed the family car into a parking meter. "Are you trying to tell me something, missy?"

"No, no. Just teasing."

"Thank God. Listen up, Molls. You're doing everything right. Get as established as you can before you get bogged down with everything else."

"Okay." I raise my fist in a power salute.

"And after that near heart attack, I'm done for the day. Good night, kid."

"'Night."

I go over to his canvas bags and sort lazily through the new offerings. Shoved down to the bottom of the bag, between a tin of Moravian spice cookies and a bag of peanut brittle, is the day's mail.

I'm putting a uniform stack of letters on the buffet when I see the envelope from United Bank. I open it: the minimum payment on their home equity loan is two months past due. I slip the bill in my pocket, knowing that I can pay it without a confrontation; my parents are hard workers, but they do seem to lose track of the details. I'm not sure whether this is a side effect of constantly scrambling or simply being in denial.

Whatever the case, it has allowed me to quietly pay off quite a few of their bills without being detected. My dream is that in twenty months—after receiving the Payne-ment—I'll be able to wipe out their entire loan, silently. I never used to understand the anonymous donor thing, but now I do: no awkward scenes, uncomfortable expressions of gratitude or rebukes about how the money should have been spent. Everyone just walks away breathing a sigh of relief.

I flip around the channels until I land on an *Elf* marathon. For some reason—maybe the poignancy of an overgrown Will Ferrell reuniting with his dad, maybe the newfound realization of just how little my dad wants grandkids—I catch myself thinking about Fern Walker, who is missing yet another Christmas with her children.

Before I can stop it, my mind moves to Karen Block. As always, when I think about her, I am almost suffocated by a queasy comprehension of the world's failings. *Elf* takes on a sinister pall. How have I never realized how tragic this movie is? A special-needs man-child is abandoned by his mother and then shunned by his father.

I press the remote until I get to MTV. Better. It's one of those mindless reality shows about a teenager named Ashleigh with a manufactured problem: she is athletic, but she longs to wear heels and a tiara. *So wear frigging heels and a tiara,* I think, forcing my mind away from Karen Block, from Fern. It's not my problem; I'm sure her lawyer is deep into building a parental alienation case soon and she won't be in the same situation next year.

I focus on the show. It takes a while, but as I watch a stammering and giggly Ashleigh ask out the captain of the football team, I feel my equilibrium return.

the acoustics in the ladies' room

By late January, the days that I spent in Hillsborough over Christmas seem like something I've heard about second-hand. As Liz had promised, the New Year makes people take stock of their lives: gym membership, closet cleaning and kicking out their spouses.

I'm alone in the elevator after dropping off an agreement with Word Processing. I can't help but glare at the Factsination! screen, which, ever helpful, informs me simply that *unmarried people are 70 percent more likely to die of heart disease.* As the doors open on the tax floor, Hope steps in. "You look pissed," she says. She's chic as ever in a crisp gray suit, but her face is pale and her lips are chapped and bitten.

I relax my features rather than attempt to explain my complicated relationship with Factsination! "How are you? I haven't really seen you since the Christmas party."

She grimaces.

"That bad?"

"I've been better. Lillian's not happy with me right now."

"What? Why?" Hope is a hard worker. She doesn't sweat the small stuff, but she constantly pulls all-nighters and has a lot of responsibility, which I have always interpreted as a sign of her competence. Maybe she isn't as on the ball as I had thought.

"It's not just one thing, but at the moment, she's mad because

she doesn't like the way I handled the Hermann settlement pro-
posal. And now she wants to look at a prenuptial agreement draft
that I did."

"Can I help with anything?"

"I think I have it under control," she says as we get off on
thirty-seven, "but thanks."

Lillian usually keeps as far away as possible from the actual
nuts and bolts of the work. It's hard to imagine her wanting to
see the first draft of anything.

Two days later, Lillian calls me on her cell phone from a seminar where she's speaking. "Molly, a favor."

"Sure."

"Can you handle one more case? Frankly, I need your work
ethic."

"Of course." It's not like Lillian to ask before assigning work.

"I knew you'd be there for me. You're really turning into
something. Go ask Kim for the Hermann file."

"Oh. The Hermann file." Hope's case.

She senses my hesitation and her sharp tone softens, sharing a
confidence. "Between you and me, Hope doesn't seem up to the
challenge of seeing it through—or much else, for that matter. It's
a mess. She really fucked up the support provisions, but I know
you'll fix it."

After I hang up, I go into Liz's office and shut the door.

"Um. Lillian just gave me one of Hope's cases."

"Welcome to the club." She gestures to her windowsill where
three files sit, newly removed from Hope's office.

"It's a trend?"

Liz nods.

"Should I tell Hope?"

"No need. She already knows that it's being done and it will
just get her upset."

"What's going on? I thought Hope was a good lawyer."

Liz sighs. "She is. This isn't about that." She pauses, selecting her words with care. "You should be . . . careful with Lillian. When she likes you, things are great, but if something rubs her the wrong way . . ."

"What did Hope do?"

"According to Hope, nothing. But you know how Hope is—she doesn't really play the game. She might have turned down some of Lillian's invitations or not been as 'there' as Lillian wanted." The phone rings. "Oh, I have to take this. Talk later, okay?"

L ike many big fancy firms, Bacon Payne makes the offices as comfortable as possible so that we employees will never need to leave.

In addition to the dining room, the New York offices have a gym, with yoga classes scheduled in the early morning and late at night; free breakfasts on Tuesdays; free sandwiches on Thursdays; and themed happy hour on Fridays, along with pantries stocked with snack food on every floor.

Some of the amenities sounded better in theory than they are in practice. When you get right down to it, does anyone really want to strike a downward dog pose—in spandex—behind the partner who just made you cry?

Nobody could disparage the Bacon Payne restrooms, however. They are nothing short of glorious.

I've been to many of the fanciest law firms in New York, and without fail, no matter the plushness of the carpets or the exquisiteness of the artwork decorating the walls, once the restroom door is pushed open, the scene is industrial-deco at best: fluorescent lighting and chipped laminate stalls cut off at the knees in off-putting colors like maize yellow or powder blue, punctuated by rusted locks and gunked-up bag hooks.

Not at Bacon Payne. First, you enter the anteroom lounge, which has thick gray carpeting, two full-length mirrors, a couch and a vanity. On the vanity is a basket with sanitary napkins, hair spray, Tylenol, Advil and ever-changing hand lotions, as though we're all attending a wedding instead of relieving ourselves during a sixteen-hour workday. Beyond the lounge are the commodes themselves, poised chicly on an onyx marble floor with full-length ivory doors. Offering dignity and privacy, the Bacon Payne ladies' room is far nicer than my home bathroom, which is probably the point.

My ear is bright red and ringing. I've had the phone receiver pressed against it for the past two hours while stuck on three successive calls about which parent has responsibility for Harold's college tuition and SAT prep courses. Harold is five.

I've allotted myself three minutes to chill out, sit in the cushy chairs and sample the different hand lotions. Today's flavors are pink and berrylike or citrusy. I have no idea who puts them there.

My work schedule has been unrelenting lately. I and the other matrimonial associates spend our days doing actual work—handling clients and going to court. Consequently, all my drafting work—and there's a lot: motions, court papers, deposition outlines, settlement agreements and proposals—is pushed to the off-hours, evenings and weekends.

I've gotten into a routine.

I get to the office between eight thirty and nine thirty. Breakfast is coffee. Lunch is from the cafeteria and eaten at my desk. Dinner, usually Chinese, sushi or Italian, is ordered en masse by Lillian's "girls." When the food arrives—usually around eight—Liz, Rachel and I file into a conference room, plastic black takeout containers in tow. Hope joins us occasionally, although these days she has been eating at her desk.

I work six full days a week and am usually home for the evening between ten o'clock and twelve o'clock. When I have motion papers due, I work the entire weekend. And three times since I've started, I've had so much work that I've pulled an all-nighter. It's a lot of hours, but still fewer than the corporate group.

I squint in the mirror and dab at a mascara smear under my eye, only to realize that it is a dark circle. I must be tired, because I'm hearing things. I swear someone is yelling, which never happens in the sterile and staid halls of Bacon Payne. Still hear it. Wait—is that Lillian? I move closer to the door and lean my ear against it.

"Horrible! Just a fucking travesty!"

It is Lillian. I've never heard her yell like this. I open the door a crack and hear another, quieter voice.

"I'm sorry. Just let me try to fix things. How can I—"

Shit. It's Hope. With the door open, I can hear them clearly but not see them. They must be in the hall adjacent to the bathroom hall, smack in the middle of the offices and secretary carrels. If their fight is audible from the bathroom, it is everywhere else on the floor too. I freeze.

"No, Hope! I don't want to fucking hear it. You messed up. You messed up! You just glide through life, not caring about anything, thinking everyone will just hand you things. Well, this is a meritocracy and you haven't earned shit."

"But I was just trying to—" Is Hope crying?

"You think anyone respects you? They don't. Everyone knows you're just a pretty face. Just a pretty face, expecting the same handouts Mommy and Daddy give you. How much attention goes into what you're wearing, Hope? How much time and money into picking out that pretty little pendant necklace, that neat little dress, fitted just so, and those shoes! So much attention to how you look and what you're wearing. You're an empty, shallow girl."

Wow. Compared to this, the corporate group's *fuck you, stupid*s are like a warm hug.

I leave the bathroom and turn right, taking the internal staircase to thirty-eight, crossing the hallway upstairs and going down another internal staircase to get to my office without having to walk past them. By the time I get back, it's quiet.

I e-mail Liz.

are you there?

No response. I remember that she's out of the office for a deposition and I e-mail Rachel.

did you hear that?!

who didn't? Right outside my office, 5 ft from me. am trapped.

I pick at my cuticles and try to read a fax, but can't concentrate. Nothing registers.

I click "Send/Receive" on my monitor screen several times until something appears. It's another e-mail from Rachel.

lillian is on her way out of the office for a meeting, probably gone for the day. hope is packing up her things.

When I get to her office, Hope—her eyes red and watery, her face blotchy—is taking down picture frames. Rachel is already there, unfolding flat cardboard into Bankers Boxes and lids.

"You're leaving?" I ask. "Did she fire you?"

"She didn't come right out and fire me, but how could I work here after that?" Hope tries to smile, but her lips quiver instead. She looks at Rachel. "You know how it goes. I'm dead now."

How it goes? Has this happened before?

I grab a tissue from Hope's desk and hand it to her. "What are you going to do?"

"I don't know. I've been interviewing at other firms since the cold freeze started, just in case. I almost have an offer from Knight, Weston & Woodley. Something will work out."

Rachel nods. "Oh, that's a great place. You'll be fine."

I nod too, but am chilled by the thought of poor Hope having to start from scratch at another law firm.

"That was awful, though. Was it the worst?" says Hope.

Rachel pauses and considers. "Not even close. It didn't approach the Jennifer London level. Remember how she played us that voice mail message Lillian left her saying no one would ever love her because she was too desperate and clingy?"

"Yeah." Hope makes a sound between a giggle and a hiccup. "And at least it wasn't outside of the cafeteria."

Rachel unfolds another Bankers Box. "That was before my time, but I heard about it." She explains, "Bethany Carter took a three-week honeymoon after having the balls to get married, and Lillian cornered her right when she got back and told her that she was destined to become"—she makes air quotes with her fingers—"a jobless hausfrau."

"She does this a lot?"

Hope nods. "Oh, yeah. This is her MO. Anyone who is less than one hundred percent available gets on the shit list. And once you're on the shit list, forget it. I felt like I'd proven myself, you know. Like she genuinely liked me and was happy with my work. So I guess I let my guard down—I excused myself from her office when I had heard an inane war story before, missed a girls' night once this fall to see my friend who was visiting from Boston. I guess I tempted fate."

"That's crazy. You're here all the time."

"I know. And when she started to give me the cold shoulder, I thought maybe if I didn't challenge her and tried to play doormat, it would be okay." She grabs a box and slams it down on her desk. "That fucking cunt. I spent three and a half years of my life catering to her every whim. I hate her."

"What about Liz?" I ask.

"What about Liz?"

"Well, she's worked here six years. Has Lillian freaked out on her?"

Hope looks at me like I'm crazy. "I love Liz—don't get me wrong—but she drank the Kool-Aid a long time ago."

"What about Henry?" I know I am bordering on being insensitive, but my foundation is shifting. It's like finding out that my parents are part of the witness protection program or something.

Hope starts to look through her bookshelf. "I don't know. He's a guy. And she relies on his finance expertise. I think it's different."

Rachel stands up "Well, I, for one, adore your dress. What was with the fashion motif in that rant? She must have nothing else on you."

"I love you for trying, Rach, but it's a little soon for me to laugh about my induction into the Starling roadkill hall of fame."

Rachel looks around and grabs the silver cup that held Hope's lead pencils. She lifts it up and points it in Hope's direction. "To Knight, Weston. May there be fewer psychopaths and an abundance of early nights."

"Hear, hear," I say.

Hope grabs another tissue and blows her nose.

the finer points of a cat motion

L illian is out of the office a lot in the month after her explosion. Aside from Hope's absence—which goes unmentioned—
everything falls back into the usual rhythm of life on the
thirty-seventh floor. I'm so caught up in work that it's easy to
keep my head down.

Everett has faded into the background. My only interaction
with him this week was when I asked him about his trip to Phoe-
nix for a seminar. ("Crazy awesome" was the response.) I am focused and busy, but every now and then I remember Hope's
hallway shaming and feel a coil of uneasiness in the pit of my
stomach.

As always, by mid-February, Manhattan has retreated from
the cozy white-lighted holiday crispness of the early winter
months into abject dreariness. The city has been hit by a series of
blizzards and my walk to work across Forty-ninth Street is
treacherous. The snow is piled up on the sidewalks at each inter-
section: mini dirt mounds the color of chocolate milk block the
corner sidewalk. I feel like I'm in one of those documentaries
about Shackleton each time I cross the street, scaling the mountains by trudging through the slush-filled footprints of the trav-
eler who went before me, wind whipping in my hair as I try to
leap across the big murky puddles on the other side.

My boots are not working for me: I left my building with

fleecy toasty feet and I arrive in the office with frozen and wet toes and damp socks that I remove and place on the on the radiator. Someone, most likely Kim, has dumped the Billings file in the seat of my chair. I shudder at the memory of moving day—the sticky notes, the sniveling—and play my messages on speakerphone.

"Liesel Billings here. Lillian said you'll file my cat motion by the end of the day. I don't see why she can't just do it, but according to her, you're capable enough. Get back to me immediately. I've called twice already this morning and listening to your annoyingly cheerful outgoing message is getting old."

Although I have tried to forget her, my day with Liesel and the sticky notes looms large in my memory. I lean forward, the sheer rudeness of the message almost distracting me from the fact that I have no idea what a cat motion is, let alone how to file one by the end of the day.

I listen to the next message.

"Um, hi, Molly. This is Fern Walker. I'm not sure if you remember me. We met late last year. Anyway, so sorry to bother you, but I have a question about some of the names on the list of lawyers you gave me. Could you call me when you have a chance? Thank you so much."

My stomach sinks; Fern should have hired someone weeks ago.

I pick up the phone to call her, but then I think of Hope, splotchy, red-eyed and packing her boxes. Liesel would probably love complaining to Lillian about me, but it's the last thing I need. As I dial her number, I remind myself how much more experience and confidence I have than when I first met Liesel. I am telling myself that I can manage her when Liesel barks her name into the phone.

"Hi, Liesel. It's Molly Grant from Bacon Payne, returning your call from earlier."

"Molly, wow—nice to finally hear from you. You sure do get

a late start around there. Nice to know my hundred-thousand-dollar retainer allows you the life of leisure."

It's eight forty-five in the morning. "I'm here."

"Have you read the papers in my case?"

"No, not yet."

"Well, that's just great. What have you all been doing? You don't know me but——"

"Actually, we met last year. I helped you——"

"Don't cut me off. I hate it when people cut me off. As I was saying, you don't know me, but I have no patience for bullshit."

"I'm sure. Why don't you tell me a little about your thoughts on the motion? I'll review the papers as soon as we get off the phone."

"I know the law as well as any newborn associate. My idiot husband has no basis for the suit. We have an ironclad prenup, and the cats are mine. I've already done my reply, so it really shouldn't involve much work for you."

"The cats? From the cat room?"

"Of course the cats from the cat room. What other cats would we be talking about?" Perhaps cat rooms are common among the wealthy; Liesel's voice betrays no surprise that I, to her mind a complete stranger, know about the cat room.

"Can you tell me a little about the cats?"

There is a long pause and no hint of humor in her response. "They have four legs and fur."

"Is there anything about the cats that Stewart specifically mentions?"

"He says that because the cats offer income stream—we don't show them, but they have lineage—and he did a lot of caretaking for them, they're joint property and he's entitled to them. But he's not entitled."

"How many are there?"

"Three. I can't believe I have to explain this all to you again. I'm so sick of talking about it."

"Just a few more questions, I promise. Did you get the cats after the marriage?"

"Oh. My. God," she says in the tone of voice of someone about to slam her head against a wall. "One cat during the marriage, two before. But they're mine. They're all in my name and it's on page seven on the prenup: all of my separate property remains mine. Mine. Mine. Mine. The cats are mine."

I switch topics, hoping to elicit a response that sounds less like the spoiled blueberry gum girl from *Charlie and the Chocolate Factory*. "When are the papers due?"

"In a few weeks. Your job is to just sign it and copy the exhibits."

"I think we should set up a time to meet. I can interview you, get the pertinent information for your affidavit—"

"You won't have to interview me."

"It might just be a good—"

"Enough of this. It's all in there. We can talk in a few hours after you finish everything. And there's one more thing."

"Yes?"

"My idiot ex-husband has a connection to this miserable scab of a reporter. Ari Stern from—"

"Oh, I know his column, from the *Independent*?"

"Don't cut me off, but yes. He writes those miserable little 'Nitty-Gritty City' pieces. Stewart will try to play this out in the press, so be prepared for an ugly PR battle. Do you think you can handle that?"

"It doesn't hurt to be prepared, but he probably won't get much leverage from press. Usually that's more of a factor with public figures."

"What are you saying? That I'm not a public figure?"

That is exactly what I'm saying, but I hedge. "If you were up for reelection or needed to maintain an image so people would buy tickets for your movies, it might be more of an issue."

This mollifies her. "Tell me the game plan."

"The plan?"

"You *are* a rube, aren't you? What's the game plan for dealing with the press?"

"We don't comment to the press."

Liesel pauses. "You're not great at thinking on your feet, which, frankly, could be a problem. I'll give you some time. Formulate a plan and we'll go over it later."

By the time I call Fern back, I've experienced so many flashes of anger that my feet have thawed to a normal temperature.

"Oh, thank you for returning my call so soon."

"You're welcome. What happened?"

"Well, I retained Phil Klotstein right after we met, but he hasn't exactly started yet."

"Why?"

"He's not really great at returning my calls. I just wanted to see what's normal to expect in that realm."

"People get pretty busy. How long does he take to get back to you?"

Pause. "I've called him a total of fifteen times in the past month and he hasn't gotten back to me. And I haven't had a lot of luck with the other names on the list."

"That's a little extreme. Has he done anything on the case?"

"He sent a letter to Robert's attorney. That was it."

"Who's Robert's attorney?"

"Risa McDunn."

"Don't know her."

"I think she's based somewhere upstate. Well, I was wondering and hoping, and I have to ask—is there any way you'd be able to take this case? I felt a real connection with you when we met."

"I'd love to represent you," I say, meaning it. "But I can't. Let me talk to some of my colleagues, though, and get some more names for you. Are things better at all?"

Fern pauses. "They're worse. I haven't seen or talked to my kids since last fall. When I call, I can hear Connor screaming in the background that he won't talk to me."

I hang up the phone after promising to see what I can do.

Having decamped to the dining room to avoid Liesel's barrage of calls, I sit over grilled cheese and tomato and review her motion. According to the affidavit of Liesel's idiot husband—aka Stewart—the cats (Pepe LeMew, Pickles von Ketchup and Princess Fifi) are not Liesel's separate property, but a source of marital income. Further, given that Stewart's job during the marriage was—he claims—full-time groomer, caretaker and coordinator of all things cat, his effort has been sufficient to transmute the cats into marital property.

In response, Liesel, who does seem to grasp the basic point/counterpoint required by motion papers if not the basic civility of them, explains that their prenuptial agreement explicitly states that all property in Liesel's name remains her separate property. Because under New York law, the cats are property and titled in Liesel's name, the cats are hers. Further, even though the cats are fine feline specimens, they have never been entered in any goddamn shows, ever, because of the "unnecessary stresses of show life" on the cats, so what on earth is Stewart's freaking problem anyway?

I am wondering how to artfully rephrase the part of the motion where Liesel calls Stewart a "money-grubbing sociopath" when someone asks me something about joining a group. I look up and Henry is at my table, holding a tray with an omelet and some coffee.

"You're joining the early lunch group?" he repeats.

"I didn't know there was a group. Who's in it?"

"Me. Them," he says, gesturing with his chin to the only other people in the room, two women at a table talking quietly over a muffin. "And, of course, Marc." He nods in the direction of the cashier.

"Huh," I say, looking around at them. "Yes, you guys seem very tight-knit. Is it hard to crack the inner circle?"

"We do a small ceremony." He gives a one-shouldered shrug. "You know, a sworn oath, some blood brother stuff."

"I want in. Is this when you eat?"

"It is." He shrugs again and smiles in a way that's almost bashful. "It's quiet."

"It's nice." The dining room at eleven o'clock offers a mood of tranquillity that is rare for Bacon Payne. "Care to join me?" I push out a chair with my legs.

"Sure." He sits down and looks at my paper. "What's that?"

"Oh, it's a motion a client wrote and wants me to submit. I'm just supposed to proofread it, basically."

"Well, that sounds like an excellent idea."

I laugh. "I know. I'm spending more time trying to figure out how to manage her. Anyway."

"You can't make someone like that happy."

"I know that on an intellectual level. It's just . . . I've concluded that you have to be on your best behavior here. Not much room for mistakes."

He looks at me. "You mean the thing with Hope?"

I am surprised. Henry usually seems so above the loop. The Hope scene was fairly seismic, though.

I nod. "Did Lillian ever treat you like that?"

"Well, Lillian's not the easiest to work for. She was pretty demanding the first few years. And I definitely jumped in response."

"But it got better?"

"Yeah, it got better. Or maybe my tolerance got higher. And over the years, I've tried to keep a low profile."

"Yes, I've noticed." I smile, looking around the room. "You eat lunch at eleven so you can avoid us all. Why are you sticking it out? Oh, wait. It's the allure of the Miró, isn't it?"

He shakes his head and laughs. "You got me. I came for the food and stayed for the art collection."

"No, really. Why?"

"I'm up for partner this year. I've put in eight years of hard work here for that very specific reason." He smiles and raises his eyebrows as though in jest, but his eyes are serious.

"Ambitious." Most senior associates act much more casual about their beliefs in the inevitably of partnership; the odds are too slim to admit to caring. "Oh, hey—I have a question. You know that parental alienation case we talked about?"

"Yeah, Robert Walker."

"Well, she hired Phil Klotstein on my recommendation and he's not returning her calls. Who should I send her to?"

"I'll call Cathy Meyers to see if she's available. She owes me one."

"Thanks. I appreciate it. You know Risa McDunn? She's representing Robert Walker."

"That's an interesting choice. She's a little mysterious, actually. She used to be a big partner at Thatch Howard, but about ten years ago, she chucked it all and moved upstate to start her own practice in Orange County. Or Rockland? I'm not sure. Anyway, she gets some huge cases but only takes one or two a year in the city."

His BlackBerry starts to ring and he peers down, absorbed. "I have to deal with this, but I'll let you know what Cathy says."

"No! No! No!" Liesel shouts. "The paragraph after that. What you should do is list exactly how many times I had to nag Stewart to do things for the cats. He wouldn't even remember to clip their nails if I didn't tell him to."

It's Sunday. I've spent much of my weekend on the phone with

Liesel, going over my changes to her draft. We have a little routine: I suggest something; she rejects it; I try to explain my reasons; she insults me.

"But, Liesel, again, we shouldn't spend much time saying that Stewart was bad with the cats. Our best argument is that the cats are property and covered by the prenup and—"

"We should spend as much time on it as I want. I'm the one who worked to afford the cats and maintain their lifestyle. If it were up to him to support them, they'd be living in a box right outside the Bryant Park subway, asking for food on a cardboard sign. I am the doer; he is the lazy scrub on the couch. That's what I want the judge to know."

"What the judge really needs to know is that the clause in the prenup—the one that says if Stewart does a substantial amount of work on behalf of a joint business, that business will be joint property—doesn't apply to the cats."

"But I've told you fifty times. We didn't include that clause for the cats. That clause was for the Internet matchmaking that Stewart wanted to do."

I put my head in my hands for a moment before responding. "I know that, Liesel. We should win this, but we have to be strategic about it. It doesn't make sense to fill the papers with a bunch of extraneous information about whether you nagged Stewart to take care of the cats or whether he took his own initiative. The judge won't care."

"Molly, how old are you?"

"What? How is that relevant?"

"No, you're so hell-bent on telling me what to do. You need to answer my questions too. It's quid pro quo here."

Pause.

"Or maybe I should tell Lillian that you're not able to handle my case." She waits for that to sink in before repeating the question. "How old are you?"

"I'm twenty-nine, Liesel."

"Well, I'm forty. You might have done a few more motions than I have, but I have eleven years on you. You don't really know about life. Trust me. We need to talk about the cat care. We need to tell the judge that Stewart never remembered on his own. It says a lot about his character."

I feel my blood start to simmer. I've been containing my anger at Liesel since our conversation a few weeks ago and the dam is breaking; I twitch a little, my knee bouncing quickly as I nibble at a jagged nail on my index finger. But I can't tell off Liesel. What if she complains to Lillian about it? "Okay, Liesel. We'll think about it. Let's move on."

the health benefits of smoking

Somehow, Liesel and I cobble together the motion by the return date. I get her to accept most of my revisions by pretending that they were Lillian's ideas. But she still calls me daily—and often for over an hour—to discuss whether Stewart's papers are in, what do I think they will say, have I reviewed her other documents, why am I so slow, why am I being so passive, why am I so polite to Stewart's lawyer, have I ever meditated, it might help me loosen up and gain wisdom, and she has a great guru, his name is River, I should try him.

Perhaps I will call River. I wonder if he needs a Xanax after an hour with Liesel.

Here's the thing about Liesel: if she displayed evidence of even a shred of humanity, she would be a real role model. The youngest (and first female) managing director ever at Constitution Bank, she helped guide it through an initial public offering, resulting in her being worth nearly nine figures by the time she was thirty-eight. Rather than rest on her laurels, she immediately started her own private equity fund. She works incredibly hard, and I'm pretty sure she's fought for every achievement. (I am basing this on Lillian's initial consult notes in the file on which she had written "SELF-MADE" in capital letters on the top of the page, circled three times, underlined six.)

Alas, Liesel has yet to display a shred of humanity.

I've managed not to scream at her so far, but I'm losing it. For about a week, I didn't return her phone calls so promptly in the hopes of lowering her expectations about how responsive I could be. "Client Obedience-Training Basics," Rachel called it. "Just like a new puppy."

Liesel was clearly no new puppy. She responded by sending an e-mail to Lillian, CC'ing me, the gist of which was that she needed to talk and, for some reason, was having a lot of trouble reaching me. She hoped it wasn't a pattern and that everything was okay.

I called her back within minutes.

Rachel and Liz both assure me that this is just part of the deal. Some clients are bullies, and some drive you crazy. Liesel is the whole enchilada—a crazy-making bully. My job, as I keep reminding myself, is to suck it up and take it.

I check my e-mail. Of course, there's a message from Liesel to Lillian asking that I call ASAP. I pick up the phone.

"Hi, Liesel. It's Molly."

"Did we get the papers yet?"

"No, Liesel. We're not supposed to get them until the fifth, remember? We spoke about this yesterday."

"Hey. A little sensitivity. My husband is trying to steal my cats."

"I am well aware of that, Liesel."

"Watch your tone. You know, client management is a big part of your job."

I take a deep breath and force my voice to be even, calm. "I promise I will tell you as soon as we get the papers."

"Oh, and also you need to call Stewart's lawyers. I've decided I'm not making this month's support payment as long as this motion is going on."

I swallow hard. "Liesel, you can't just not pay support. Wait one month and I'm sure you'll be awarded counsel fees for this motion."

"God, why do you always take his side? If he's making this stupid motion, he doesn't deserve any support."

"I understand, but it helps our case if you haven't defaulted on the terms of the agreement."

"Molly. You know what lawyers are supposed to do?"

"Give their clients good advice?"

"No, Molly. You, as my lawyer, are supposed to zea-lous-ly ad-vo-cate for me." She draws out the syllables as though I'm a toddler. "That means if something is important to me, it should be important to you. It's funny. I used to not understand why people in finance were better compensated than lawyers. I mean, we all go to the same colleges and consider the same career paths. Now, though, I don't know. Having worked in finance and going through this experience, I feel like, if anything, lawyers are overrated. People in finance have a head for business, you know? Lawyers just seem—a little . . . slow. Anyway, call Stewart's lawyers and then call me right back."

I close my eyes and inhale deeply. Then I walk down the hall to Lillian's office, going quickly so that I get there before I lose my nerve.

Lillian is behind her desk, animatedly talking to Rachel and Liz. They're perched on the couch, listening silently, identical wide impressed smiles on their faces.

". . . And I told him that even if I represent the governor, it doesn't mean that I get a tax break, so he should definitely take that into account."

Liz and Rachel laugh in simulcast.

"What did he say?" Liz says as Rachel simultaneously says, "That's too funny."

"Molly! I was just about to buzz you. Congressman Larson sent over some chocolate-covered strawberries." She points to a box on the table in front of the couch. "Take, take. What do you say, girls? Should we do a little impromptu tea right now? I have about twenty minutes."

"Of course!" "Great!" "Definitely," we all say at the same time.

Wearing only nude trouser socks on her feet, Lillian pads over to the chair opposite the couch. She grabs a strawberry and bites off the bottom.

"Did I ever tell you girls about the time I represented Ben Brick?"

"No." "I don't think so." "You represented Ben Brick?" Liz, Rachel and I are like Greek chorus misfits, unable to achieve unison.

"Well, I thought of it today because he has a movie coming out so I keep seeing his name. Anyway, it's a great lesson. . . ." She launches into the story, something about Ben Brick not telling her that he had a gay lover on the side and that fact coming up at trial, resulting in a big fight between Lillian and Ben Brick, during which she called him an asshole and he cried. I would have loved the story a year ago, but my mind is still preoccupied with Liesel.

When Lillian stops talking, we all murmur approvingly.

"Speaking of difficult clients, I have one now."

Lillian turns toward me. "Oh Molly, I'm sorry to hear that."

She doesn't really sound sorry. She sounds a little steely, actually. I plunge in. "Yeah. It's really difficult, right? When clients make it almost impossible to do your job. Sometimes you think exploding at them would be the best way to get them to listen."

Liz and Rachel are both looking at me with surprised expressions.

Lillian shakes her head. "Maybe you're still new enough to need this lesson, Molly, but the job is the clients."

Okay. What the hell does that mean?

She continues. "You'll learn as you work here more, but it's very important to keep clients happy. It's everything. If you don't get your clients to like you, you're not going to amount to much."

There's my answer: even though Lillian just told a story about yelling at an incredibly famous client, that privilege doesn't extend to me.

I nod. "That makes sense," I say, although it makes me feel sick. "That must be where the chocolate-covered strawberries come in, to ease the pain." I grab a strawberry and sink back into the couch.

Lillian smiles broadly and pats her hips. "Tell me about it, Molly. There are years of chocolate-covered strawberries on here."

Liz and Rachel laugh a little too long. I can feel their relief.

I force myself to stay until the party breaks up and then, without grabbing my coat, head immediately to the elevators.

It's freezing when I leave, a blustery March day that's way more lion than lamb. I walk around the block, hands in my pockets, leaning against the wind. I round the corner to the service entrance and of course, there's Kim, standing right by the door, hunched over and hopping back and forth to keep warm, a cigarette between the thumb and finger of her right hand.

I stop and look at her. "How do you do it?"

She doesn't miss a beat, clearly less surprised than I am at my question. "It's a job."

"Really? You can go home and put it away, just like that?"

She takes another puff. "Good pay, constant overtime, benefits. Could be a lot worse."

I nod and start to walk back inside when she calls out, "Molly."

I turn, realizing she's never used my name before. Or maybe it's just that she's never spoken slowly enough for me to realize it.

"I didn't start smoking until my fifth year working for Lillian."

I nod in understanding. "The stress?"

She laughs. "No, it's the only way I can get four seven-minute breaks during the day. Four glorious breaks. Take it however you can get it."

When I get back to my office, I have two voice mail messages.

"Molly, it's Liesel. Where are you? I'm canceling Stewart's support payment later today. If I don't hear from you, I'll assume you agree that it's the best course of action to take. Also, there's an item in the 'Nitty-Gritty City' column that I know is about me." She starts to read in a violent staccato. *"What downtown celebrity and her financier husband are rolling up their sleeves and gearing up to fling dirt in their upcoming divorce trial?* Remember? I warned you that this would happen. You need a press plan."

I wag my head in disbelief. I can think of ten Bacon Payne clients who sound more like the description in the column than Liesel does.

The next message starts.

"Hey." It's Henry. "I'm in court today, but I wanted to let you know I got a message from Cathy Meyers. She has some conflict— I guess at one point her partner represented Robert Walker in one of the previous actions. Only for a millisecond, but it's a no-go. But I have a few other people to call. We'll find someone good for her, someone really dedicated—we'll get her what she needs."

I know what I'm supposed to do; I know my part. I've been trying to play it for months—be the obedient do-gooder, packaging up Fern for the next recipient. But the case keeps boomeranging back to me. Or maybe I keep reaching out to catch it.

When I took the job at Bacon Payne, I knew there would be expectations, a price exacted for the prestige and the high salary and the big bonus payment. "There's no such thing as a free lunch on Wall Street," a professor had told me jokingly before I moved up here. But I didn't want a free lunch. Hard work, giving one hundred percent, being on perpetual call—I was prepared for these things. The arrangement, I thought, was simple and fair.

But it doesn't seem that way anymore. And for some reason this year—the one that should kick off my downhill coast to the finish line—I'm stuck. It's as though right before the last leg, I find myself on the side of the road, sitting cross-legged in the mud, pondering cloud shapes, having a horribly timed existential crisis about why I even entered the race in the first place.

I squeeze my eyes shut as hard as I can and cover them with the tips of my fingers, hoping for some sort of sign to help me focus, to help me get back on track. All I see against the darkness is a flash of images: the desperate look in Fern's eyes and Karen Block and Liesel and Lillian and all the Bacon Payne partners whose judgment I've substituted for my own over the past four years. And what have I done in the face of this? Nothing: nod politely and ineffectively, tiptoe around the firm. Were these the same terms that I agreed to four years ago, the ones that seemed so simple then? I don't even know how to answer the question. All I know is that something has to change.

Someone dedicated, Henry had said.

I open my eyes and pick up the phone.

part two

the triumph of the human spirit

The veins in Henry's hand pop as he squeezes a green stress ball with a Westlaw logo printed on it. I've never seen anyone actually use a stress ball in a time of stress, but he is pretty agitated. "Seriously, this is the stupidest idea I've ever heard."

"I don't think anyone will find out. Besides, it's my ass on the line if anyone does."

"Then why did you tell me? I don't want to know if you're going rogue."

"Henry, calm down. Your temple is throbbing. Think of peace and light, peace and light."

He glares at me.

I stand up. "Okay. I'm sorry. This conversation never happened."

"Sit down. There's nothing to figure out. You need to call Fern back and tell her that you can't represent her. Tell her you misunderstood Lillian and give her the name of another lawyer. Otherwise, you're done." He is almost shouting. I'm glad I shut the door.

"But, Henry, if my job is simply buffering Lillian against the Liesels of the world, I don't want it. I want to represent Fern. I was just hoping you could give me a little advice on how to bring it in as a pro bono matter, but don't worry about it."

I sound much more resolute than I feel. It's an idiotic plan, no question. But even as I see its flaws, I am bound to it. I wonder if this is what people feel like when they're about to climb Mount Everest: backpacks on, walking in lockstep, marching forward, but ever cognizant of the fact that hundreds of people before them have bit it doing the exact same thing.

There's no way I'm rescinding on representing Fern. She was so happy when I called that she started sobbing. Nor can I just walk away from my Payne-ment. I need to leave on my terms, *after* I get my money, after I pay off the Grant family debt, all acquired in the name of my quest to join this most glorious of professions and become a lawyer.

I see a real chance for it all to work out. First, Robert Walker's attorney is a recluse, not part of the matrimonial cabal. Second, Lillian is especially uninterested in the details of our pro bono cases, refusing to discuss them as long as we're meeting the firm's hour requirements. I figure as long as I keep everything quiet, it will be seamless.

Henry rolls his eyes. "Okay—here's a question. What are you going to do when Robert Walker sees that Bacon Payne is representing his ex-wife and the corporate department finds out?"

I am silent, not having thought of that particular twist.

"Molly, just pack up your things now. This is not going to end well. I hope Fern Walker—whom you've met, what? Once? I hope she's worth it."

"It's not really about Fern. I mean, I like her and want to help her, but it's what she represents."

"What does she represent?"

I'm not about to tell him the truth, so I fudge. "She really needs help, Henry. And no one will touch her."

"But we can find someone. Why you?"

"I don't have any other life. Working here—being a lawyer—is the only thing I do. And if I can't help someone like Fern, who, God save her, has been trying to get decent representation since last November and whom I actually like, then what's the point? I know that this whole thing might end badly, but for me . . . right now, it's worth the risk." I swallow. "Working here? It's corroding my soul."

"Isn't that a bit dramatic?"

I consider for a moment. "No."

"I've been there. I get it, I do. Working here, for these people . . . it's not always the easiest. But why not just quit?"

I look down. "I have to get the Payne-ment."

"The what? What'd you just mumble?"

"The Payne-ment. You know, the fifth-year bonus. I have just over a year left. No way I'm walking away from it."

"Okay, if you think getting a few hundred thousand dollars—before taxes—makes it worth your while to cross all sorts of ethical and professional boundaries, I don't know what else to tell you other than that it was a pleasure to work with you." He shakes his head and turns to his computer, his profile stony and grave, Mount Rushmore's fifth face.

"Some of us need to worry about money." In my head, the words are zingers, a rebuke, but to my embarrassment, they come out soft and wistful.

Henry acts like he didn't hear, but I can tell that he did by the way his jaw softens after he swallows. He doesn't say anything, though, so I leave.

That night, I barely sleep. I know that Henry is right; with Bacon Payne splashed all over Fern's papers, there's no way I can keep this low-profile. I am about to do something I've spent the last three and a half years trying to avoid: swan diving into a blaze of infamy.

I must have sounded silly to Henry. But that is preferable to telling him the truth and explaining what I did to Karen.

The worst part is that I didn't even give her a second thought. I didn't think about Karen Block once after our meeting, and I probably would've forgotten all about her.

Two weeks after she came to the clinic, though, I was watching Channel Four news and I saw it. Tim Block, assistant manager of the Food Lion, had shot his estranged wife, Karen, in a parking lot as she was getting into her car. Twice in the head, once in the stomach. She was dead at the scene.

The morning after our conversation, Henry e-mails me to meet him in the dining room at eleven o'clock.

When I get there, he is sitting at a table reading through a document. I grab a coffee and join him.

"You look especially tired this morning," he says.

"Thanks. You wanted to say good-bye again?"

"You know, you're confusing. You act all meek and obedient, but you're actually crazy."

"Um, thanks?"

"Not really a compliment. It's a very stupid idea."

"I know."

"I mean, insane."

"Okay, Henry. I get it."

"I thought of something, though. You didn't sign an agreement, right?"

"What?"

"When you started working here, there was no agreement?"

"Right."

"Well, there's nothing requiring you to work exclusively for Bacon Payne."

"Yes, Henry. With my five hours of free time a day, why don't I get another job?"

"So why can't you establish your own law firm? Your first case can be *Walker v. Walker.*"

"I can do that?"

"Oh, I'm not recommending it. You'll definitely get fired if anyone finds out. But it is a way to keep Bacon Payne's name out of things."

"Starting my own firm. What's involved with that? Do you know?"

"You definitely need liability insurance. Also, you have to make it very clear to Fern that she's hiring you, not Bacon Payne."

I don't think Fern will have a problem with that. She never mentions Lillian when she talks about hiring me. "There were two people in my law school class who started their own firm last year. I can talk to them about what's involved."

Henry nods. "And of course, I'll help you with the law if you need it."

"Henry, why are you doing this?"

"I'm so programmed to just fulfill expectations here. I've been doing it with blinders on for nearly a decade. What you said yesterday—it's nuts but it made some sense. And it's so rare to see any associate here do anything gutsy or risky, especially for the cause of justice." He chuckles. "Yesterday in my office, you were like one of those preview voice-overs." He deepens his voice. "In a world of injustice, one young lawyer is driven to change things."

I lower my voice. " 'Fighting for the triumph of the human spirit and the will to live.' Isn't that how they always end?"

He smiles briefly and then gets serious. "I'm on board to help. But I have to tell you, Molly. I don't think it's going to end well. Just promise me you'll be prepared for that."

"I promise."

The next morning, I track down Andy Smith, my former law school classmate and cofounder of Rappaport and Smith, LLP—for all your legal needs, with special expertise in family court, personal bankruptcy, corporate, employment and traffic law. Apparently, there isn't much involved in hanging up my own shingle, as long as I go bare-bones.

I register my professional corporation with the state. I procure some professional liability insurance, along with a firm bank account, a corporate American Express card and accounts billable to my firm at a service that files documents, an express mail service and an office supply company. My billing and accounting will be easy, because I only have one case. Andy thinks I can just do everything with Excel or a calculator.

On my home computer, I cobble together some templates for generic letterhead and simple business cards and a retainer agreement. Fern and I discuss the terms of my engagement: she will pay all costs and disbursements up front. I will not ask for a retainer check, but will keep a running tab of the bill. In my mind, this is a pro bono case, although Henry tells me I'm crazy, that custody battles take up a lot of time. Whatever. I've gotten used to Henry telling me I'm crazy.

I lock down a firm e-mail address through a free provider and buy a cheap cell phone for my office line. Andy and his partner generously give me the passwords to their online accounts for legal research in exchange for the promise of a steady stream of drinks.

I briefly toy with the idea of using my home address as my office address. If I can convince my doormen to call me if I get any motion papers served on me, it should be okay. But then I picture what will happen if any papers come when Rocky, the morning doorman, is on duty. He'd spend ten minutes flirting or joking with the messenger. Then the papers would become a place mat for his greasy hero du jour, while he sauntered back to 1G for his afternoon toke break.

I reject that idea. For eighty dollars a month, I find a virtual office address at a suite in a building on the same block as Bacon Payne. Because the place is so close to work, I'll be able to duck out to pick up my mail or papers without putting on my coat, which could arouse suspicion.

This will work, I tell myself as I sign the lease.

By Saturday, Molly Grant, PC, is open for business.

no sleep till brooklyn

The clerk has been thumbing through my papers without blinking, breathing loudly through his nose, for the past five minutes. I bite my cheek as he wordlessly picks up the six-inch-thick motion, tucks it under one arm and walks to the back of the room. He disappears behind a wall of filing cabinets, the tops of which are piled with stacks of uneven documents that look about to slide off and create a loose-leaf blizzard.

"Christ, you've gotta be kidding me. Today, people," mutters the man on line behind me. "Whatcha got in there?" He stares at me accusingly.

Oh, nothing much. Only Fern Walker's motion for sole custody against Robert Walker, King of Cable Media, I want to shout. Instead, I raise my shoulders to indicate that I don't know what the clerk's problem is, as I run through a checklist in my head: yes, I had included an Emergency Affidavit; yes, Fern's Client Affidavit was notarized; yes, my Attorney Affirmation was signed.

So what's the holdup?

I shift my weight nervously and note the irony. Now that I have the most understanding boss in the world—me—and a client who will not blame me if the papers get rejected, I care more than ever about getting these filed today. I mentally prepare myself to suck up to the clerk, trying to gauge if he'll go for a clueless and sweet vibe. They usually do, but this one seems especially dour.

The clerk returns, expressionless. "Take it to Brooklyn," he says.

"What? Oh, no. Really? Judge Strand did the Judgment, so I thought for sure he'd be the proper recipient of the motion and both parties live in Manhattan—" I smile in what I hope is a winning, nonthreatening way.

"Yep. Judge Strand. Brooklyn."

"But I just checked and—"

"Transfer."

"But when?"

He sticks a finger in his ear. "Dunno." He looks behind me, done with our conversation. "Next."

I sigh. A schlep to Brooklyn means that I'll be even later getting back to the office. I'll have to reschedule my early-afternoon calls, including a dreaded appointment to speak with Liesel about something urgent involving her cat and the vet. I'm not sure how either one of those things is within the purview of her divorce lawyer, but bless Liesel, she will somehow make her cat's health my problem.

Although maybe this is good news. Most of Bacon Payne's practice is in Manhattan and on any given court visit, I am guaranteed to bump into several people I know, either adversaries or coworkers. I've only been to the Brooklyn Supreme Court once, back when I first started. I was getting an adjournment for Liz and I might as well have been in the Family Justice Services Branch of Saskatchewan, except of course that people were still rude and said "ya know" instead of "eh."

I leave the courthouse and walk into the Brooklyn Bridge subway station. Bacon Payne associates travel only by town car, so hopping on the Number Four train in the middle of the workday is like being unleashed. I can tell that summer is nigh by the smell of the subway car: a mixture of garbage, body odor and heat—eau de city underground. There is a small, almost-person-sized space on the blue bench. I squeeze between a woman with sandals and huge gold U-shaped earrings and a teenage boy with scruffy spiky hair and a high collar. I sit back and feel their bodies retreat into their seat borders, reluctantly making room for me.

With my elbows pinned at my side by my seat companions, I flip through the motion papers once more. I've been through them fifty times already, but I can't help myself. We ask that Fern be granted sole legal and physical custody of Anna and Connor, meaning that not only will she be the one making decisions for them; they'll live with her too.

Given that this case has involved trauma for the kids and will continue to do so, we've asked for a phased-in custody transfer to be coordinated by a psychologist and for ongoing treatment for all the family members, to be paid for by Robert, of course.

We've also asked that Robert pay all court costs, attorney fees and child support.

The train screeches into the Borough Hall station, making me wonder for the gazillionth time how much damage I'm doing to my ears by living in New York City. I climb the stairs to the outside world, emerging steps from the Brooklyn Supreme Court.

The feel is very different from Manhattan Supreme Court's grandeur—the massive *Law and Order* pillars and dramatic rotunda murals depicting justice via fair-skinned people in flowing robes. The Brooklyn building is a boxy gray concrete structure with rows of tiny square windows alternating with rows of even tinier square windows—the type of place that conjures red tape and clock-punching and humming fluorescent lights, but that's okay. Brooklyn Supreme Court doesn't have to look like the birthplace of justice as long as they know how to dole out some.

I yank open the door to the courthouse and flash my washed-out photo ID to an officer with a bored expression.

Crammed into a very crowded elevator, I bump up, local-style, floor by floor, until the doors finally open on ten. I push my way out of the doors, the weight of the motion heavy in my arms.

does anyone *not* like stars?

I'm back in Manhattan, emerging from the subway, when my phone rings. I assume it's Liesel because it usually is, but it's a Manhattan number, unrecognizable. I clear my throat to sound as official as possible before picking up.

"Molly Grant."

"Uh, hey."

I recognize him immediately, but pretend not to. "Who is this?"

"Caleb."

"Oh, hey."

"So, it was good to talk to you the other day."

Here's how it had happened: I had called Duck's cell phone two days ago and she had answered and said hello. Nothing out of the ordinary, until I heard a male voice in the background.

"You talking to Grant?" it demanded.

"Uh-huh," said Duck.

"Where *are* you?" I had asked her, suddenly light-headed.

She sighed, second-guessing her decision to pick up my call. "Caleb's new office space, taking measurements."

I heard his voice. "Tell her we have an extra ticket to the Klezmaniacs, if she wants to come." It was a private joke, referencing an interminable klezmer concert, a requirement for his Ensemble Melodies of Religion class, that we had driven to in Rutland, Vermont, my junior year.

"Only if he promises to lead the audience in a scarf dance, like usual."

Duck repeated this and Caleb chuckled. "Only if she wears a—"

"Here," said Duck, flatly, "tell her yourself."

"Hey." Caleb's voice was closer in my ear. "Your friend seems rather touchy."

"Well, she gets focused when she's working."

"Where are you?"

"Trying to work, although now, thanks to you, my head will be filled with the magical strains of flute meets violin—"

"Meets drum block, meets cymbal, meets crazy hook. Sorry about that."

"You should be."

"Hey." Pause. "Can I call you sometime?"

"Sure." I gave him my number, trying to push away the image of Duck, who I knew was still within earshot, probably shaking her head over her measuring tape.

Since the call, I had replayed our conversation several times, but now, I try to sound like I haven't. "Good to talk to you too."

"So, you up for grabbing some grub, catching up sometime?"

"Sure. When?"

"Um." Long pause. "The fourteenth?"

"Let me just check my schedule." I wait a couple beats. "Yep, the fourteenth works."

"Well, all right, then. See you around nine."

"Wait, where?"

"I'll e-mail a place."

Even though I'm due back at Bacon Payne, I can't help myself. I stop in my tracks right there on Forty-eighth Street, lean against the side of a building and do an Internet search, something—I realize with pride—that I haven't done since last month. No new photos, but there is one mention on a random society Web site: Mr. Caleb Frank and Ms. Anastasia Peppercorn, still apparently in cahoots, are jointly listed as Angel Benefactors of the Aristotle Foundation's Annual Benefit.

If my preliminary research hadn't tipped me off to the fact that my dinner with Caleb is not a date, the location would have. We are at the Burger Joint at Le Parker Meridien, a tiny little hole-in-the-wall. Great burgers, good fries, yes, but to get them, we had to stand in line for forty-five minutes, making awkward conversation about New York restaurants and mutual friends from college.

Now we're crammed next to each other on one side of a tiny table for four. Mike, one of the guys sharing the other side of the table with us, is a blond, red-faced beefy man. He and his dining companion, Chip, work in management at Kroger's corporate offices in Cleveland, really enjoyed *The Lion King* and are both divorced. I learned all of this after Mike spilled his beer on me and, by way of atonement, filled me in on the details of his life.

"So," I say.

"So." Caleb lazily dips a fry in some ketchup.

We look at each other.

"You're at Bacon Payne?"

I nod.

"That's, like, a strong firm. You know Dominic Pizaro in corporate?"

"Of course," I say, as though Dominic and I hashed out corporate structure maps together plenty of times.

"Yeah, worked with the guy a little bit. He was pretty sharp."

I play dumb as Caleb explains his illustrious career. In business school, he and his buddy would spend all this time on their asses, playing video games and blowing off class. Well, his buddy loved tooling around with computers and one day had this great idea for a new kind of joystick for the Xbox. So, Caleb said, we should totally do our business plan about that, because they had to do one anyway as an assignment for school. The professor contacted a friend who was a venture capitalist, and the next thing they knew, they had a company, Da Styck, Inc., which they then sold to a megaconglomerate, making a gazillion lucky investments with the proceeds. Enter Dominic Pizaro.

"So what are you doing now?" I say.

"We're looking at other opportunities, working some stuff up."

"Sounds good."

"So, you're not married yet, huh?"

"No," I say, laughing. Does he honestly think I'd be here with him at ten fifteen on a weeknight if I were married?

"You dating mostly serious types? Lawyers and bankers?"

I do a vague head move that's neither nod nor shake. I'm not about to say that my current type is fictional. "My hours are pretty long, so at this point it's kind of all about the job. What about you?"

"My hours aren't that bad. Sometimes travel, but pretty humane."

"No, I mean, are you married?" Even though I know the answer, it's not as ridiculous a question for Caleb. Somehow, I can picture him meeting an ex-girlfriend for dinner while his wife stays home with leftovers.

"Married? Uh, no." He looks at Mike and Chip out of the corner of his eye, and then leans across the table, his hands gripping the side. "So, Mol." He lowers his voice and I lean my head closer, tilting my ear toward him without losing eye contact. "Is this the most awkward conversation you've ever had?"

I laugh. "It's up there."

"Can I level with you?"

"Level away."

"I've been wanting to call since last fall. Seeing you brought back some memories."

"Why didn't you?"

"Complications." He is straight-faced, as though this actually answers anything, and I can't help myself. I snort. A flicker of annoyance crosses his face, bringing me right back to where we last left off, as though neither of us has evolved one iota since college. And I don't want or need that feeling—what would be the point?—so I smile, waving my white flag.

"So what kind of memories did it bring back?"

He smiles too, almost shyly. "The good kind. Loon Mountain? You remember that?"

I nod. The truth is, although I know that we decided on a whim to drive to New Hampshire for the weekend, I have no recollection of the ski conditions, how we got along, whether our conversation was as awkward as tonight. My sole memory from the trip is this: for some reason the orange gate was skeptical of our E-ZPass and we got stuck at a tollbooth; it was late and dark and isolated. Without words, we looked at each other, unbuckled our seat belts and jumped into the backseat, fogging up the windows and ignoring the few headlights of other cars.

I am happy keeping this thought—and the full-body flush it triggers—to myself, but Caleb looks at me pointedly and presses his knee against mine under the table. He laughs and shakes his head. "It's been, what? Ten years. Every time I go through a goddamn tollbooth . . ." He shakes his head.

"Am I really supposed to believe that you remember anything from college?"

"What would make you say that?" he says, his hazel eyes growing big with mock indignation.

"Certainly not the haze of smoke around your head back then. Nor the bags of magical fungus in your apartment."

He chuckles. "Huh. Right. So, if my memory can't be trusted, what do you think happened with us?"

My eyes wander off to Chip and Mike, who must be eavesdropping, based on how quickly they look down at their burger wrappings. "You really want to do the postmortem?"

"I do. I want to do the postmortem. You know why?"

"Because nothing is as much fun as a good postmortem?"

He treats my question like it was a serious one. "No. Not because it's fun, but because you know what seeing you made me realize?" He shifts his knee away from mine, making my leg feel suddenly cold, even though it's probably eighty degrees in the restaurant. Keeping his eyes locked on my face, he lightly covers my feet with the tips of his shoes. "I've really missed you. It's not so easy to connect with people the way we connected." He presses his feet down gently on my toes. "So, Ms. Grant. What were our college missteps?"

I decide against relaying the first fifty missteps, exclusively Caleb's, that come to mind. "We weren't . . . on the same page."

"Not on the same page," he says, drawing out each word. He laughs. "Is that your corporate-speak way of saying I was young and stupid?"

I didn't start out as one of those girls in college, the kind that hangs up a neon sign proclaiming "Taken" at the first spark of interest in a guy. Initially, I assumed things with Caleb would be casual. But one night at three in the morning a few weeks after we met, I woke up to a soft scratching at the window. At first, I was freaked-out—I lived on the ground floor and wished I hadn't laughed off the protective bars that my dad offered to install.

Duck was sleeping through the intrusion—I could tell from the way her body was lumped, immobile, under her comforter—so I sat up in bed and peered out the window. There was Caleb, his curls escaping out of a baseball cap that sat low on his head.

I gestured that he should go around to the front so I could let him in, but he held up a bottle of wine and a blanket and tossed his head backward to indicate that I should come outside instead.

"Prebreakfast picnic?" he said, and we walked, hands clasped, to the quad. He spread out the blanket and, this being college, unscrewed the cap of the wine.

"What's this about?" I had asked.

"I like these stars," he had said, casually pointing up to the sky, with a flick of his index finger. "And I like you"—he pointed to me—"and I was thinking to myself that it might be really nice to look at the stars I like with a girl I like."

It was, I knew, a grand romantic gesture, the first I had ever really received. Later, when I tried to describe it to Duck, she smiled and nodded, but I could tell by the way she failed to clutch her chest and swoon that I hadn't been able to properly articulate the moment's magic. Which was fine, because as long as Caleb and I both felt it, it didn't matter if anyone else did.

Of course, a mere two weeks later, I watched Caleb leave the Sex on a Beach party with Chloe Small, the two of them entwined at the head like pipe cleaners. In retrospect, that should have been enough, but it wasn't. Eventually, though, with the passage of time and after hearing Caleb profess his "like" of many things, including a bag of salt and vinegar potato chips and a fleece sweatshirt, I eventually got it: Caleb had not been promising anything more that night than exactly what his words indicated. Stars he liked. A girl he liked.

I rest my chin on my hands. "I wouldn't argue with young and stupid."

"It was me. I'll wear the scarlet letter. I was young and stupid." He keeps one hand on my leg and reaches for his beer with the other.

"Let's be fair. We both were."

"Maybe. But, Molly, the thing is, I'm a little older now, and a lot less stupid."

"Is that so?" I reach for a fry without breaking eye contact.

He does the same. "It is so."

He lifts his bottle. "To real connections."

"To connections."

Although I've spent years telling myself I've imagined the heat of our connection, I feel it again now, our eye lock making me feel warm and floaty and like we're the only real thing in this restaurant, despite the fact that my left sleeve is still damp from the beer-spilling Kroger executives. Maybe his relationship with Anastasia Peppercorn has taken a turn for the professional and they're just charity buddies, going around donating to worthy causes together. I mull whether this is possible, somehow managing not to laugh out loud at myself for doing so. I reach under the table for my bag. I recognize this feeling; it is nothing more than lust.

Caleb pouts. "You're leaving?"

"I have to go, Caleb."

"Then come over to see my butterfly collection." He cocks his head and arches an eyebrow, deliberately and exaggeratedly.

I am more tempted than I want to be. But I know him too well. Being obsessed by the idea of Caleb is one thing; willingly submitting to the heartache again is another thing.

I laugh. "Not tonight. I've got to work."

He nods, unsurprised. "Don't think you're off the hook, Ms. Grant. I'll be in touch."

a genuinely nice guy

I love summer, and not just for the obvious reasons like the beach, ice cream and barbecues. I love it because it's possible to nonchalantly leave my office without a coat, casually tell Liz that I'm just popping down to another floor for a minute and, instead, slip out of the building.

Which is exactly what I do when an e-mail comes in from my virtual office, notifying me of the first official communication on the Walker case.

I speed-walk the two doors down, more from nerves than anything else, snatch the fax from the receptionist's extended hand and skim.

It's from the court. Oral arguments on the motion are scheduled for July 16, with Robert Walker's reply papers to be served on us at the end of June, in a few weeks. I run down the street to Bacon Payne and stop first in Henry's office.

He looks up. "Are you sweating?"

"A little."

He puts down his pen. "I'm intrigued."

"I got the date."

"O-kay. The date?"

"The date. The return date. From Brooklyn."

Understanding dawns on Henry's face. "What is it?"

"July sixteenth."

Henry smiles. "Sounds auspicious. Still before Strand?"

"Yep."

He pulls up his calendar on his computer screen. "You know, I'm around the weekend before. Do you want help prepping?"

"Really, Henry? It's a summer weekend. Don't you go to the Hamptons or something?" Surely that woman he brought to the holiday party has a perfect summer wardrobe: white linen pants and green and pink print dresses that aren't going to wear themselves.

"I can donate to the cause for a couple of hours. I've seen enough to know that you'll be a mess."

"No question. How many times have you been before Strand?"

Liz pops her head in. "Strand? Are you guys talking about his transfer?"

I look at Liz. "Do you know anything about it?"

"No, I just heard. Is he taking his cases with him?"

"Dunno."

"Wait. Why do you care? Have you been assigned to him for something?" Liz's dark irises shift to the left and I know she's mentally cataloging my cases.

"No." I hate lying to her. "I had just heard something about the transfer and was asking Henry if he knew anything about it."

"And I don't, so everyone can just get out of my office and go back to work." Henry starts to type on his computer.

Liz mutters something about antisocial grouches and I follow her to the door in a pretend huff, glancing back at Henry in gratitude.

He frowns at his computer screen, his fingers flying across the keyboard, but I'm not buying it. Underneath the brusque persona is a genuinely nice guy.

It's just weird to have Henry sitting on my couch, his feet propped on the coffee table in a familiar manner, a bottle of water in his hand. Adding to the strangeness, he is wearing shorts, beat-up sneakers, no socks and a faded blue T-shirt with lowercase letters arranged in a way that means nothing to me but I assume is a wry insider's statement on something.

His outfit is perfectly appropriate for a Sunday work session at my apartment. I myself am wearing cutoff shorts that had a run-in with some bleach during a law school laundry session. When I opened the door to my apartment, though, it was a jolt to see him there, all casual-like. I could tell from the brief pause and the way his head dipped down toward the teal carpet in my hallway that he felt awkward too. Either that or he was horrified that my hair was still damp from the shower.

All the associates in the matrimonial department see one another so much in the office that we rarely socialize in our limited time off, and there is something jarring about crossing the boundary. Plus, now, I can't help noticing that Henry is, well, nicely built. Broad shoulders. Muscular legs that, when examined closely as I have surreptitiously done, are the perfect amount of hairy.

He looks around. "Nice place. I would never know from the mad stacks of paper in your office that you could produce a room this"—he searches for the word—"habitable."

"Oh, my best friend is a decorator. She just sort of Tasmanian Deviled herself one weekend. When she was done whirring around, this is how it looked." Also, twenty minutes earlier I hastily shoved all my piles of clutter and unopened mail into my closet and kitchen cabinets.

I regard Henry. "Don't you usually go away on summer weekends?"

"Sometimes. I needed to bill some hours this weekend."

"Partner track." I nod. "Did you do it?"

"Almost. Just a couple to go, but I have a conference call later tonight with a chatty client, so things look promising. So, how are you holding up?"

"I'm doing okay." In fact, my plucky resolve of two months prior has been replaced by abject terror. Even though my name is already attached to the papers, there is something so irreversible about actually appearing in the flesh before Justice Strand, opening my mouth and speaking. When I stop to think about what I'm risking, I freeze, so instead, for the past two weeks, I've fantasized about falling into a subway grate or getting brushed by a cab while crossing the street. Nothing terminal, just a few broken bones, so I can have a good excuse to find Fern another attorney and spend Friday comfortably in traction at Mount Sinai hospital.

Henry looks at me closely. "You freaking out?"

"A little."

He nods. "Not the easiest route, this whole plan you've got."

"Can we start with my outline?"

I hand it over and he flips through it. "Whoa. Overkill."

"I know—it just makes me feel better prepared."

"Not much of substance will be decided. Strand can't change custody unless he determines it's in the kids' best interests, and he won't do that without an actual hearing. But you do want to start to tell Fern's story and get out her key points."

We review my talking points—essentially, that Fern should have custody because Robert is turning the kids against Fern and harming them by doing so—and the specific relief I should request. We're on hour two and Henry's walking me through the process by which Strand will appoint neutral experts—attorneys for the kids and a psychiatrist to assess what would be best for them—when I order us some food.

Henry isn't much of a fixture at our nightly dinners, but I've started to invite him to eat with us. As with Liz and Rachel, I have a better sense of his habits and preferences than I do for most blood relations, so I know what to get: two corned beef and turkey sandwiches on marble rye, two cream sodas and two black-and-white cookies. When the food arrives, I bring the bag to the table and start unwrapping the sandwiches.

"So, Strand," I say, licking Russian dressing off my thumb. "I've never even seen him."

"He's just . . . well, some call him Andy Griffith."

"Why? He's a whistler?"

"He sort of acts like his courtroom is, you know, Mayberry— small town, why can't everyone just get along? You'll see. I think if you do your whole polite and pleasant thing, you should do all right."

"My polite and pleasant thing?"

"Yeah, you know." He smiles brightly, bobbing his head and blinking his eyes.

"Good Lord, Henry. Was that supposed to be me?"

He nods as though he's just espoused a simple truth and then, laughing, comes over to the table to take a half of sandwich.

"Okay. Moving on. Risa McDunn? I haven't been able to find out much about her. She doesn't have a Web site."

"Maybe it's better that way. You don't necessarily want her looking you up."

"Agreed."

"Well, she wrote that book," Henry says. "The one with the graphic title."

"Trust me, I've read it." Risa McDunn—and I directly quote her publisher's Web site—is not just a lawyer; she's also the best-selling author of the classic *Don't Be Afraid to Split the Baby: How to Win Your Child Custody Litigation.*

"What's it like?"

"About as nuanced as you'd expect from something with a title that makes you envision an infant cut in half. Very evocative chapter headings, though, like 'Making Your Spouse Pay' and 'Dirt You Can Buy from a Private Eye.'"

"She sounds very creative."

"She must be. In her reply papers to Fern's motion, she managed to list about fifteen reasons why Strand should throw out our case. But she must have a streak of humanity somewhere, because she likes dogs. Unless she's one of those people-hating dog lovers."

"One of what, now?"

"You know the type—hates people, thinks they're responsible for all the ill in the world; loves the innocence and unconditional love of dogs."

"You sound a little crazy. Although I am curious about the source of your information."

"Her book jacket. She mentions them in the third sentence." I adopt my best Home Shopping Network announcer voice. " 'Risa McDunn is one of the leading experts in family law. She has her own firm in Orange County, New York, where she works and lives with her two Irish wolfhounds.' "

He stops midchew and swallows. "You memorized that?"

"I know, horrible time management. I'm just a little hungry to know what to expect from her."

"Well, I've never had a case with her, but I've heard that she's a bit batty. Doesn't change how strong your facts are, just might be a wild ride." Henry swigs his cream soda. "Everett's actually had a case with her. A couple of years ago."

"It's okay. I'm not that desperate."

"He's not as bad as you think."

I make a face.

"I know, I know. You were his most recent victim, but you have to realize by now that he's just doling out the same shit that's been heaped on him."

"What was he like before he was partner?"

"He's always been a little on the awkward side. But the nastiness has increased each year that he works with Lillian. I think at some point he realized that if he just became her doormat, she would keep him around. I've heard that he waters her plants when she's away, no joke."

"I still don't get why he's partner. Why not keep him as counsel or something?"

"You want the real story?"

"No, Henry. I detest office gossip." I smile innocently. "Anything but the real story."

"Okay. This was about six years ago, before any of you started. Everett was engaged——"

"What?"

"Everett was engaged."

I inhale sharply. "Seriously?"

"Oh my God, Molly. It can't be that shocking. Let me tell the damn story."

"Okay, sorry. Go on."

"So, anyway. Everett was engaged to a fetching young lady."

"What was her name?"

"Um." Henry squints. "Becky. No, Becca, I think. Does it matter?"

"No. Just makes her seem more real. And she was fetching?"

"Not sure about the fetching part. It's subjective, right? And, I mean, this is Everett. She must have been at least a little quirky. But for the purposes of this story, yes, she was fetching. Anyway, Becca lived in another state." Henry holds up his hands in anticipation of my question and squints again. "Maryland, I think. Let's say Maryland. At some point, Everett went through the watershed moment that every Big Firm associate goes through—— why am I here? Is it worth all this work? What am I doing? Nothing you'd be familiar with on any level." Henry looks at me with a grin.

"Not in the slightest. Watershed moments are for wimps."

"Couldn't agree more. And so, during this period of self-reflection, young Everett chose love, or at least escape. He decided he was going to throw in the towel at Bacon Payne, move out to Baltimore or wherever Becca was and get a job at a nice firm with reasonable hours."

"What, did he get lost on the way?"

"Nope. Around the time that this was happening, Lillian was going through her divorce from Stan Armor. Ugly time, it was before she met Roger. So picture it, she's even needier than usual, Everett is her right-hand man and when he starts talking about giving notice and moving, she freaks out and convinces herself that he is irreplaceable."

"No way. She told him she'd make him partner if he broke up with Becca?"

"I think it was a little more nuanced than that. More like she told him that she needed him around, he asked about his partnership chances, she promised it to him and that was his true watershed moment. He made the deal, agreed to stay around, and he and Becca eventually broke up at some point after that, most likely as a result of his refusal to move, his insane hours and his utter devotion to another woman.

"And now, they're trapped together. Lillian resents that she wasted her chit on making him partner and wants to remind him every second that she owns him. And Everett is completely dependent on her. He has none of his own cases, and feels like he has to take whatever she dishes out."

"Depressing. That made me feel bad enough for Everett to need some cookie." I rip off two pieces of the white part of the cookie and hand one to Henry.

"Told you."

"So, when was your watershed moment?"

"Not sure. I certainly haven't been moved to make a wacky choice like some people I know."

"But like the thought process you were talking about—why am I doing this? My hours suck, blah, blah. You ever question that?"

"No. I've just sort of looked at it as something to get through. I've wanted to do this since I was a little kid."

I know that both of Henry's parents are partners at big New York law firms, so I guess this world is his comfort zone. I, on the other hand, wasn't even aware of big firms until law school. But maybe he didn't learn about fondue pots as early as I did.

"Why matrimonial?"

"Honestly, I always expected to do corporate work, but it bored me when I was a summer associate. I like the mix-up of transactional work and litigation. And I like dealing with different types of people. After my summer, I asked Lillian if there was space and she said sure. I think she liked that I have the joint JD/MBA. She thinks it sounds good for the department."

"Yeah, because they're both from Ivy League schools." I've heard Lillian point this out to at least six clients. "Is that why you're not like Everett?"

"Um, well, I also don't wear glasses. And I try not to yell at people in the hall, although it is hard sometimes."

"No, I mean for Lillian. Why does she leave you alone?"

"She doesn't entirely. I mean, she's Lillian—she definitely made me earn my stripes. But I've built up my own book of business."

"You have? How?"

"It's nothing magic. Just family connections that I've made through the years and then word of mouth. And for a certain circle, just working at Bacon Payne is enough to make them hire you."

"I'm surprised that Lillian isn't threatened by you."

"She probably is. But while I certainly don't want to piss her off, my partnership chances don't really rest on her."

"How is that possible?"

He smiles. "Dominic Pizaro has been best friends with my dad since law school. I've been playing basketball with him almost every Thursday evening since I was twelve."

"Dominic Pizaro? The one from the firm?"

"Yes, that one. How many people are there in this world named Dominic Pizaro?"

I laugh. "Never been so happy to hear about nepotism. I guess you have job security even if I've pulled you into this mess."

My buzzer rings and Henry looks at his big black sports watch. "How is it five o'clock already?"

"No clue how that happened." I open the door for Duck, who's talking as she waltzes in, something about my doorman and his wedding. I try to follow along, but she stops when she sees Henry standing by the door.

"Oh, hi," she says as I say, "This is Duck."

"Henry." They shake hands. "Great to meet you."

"Henry is a saint who was helping me with some work."

"Of course he was. God forbid you would take a Sunday off, you automatons. Henry, come and see a movie with us. We're planning to see—what is it?—*East Spy, West Spy*, that new Ben Brick movie, but we are open to anything that is mindless and is showing around seven."

"I'd love to, but I can't. Maybe another time."

Duck rolls her eyes. "I haven't been able to get this one"—she pats my shoulder—"to see a movie since six months ago, so I'm not holding my breath, but sure—another time sounds lovely."

Henry looks at me. "Thanks for lunch."

"Thanks for coming over. Can you tell how ready I am now?" I know my smile looks like one of those squiggly Charlie Brown ones.

"It'll be fine. Bye, Duck."

As Henry leaves and I shut the door behind him, Duck comes over and stands directly in front of me, her eyes wide. "Um, hello? He's hot. Like, really hot. How have you not mentioned him before?"

"I have. That's Henry."

"Yeah, but why have you not mentioned the hot part?"

"Please. You're ridiculously transparent."

"What?"

"You're trying to get me interested in someone who's not Caleb. But I'm not interested in Caleb. I said no."

"Of course you're not, which is why you ask me oh so casually about every detail of his office renovation." She blinks innocently. "But I have no ulterior motives. I'm just asking why you haven't mentioned Henry's dashing good looks."

"It's not relevant. Stop giving me that look. He has a girlfriend."

"Do you ever socialize with guys who don't have girlfriends anymore?"

I ignore her, but Duck continues as though I've responded. "He can't be serious with her. If he is, then why are the two of you alone in your apartment on a summer weekend?"

"Jeez, Duck. Are you also steamed that I was entertainin' without my white gloves and a crinoline? We were doing work."

"But you're not denying you think he's cute."

"Of course he's cute."

"Aha!"

"Again. He. Has. A. Girlfriend."

"He does? Gawd. Why didn't you just say so?" Duck smiles at my exasperation. "Go get your bag so we can get out of here." She gives my tank top and shorts an exaggerated once-over. "Not like you put any effort into your study outfit. I guess that's as clear a sign as any that you're not harboring a crush."

"Exactly," I say, grabbing a cardigan and my bag. "Nothing to see here. Let's go."

my visit to mayberry

The night before Fern's court date, I finally doze off at three o'clock in the morning, only to dream about frantically wandering around my college campus, being unable to get to the room for my Abnormal Psych exam. When I finally find it and push open the door, I have floated onto the set of *Jeopardy!* and am behind the electric blue podium as Alex Trebek barks confusing questions about somatoform disorder and antisocial personalities.

A few hours later, I jolt awake. My entire week has been a long dark tunnel winding toward this morning: Oral Argument Day. I get out of bed, blast hot water for a brief shower and twitch my way into a navy suit. After forcing down some dry toast, I promptly throw it up, and decide to get the hell out of my apartment. I emerge from the subway at the Borough Hall station almost two hours before our appearance, more than enough time to purchase herbal tea at a coffee cart and park myself on a bench in the hall outside Strand's courtroom.

An hour and a half later, Robert Walker, *Forbes*'s 256th-richest American, walks in. He's alone, which is strange. Lillian always meets her VIP clients at the office and strides into court like the Mod Squad, the client flanked between her take-no-prisoners legal team.

Relishing my brief moment of anonymity—in twenty-five

minutes, Robert will know to forever be on guard in my presence—I pretend to look down at my papers as I check him out. Duck would probably describe him as a human potato: big lumpy features, thick, short, graham cracker brown hair that looks too uniform in color for his sixty-five years.

I hear the panning percussion of Jimmy Buffett's "Margaritaville"—this has to be the first time it's played in the Brooklyn Supreme Courthouse—and Walker picks up his phone. So he's one of *those*, a type-A shark masquerading as a beach bum: deep-sea fishing on his fifty-foot yacht; putting an avuncular arm around the resort's golf caddie, with whom he's on a joking and first-name basis five minutes after meeting; and then, having convinced the world what a good dude he is, discarding his wife, terrorizing some employees, damaging his kids. He answers with a gruff "Yeah," nods once, hangs up and starts firing away on a BlackBerry. He is still typing when a tall-heeled woman clicks up to him, carrying two coffee cups.

No, definitely not Risa, I conclude, after she leans in to straighten his tie. He holds up a hand to stop her, finishes typing and then allows her to resume the grooming. This must be Claire Dennis. Risa's reply papers had rhapsodized about her—part earth mother, part PTA machine, Claire is Robert's girlfriend of two years and, according to the papers, a consistent maternal presence in the lives of Anna and Connor.

Claire is in her mid-to-late thirties, a delicate little pink sea-shell of a person. It's how Fern must have looked before she ran smack into life's hardships: petite, proportional and freshly pretty. Claire's shoulder-length brown hair is pulled back into a sophisticated low ponytail—no bumps or frizz—and her court attire is oh so appropriate, a short-sleeved dark gray dress, nipped in at the waist and accessorized with high black pumps.

After straightening Robert's tie, Claire hands him the coffee cup and then reaches into her textured reptilian navy bag for a small container of Aleve. He dutifully puts a pill on his tongue and washes it down with coffee. She sits very close to him on the bench and occasionally pats his leg or rubs his shoulder. They nestle there sweetly, looking the picture of either father-daughter devotion or romantic contentment, depending on how much you know.

I'm watching them out of the corner of my eye when Fern arrives. She walks by their bench, her eyes fixed on me, deliberately not looking at the lovebirds to her left. When we hug, I see, out of my peripheral vision, Robert Walker stiffen.

"How are you?" I say. Each week, Fern's eyes have gotten less watery, her gaze more direct, her voice firmer. The fight has made her stronger, galvanized her.

"I'm good," she says. "A little nervous, but honestly, I'm glad it's finally here. You?"

"I'm ready."

"So that's Claire?"

"Either that or a very affectionate assistant."

"Is his lawyer here?"

"Not yet." I check my watch. Nine twenty-five. "Do you want to go over anything again?"

"Nope. Let's talk about something entirely different, please."

"I keep forgetting to tell you. I went into your shop, Petal and Stem."

Fern smiles. "Which location?"

"The one on Lex."

"Oh, that's the first one my boss, Brian, opened. He's actually there a lot. Did you see him?"

"Fern"—I start to laugh—"I have no idea. I'm just trying to make conversation. I was there months ago, ordering flowers for Secretary's Day."

"Administrative Assistant's Day," she corrects me as an officer swings open the doors, signaling that the court is open for business. "Please, talking about work is relaxing me. Do you remember who rang you up?"

"A young girl, I think. Brown hair."

"That was probably Jenny, Brian's daughter. Did you see Brian? Tall, gray hair? I went to high school with him."

"Is that a coincidence?"

"No, we've been in touch since we both moved up here. And then he gave me a job when I needed one. And then, he gave Lolly a job."

"Your sister, right? Is that her real name?"

"Her real name is Laurel Dolly."

I repeat this, but my voice goes up at the end like I'm asking a question.

"I know. It doesn't really flow. Dolly was my mom's favorite aunt. Plus, she was hooked on the plant motif for us—"

"Fitting for your later work."

"Exactly."

"So did Lolly move up to work at Petal and Stem?"

"Not exactly. She moved up when I was pregnant with Connor. Actually, Robert had promised her a job, which never materialized when everything fell apart, so then she took care of me, and Brian hired her for a bit." Her voice drops several decibels, although it hadn't exactly been loud to begin with. "She hates Robert. Passionately."

I don't get a chance to reply that I don't really blame her, because I'm watching a woman walk over to Robert Walker and Claire. If that's Risa McDunn, she isn't the severe, suited Amazon I've been picturing. She's small, with what my mee-maw would have called an ample bosom, but what's most noticeable is her outfit. It's straight from the wardrobe department of *Little House on the Prairie*: long, pleated lavender skirt, ivory blouse buttoned up to a high collar that must be itchy torture on this hot July day and pointed beige shoes. No bonnet or parasol, but they would not be out of place.

Risa is trailed by a lanky man with floppy blond hair. Everything about him screams associate: his hopping, uncomfortable stance; his protective grip on the black litigation bag; the way his head is constantly leaning in toward Risa and Robert, resulting in a stooped, kind of giraffe look.

Robert Walker points at us, flicking his index finger against his thumb, like disposing of something sticky and gross, and Risa's eyes glide from my head down to my shoes.

I walk over, hand extended. "Molly Grant."

She shakes it, without a smile. "Ah, Molly." She peers at me as though she's been commissioned for a reading of my aura.

I turn to Robert Walker. "Molly Grant. I'm representing Fern."

He shakes my hand as though it's a dirty tissue to be crumpled, his eyes over my head the entire time.

I nod at Risa. "Should we go talk down there by the benches?"

She's expressionless for almost a minute. Then, as though I'm a waitress who has asked if I can get her anything else, she tilts her head to the side, purses her lips and shakes her head no, smiling politely. Usually this is when the attorneys kibitz: we find a neutral space away from our clients and try to persuade the other that he or she has no case. The tone is always different—I've laughed, gossiped, been called wrong, stupid, immature and too young to know any better. Until today, though, I've never been ignored.

I return to the bench, my eyes wide with disbelief.

"Bad?" says Fern.

"More like—" I pause and hum the theme to *The Twilight Zone.*

"Fitting," says Fern. "Because that's how my whole life feels."

Eventually, the clerk emerges and shouts, "Lawyers on Walker."

I stand up and Fern whispers, "Do I just stay here?"

"For now. They'll call you in at some point."

She nods and I follow the clerk behind the courtroom, into

Strand's chambers. I feel like I'm in a jury duty video: Justice Strand sits behind a huge walnut desk, the American flag waving behind him. He has a wide toothy smile, and perfect posture under his robe. Mike, Strand's law clerk, sits to his right, chin up, papers in his lap.

Strand waves his hand in the direction of the chairs in front of his desk. "*Walker v. Walker*, have a seat, counselors."

All three of us murmur greetings. Risa and I sit down.

"So, hello. Welcome to my courtroom. What can I help you with today?" He smiles broadly and pats our motion papers, which are stacked neatly on his desk in front on him.

He has just completed the last syllable when Risa pounces.

"Your Honor. We desperately need your good sense. My client has single-handedly raised his son and daughter for the past three years. Ms. Walker has not been in the picture for the simple reason that she's mentally ill. She's been diagnosed, Your Honor—depression, homicidal thoughts—not a safe environment for children. Terribly sad situation for everyone involved. Anyway, she abandoned her children years ago because she couldn't deal with them and now, suddenly, she has decided to upend everything again. But she can't handle it, Your Honor, and the kids don't even know her—"

I jump in. "Your Honor, this is simply untrue. Ms. Walker, my client, I mean, the mother, is not mentally ill—"

"Counselor. Don't interrupt me. Let me finish. Your Honor, may I finish?" Risa keeps her eyes on the judge.

Justice Strand's smile wavers. "Yes, you may finish." He looks at me apologetically. "Please, let her finish. No interrupting in my courtroom. Only courteous behavior here."

"Yes, Your Honor."

"As I was saying. Her client is mentally ill, sees hallucinations, can't be around knives, that type of thing."

"What? This is crazy. That's a lie—"

Justice Strand eyes me sternly. "Ms.——," he starts, before realizing he doesn't know my name. He looks down at the papers as Mike quickly says, "Grant."

"Ms. Grant," Strand continues. "You're not doing your client any favors. No interruptions. You'll have your turn later."

Risa nods as though justice has been restored. "Thank you, Your Honor. So the father, Robert Walker—incidentally, Your Honor, a community pillar, I'm sure you're familiar with him—hundreds of people would speak for his integrity, competence, valor, heart. Really, he is just an incredible human being, a beacon to all. Every time he and I meet, I am blown away by his character. And I do not say that about just anyone. Anyway, the father was devastated at his ex-wife's desertion, but he stepped up. He's become, well, he's become superdad, prioritizing these kids, being their rock, their champion.

"So, this is a case that requires a lot of thought, Your Honor. Not only is there the very basic matter of the kids' safety if Ms. Walker's inappropriate requests are granted—there's also the very real concern of upsetting the routine of two tiny little kids from a broken family, who have been through enough. These kids, these poor, poor kids—their mother is a sick, sick woman—homicidal." She looks around the room, making sure we all understand what's at stake. "It's quite a burden for these poor kids to have. A homicidal mother. We have to proceed with caution."

The stooped giraffe, whose name, it turns out, is Graham, nods emphatically and slowly, as though he's found a great batch of leaves to snack on.

Justice Strand frowns. "Of course. We certainly don't want to do anything rash that will upset the kids."

"No, Your Honor. You need to dismiss their motion."

"Your Honor, may I speak now?" I say.

"Yes, of course. So, how is Ms. Walker doing? Is she on medication?"

"Your Honor, the mother is not mentally ill. Ms. McDunn is mistaken about that."

He looks confused. "Having homicidal tendencies does point to mental illness. You don't need to worry about the stigma, counselor. No one thinks it's your client's fault."

Risa jumps in, "I have documentation—"

"Your Honor, I assume I can finish without being interrupted?"

He looks relieved at knowing the answer to my question and points at Risa. "No interrupting, Ms. McDunn. Everyone gets a chance to speak in my court. We've covered the rules here already."

"The mother had postpartum depression two years ago, when her son, Connor, was born. She has no other mental health issues whatsoever."

"But what about the violence?" Justice Strand says.

"She's not violent, Your Honor. She is a gentle and loving person. She's in perfect health. Mr. Walker has deliberately frozen her out of her own kids' lives. It's a textbook case of parental alienation, and all she's asking is the chance to be their mom. Because of him, she's missed too much already."

Risa is up, out of her chair. "Parental alienation? This is not parental alienation. This is a case about a father's protection of his children. Your Honor, I wrote a book about custody. I am an expert on identifying parental alienation, and this is not it."

Justice Strand frowns as though trying to figure out why we can't just get along.

"I care about the best interests of the children," he says. "And you're both telling such different stories about what's happened here. Can you settle this?"

"I'm sure we can, Your Honor. The father is absolutely willing to continue Ms. Walker's visitation. It does need to be supervised, of course, for security reasons."

I shake my head. "We won't agree to anything other than custody returned to the mother."

Justice Strand sighs. "Well, then, I can't really decide anything until we have a hearing on the best interests of the children."

"Your Honor, that's ridiculous. There's enough to dismiss this motion *prima facie*," Risa says.

"No, there's not, Ms. McDunn. There's a request to change custody and an accusation of parental alienation. And you know I can't just dismiss it. So, you need to get some dates from my court clerk out front. And I'll need you to stipulate to a law guardian and forensic. Can you do that or do I need to select one for you?"

I nod. "Yes, Your Honor. I'm sure we can stipulate to that. What about establishing some counseling or visitation now for the mother and the children? She hasn't been able to see the kids since last fall."

Justice Strand raises an eyebrow at Risa.

"Absolutely not." She steps backward, as though she can't even be in the same room as that suggestion. "It's a basic safety issue. For the kids."

Justice Strand looks thoughtful. "I'm concerned about the violence. What about the knives? You know, let's just continue supervised visitation until the hearing, just to be sure. You'll get your hearing soon enough."

"We need a neutral therapist to supervise, not Mr. Walker's nanny, which is what's been happening." I hand over a list to Risa and Mike that has five names of psychologists specializing in children of divorce. "None of these has any connection to Ms. Walker."

Risa crumples up the list without looking at it. "The father is not going to agree to have some therapist he's never heard of talking to his children. Why would he agree to that?"

"That's why there are five names on there. I'm sure we can

agree that at least one of them is sufficiently qualified to clean up the mess he's made."

Justice Strand slumps down in his chair. He looks up wearily. "Ms. McDunn, I suggest you try to persuade your client to at least look at the list or come up with some names of his own. And as far as cost goes, it's going to be an uphill battle for him to claim that he's not the moneyed party here."

I am heartened by this, the first sign Strand has given that his thoughts are independent from Risa's.

Risa shakes her head vehemently. "But their separation agreement says that the party in breach of the agreement will be responsible for costs, and Mrs. Walker's in breach."

Justice Strand stares off in the distance, mourning his hopes for a nice breezy settlement conference. *Dude,* I think, *you are in the wrong business.* "I'm not inclined to rule on counsel fees until after the hearing." He shoos us away. "Go find some common ground."

Risa ignores the order to compromise and leads Graham—who is glaring and huffing at me like a ninth-grade drama student in a production of *The Crucible*—to a bench on the far side of the hall where Robert and Claire wait. I join Fern and recount Risa's arguments for her.

"I have to know," I say, "where on earth did you meet that guy?"

"CBS. I was his assistant."

I try not to gag. "Great, so he's guilty of sexual harassment too?"

"It wasn't like that."

"Yeah. I know *my* parents would be just thrilled if I told them that my new boyfriend was their age and also my boss."

"Don't forget married," Fern says, biting her lip.

"Oh. Fern."

Fern nods. "To Vicki, his second wife. But they had problems before we started anything."

"I'm sure they did."

"He doesn't seem like an obvious choice at this moment, but I swear, he can be incredibly charming. You probably won't see that side of him, though."

"Probably not."

"And he's super smart and sharp, completely in his element at work. Everyone had a crush on him."

"If you say so."

Fern sighs. "Trust me, I understand your skepticism, but he's really not a monster. He just gets very defensive and paranoid and likes to be in control."

I tilt my head to the side. "Isn't that what Mussolini's wife kept telling everyone about him?"

Fern jabs me in the ribs with her elbow, but she's smiling.

Eventually, Mike emerges from the courtroom's double doors and calls us all back in. Justice Strand sits at his bench, looking reinvigorated and in command as he introduces himself to Fern and Robert, although his smile dims when he hears that we have not reached consensus. Ready for us to leave his courtroom, he rattles off a series of orders: someone named Roland Williams will be the attorney representing the interests of Anna and Connor, and a Dr. Gary Newkirk, a forensic psychologist, will assist Strand in his determination of what's best for the kids; Emily Freed (after much back and forth from Risa) will be the therapist who supervises Fern's visits with the kids.

We get some dates for our hearing, and then it's over. We've been here for almost five hours without eating or drinking anything. My head throbs from dehydration and lack of nourishment.

Robert Walker and Risa confer, huddled close together. Claire stands behind Robert, rubbing his back. It must gall him to spend the entire morning at court, waiting. And there is more to come: random deadlines; court appearances where he's forced to show up but will not be asked to say a word; enough bureaucracy to make anyone feel small, powerless and frustrated. Robert Walker probably hasn't been in touch with any of those emotions in a while.

Fern has, however. She and I share a satisfied smile, our subtle substitute for a high five. We have a hearing date and that is a victory.

godzilla vs. mothra

Lillian has blocked out the entire day to prepare for what we're all now calling the Cat Hearing, which is three days away. I don't know how one small conference room will contain both Lillian's and Liesel's sizable alpha egos. It's a matchup of headliners—my personal Godzilla vs. my personal Mothra—and I anticipate being curled up in the fetal position by mid-morning.

After Kim buzzes me, I knock lightly on Lillian's door to let her know that Liesel is waiting in the conference room. Lillian stalls, making a few brief phone calls and sorting her papers with the kind of noisy fruitlessness that indicates she's not even looking at them. Finally, after ten minutes, she grabs the outline for Liesel's testimony that I left on her desk last night and, grumbling, gets out of her chair.

"I really don't have time for this," she says.

"I know."

"And you did a great job on the discovery. I don't need to be involved."

"Thank you."

She shifts, straightening her jacket. "Talk about divas. I had to move my entire schedule around to do this hand-holding."

"I know," I say again, even though I am pretty sure, aside from the Cat Hearing, Lillian has nothing other than the usual: a few luncheons, a manicure and several initial consults. It is rare for Lillian to return to a case after she's cast it off, but upon hearing that I would be arguing her motion solo, Liesel pitched a fit, sending a torrent of e-mails, letters and phone calls, declaring that if Lillian didn't do the argument, Liesel would retain new counsel. ("Molly," she had said, "you are not cutting your teeth on my cats." And as distracted as I was by how disgustingly furry that sounded, the irony was still not lost on me: I had already taken on Robert Walker, but could not be trusted with the fate of Pickles von Ketchup.)

Lillian had fought back. She tried to pawn off Liesel on Everett, Liz, even Henry, but Liesel wouldn't budge. Not wanting to lose Liesel's steady monthly receivables, Lillian eventually capitulated. And to my surprise, today she is rolling up her sleeves for some pure, old-fashioned work.

Liesel steps out of her conference room chair and walks over to Lillian. As always, I am struck by how normal she appears: round brown eyes, boring red sweater set, messy bun—the type of person who could be counted on to bring consistently reliable homemade brownies to her book club meeting.

Beaming, Liesel puts a fluttering hand to her chest. "Lillian. It is such an honor. Thank you so much for making the time. It means everything."

In a flash, Lillian's expression changes from put-upon to charmed. "Of course," she says. "And don't you worry about this jackass and his lawsuit. He's toast. We're going to take care of you."

"I know you will. I have such faith in the team here." Liesel turns to me and holds out both hands. "Molly," she says as though we're long-lost pen pals. "Always wonderful to see you."

It's as surreal as if, instead of burning villages, Mothra and Godzilla had joined forces to coordinate a canned-food drive. "No, really, Mothra, let me design the flyers. I *insist*." Liesel engulfs me in an awkwardly brittle hug. I manage to blurt out something pleasant sounding before Lillian adjusts her glasses, opens the outline and begins asking Liesel questions. After about thirty minutes, Liesel raises her hand.

"Feel free to jump in with any questions, Liesel," says Lillian as though she's granting Liesel three special wishes.

"It's very important to me to be able to discuss all the things I did for the cats and especially how I had to constantly remind Stewart to help out. He never had their best interest in mind. Pickles had a fatty tumor once and I asked him to take her to the vet. Seventeen times I asked him. I know it was seventeen because I counted, but he absolutely refu—"

Lillian holds both hands up. I almost duck my head anticipating the explosion from this interruption, but Liesel stops, tilts her head and smiles politely. "Yes?"

"Is a fatty tumor harmful?"

"No, but that's not the point of the story."

Lillian smiles kindly. "And isn't that good news, dear? That Pickles is in good health? But we don't want to include too much information about how much you had to remind Stewart to take care of the cats, because it's off topic. Perhaps we'll get in a quick mention, but really, we want to make sure to emphasize the right things."

Liesel nods thoughtfully.

We resume the preparation without incident and in fact need to stop only twice more: once to advise Liesel to use a gentle tone with Stew's lawyer during cross-examination ("Think of him as your boss's slightly slow third-grade son—even when he gets obnoxious, you have to be polite") and once more, to tell her what to wear ("professionally tasteful, but not too severe").

It goes so well that three days later, on the date of the hearing, I am optimistic, right up until I spot Liesel waiting outside the courtroom for us. She looks professional, but has skewed a little severe—black suit and slicked-back hair.

"Hi, Liesel." I smile and step forward. "Sorry we're a couple minutes late. We had trouble getting a—"

She taps her foot repeatedly, frowns and looks at her watch. "I guess when it's your life, it's important enough to show up on time."

Lillian's eyes flash and she says nothing as she walks ahead quickly and pushes open the courtroom doors.

Justice Love, a maternal-looking woman with gray hair, is at the bench, presiding over another matter. Lillian darts off to say hello to Ethan Crosby, who is crammed into one of the spectator benches next to Stew. His associate Erika, whom I haven't seen since moving day, is behind them. I head over to Linda, the court clerk, to say hello and tell her we're here.

Within minutes, the other parties wrap up their business and Linda calls out for the parties on Billings. Justice Love addresses both Lillian and Ethan in a clipped, professional tone that makes me almost forget that Justice and Mr. Love were guests at Lillian and Roger's Hamptons home last summer.

During direct testimony, Ethan tries as hard as he can, pacing across the courtroom on his tree-trunk legs, furrowing his white brow in concern as Stew testifies about how much Pepe LeMew, Pickles von Ketchup and Princess Fifi mean to him.

Stew trots out the arguments from his motion papers—that he and Liesel always intended to make the cats into a profitable showing and breeding business and that, as such, they are joint property. I'm getting whiplash from his testimony: during some points, he gets very emotional about the cats, referring to them as his "everything"; at other points, it's like he's talking about bars of gold. Lillian, her glasses on, scribbles notes on the legal pad that I had set up beside her. When Ethan finishes, she doesn't even bother to glance at what she's written, walking right up to Stew.

"Hello, Mr. Billings." Her tone is friendly, sincere.

"Hello," Stewart says, blinking rapidly.

"You testified about Article One, Provision Four, of Exhibit One, the Prenuptial Agreement?"

"Yes." Stewart swallows.

Lillian hands the court officer the agreement, who presents it to Stewart. "Could you read that for me, please?"

" 'In regards to any joint venture started after the date of the marriage, and to which joint venture both parties contribute in any way, including but not limited to contributions of monies, time and/or effort, same joint venture shall be and remain joint property.' " Stewart's voice gains confidence as he reads and when done, he looks up triumphantly.

"You started a joint business during the year after your marriage?"

"Yes."

"It was called Game, Set, Match Up?"

"Yes."

"It was a matchmaking service?"

"Yes, matchmaking through tennis lessons."

Lillian pauses and I imagine all of us in the courtroom, save Stewart and Liesel, are contemplating the mechanics of combining these two services. "And does it still exist?"

"No, it folded about eighteen months after we started it."

"And when you started the venture, did you file with the State of New York?"

"Yes."

"You incorporated?"

"Yes."

"And did the corporation issue stock?"

"Yes."

"And who owned the company's stock?"

"My wife and I did."

"Both of you, jointly?"

"Yes."

"And did you file a corporate tax return for each year you operated?"

"Yes."

And it goes on like that. Politely, cleanly, effectively, Lillian first makes clear the legitimacy of Game, Set, Match Up and Stewart's expectation of income from it, however frustrated. Then she walks Stewart through the acquisition process and the cats' lack of show experience. There's no dramatic moment—nothing like in *A Few Good Men*, when Jack Nicholson roars that Tom Cruise can't handle the truth—but Lillian meticulously picks away at Stewart's testimony. By the time she's finished, it's impossible to imagine that Stewart and Liesel ever had plans for the cats beyond scratching behind their ears and occasionally waving around a laser pointer for them to chase.

After Stewart's turn on the stand, Liesel is sworn in. Her delivery is slightly hostile and defensive, but she credibly establishes that the cats were purchased—in her name—to be pets. Lillian completes her questions and Ethan eases up from his seat with considerable effort. When, after about fifteen minutes, he asks Liesel who was responsible for grooming the cats, Liesel's lips purse.

Seeing her expression, Ethan moves closer. "You didn't like the way Stewart groomed the cats?"

"Objection," says Lillian. "Out of the scope of direct testimony."

"Ms. Billings testified that she spent time on the day-to-day care of them. I'm just exploring that, Your Honor," says Ethan.

Judge Love nods. "I'll allow it."

"What I didn't like," says Liesel, leaning back conversationally, "was how he'd say he'd groom the cats and never did."

"He didn't follow through?"

"That's putting it delicately. He is a complete loaf of a human being. I would have to ask him fifteen times to do anything. I mean, I was working all day, paying for everything, and he couldn't even take care of the cats. It was too much for him. So yes, the day-to-day care and distribution of jobs was a source of tension."

"Fifteen times? That sounds like a lot."

Liesel snorts. "Please, if anything, that's a lowball estimate. Once"—she shakes her head at the memory—"Pickles had a fatty tumor, so I asked Stewart to take her to the vet."

It takes some effort to stop from repeatedly banging my forehead against the defense table.

"Pickles had a tumor?"

"Objection," says Lillian, "way off course."

Liesel rolls her eyes and holds up her hands at Lillian. Judge Love, who has been scribbling on a pad in front of her, slowly turns her head toward Liesel in stupefied disbelief. Ethan's sizable mouth drops open. Oblivious, Liesel continues, leaning forward in the witness seat. "It was a fatty tumor, not harmful, but unsightly. They protrude and continue to grow until they become a real problem. How many times do you think I asked Stewart to take Pickles in? How many times? Seventeen. I know because I made a spreadsheet of each time I asked him." Liesel spits and fumes like a Joan Crawford impersonator. "Finally, I had to hire someone else to take the cat to the vet. Can you imagine that? He"—Liesel points to Stewart—"has no job and I still have to arrange to outsource a vet appointment. And he claims to love these cats?" She stares down Ethan Crosby as though he's personally responsible for Pickles's tumor; apparently she doesn't give a crap about sucking up to her boss's third-grader.

Lillian stares at Liesel through narrowed eyes, her fists gripping her pen so tightly that her knuckles are white.

Ethan nods as though he completely feels Liesel's pain. "So if it wasn't a dangerous tumor, why was it so important?"

"Because Pickles is an F1 Savannah pedigreed purebred. She was bred from a long line of show cats, including three Grand Champions and five National Winners, and cost me twenty thousand dollars. If she had a tumor hanging off her goddamned gut, she'd be worth nothing, a complete and utter waste of decades of work."

Ethan steps back, looking more surprised than victorious. He clears his throat uncertainly. "No further questions."

On redirect, Lillian tries to clean up, emphasizing that Liesel and Stewart had not made any money from Pickles, no matter how expensive she had been.

I expect a scene as I pack up our files, but Lillian flutters around saying her good-byes as she normally does. We file out of the courtroom and into the elevator. As the doors close behind us, Liesel smiles confidentially. "That went well."

"We're not discussing it here," Lillian says.

Liesel purses her lips in annoyance but, amazingly, says nothing as we emerge from the elevator and walk in awkward silence through the rotunda and down the steps of the building. On the sidewalk outside, right next to the security station, Lillian stops abruptly and turns around, crossing her arms across her chest and giving Liesel a deliberate once-over.

"It went well? It went well for me. I put on the best damn case anyone could for you. But you? You were hands down the worst witness I have ever seen in my life. Interrupting your own lawyer? Holding up your hands at me? I know you've made yourself a lot of money, sweetheart, but you must be the dumbest bitch I've ever represented, and I've represented some real dummies."

Liesel's face drains of color until it's a violent, vampiric white. "It had to be said. He was making it sound like I was crazy to be upset."

"Bullshit. That's his job. And your job was to talk about what

I told you to talk about. All you had to do was listen to my instructions and pretend to be pleasant for a fucking hour. Too much of a challenge for you, apparently."

"I was telling the truth."

"I'm glad you feel good about it, but just so you understand how this went—this should've been a slam dunk, but after your la-la land performance in there, Pickles von Pepe or whatever the fuck you named her might well be spending her days with that doughnut you married." Lillian barks out a caustic laugh. "I really get why Molly can't stand you."

I fix my eyes on the building across the street and feel my cheeks redden.

Lillian continues. "Probably the only person who likes you right now is Ethan Crosby, because you gave his case a fighting chance in hell. We will remain your attorneys on record until the decision comes in, but after that, we're done. Come on, Molly."

I touch Liesel's arm and whisper, "Sorry," but she doesn't respond. As Lillian walks away, Liesel stands frozen in the middle of the sidewalk, her jaw hanging open.

Scurrying after Lillian, I feel terrible and I'm not sure why. My days of handling Liesel are over, and that is cause to rejoice. As many times as I've imagined ripping into her in the way Lillian has just done, though, there was nothing satisfying about it. I feel a little ashamed, actually. Watching her crash and burn on the stand made me cringe, but it also made me realize that beneath her negligible interpersonal skills, Liesel is crying out for an audience. Granted, it might have been a bit smarter to unload on a therapist rather than her husband's divorce lawyer, but she's staying on message: she needs the world to know that she's in pain and it's Stewart's fault.

There's no amount of money that would make me represent Liesel again, but still, some part of me wishes I had had this epiphany before today.

the shade of no boundaries

The phone connection to my mom is crackly and fading in that way that immediately identifies she's not only on a cell phone but also in transit and indeed, she tells me, "I'm here!"

I look out the window of my office, half-expecting her to appear outside my window, levitating by the thirty-seventh floor. "How was the flight?"

"Heaven."

"Which part—the middle seat or the three-hour delay on a hot tarmac?"

"I sat. I read. I sipped the drink someone thoughtfully brought to me."

"Where are you now?"

"Aymade is driving me." A friendly male voice corrects her pronunciation and she repeats after him. "Ah-med, oh sorry, like red, I get it. Ahmed is taking me down the FDR Drive now. What time is dinner?"

"Six."

"Isn't that too early for you to leave work?" My mom sounds worried, like my priorities are all wrong, joyriding instead of studying for the big test tomorrow. "Molly? I don't want to get you into trouble."

"It's August. It's slow. It's fine." We have the same conversation each visit, but I especially appreciate the irony now; as if, with all the fireballs I'm juggling, leaving the office at six on a Friday would be the thing to fell me. "How's Dad?"

"Sad he had to stay, but hopefully distracted by working on payroll."

For as long as I can remember, the demands of Cheddar and Better have dictated an alternating "man-on-man" visitation schedule: Mom hangs with me; Dad babysits the store. Partner swap. Repeat. One unforeseen benefit of this is that I can assure my clients with a straight face that little Emma will be no worse off after spending Saturday alone with Dad and Sunday alone with Mom. If anything, I tell them, it will strengthen and deepen their children's individual relationships with their parents, encourage real and honest conversations. Perhaps I should start telling my clients that their coparenting schedule will imbue their children with an independent spirit, as I have no plans to engage in a deep and honest conversation with my mom this weekend. My goal is to get through the weekend without disclosing the following: my role in the Walker case, my fear of Lillian, my flirtation with Caleb, about whom my parents know nothing.

The rest of the afternoon ticks by, and I'm in the middle of a conference call with Sully, a private investigator—Kira Wades has been adamant that her husband has offshore accounts, which we've been trying to track down—when I hear effusive laughter from a few doors down. It's a little too loud, a little too forced— *Ha! Ha! Ha!*

Lillian must be on a walkabout.

When Lillian is truly bored, she breaks free of her office and goes roaming around the halls. It's like a geriatric rock legend going on tour; it doesn't happen all that frequently, but when it does, we—her adoring public—are supposed to show up and swarm the stage (i.e., locate the office where she's landed and crowd in like skipping, smiling teenagers in a music video), no matter how feeble the show actually is.

On the other end of the phone, Sully hems and haws about how this search didn't find anything, but maybe if the client throws, I dunno, another couple thousand at the search, he'll be able to get me some information.

There's a shriek from down the hall—*"You're too much! Ha! Ha! Ha!"*—and I shift in my seat. It's like missing someone's birthday party, even if you never really clicked with the birthday girl; even if they're having it at the roller rink and you hate skating; even if they're serving one of those giant submarine sandwiches composed primarily of bread that tastes like cardboard. It's screwed up, but you still don't want to show up at school on Monday when they're all reminiscing about the group skate to Journey, so I hang up with Sully and rush down the hall to Rachel's office.

"Lillian's evening plans were canceled," says Liz, and I can tell by her tone that this is a warning as much as a celebration. "And she's taking us for manicures!"

"Wow."

"Five thirty." Lillian grants a beneficent smile. "Kim's calling Svetlana now. We knew you'd want in, so I'm having her make four reservations."

"Great," I say, my voice ringing with phony joy as my brain skips ahead to my evening plans. If I tell my mom that my boss required my presence, she'll understand and we can just push dinner back a half hour. It will be fine.

"Molly," says Rachel, her brow creasing, "what about your mom?"

"Your mom?" Lillian looks intrigued. "What's happening with your mom?"

"She just flew in for the weekend, but it's okay. She doesn't expect to see me until dinner, so I can still come."

"Invite her!" Lillian gets a compassionate gleam in her eye as though she's piping in fresh water to a remote Kenyan village instead of offering a double coat of pink polish. "I'd love to meet her."

"Oh, that's so generous." I emphasize the *o* in "so" a little too much, bordering right on the verge of phony. "But you really don't have to."

"Molly, enough." Lillian's voice is a little snappier. "Tell your mom to meet us there. I won't have you missing time with her for no reason. Family is too important."

I nod, not too trapped to appreciate the humor of Lillian—she of the estranged daughter and serial marriages—opining wise on the power of family. My mom will hate manicure night. But there is no contest: her comfort, like everything else that should be more important, is secondary to Lillian's demands.

I beg off traveling en masse with The Girls to the Salon at Fifty-fifth and Fifth, and even Lillian agrees that I should wait and escort my mother there. A few minutes after Lillian, Rachel and Liz file out, I head down to the lobby.

Of course, my mom is already there, outside, leaning against the glass door, her face raised up to the sun, soaking it in. As I exit the revolving door, she turns around and breaks into a huge smile. "Ha! I get such a kick out of seeing you emerge from this fancy building in a suit."

I know this and it's exactly why I wore one today, even though nothing in my workday required it. She wraps her strong arms around me and pulls me to her, her touch refreshingly cool and firm even on this muggy wet blanket of a day. Taking a step backward, she places her hands on my shoulders.

"A little pale for August," she says in a voice that's half concern, half pride. "Same ol', same ol'?"

I nod and shrug. My hours and lack of sleep have been a constant of family discussion since the summer before tenth grade, when ninety percent of my dinners seemed to be scarfed in the

Cheddar and Better stockroom (my SAT prep class was sandwiched between preseason soccer practice, volunteering at the library and my shifts at the store). My parents have always seemed a little in awe of my hard work but have a far less glamorous view of their own long hours. The subtext, of course, is that my hours are in the name of forward motion, a strong and sure freestyle stroke toward the horizon, while theirs is treading water, stagnating in the middle of the ocean with no land in sight.

"You look good," I say. My mom is tan and freckled under her faded blue cotton sundress and heavy cork-soled sandals, her hair streaked blond. Even amid the stretches of Midtown concrete and glass, she looks natural and clean, as though she spends her days surrounded by sparkling rivers, purple mountains and stately blue green trees rather than an eight-hundred-square-foot storefront in a strip mall.

When I was in third grade—before the middle school years of being embarrassed by simply having parents—my mom signed up to chaperone our spring class trip to the lake. It was everyone's favorite day, the spring warmth hinting at summer vacation, our only responsibilities a very manageable combination of nature walk, three-legged race and cookout.

My mom led the nature walk that year, and a handful of us third-graders trailed behind her, tripping over roots and scrambling over rocks. She paused occasionally, to identify a tree and ask us which animals we thought lived there, or to point out the illuminated flash of a fish retreating into the sun-capped water. She knew everything, it seemed, and I could not remember ever seeing her that patient or smiling. I was concerned, in the irrationally innocent way of someone who didn't yet get the captivity of obligations, that she'd choose to stay at the lake campground, slipping away to hide behind a rock when the rest of us boarded the school buses back to the school parking lot. Afterward, when we were safely home, I had asked her why she didn't work at the state park. She had caught my chin with her hands, forcing eye contact. "Do you want to choose where you work, Molly?" I knew the answer was yes, so I nodded. "Good," she had said, releasing my chin and gently pushing my back, propelling me out of the kitchen. "Go to college. College will let you have a choice."

"Thanks," she says. "I've been making a point to walk in the mornings with Mindy Sturvidge. So, what's this we're doing? I don't understand."

"Manicures with my boss."

"Manicures? As in—" My mom holds up her hands with an incredulous look.

"Yep."

"This is something you guys . . . do?"

"It's only happened once before. That time it was pedicures." I assume, but don't say, that our group beauty regime is based on Lillian's needs. The pedicure jaunt came immediately after Lillian's purchase of some designer sandals.

My mom nods. "Lead the way," she says, gesturing down Park Avenue, and we start walking. "So," she says in a tone that's forced casual. "Do you socialize a lot with your boss?"

"Not a lot. Every now and again she just likes to do nice things for us, you know, take us out to dinner or drinks, go get our nails done."

"Huh. Rewards for good behavior? A motivation technique."

"I guess so." I've never thought of it that way. I've always imagined that Lillian hangs out with us when she's lonely. Loyal friends on salary.

"Too bad she doesn't just give you cash as a reward," my mom says, raising one eyebrow.

"This stuff is actually kind of fun. It's bonding." I grab my mom's left hand and examine it. It looks much older than the rest of her: wrinkled fingers, age spots, short, no-nonsense nails. "Have you ever gotten a manicure, Mom? You know it means sitting still while someone rubs lotion into your hands."

"A mani—what's it called?" My mom widens her eyes, a jok-ing babe-in-the-woods impression, and then one side of her mouth turns up. "Yes, I am familiar. I had one forever ago. Aunt Kara made all her bridesmaids get them when she got married to her first husband. You remember Uncle Mitch? Everything about that wedding was ridiculous." She rolls her eyes at the memory.

"You don't have to get one."

"Why not?" My mom looks defiant, as though she's agreeing to bungee jump. "This is a vacation. Aren't manicures a very vacation-y thing?" She wiggles her fingers. "I can have bonding fun with the best of them, especially Lillian. She's been so good to you."

"That's right," I say. And each of us having convinced the other of our excitement, we march our pasted-on enthusiasm to the salon.

Lillian, who's sitting between Rachel and Liz, gets up when we come in, dripping water from the little finger bowl where her right hand has been soaking.

She prances over to the entrance and wraps her arm around me, pressing her hand on my elbow so that I can feel the wet eucalyptus warmth of her fingerprints. Keeping her arm around me, she reaches around to my mom.

"I'm so glad you could join us," she says, beaming.

"Gwen Grant," my mom says, leaning in awkwardly to Lil-lian, then pulling back and extending her hand for a shake. She waves to Rachel and Liz, both of whom chime greetings from the manicure table, their hands splayed out before them as they half rise out of their chairs like they're stuck in stocks.

Lillian lets go of me but keeps her arm around my mom, in-troducing everyone as I stand by silently. She takes my mom's hand. "Your daughter," she says, letting go of me to press her hand to her, "is wonderful."

"Well, thank you. That's nice to hear."

"So much fun and reliable. A real member of the team."

"I hear it's a great team."

"And you—" Lillian looks back and forth between us. "Spitting image! Two Breck Girls."

"You really do look alike," says Rachel.

We're used to these comments, my mom and I. We have identical hairstyles—shoulder-length blond hair, parted in the middle—and are the same build and height. People call twins on us a lot. We respond as we always do: both straightening up and saying—almost in unison—"Thank you, what a compliment," punctuating it by a self-conscious half laugh. I don't know if Mom agrees with the appraisal of us as spitting images, but I don't. The way my mom's blue eyes are clear and wide, emitting cool competence; her unapologetic laugh lines; her cool, steady hand; her strength—these are hers, not mine. My mom glances down at her hand, still joined with Lillian's, with a hint of confusion. Presumably, she's wondering when it's customary for New York handshakes to end.

Instead of letting go, though, Lillian uses her grip to pull my mom over to one of the chairs. "Let's segregate. Young'uns, you sit over there at this table, and we ladies of a certain age will stick together."

Lillian has about twenty years on my mom; as a matter of technicality, she could be my grandmother. My mom looks as though she's about to say something but stops when she catches my eye, making me wonder what message I unwittingly transmitted to her. She shrugs—*just go with it*—and follows Lillian over to the table where Svetlana and her colleague flurry around, setting up bowls of water and lotion, grabbing tools from the sterilizer.

I take the seat between Rachel and Liz that Lillian has vacated. Rachel, her head leaned toward me, whispers so low I can barely hear it. "She's a little fascinated by your mom."

"Lil' bit." I exhale the words as quietly as I can.

"I go for the neutral colors," Lillian is instructing my mom, lifting up bottles of polish and holding them to the light. "Better to leave the garish stuff to the younger set, right, Gwen?"

My mom does not appear insulted. "Neutral tones are definitely more my speed, Ms. Starling."

A shocked expression crosses Lillian's face. "Please. You have to call me Lillian. I see your daughter nearly every single day."

"Okay," says my mom in an even tone that makes me wonder if she is thinking the same thing that I am—that I see the coffee cart man outside my building every single bloody day and *that* hasn't translated into chumminess. Quite the contrary: he seems surprised every time he hears my order. She gestures to Lillian's ensemble, an off-white suit with nude pumps. "I love your style, so just polish me whatever color you've picked out."

"Svetlana will take care of it all." Lillian promises this with a confirming nod at Svetlana, who smiles, briefly and close-lipped. "How is Molly's dad occupying himself while we pamper? I mean, he could have come too, of course."

"He wouldn't be caught dead." My mom and I both laugh at the thought of my dad squashed at the table, looking confused, his large hands being buffed by one of the ponytailed, white-coated nail technicians, and she replies, "He's back in North Carolina. With the store, we try not to have both of us gone at once."

"You have a store?"

My mom gives me an odd look, questioning, I'm sure, how I've spent such quality time with Lillian and not mentioned this fact. "Yes, we have a little specialty kitchen store."

"That sounds charming." Lillian, genuinely fascinated, launches into a series of rapid-fire questions that are surprisingly knowledgeable for someone whose silverware is probably handled only by a housekeeper. What brands do they carry? Do they have cooking demonstrations? What is my mother's favorite cheese? Are the hours torture? Who does the hiring and firing decisions?

Finally, Lillian stops, resting back against her chair. "I'm really impressed. Building a shop is hard work. It's like having a baby." She winks at me from across the salon and I unsuccessfully try to imagine Lillian taking a maternity leave, tending to a newborn's needs. "I see where Molly gets her work ethic now."

"It's not a perfect situation." My mom's tone is matter-of-fact. "Unfortunately, we just don't have an employee we trust enough to leave the store with." The subtext of course is that they can't actually afford a manager; their staff is composed of college kids doing shift work. It's unsaid, but when I hear Lillian's follow-up question, I know that she has intuited this.

"Where are you staying? There are so many great hotels in Midtown."

"I stay with Molly."

"Oh, Molly has a guest room?" Lillian sounds impressed.

My mom shakes her head. "A studio."

"How wonderful," says Lillian, as though she's downright moved by our bond. "Like a slumber party."

"Like a slumber party," says my mom in a fond echo.

I meet Lillian's eyes and try to read her expression. Not sympathy. Not pity. But dawning comprehension, as though she's placing me, has put a piece of the puzzle together.

Later, after Lillian makes a show of pulling out her American Express card and insisting to us that all of the manicures are her treat—she wouldn't dream of it any other way—and several rounds of kisses and embraces between the five of us, as though we're all headed off to war instead of the weekend, my mom and I hurry down Fifth Avenue toward our restaurant.

"So how bad was that?" I say as soon as we're a block away from the salon.

"I don't know," says my mom. "It was kind of fun." She holds out her nails, a pale glossy plum called No Boundaries, in front of her. "I don't even hate the color so much. I'll tell you, though, that Lillian?"

"Yeah?"

My mom pauses, long enough for me to identify a sliver of emotion passing through me—it's hope. I am dying for her to open the door, to say something caustic and derisive about Lillian, the salon, New York City, anything.

Because then I could laugh in agreement and come clean: about Lillian's suffocating expectations, about Fern's nightmare and about how I might be able to help her. I can't introduce a discussion on any of these topics, of course; I'm not about to volunteer that I'm anything other than the very personification of the Grant family's upward mobility—if I'm not, then what was the point of their sacrifice? But if she brings it up . . .

"What about Lillian?" I lead, trying to keep my voice neutral.

My mom tentatively touches her thumbnail with the tip of her index finger, testing the polish's dryness. "She's good people, huh? I mean, a lot of noise, all that talk about beauty routines and the Svetlana stuff, but deep down, she's got substance. I can see why you're so loyal to her."

I nod, unable to bring myself to verbally agree. "You really liked her?"

"I did," says my mom. "But I'm easy. I like anyone who appreciates my daughter, which Lillian most definitely does. If you stick with her, just stay the course and watch carefully, I bet you can achieve everything that she has."

And we leave it at that.

the insufferable heat wave

In the months since my nondate with Caleb, I have been a search engine monk: no extracurricular Internet research on anything except the Walker case. I had actually begun to consider the idea of going back on the dating market, even agreeing to a blind date with some cousin of Holt's coworker. After today, though, no way.

As I sit next to Fern on the pilly brown and orange couch in Emily Freed's waiting room, I'm reminded of the blind dates I went on when I first moved to New York. It's all coming back to me—the in-your-face awkwardness, like a roadside accident that it's impossible to look away from, and the way time passes at the speed of congealed molasses.

Fern and I are both dressed nicely and are doing our best to emit friendly, calm vibes. Claire perches on a ripped avocado green chair opposite us. It's one of those "difficult" colors that I've heard Duck talk about, but Claire's neat white pants and summery sky blue tunic make it look cool and fresh. Graham stands next to her, hovering protectively like a gangly attack mantis.

So far, we win gold stars for attempting to appear as though this situation falls within societal standards of normalcy. Graham has been a willing participant in exchanging stale pleasantries, volunteering that this crazy August heat wave has been insufferable. Despite this, there's an African elephant in the room. We are waiting for Emily to emerge from her office and fire the starting gun for Fern's first court-mandated visit with her children.

I break the silence. "So, is Risa coming tonight?"

Graham's mouth becomes a small narrow line. "Not tonight."

Of course not—without Robert here, what's the point of a show? "And where are the kids?"

It's Claire's turn to frown. "When she's ready"—she nods toward Emily's closed door—"Hannah will bring them in."

Fern shrinks back into the couch, her face tight. I'm not sure whether she's offended at Claire's presumptions, just nervous or both. Claire examines her nails, palms up, sighs and retrieves her phone from her bag. There's a nonchalance to her gesture that belies her words and I wonder what she's thinking, whether it's surreal for her, to be involved in this fight. One day she accepts a job at Options, presumably thinking only that it's a good career move. Jump ahead a couple years and she's living with the head of the company, a substitute mother to his kids. It would be a lot to handle. Claire catches me staring, her flared nostrils indicating that she is not, at the moment, putting herself in my shoes, or imagining whether our perceptions of each other might be different had we met on adjacent treadmills at the gym rather than in the courtroom.

The door opens and Emily steps out before recoiling a full step backward. We're not the intended inhabitants of this waiting room—four full-grown adults crammed into a tight space filled with stained stuffed animals, picture books and decades-old *Highlights* magazines.

"Where are Anna and Connor?" Emily says to Claire, whom she met last week during the kids' pregame visit.

Graham strides forward. "Ms. Freed, I'm Graham Allesser, Mr. Walker's counsel. I'm here on behalf of Ms. Dennis."

Emily nods politely but her eyes dart around as though she's looking for the hidden camera. "You can go."

Graham clears his throat and fixes his eyes on a point across the room. "Sorry, Ms. Freed. Ms. Dennis wants to make sure the kids are okay. She thinks it will go better if she's here."

Emily shakes her curly ponytail and exhales through her nose. "Whatever. But lawyers—out of my waiting room. Mom, come on in"—she gestures to Fern—"and whoever has the kids, get 'em. They're needed for this."

Fern stands up, rather shakily, and with a wan smile directed to me disappears into the room.

Graham, still in the same spot, winks both eyes. "But where should we go to wait?"

"Not my problem."

Graham and I walk just far enough around the U-shaped hallway to be out of sight.

"Listen," I say. "Why don't we both leave? It's not like we can really do anything today anyway."

"Go right ahead," he says, extending his arm down the hall as if to say, *After you.*

I roll my eyes and slide down the wall to sit on the floor. We grab our BlackBerries and ignore each other until the wailing starts. When the elevator doors ding open, it gets louder: a tonsil-vibrating yell, an accompanying shriek and urgent adult voices. Graham and I both peek around the corner.

A blond ponytailed young woman—Hannah, I presume—carries Connor toward Emily Freed's office as he bellows, kicking his legs like a pudgy pissed-off roadrunner. At least Connor is portable. Anna has grabbed on to Claire's pants leg and is doing her best to pull her back into the elevator. Claire, pained, stops and squats down. "Sweetie. Anna, honey. The judge has ordered this. Sweetie, you won't be left alone with her, I promise. Mama will be right there the whole time."

Emily Freed's door opens and the whole screaming gang limps through the door of her office, which hiccups shut. Graham and I look at each other, stunned enough for the moment to forget our allegiances.

"That was nuts," he says.

There's muffled screaming for a little while, which recedes, then flares, then recedes, then flares again. Graham and I eye each other uncertainly. He makes a few furtive steps toward the door, only to retreat when the crying stops. Finally, the screaming escalates again and Graham takes long, determined steps toward the door as though he's worried he'll talk himself out of going in.

He opens the door just as Emily starts to walk out.

"Ah, Mr. Allesser. You're still here." Her voice is flat. "Ms. Dennis needs to leave the building and not come back for forty minutes." Emily has her hand on Claire's back and gently pushes her out of the door. Hannah follows, looking a bit dazed.

"Ms. Freed, with all due respect, Ms. Dennis has every right to be there. She promised the kids—"

Emily shakes her head. "I don't know or care about her rights. All I know is I'm supposed to supervise and ease the visit between these children and their mother. If this one bursts into the office every minute, I can't do my job."

She and Graham stare at each other for a second.

Emily speaks, breaking the standoff. "I can either tell the judge that you interfered with the visit or you can get the hell out. Your call."

Claire sniffs and dabs her swollen red eyes with a rolled-up tissue. Emily's voice softens. "There's a coffee shop around the corner. Why don't you go wait there?"

Graham puts his arm around Claire and she collapses into him, sniffling against the backdrop of the screams. He pushes the elevator button.

When it dings open, Graham and Claire shuffle in, Hannah trailing after them. Before the doors close, Graham stops them with his hand and sticks his head out.

"You coming?" he says to me.

Claire is quietly sobbing in the elevator. I look pointedly at her. "I'll take the next one."

He nods.

I sit back down in the hallway and listen. Within ten minutes of Claire's departure, the screaming stops. I picture them all in there, eyeing one another cautiously around a game of Candyland; Fern tentatively bridging the gap by asking gently about Connor's favorite color, Anna's teacher's name. They are questions she shouldn't have to ask, but still, for the first time, I know that it's not too late for her to find out the answers.

wwmd (what would machiavelli do?)

In the week after my mom's visit, I'm back to my spy games, ducking out of Bacon Payne's building, and soaking up the late-summer sun during my two-hundred-foot walk to the headquarters of Molly Grant, PC, for a mail check. I've been doing this so much that for the first summer since I moved to New York, my wrist bears the faint lines of a watch-strap tan.

I pull open the heavy glass door with CENTRAL OFFICES written on them in white lettering. Dottie looks up from behind the desk, smiles and disappears into the back office. She comes out carrying a thin beige envelope and pushes it toward me with a cheery "Here ya go."

McDunn and Associates is written on the return address in a flowery cursive. I've called Risa about fifteen times since our court date, to no avail. Each time I dial, the phone is picked up by one of two voices—Cold and Colder. Cold is a receptionist with a clipped British accent who feigns complete ignorance about when Ms. McDunn will be available to talk. Colder is an outgoing voice mail message in which a different, even chillier British voice informs me that Ms. McDunn is not available but I am free to leave a message. Several times, I have called and asked to speak to Graham, but he's never around either.

I wonder exactly what Risa is doing at these moments when she's unavailable for a work call—trimming topiary in the shape of her wolfhounds? Holing up in a bunker with Robert Walker, the two of them in army fatigues, chomping on cigars and point-ing at strategy diagrams pasted on the wall? My least favorite scenario is that she's standing by the receptionist desk, dissolving into giggles each time I call.

Even though Risa won't deign to chat with me, I don't feel ignored. Last week, she served me with a ten-inch-thick docu-ment requesting that the case be dismissed in light of new infor-mation regarding Fern's mental state, that the visitation schedule cease immediately and that Fern pay for fifty percent of the court costs. It was all bunk, but I still had to respond.

I rip open her letter and read it, standing on the nubby red carpet of the Central Offices lobby.

Dear Ms. Grant:

I have received the message that you called me but have been unable to reach you. Please call me at your convenience to discuss the Walker matter.

Very truly yours,
Risa McDunn

"Are you freaking kidding me?"

Dottie looks up and frowns.

"Sorry." The letter tucked in my bag, I head back to Bacon Payne, muttering—quietly, for Dottie's sake—about Risa's mad genius: after ignoring my pile of phone calls, she's somehow flipped the obligation back to me and memorialized that obligation in a form to show the court. Still talking to myself, I pop into Jodi's Deli—the midpoint between my two offices—hoping to find some peace of mind amidst the store's rows of dusty apple-flavored soy chips and Lorna Doones. I'm at the register paying for my sandwich—the virtuous-sounding Garden Veggie Delite—when my Molly Grant, PC, cell phone rings. I pick up with one hand, grabbing the flimsy green cellophane bag with the other. "Molly Grant."

"Roland Williams here."

I hurry outside the deli, cell phone clutched to my ear, and find an empty spot under the awning to talk.

"Hi, Roland. Nice to meet you over the phone." This is what I know about the court-appointed lawyer for the Walker kids: he worked in the family courts for legal aid for twenty years, after which he cofounded his own firm, Williams and Douglas, LLP. He's active in the Brooklyn Bar Association, he's well regarded in Kings County and he happens to be black, which is notable only because of the homogeneity of the matrimonial bar. Bacon Payne corporate group, white-bread in its own right, looks like the United Nations compared to most Bacon Payne matrimonial cases: white judge, white lawyers, white clients, white experts, white witnesses.

He launches right into it. "I'm calling to set up a meeting with my clients. Can you help me arrange that through Ms. Walker?"

"Well, the children currently live with Mr. Walker, so it might make sense to call Risa McDunn."

"Yes, I've tried, but my attempts have been unsuccessful."

"Oh, well, nice to know I'm not the only one getting the silent treatment there." I chuckle, stopping when I realize Roland is not laughing along with me. I strip the humor from my voice in an attempt for a more professional tone. "My client sees Connor and Anna twice a week, so maybe we can try to work out something during her visits." Fern won't want to give up her time, but it's important to cooperate with Roland. I've seen it before— an expert's opinions of the parties and their attorneys influencing her feelings about the case.

"I didn't realize that was the extent of her visits."

"Well, that's it for now, but things are going great. We're working on more time and Emily Freed—that's the neutral child specialist—she's helping to undercut the effects of the parental alienation—" The transitions have been rough with both kids, especially Anna, shy and teary at the beginning and end of the visits. Fern says the good time in the middle—reading together, coloring, once even venturing to a playground, where Emily Freed retreated to a faraway bench—keeps expanding.

"Ms. Grant. I'm really not interested in hearing the slant. I was just hoping for some logistical assistance, but I'll write a letter to both you and Ms. McDunn about scheduling something."

He hangs up and I notice Everett approaching me from the door of the deli, flimsy green bag in hand, his pasty skin fluorescent in the bright sun. Crap. How much did he hear?

He lifts his face up to the sun and squints. "Hey! Molly. You got food from the deli? *Moi aussi.* Isn't this day awesome?" Now that my hazing period is officially over, Everett treats me like a frat brother from a bad eighties movie, the same as everyone else he considers a bud. "So, I've been meaning to tell you, big congrats on that decision."

"All Lillian." It has been three weeks since Liesel's oral argument disaster, and we received Justice Love's decision yesterday: the cats are separate property and Liesel gets to keep them all. I left Liesel an awkward voice mail and e-mailed her a scanned copy of the decision, but haven't heard from her, which is actually a relief. Not having to talk to Liesel is like that moment when a stomachache disappears—the absence feels good, rather than just normal.

"So, who was that on the phone? Adversary?"

"Um, no."

"It was about custody, though, right? You have a parental alienation case?"

"No, I just threw out the term. Don't know if it really applies."

"Oh, you want to talk about the facts? I've got a moment. We could eat inside."

Oh, God, no. I mumble something about having to get back and we turn toward the office. Kim, of course, is outside in a haze of smoke, the center of a cluster of Dementors shifting their weight on rooted legs. I smile and wave and in response she gives a barely perceptible nod.

"So what case?" Everett persists.

"Borowick." It's the first thing that pops into my head.

Everett looks confused as we walk into the lobby and press our IDs against the turnstiles. "But I thought that was amicable. Fifty-fifty visitation, the whole enchilada."

"Um, it is. Well, it was. Things have gotten tense. Well, not too tense. Just a little more tense. Just sort of weighing strategy, you know. Batting things about. Anyway, I'm sure you're right. Yep, it's amicable."

Everett's forehead starts to wrinkle.

We get in the elevator and I point to the Factsination! screen. "Hey—look at that!"

Everett turns, but too late. The screen has changed. He reads out loud. "Did you know that Italian Renaissance historian Niccolò Machiavelli loved creating carnival songs, poetry and comedies?"

I start to snort, but obscure it with a cough. "No, before that— the number one movie last weekend was *Fifi and Sandy.* Is that the dogs who open a fast-food place?"

Everett perks up, which makes sense; he and the Factsination! monitor actually have similar conversational skills. "Yep, they find an abandoned restaurant and become short-order cooks. Wow—eighty-one million." He whistles. "That's amazing. And number two was *Devil with a Gun.* I think that was number one last week. I saw that here, on the elevator screen. Did you?"

"Missed it. Is this *Fifi and Sandy*'s first week?"

Improbable as it seems for someone who sees one movie a

year, I manage to discuss box office profits all the way up to the thirty-seventh floor. It's a ridiculous conversation that leaves me with enough excess brainpower to scold myself. If I'm going to survive for one more year, I will have to become a better liar. In the words of that great jokester Machiavelli: the ends justify the means.

underground beatz

As soon as I hear Liz leave for the night, I pad down the hallway to Henry's office. He and I have become a lot closer in the months since I took on Fern's case, part of which, I know, is the intimacy of sharing a secret. I still eat with Rachel and Liz on a nightly basis, and we discuss the daily grind that made up the day—client drama, of course, but also head colds, poor nights' sleep, new clothes, weekend plans, movies, bad dates (well, Rachel's the only one who actually goes on dates). Not being able to talk to either of them about the Walker case acts like a protective moat around the friendship, though; there is only so far it can go.

But I genuinely like Henry in a way that transcends being work friends. I enjoy his company enough to try and cajole him out of the office tonight to meet Duck and Holt at a beer garden downtown. He's already looking up when I appear in his doorway, my flip-flops having heralded my arrival with all the elegance of a teenager smacking her Bubble Yum.

"That sound your shoes make?" he says. "Could be a Guantánamo torture technique."

"Weekend wear." I perch on the arm of his guest chair. "My subtle acknowledgment to the fact that it's Sunday."

He rejects this notion with a quick smile and headshake. "Not so subtle, my friend."

"Henry," I say. "It's seven thirty. You've been here ten hours. Everett is gone. Liz is gone. We're the only ones left on the floor."

Henry leans back. "I see that Disney Channel gleam in your eye. You're thinking the same thing I am, right?" He leans forward, a look of mock shock on his face, wagging his finger. "Toilet papering Everett's office?"

"Compelling idea, but no." I stand up. "I'm taking you where the air is fresh and the hills are green. Grab your stuff and meet me by the elevators."

Fifteen minutes later, we're underground, waiting on the platform for the 4 train. Henry has a serious expression. "I think," he says, inhaling deeply, "that if this is where you go for fresh air, we need to talk."

"Yeah, I lied about that. No green hills, no fresh air."

"So." He rubs his hands together. "Where's this adventure taking us?"

"The Seaport." I hold up my hands before he can respond. "Mea culpa for the false advertising. I thought it was necessary to entice you."

"You overestimate my desire to be in the office. I would've been game if you had told me we were riding the 4 train back and forth to go rat-spotting."

When the train—one of the ones that looks like a slice of the 1970s, seats in alternating shades of orange—pulls into the station, Henry and I sit perpendicular to each other, his legs stretched out under my seat. "Please, Henry. You love being in the office."

"I don't."

"You do. The way you've personalized things. All those family pictures, the artwork, the cozy rug."

He makes a face that indicates I'm a crazy person before realizing that I'm joking. "Ah. I see. You're being sarcastic."

"It must be shocking. Not that sarcasm is, like, your default conversational mode or anything."

"Whoa." He blinks. "Was that a criticism of my sarcasm wrapped in a sarcastic delivery?"

"I think it was." I reach my hand around to pat my shoulder. "A sarcasm sandwich."

"How meta." He widens his eyes as though I've overtaxed his brain. "But back to the office thing—you haven't exactly decorated either. No needlepoint pillows, no rainbow wallpaper, no posters with fluffy kittens and inspirational sayings."

"The stuffed unicorns don't leave room for that kind of thing."

"I suppose not."

"Seriously, though? I'm not trying to work there forever. If I did, I'd make it a little homier."

"Homier." He holds up one finger. "That's a dangerous word. Work should be here"—he holds his hands apart and sets them to his right, as if putting down a box—"and home and all things homey should be here." He makes the same gesture, but to the left. "That's what's so challenging about Lillian's management style. Friendly banter is okay, I guess, but beyond that? It's all ammunition and exposed Achilles' heels."

"Work is a battlefield."

He shrugs, as if to say he's just calling it like he sees it.

"But that's impossible to maintain, Henry. Spending sixteen hours a day with people, you have no choice but to connect."

"Work is work."

"Then what about Dominic Pizaro?" I hold my hands wide apart, holding a large imaginary box that dwarfs Henry's imaginary boxes.

"That's different. And we don't really socialize in the office."

"And me."

"You?"

"We're friends."

He doesn't answer, twisting his mouth, knitting his brow and moving his head in the slow swing of a pendulum as though weighing my statement.

"Wait a second," I say, indignant. "You follow me out of the office without even knowing where we're going and you're telling me that we're not even friends?"

"That says more about my judgment than our closeness."

I kick his leg with my foot.

"No," he equivocates. "I wouldn't say we're *not* friends. But aside from the kamikaze way you practice law and your flexibility with the truth about where we were going, what do I really know about you?"

"*You* know *my* deepest darkest secret. Aside from your fondness for sarcasm sandwiches and the fact that your social skills, while hidden very deeply within you, are actually fairly substantial, what do *I* really know about *you*?"

Henry smiles mysteriously. "Exactly. I like to keep 'em guessing." He pauses for a moment, tilting his head toward me. "As do you."

"Me?" I lower my eyebrows to refute, and point to myself. "Open book."

He clears his throat and gives me a look that says *hardly.*

"Ask anything. I will answer and you will see—I am remarkably uncomplicated."

"This is what I don't get about you. You're so clear about drawing lines—what you want and what you'll put up with—and yet, here you still are. How and why have you lasted this long at Bacon Payne?"

"Doesn't everybody hate it?"

"Answering a question with a question only perpetuates your mystery," he says drily. "But no, I don't hate it. I see that it's not a perfect place, but to me, it's worth it. I feel like I'm living my life there, not wasting it."

"You're stronger than I am. Or maybe not as smart."

"Your opinion of the firm, choosing to stay or leave? None of it's a referendum on your value as a human being. It's just a job. So, what's making you stay put?"

"The money," I say, but my voice goes up at the end, so it sounds like I'm asking a question instead of answering one.

He tilts his head thoughtfully. "I'm not discounting that," he says, "but is that enough? It's a lot, but come on—you're smart enough to figure out another option."

I'm trying to think of a retort when he points his chin at a group of boys who just got on at the Chambers Street stop. At first I don't know why he's directing me to look at them, but when the doors close, the subway is filled with a thumping bass and the group—three teenagers in baseball caps and red tracksuits—takes turns posing. They do contorted break-dance moves that are frenetically impressive: crazy handstands, rubbery legs jutting out at unnatural angles, swinging around the center poles.

Our eyes meet and I assume mine, like his, are open wide, thrilled to observe the spontaneous entertainment, and as our train pulls into the Fulton Street stop, his elbow jabs into my side and he raises his eyebrows in false modesty. "I can do that, you know."

"You can swing from a subway pole?"

"I can break-dance." He extends his arms, flexes the fingers of his right hand in a twitch that moves up his shoulder blades and down the other side. "And—" He stops and leans back.

"And what? What?" I lean forward. "That was the perfect wave, by the way."

"The summer when I was twelve, my friends and I? We were those kids. We put on shows in subway cars."

"You did not."

"Three of us plus mad skills equals one amazing dance group."

"I hope you weren't in charge of the publicity for it." I roll my eyes. "What'd you call yourselves?"

"Underground Beatz. With a z."

"Catchy." We exit at Fulton Street and ascend the stairs to the street. "Were your parents horrified?"

"They didn't know."

I cover my open mouth with my fingers as though scandalized. "Upper East Side boys dancing in the subway without permission."

"Your mockery only serves to challenge me." He gives me a long sideways glance through narrowed eyes as we cross Broadway and head across a concrete plaza in front of an office building. In the middle of the plaza, he stops, lifts his messenger bag over his head, hands it to me and holds up one finger. "Prepare to be impressed."

"If you say so."

He stretches his arms over his head, shakes out his limbs and then executes a perfect moonwalk.

Someone from one of the park benches lining the plaza claps and shouts, "Move it, corporate dude!"

Henry bows, returning to claim his messenger bag.

"Bravo." I hand him the strap.

He shrugs casually, adjusting the collar of his button-down like he's not going to argue with my assessment, and starts strutting toward the Seaport.

"Wait." I step out of my flip-flops, hand Henry my bag and, bare feet on the pavement, reach my hands up and execute two cartwheels, followed by a front handspring, something I haven't done—or wanted to—since middle school.

"Still got it," I say as the same voice from the benches—Henry's fan—chimes in.

"Lady, you crazy," he says. "What you doing taking off your shoes on a city street?"

"Nice," Henry says, "although I think he has a point about the basic health concerns of that."

"Yeah." I look at my palms, dirty from contact with the side-walk. There's a squashed piece of detritus on my hand that I don't want to start to identify. "Didn't think it through."

He takes my palms and wipes them on his shirt.

"Thanks." I hold his gaze for a moment.

"Probably not the most effective cleansing."

"Still," I say, knowing that—as considerate as the gesture was—it's not really why I'm thanking him.

deus ex machina

Even though it's a beautiful, warm late September morning, I sit frozen at my desk, trying to figure out how the hell I can be at the two thirty compliance conference in *Walker v. Walker* when Lillian just demanded my presence at an impromptu girls' lunch. Today. At one o'clock.

She's giving a little talk at the City Bar Club and we girls haven't gotten to see her speak in a while, so wouldn't it be great if we all meet her there at twelve thirty? That way, we can hear the end of her speech and then just run across the street for bonding over microgreens, dressing on the side.

The Walker matter's been cruising along for a few months, and so far I've been incredibly lucky: no deadlines missed, suspicions aroused or huge conflicts between Fern's needs and my Bacon Payne caseload. I wasn't prepared, and I mumbled something to Lillian about having court in the afternoon. What case? Lillian had asked, at which point I regained my senses. I couldn't conjure a name as I had with Everett, because Lillian could be counted on to ask Kim to print out the court schedules.

I pretended to check my schedule, slapped my head in abject fear (although I think Lillian interpreted it as goofiness) and sang, a little too brightly, that I had the day's schedule wrong in my head. She'd flashed me a little smile, looked at me somewhat sternly and told me to get it together; she'd see me at twelve thirty and that I should check with Kim before I left to see if I needed to bring anything over.

Like Charlie Brown running full speed toward Lucy's football, I pick up the phone to call Risa. If I can get her to agree to just delay the conference by an hour, I'll be fine. Colder—the clipped-sounding outgoing voice mail message—answers. I press redial for several minutes and eventually Cold, the live receptionist, picks up.

"Risa McDunn and Associates."

"Hi, I'd like to speak to Risa, please."

"And who may I say is calling?"

"Molly Grant," I confess, although I am tempted to say Oprah and see if the service improves.

Without even pretending to pause, she says, "Ms. McDunn is not available to take your call. Good day."

"Wait—"

Pause. "Yes."

"I'm scheduled to be in court with her this afternoon and I've had an, um, family emergency come up, so I desperately need to just delay our compliance conference or even adjourn it, whichever works better for her. Please, I'm begging. I know she's really busy, but please." I smile hard as though Cold can see my pearly whites through the phone.

"Well, Ms. McDunn doesn't customarily agree to adjournments this close to the court date."

"Please. Can you give her the message or forward my call?"

Pause. Sigh. "All right. If you call back in ten minutes, I will have tried to reach her to convey your message. Ms. Ruben, was it?"

"Uh. No. Molly Grant. G-R-A-N-T. *Walker v. Walker.* Thank you so much."

Ten minutes later to the second, I call back.

"Risa McDunn and Associates."

"Hi again. This is Molly Grant. I called earlier about the adjournment in *Walker v. Walker.*"

Pause.

"You said that you would try to reach Ms. McDunn."

"Who is this?"

"Molly Grant. I have a court appearance today with Risa. You told me to call back. In ten minutes. Which is now."

"Let me look through my notes." I hear some papers shuffling. "Right. I wasn't able to reach Ms. McDunn. She is very indisposed, but I did check with Mr. Allesser"—she stops to let the generosity of her gesture wash over me—"and he said that Ms. McDunn would not be amenable to an adjournment or delay."

"That's it? She's just not amenable to it? He knows without asking?"

"Oh, yes, he also said that Mr. Walker is a very busy man and his schedule can't be changed on a whim like that."

"Okay. Well, thank you so much for all your help."

"You're quite welcome," she says, missing my sarcastic tone. "Good day."

I am fucked. And I have just billed twenty minutes on *Walker v. Walker* while in my office at Bacon Payne. And used my Bacon Payne phone to call out, which could have been really stupid but for the fact that I was pretty sure Cold the Receptionist had not deigned to remember my name, let alone check my caller ID.

I e-mail Henry *SOS.* A few minutes later, he appears in my doorway.

"What's wrong?"

"Shut the door," I say, dropping my head in my hands. I tell him about the conflict.

"Hmmm. Well, maybe the lunch won't go that late."

"I know, but if it does . . ."

"What if you just don't go to the lunch?"

I shake my head. "As of this moment, I'm still below radar. If I don't go to the lunch, I'll get on the shit list and that means—"

"Yeah. You've been lucky so far. You wouldn't last a week with anyone scrutinizing your schedule. Okay, let's think. Did you try Risa?"

"Yep, she is not amenable to an adjournment or delay," I say in an atrocious British accent.

"What happened there? Did you just go on vacation to Austria in your head?"

"Nah—bad imitation of her horrid receptionist."

"So what's the plan now?"

"Um. Hope that lunch doesn't go too long. Maybe I can choke on something while eating." Someone knocks on the door. I grimace and nod at Henry, who leans back in his chair, stretches out his arm and pushes open the door with a casual flick of his wrist that evokes a Frisbee toss.

"Oh, hey, guys." Rachel looks back and forth from me to Henry. "Sorry to interrupt."

"Oh, no interruption. I just closed the door to show Henry a loud YouTube video."

Rachel steps backward in mock surprise. "Henry wanted to see a YouTube video?"

Henry nods. "Nothing I love more than a good YouTube video."

"Which one? I wanna see." Rachel starts to walk around my desk to see my computer.

"Oh, I couldn't get it to work. It was one with a baby. And music. Totally adorable." I figure that's a safe bet. Seventy percent of YouTube videos are some sort of baby action set to music.

"Dancing baby or guitar baby?"

"Guitar," I say.

Henry looks at me, eyebrows raised. I am getting better at serial lying.

"Oh," Rachel says, disappointed. She sits down in the guest chair next to Henry. "So, are you feeling girlie enough for this lunch we've got?"

Henry stands up. "That's my cue." He looks at me. "So, as far as your custody question, let me think about it and see what I come up with."

Rachel watches him leave and then turns toward me. "What's up with you two?"

"Nothing," I say.

"Really? You're always . . . fraternizing."

"We've just become buds," I say, opening my bottom drawer to pretend to look for something as I feel the beginning prickles of a blush on my cheeks. I bend down, moving things around until I feel my cheeks cool. It shouldn't surprise me that Rachel has noticed the amount of time Henry and I spend in each other's office; increasingly, I treat his couch like my own personal lounge chair. What Rachel doesn't know is that the office visits are the tip of the iceberg; throughout the workweek, Henry and I volley a steady banter of texts and e-mails, one long-running conversation without salutations or sign-offs.

I scowl at Rachel. "Seriously, we're work buddies. I ask him a lot of questions and he gives good advice. He's really nice."

"I know. He's just always kept to himself."

I shrug, rather than remind Rachel that Henry has a girlfriend. I know—because Duck and I have had this conversation no fewer than ten times—that when I say these words, I will whine like a fifteen-year-old whose parents *just don't get it*, a tone that only seems to invite further speculation. The whole thing is ridiculous, as though just because Henry is male, he and I can't be friends without there being romantic subtext. I laugh at Rachel, making sure to meet her eyes. "Well, he's probably never seen anyone in such dire need of assistance." At least *that's* not a lie.

"If you say so. Want to leave at ten after twelve? That way we can see enough of the talk but not too much."

"Okay."

Rachel examines me closely. "You all right?"

"Um, yeah, just stressed about an annoying call I have to make."

"Oh, good luck. See you in a few."

At twelve o'clock, ten minutes before my march toward the gallows, Kim buzzes me to say "Lunchisoff" in a quick, monotone delivery that does not do justice to the dramatics of the moment. She hangs up before I manage to ask her why.

Shaking with excitement, I go find Liz next door.

"Our lunch is off?"

"Yeah, apparently."

"What happened?"

"Oh, Lillian has an important client call."

"What case?"

"What do you think? Another fire drill in Murty."

"Really?"

Liz laughs, "Wow—you look so happy. You didn't want to go that bad? I was looking forward to it, as pathetic as that might sound."

"Oh, me too. I'm just really busy."

With Murty, I know I'm safe. Adam Murty is a U.S. senator from New York who last summer had checked into the Hay-Adams, a swank Washington hotel, with his twenty-seven-year-old legislative correspondent. He certainly was not the first politician to have an affair with a comely employee, but he was one of the few about whom *Celeb-dirty* magazine had published an exposé. An amateur photographer, rumored to be a Republican lackey, trailed him to the hotel and somehow caught pictures of "the Senator and His Staffer" (the scandal's media moniker) entering the room, midnuzzle, his left hand grabbing her "heart-shaped ass" (to use Howard Stern's poetic description).

The picture was splashed everywhere and it would have remained a mere political scandal, except that Adam Murty's wife is Francine Claste, a film actress with a severe bob, an intense gaze and a recurring role in award-nominated period films. When Francine opted against standing by her man and filed for divorce immediately after the pictures were published, their split became the story. Since then, the case has eclipsed the tabloid level of press; it's been followed by even *The New Yorker* and the *New York Times*, both of which usually ignore our cases in favor of the First Amendment ones.

The Murtys are rich, but Adam certainly isn't our richest client. All the press surrounding the case, however, makes everything about it—each motion, each deposition, each phone call—huge; it is probably the most important in our department. Lillian does not want Adam Murty to fire her, because that will make the evening news. As a consequence, she bends over backward to make sure Murty is a happy client.

I leave Liz's office incredulous; this is the type of deus ex machina that happens in the movies, not real life. Not stopping to question my luck, I hurriedly pack for court.

By the time I emerge from the Borough Hall subway stop, my nerves have settled. I check in with Fern, who is camped out on our bench, and then make mildly successful small talk with Mike, Justice Strand's law clerk, who apparently travels the eastern seaboard participating in barbecue cook-offs. He's walking me through how he changed his spice rub from last year (more turbinado brown sugar!) when Roland Williams shows up.

"Ah, we were just talking about Walker," says Mike.

I introduce myself to Roland, who gives me a warm enough smile. "It's nice to see you."

"Did you receive the letter from Emily Freed?" I ask. She had written a brief recommendation that Fern's visitation be increased and unsupervised.

He nods, the smile freezing on his face. "I'm sure we'll all have a chance to discuss it with the judge," he says, walking away toward a bench across the hall.

By ten after three, there is still no sign of Robert Walker or his attorneys. Roland sits across from us, frowning over a brief but not looking up. I walk over. "Excuse me, Mr. Williams. I was just wondering whether you've received any word from Ms. McDunn."

"No," he says, looking at his watch. "I do have a four o'clock, though."

I tell Mike with a sigh that everyone else is here, but we're missing the defendant and his attorney.

He gives me a forgiving look and smiles. "Oh, it's no problem. The judge has a busy schedule this afternoon, so he won't be waiting. Just let me know when they get here."

For the love of barbecue, Mike, come on. I press forward. "Well, defendant's attorney is actually forty minutes late. Neither of us has heard from her."

"Ah, okay. Well, if she's not here in a little bit, we can always call her." Mike shrugs, making clear that this is not going to be his problem. Had I been late, Risa would be screaming to the entire hallway about my tardiness and unprofessionalism. She would force Mike to make it his problem. I open my mouth, trying to conjure a fight, but I end up smiling at Mike and retreating. I just can't bring myself to channel Risa, which makes me feel guilty, as though I'm not fighting hard enough for Fern. Increasingly, I wonder if I have what it takes—do you have to be a sociopath to be a really good divorce lawyer?

At twenty minutes after three, nearly an hour after our scheduled call time, they finally arrive. Today, Risa's look is an homage to Victorian equestrian fashion, hold the riding crop. She's got a full sky blue skirt down to the tops of her laced-up tan ankle boots and a white high-necked shirt with epaulet shoulders. The shirt is tucked into a light blue cummerbund that provides a tiny indentation of cinching around her waist. And her hair! Red ringlets gathered in an elaborately woven braid that must have taken hours and could easily explain her late arrival.

I'm halfway through the door, with Roland behind me, when Risa nods to Graham and he lugs out of his bag a thick document.

"Justice Strand, we have an emergency order for your signature." Graham holds the document out to the judge. When Strand doesn't reach for it, Graham drops the papers on Strand's desk, where they land with a thud.

Justice Strand blinks a few times. "Wait a minute, wait a minute." He holds up his hands, frozen in a pause. After a while, he smiles, as though an invisible hand pressed a reboot button on his back. "Good afternoon, counselors. We've crammed more chairs in here for you. Please have a seat."

We all sit. And he nods again, secure in the return of civility to his courtroom.

"So, Ms. McDunn, what is the big emergency?"

No way she's going to grab the floor like last time. I lean forward.

"Well, before she tells you, Your Honor," I say, channeling Kim and speaking as quickly as I can, "I want to bring a letter to your attention. We all received it."

Risa parries. "Your Honor, with all respect. You need to hear about my motion first. It pertains directly to this inappropriate and unethical letter—"

"Ms. McDunn just interrupted me, Your Honor. In your court. We established last time that interrupting is not appropriate. May

I finish?" God, I feel like a shrill first-grader. *But I was playing with Custodial Parent Barbie first, Mr. Strand.*

"No, Your Honor, I was interrupted. I was telling you about the motion when—"

Justice Strand screws his eyes shut. He opens them and focuses in on Roland, who is sitting there unruffled, in great contrast to us mannerless womenfolk. "Do you have a copy of the letter, Mr. Williams?"

Roland hands it over, above Risa's objections, and Justice Strand reads it.

"Mr. Williams, what are your thoughts on this whole . . . visitation issue?" Justice Strand wipes his hands together as though he doesn't want to get them dirty.

"I think there is no reason to disagree with increased and unsupervised visitation for Ms. Walker, as long as it's temporary."

Risa is outraged. "If he were a true advocate for his clients' interests, he wouldn't let them anywhere near Ms. Walker. She's dangerous."

I clear my throat and note that Emily's recommendation is in line with the minimum schedule in Fern and Robert's existing separation agreement.

Justice Strand holds up his copy of the letter. "Ms. McDunn, if you need me to order it, I will, but I would advise your client to agree to the increase. The more he argues about whether his ex-wife is fit to see her children, the more he looks like he's withholding the children without regard for their best interests."

According to Factsination! *Nine out of ten doctors say balance is the key to a happy life!* I blink my eyes and reread, more than a little surprised that nugget got past the Bacon Payne Politburo. The elevator doors open on the thirty-seventh floor and I walk down the hall, clutching to my side a file folder, Fern's new visitation order safely contained within. Her time with them has been officially expanded to include alternate weekends and three midweek visits.

Henry is leaning against the wall, talking to an associate from the tax group, Ed Something.

Just then it hits me. Of course—Henry is on the Murty matter. He is my deus ex machina.

"Hey." He and Ed Something both turn toward me. "How was your meeting?"

"Great. How was your call?"

"What?"

"Your midday call? On Murty? I heard it was a really big deal." I blink innocently.

The tax associate continues to smile politely, nodding impatiently in the hopes that I'll hurry up and end this generic exchange so he and Henry can resume their conversation.

"Oh, *that.*" Henry smiles, caught. "Yeah, I talked to the client this morning and reminded him of some of the things he needed to discuss with Lillian, so we were able to schedule a time the whole team could talk for midday."

"I bet the client is eternally grateful."

"Don't know. I haven't heard from him, but I agree with you. He should be terribly grateful," says Henry. "He should give me a medal for my efforts to make his life easier."

"Isn't the real gift that you won't have to visit him in the mental institution, which is where he was headed without your help?"

He pretends to consider that. "True. However much of a pain it was to have the call, it was nothing compared to the pain of listening to my client lose it. I've seen that and it's a horror show."

Ed Something pivots his head back and forth, trying to follow along.

"Your client owes you a lunch."

"I don't know. My client will probably just use the lunch to talk about his case some more. He's kind of one-note. I would love more than anything to expand his mind, get him to talk or think about something else, you know?"

"Well, you're incredibly well-rounded," I say, looking at him pointedly. "Maybe you could ask this client to join you in one of your many time-intensive hobbies. Macramé? Sea monkeys? Gardening? So many to choose from."

By this point, Ed Something looks upset and confused, so I squeeze Henry's arm. Grinning, I walk back to my office and the fifty-five e-mails that have accumulated in my absence.

ms. longstocking's very adult adventures

On the way over to Duck's annual Halloween party, I run into one of those Halloween express pop-up stores. I did not have energy to plan my costume this year, what with all my *telenovela*-esque lies and subterfuge on behalf of the Walker case. Alas, looking for a costume at six o'clock on Halloween is like going grocery shopping right before the first snowstorm of the season—bare, picked-over shelves—any remaining loaf of bread, no matter how fresh and soft, is going to be mashed and misshapen into something unappealing.

Instead of one of those harmless, no-thought-required, costume-in-a-plastic-bag options, all I see is the slutty trifecta: slutty nurse, slutty pirate and slutty go-go dancer. I refuse to wear something so short that I won't be able to sit down or so low cut that I can't bend over, so I rummage around and leave with a motley assortment: a Groucho Marx disguise, a bright red wig, a bandanna, some face paint.

Duck opens her front door with a grimace. "You're going to kill me. I let slip to Caleb that we were having a big Halloween party."

"And?"

"And he said he wasn't doing anything and wanted to come, so I had to invite him. I'm so sorry."

I shrug, but my heartbeat kicks up a notch.

"I just assumed he'd be going somewhere else fabulous, so I thought it was safe to mention."

"It's fine." I feel a junkie's itch crawl up my fingers and think fast. "Seriously, not an issue. I have to send a quick e-mail for work, though."

"Of course you do." Duck opens her chrome refrigerator and, holding the door with her hip, starts unloading bottles of wine and beer onto the kitchen counter.

I sit down at the table and pull out my BlackBerry. I type in Anastasia's name first, as I always do—she gets more press. She's been active since spring: summer parties in the Hamptons, Edinburgh and the Mediterranean and fall stops in New York, London and Miami. I find no pictures of her with Caleb, but several with a long-haired man named Bertrand Mallet. A Page Six blurb from mid-October reports canoodling between "our favorite Peppercorn party princess and her dashing Parisian pal."

A little too enthusiastically, I do my Caleb due diligence. I find nothing, save a brief note of his attendance at the Friends of the High Line benefit.

I kick myself for opportunities lost. Maybe Caleb was free to flirt with me in June; maybe that charity event he and Anastasia jointly donated to meant nothing, or was a relic from happier times. In an instant, my expectations for the evening elevate. But, oh, crap, my costume. I wonder whether I have enough time to run out and grab one of the slutty options.

I dump my bag of foraging spoils out on Duck's kitchen table. "Help."

"Um, so what's the theme here?" She touches the bandanna.

"Chaos and uncertainty?" I say.

"Well done, well done." She holds up the wig. "Hey, how about good ol' Pippi Longstocking?"

When I first emerge from the bathroom fully dressed, Duck

and I laugh until my tears leave a smear line through my apple red cheeks. Along with legions of seven-year-olds across the city, I am clad in my red wig, sloppy braids wrapped around those red sandwich Baggie ties so that they defy gravity, red circles on my cheeks and confetti-sized freckles dotted across my nose. I am in Duck's denim skirt—too short for me, so somehow, after all the avoidance, I am Slutty Pippi.

"Wait," says Duck. "What about Mr. Nilsson?"

She appears five minutes later with a picture of a monkey printed from the Bronx Zoo Web site, which we safety-pin to my turtleneck.

The guests start to arrive, and I grab a chocolate lager, which, sadly, does not taste like a Hershey's bar, and appreciate their costumes. Duck and Holt are coordinated wizards, with glittering pointy hats and wands and dramatic capes—hers purple and his dark blue. Two people are in full-fledged white furry bunny outfits, their ears stretched high above them, little poufy tails affixed to their bottoms. Several women have gone where I feared to tread. I see a slutty pirate maiden, slutty witch, slutty doctor, all wearing fishnets and showing remarkable cleavage.

Holt's New York–based fraternity brothers—a sloth of burly men all approaching forty and somehow, through a combination of divorces and Peter Pan syndrome, still single—are convincing Vikings, complete with horned hats, red shields, leather skirts and, Lord help us all, spears. I wonder if they took public transportation here and scared the bejeezus out of the other passengers.

"Hey, Molly. Haven't seen you in a while. Good Raggedy Ann costume," the one the rest of them call Bigfoot says.

"Oh, I'm Pippi Longstocking, actually."

He looks at me blankly.

"Plucky little Swedish girl from the books and movie?"

He shakes his head.

"She has a monkey friend, superhuman strength, wacky exploits?"

"Sounds like a fun chick. Hey, Luger," he shouts to his fraternity brother heading over to the kitchen, where the drinks are. "Look who's here." He points to me exaggeratedly.

Luger cups his hands over his mouth. "Orphan Annie! Howrya? Drink?"

Orphan Annie? Oh, forget it. I hold up my beer to indicate no, not that Luger will think already having a beer is reason enough to decline another drink.

I get into a conversation with Rico (dressed as a bonsai tree, with brown pants and turtleneck, hundreds of green pipe cleaners on his torso), Duck's newly hired associate, fresh out of Pratt. He identifies me as Strawberry Shortcake and starts talking about the difficulties of the first postcollege year: getting used to a daily alarm clock, not having a bazillion weeks of vacation, having to answer the phone, regardless of whether you feel like talking. I feel his pain, remembering that sharp feeling as a first-year associate when, as I was walking to work on the first happy, hopeful, sunny day of spring, it hit me like an invisible wall that I couldn't just take my reading to the Quad.

Luger blusters over, intent on discussing the grossest things he's ever seen on the subway. Although some involve small animals (rats, pigeons), most involve bodily fluid. He's ending a horrific masturbating-commuter story when I spot Henry across the room, his head visible above the crowd.

Duck insisted on inviting him. "We've had beers together," she said. "It would be weird if I didn't invite him." She promised that it wasn't an attempt to pair us off, but she'd seemed surprised when Henry checked the Evite box that said "Hell, yeah, wouldn't miss it" and indicated that he'd be bringing along a guest.

Henry and that guest—Julie, looking like a runway model—

glide over to me in unison, like costumed ice-skaters, just as Luger shouts, "I mean, the hugest, hugest crap, biggest dump ever. Seriously."

Julie winces as Henry's eyes widen. "Wow," he says. "What are we interrupting?"

"Trust me, it's not an interruption. It's a relief," I say. "Better not to hear any more, especially if you ride the subway regularly. Good costumes."

I would've never pegged Henry as someone who would dress up for Halloween, but he has rallied as Han Solo, complete with the V-necked white shirt, tight dark pants, vest and badass holster. And Julie is of course Princess Leia, her glossy hair done up in resplendent coil buns, her perfect body dipped in a long clingy white dress that reminds me of an Oscar gown.

Henry and I never talk about Julie, which I chalk up to his philosophy on compartmentalizing work life and home life. When we had drinks several weeks ago, Duck had plowed right through Henry's obvious palpable reluctance, jackhammering him with questions about how long they'd been together and what was Julie like. All I learned was that Henry had met Julie through her brother, his friend from college, and that Julie liked the Hamptons.

Henry gives me the once-over and busts out laughing. "Nice," he finally says. "Good look for you."

"Yeah." I give a little wave. "Apparently I'm a generic red-haired character."

"Who are you really? *I Love Lucy*, right?" Julie says.

I bite my tongue to keep from replying *Yes, I'm Lucille Ball during her crack-whore/hobo years.*

"She's Pippi Longstocking—note the monkey friend carefully, um, assaulted with pins and stuck to her shirt," says Henry, pointing to the picture. "Pippi, you better hope the ASPCA is not here."

"Little-known fact about Pippi—she's got a bit of a sadistic edge," I say, with an eyebrow arch, sipping my now flat beer.

When Henry leaves to get drinks, I ask Julie what she does and she takes off running. She used to work for Rosenthal, the auction house, and that was totally great, oh, the stuff she got to just work around, just masterpieces—the Picasso, the Close, the Hirst. Now she's with a smaller gallery, Krenshaw London, did I know it, no, see, that was totally her point, no one had heard of it, so, even though she did really, like, truly believe in the power of small boutique galleries as a way to showcase the right artist, it just wasn't as important as her work at the house—they totally missed her there and the hours were better than her new hours, which were, well, nothing like poor Henry's hours, which were nuts, just crazy, I mean I would not believe how hard poor Henry worked, at which I nod emphatically.

"He works really hard," I say.

"Oh, you must be the one who works with him?"

I nod. "We're both in the matrimonial group at the firm."

"Oh my God. So you've seen the Miró? I swear I almost started to hyperventilate."

"Actually, I've never—"

"Oh, you must be the one who introduced him to the hosts, um—Goose and—"

"Duck and Holt. Yep, that's me."

"We, like, never go to Brooklyn. And our friends back in the city are having a party tonight, so I was, like, totally shocked when Henry wanted to stop by here before our Halloween party. He must have really hit it off with them, right?"

"Right," I say, although I'm pretty sure that he's only talked to Duck twice. "Well, I'm glad you guys showed up."

Henry returns with three margaritas in red plastic cups and hands one to Julie and one to me. There's a moment of awkward silence that I chalk up to the out-of-place work-friend phenomenon. I look down at my feet. One is in my own sneaker and the other is in Duck's fuzzy thong slipper. Not wanting to draw attention there, I quickly look up. "So, where'd you guys get the costumes?"

"Oh, I spent weeks scouring the Internet until one of my network of costume sources—Yuri, I think, from Brighton Beach—tracked them down," Henry says.

I laugh. "Wow, it's Loose Party Henry. Nice to meet you."

"No, it was all her. I had hoped to be a hardworking office drone and just come in business casual with a cup of coffee."

Julie rolls her eyes. "Hon, that would have been so boring. Thank God you have me to dress you up." She puckers up her lips and pecks him on the mouth, making an exaggerated *mwah* sound.

Gross. I hate when unmarried couples call each other hon. It always sounds phony to me, like they're playing house. I gulp my margarita and consider excusing myself when I spot Caleb.

He's leaning against the wall, lazily sipping a beer, a half-interested expression on his face as he listens to someone tell a story. At first I wonder if he's come dressed as his college self. He has the same half-present expression that he did the first time I saw him at a party my freshman year, as though waiting for something or somebody. I had watched him smoke a cigarette, something I had until that moment found disgusting, and—in an impulse I still find bizarre—imagined myself tracing the contours of his chiseled face with my fingertips. I must have stared for some time, because my friend Olivia followed my gaze across the room and nodded knowingly. "Total sex appeal," she said, her voice leaving no room for doubt. And then she had insisted on debating which celebrity he most resembled, emphatically chanting "Bradley Cooper. Bradley Cooper. Bradley Cooper," as I lied that I just didn't see it.

I watch Caleb's eyes drift, looking around the room. *Look at me, look at me, look at me,* I will, just as I did eleven years ago. He nods at someone, I can't tell whom, and then, as if in direct response to my thoughts, looks right at me. He excuses himself and strides across the room.

"Hey," he says. He nods to Rico, who has been helping Duck redesign his office, and I introduce him to Henry and Julie.

"Hats off to not dressing up. I admire your resolve," says Henry with a smile.

Caleb looks down at his plaid shirt and jeans, as though it's occurring to him in this moment that he's not wearing a costume. "Oh, yeah," he says, expressionless.

"So, how do you guys know each other?" Henry says.

"Rico and Duck are almost finished designing Caleb's office," I say.

Caleb looks at me and raises his eyebrows, as if he can't believe that's the extent of my introduction.

". . . and we all went to college together," I say.

Henry looks back and forth between us.

"What?" I say, feeling my cheeks getting red.

"Excuse us," Caleb says, putting his hand in the small of my back and steering me over to the couch.

He sits down and pats the cushion next to him.

"It's all over your face," he says, his tone serious.

"It's supposed to be there. It's makeup," I say, but I wipe at my cheeks nonetheless.

He gives me a deep look. "I'm talking about your expression. You've missed me too."

I look down at my hand and busy myself with smearing the makeup off with my thumb. "And you're basing this on?"

He doesn't respond, so I look up. Caleb is staring right at me, unsmiling, a golden curl falling over his eyebrow. Without thinking, I brush it off his face and his smile lines crinkle, three tiny ridges that deepen for an instant and then don't entirely recede.

"Like I said. You miss me too. I know you." He reaches around my right hand for a second, lacing his fingers through mine and then using them to pry away my empty beer bottle. "I'll get you a refill. You might need it for the rest of our conversation."

"Seriously? You think you'll do better if I'm drunk?"

"Not drunk," he says, shaking his head. "We just need to manage your inhibitions. Acting on what you really want has never been your strong suit." He stands up and goes over to the bar.

Henry approaches, jacket folded over his arm.

"We're leaving now."

I look around. "Where's Julie?"

He points. She's wearing her coat, deep in conversation with Rico. "They've been talking about John Currin for ten minutes."

"So why don't you guys stay?"

"We have to get to our other party."

"Okay, well, I'm glad you came and it was really great to meet Julie." I am lying. She's kind of a bore, actually.

Henry stands there, paused.

"Who is that guy?" He nods toward Caleb, who's in the process of opening two beers.

"We used to date in college." I feel my cheeks getting hot yet again. "A long time ago."

Henry looks at me for a moment.

"So, see you Monday?" I finally say.

"See you then." I watch as he walks over to Julie and touches her shoulder; then she trails him out of the room.

It's bright, bright, bright. The sunlight slices through my closed eyelids and I force one open. My hair hurts. I reach up and tentatively touch it. Right: red wig, wire braids. I can tell without looking that I'm wearing only my robe, the blue cotton jersey one that always comes untied. I sit up in my bed and start to rake my hands through my hair, untangling the mess of red strands and wire, as I review the night.

My bathroom door swings open. I sit up straight as Caleb saunters out and my robe falls open. He's wearing striped boxer shorts and that's pretty much it.

Right. That was my night.

"Morning," he says, sitting down on the foot of the bed.

Seeing Caleb, I am very aware of the horrible taste in my mouth. "Hold on a second," I say, clutching my robe together as I scramble out of bed and into the bathroom.

I look in the mirror. My Pippi wig is still on, a vibrant red fringe half-covering the blond. The remnants of my rosy red cheeks and fake freckles are smeared all over my face, making me look like Baby Jane after a hands-free cherry-pie-eating contest. I gulp down two Advil, bending my head under the faucet for water, brush my teeth for about five minutes, pick off my wig and scrub my face three times with an exfoliating cream. I tie back my hair in a sloppy bun, which feels as refreshing as it should after a night of suffocating my hair with a braided wig.

When I finally emerge, straightening and tying my robe, Caleb is already dressed in his outfit from the night before.

"So?" he says.

"So . . . what?"

"Any regrets?"

"None." It felt great to be with Caleb, a heady combination of familiar and electric. "Do you feel like the diner for breakfast?"

He grimaces. "I have to be downtown in"—he looks at his watch—"an hour."

"Oh, okay." I turn toward the closet.

"Wait a minute, wait a minute," he says, grabbing the belt of my robe. He pulls me toward him and in one fluid move, we're directly in front of each other, close enough for him to drop the belt and slide his arms around my rib cage.

I know it right before our lips lock. I'm hijacked: intoxicated by Caleb's familiar smell (soap mingled with fresh tobacco) and the taste of his toothpaste-fresh mouth. It's like no time has passed, all memories erased, and I'm nineteen again. Only this time, I get it. He likes kissing. He likes me. I wrap my arms around his neck and tug him closer, knowing just what this is and knowing it's completely fine.

the devil wears hawaiian print

W hen Fern calls my cell phone, I am lying on my bed, risking paper cuts by rubbing my wrist against a yellowed
scent strip from a fashion magazine's March issue. I should be
working on a draft of the Wades agreement; instead, like a hope-
less teenager, I sniff my wrist and wonder if Caleb would like the
smell.

"I am so sorry to bother you," Fern says against the noise of
sirens.

"What's going on?"

"I hate to ask, but if you're around, could you come meet us? I
wouldn't ask if I didn't—"

"It's fine." I hear another set of sirens. "Where are you?"

Twenty minutes later, I walk into the pediatric emergency
room at New York Presbyterian. Fern and her kids have camped
out across a row of blue chairs that's attached at the arms like a
lineup of Rockette torsos. Anna is engrossed in a book with a
frothy pink cover, her legs—in star-print tights—propped up on
her chair. Connor sits next to Anna, entirely focused on eating an
ice-cream cone, melted chocolate dripping down his hands and
arm. Fern is holding an ice pack to Connor's forehead. The three
of them look like a family.

Fern smiles when she sees me. "Oh, thanks for coming. I'm so
grateful. I tried not to bother you, but my sister, Lolly, is in

Pennsylvania this weekend and my friend Marie is meeting her boyfriend's parents and for something like this, there was really no one else. . . ."

"No problem." I nod toward Connor. "He looks good."

"Yeah, I think he's okay."

Fern leans over Connor, her hand still holding the ice pack. "Anna, this is my friend Molly."

"Hi, Anna, great to meet you. High five!" I say, too loudly and brightly. I always feel awkward with kids, as though I'm reading lines from the script of a hokey after-school special.

Anna's eyes widen, part disbelief, part alarm. Fern nods reassuringly and Anna quickly resumes reading, sticking a strand of her long brown hair in her mouth.

Fern meets my eye, smiles and mouths "Shy," although I am sure that she thinks Anna's reaction was as much due to my vigorous greeting as anything else.

"And this is Connor."

Subdued by my strikeout with Anna, I keep it simple. "Hi, Connor. You hurt your head?"

"I gotta choclitt icecream! Choclitt! Ice! Cream!" is his response, as he continues to concentrate on inhaling the ice cream like he's Mick Jagger and the sugar cone is a microphone. There is now chocolate in his curly brown hair, all over his chubby little cheeks and all over his red turtleneck shirt. He looks like a cherubic little pig in mud.

"So, this was a playground incident?"

"Yes, Connor was climbing the monkey bars"—over his head, she uses air quotes, indicating that whatever Connor was doing would not meet a technical description of monkey-bar climbing—"and doing a really *great* job, but he lost his grip and when he fell, he hit his head against the bars. The bleeding has mostly stopped, though." Fern removes the ice pack and squints at the congealing cut. "And his pupils look normal too and he hasn't gotten sick or anything, so he's probably fine."

Anna looks up and rolls her eyes. "Of course he's fine. Connor falls, like, all the time."

Fern nods. "I know, and I'm sure he's okay, but he bumped his head, so we just want to make sure."

"But we still get to make pizza, right?"

"Yes, pizza, right after this, your choice of toppings," Fern says, using her free hand to rub Anna's shoulder.

Mollified, Anna continues reading.

"So you called me for my medical expertise?" I say.

Fern sighs. "I wouldn't put it past you to have medical expertise on top of everything else, but no, I left a message with their father to let him know we were here. I thought this was the type of information that he should know." She keeps her voice light and conversational, but her eyes start to water and I realize why I'm here. She is scared of seeing Robert Walker and wants my protection.

The punch line, of course, is that I am scared of Robert Walker too. He belongs in a horror movie. I am freaked-out enough already at the thought of cross-examining him, even though in court, as Henry constantly reminds me, it's all only words. Yes, words can be aggressive, annoying and migraine generating, but at the end of the day, how threatened can you be? The words swirl around and it's over.

That argument doesn't apply now. We are out in the real world with no bailiffs, rules of procedure or metal detectors. I'm not sure what would happen in an ER showdown, and while I am taller than petite lil' Fern, I am hardly bodyguard material. I think longingly of that key-chain Mace spray my dad bought me before I moved to New York.

I match Fern's light tone. "Yep, I'm really glad you called me."

She shakes her head. "And I called Claire."

"Interesting tactic." I try not to roll my eyes.

As a matter of strategy and parenting, Fern has done the right thing by calling Robert. I dread his arrival, but even I have to admit that he deserves to know when his kid is in the emergency room. Plus, if Fern had not told him, Risa could—and would—correctly accuse her of freezing him out in the same way that Robert's been doing to Fern. Claire, on the other hand, has no parental rights. She just acts like she does.

Fern knows what I'm thinking and her tone is apologetic. "I just wanted him to get word as soon as possible, so I called her too."

An idea hits me. "And did you call Emily Freed too?"

"Um, no. I didn't. Do you think I should?"

"Oh, yes," I say, carefully watching the kids to see if they're paying attention to our conversation. Connor is still working on the ice-cream cone and Anna just turned a page, so I don't think so.

I keep my tone carefully casual. "I think you should just call her, tell her that Connor had a little playground fall and that you think he's okay. And maybe just tell her that you're working hard to notify their dad, have left messages and will keep everyone posted."

Fern nods. "All right, I'll do it," she says, sitting back in her chair.

"Fern, maybe do it now," I say.

Fern removes the tissue from Connor's forehead, which isn't bleeding anymore, but sports a small purple bump in the middle—the nub of a unicorn horn. She takes her cell phone from her brown slouchy leather bag, gets up from her chair and walks about ten feet away from us. In a quiet voice, she leaves a message virtually identical to what I suggested. Then, at the end, she pauses and, looking at me, adds, "So, um, we might all be here at New York Presbyterian, all of us, in a little while, and if you have any suggestions on that, or thoughts, just, um, let me know. If not, I'm sorry to bother you on your weekend and we'll see you next week. Thanks."

Fern hangs up and, still across the room, starts pacing.

I walk over to her. "It's okay. It will be fine."

She stops, speaking quietly so her kids can't hear. "I screwed up everything, didn't I?"

"What are you talking about?"

"I'll never win now. Robert will make such a big deal about this. He'll say this proves I can't handle them—"

"And he'll look like an unreasonable monster when he does. Accidents happen. You acted responsibly. You have nothing to worry about."

"Really?" She looks at me, biting her lip. "You still think we have a shot at winning?"

"Without a doubt."

"Because . . . it's just gotten so good with them, but I still can't get back the time I missed. The thought of losing everything again . . ." Fern slowly shakes her head. "I don't know how I could . . . if I could—"

"I know," I say, even as I can't begin to imagine.

Eyes closed, she presses her right palm against her forehead, as though checking herself for fever. "I figured it out, you know," she says, dropping her hand. "Why we always meet on evenings or weekends, why I'm not supposed to call you at the law firm, and why you're always a little on edge when we're waiting in the hallway at court. How much trouble would you get in if your bosses found out you had taken my case?"

"A fair amount."

She shakes her head, frowning.

"I promise, it's not against the law or anything. It's just probably best if they don't find out."

"It's too much, Molly. It's too much pressure for you."

"It's not, Fern. It actually does me some good to have an appreciative client." I laugh in an attempt to lighten things. "You'd be surprised at how rare it is."

She doesn't answer.

Keeping my voice quiet, I sound as definite as I can. "Fern, if I couldn't handle your case, I wouldn't have taken it on."

She nods, inhaling deeply. "Okay," she says, making me think that perhaps I'm a more convincing actor than my high school drama teacher had thought.

I return to the kids' bench and settle in next to Anna. She's fairly engrossed in her book, something called *Muggie Maggie*, which she tells me is about a girl who can't write cursive. I ask her some polite questions about it and receive nods and headshakes in response, but I can tell she just wants to read. Connor finishes his ice-cream cone and turns into a live wire, running around and climbing on the chairs. I make an off-hand comment about a sugar high, and Anna responds in an adult tone that he's a three-year-old boy and is, like, always like this.

Finally, Fern gets Connor focused on the TV screen above our heads, which is showing a cartoon about fluffy little creatures with masks. The sound is off and the creatures just seem to be running around, but that is apparently riveting enough for Connor. He stands immobilized, staring at the screen as Fern uses a wet wipe to clean his face and slips a clean red T-shirt over his head.

The hospital doors slide open and someone enters the waiting room. As we have the other twelve times someone has come in, Fern and I jerk our eyes toward the entrance. This time, I am relieved to see a small dark-haired pregnant woman with a head scarf, pushing a sleeping toddler in a gray stroller.

I meet Fern's eye. "Maybe it will just be us today?"

She discreetly crosses her fingers.

Connor finally gets admitted and we are shuttled into an exam room. A young resident comes in, shines a light into Connor's eyes, checks his reflexes and gives him some simple commands. He tells us that the kid looks fine, he doesn't think an X-ray is necessary and that he'll be back soon.

All of a sudden, I hear yelling outside.

A female voice says, "Sir, Sir, Sir, SIR, YOU—" in a crescendo of disbelief as the door to our exam room pushes open and Robert Walker walks in, Claire right behind him. Claire is perfectly turned out in Upper East Side weekend casual—skinny jeans, high boots and an asymmetrical gray sweater.

Robert, however, is wearing a long-sleeve Hawaiian-style shirt with swirling azure and pink flowers, his potbelly shoved into linen khaki pants, above loafers and no socks, as though we've disrupted his annual November pig roast on the Hudson. The comic relief brought by his outfit lasts a nanosecond. Both kids freeze in their tracks. Anna silently leaps out of the guest chair that she has been spinning around in, grabs Connor's hand and yanks him from Fern's lap. They run to Claire and bury their heads in her legs.

"Oh, my poor babies," she murmurs, clutching them. "Oh, Connor, where's your boo-boo? Let Mama see it, let me see it." They both start to cry and cling to her.

Robert steps toward Fern. "What the fuck?"

Without thinking, I step in front of her. "It's okay, Fern. You didn't do anything wrong."

This incenses Robert. "Why the fuck are you even here, Ms. Grant?" He spits my name. "And what the fuck do you mean this hapless bitch didn't do anything wrong? Why is my boy in the hospital? You can't even watch them for one fucking afternoon? One fucking afternoon! I can't wait until that judge hears about this. You won't ever see my kids again."

From somewhere, I hear "Margaritaville." I remember that it's Robert Walker's ringtone, the world's most incongruous super-villain theme. Robert reaches into his pocket, grabs his cell phone and pushes it at Claire, telling her to shut the fucking thing up.

Claire expertly presses a button, silencing it before we find out that it's all Jimmy Buffett's own damn fault. The kids continue wailing and Fern tries to reach over to them, but Claire body-blocks her, pushing her arms out and then bending over Connor and Anna, Lady Liberty harboring the cuddled masses.

"It's okay, babies," she murmurs. "We're gonna take you home. Don't worry. We're going home."

"Actually," I say, with as much authority as I can muster, "you're going to go home. This is Fern's time with the kids."

Fern is frozen and does not respond to my prompt, even as I put my hand on her back and push her gently toward the door.

Robert moves directly in front of the door, blocking it.

Fern's cell phone rings faintly from somewhere deep in her bag.

Robert puts his face directly in Fern's, speaking softly. ". . . idiot, incapable," he continues as Fern's phone rings again.

I nudge her so she'll hear it. Fern does not move, so I step back from Robert, hope that Fern does not think I'm abandoning her and grab her bag from the doctor's desk where she has left it. I fish around until I get the phone, glance at the caller ID and surreptitiously open the phone, keeping it behind my back. I hear a tinny female voice repeating, "Hello, hello, hello," but I don't respond, concentrating on keeping the phone open in my sweaty, slippery hands.

Robert continues, his voice a little louder. He is still planted in front of the door, his face inches from Fern's, talking directly to her. "And this piece-of-shit hospital? What is in your head? I'm on the fucking board at NYU. Do you understand? The board. Why on earth would you send them here? Where is your fucking common sense? I have the chief of pediatrics in from his golf game, personally waiting for us downtown. And that's where we're going." He takes a step even closer to Fern and pushes his finger in her chest. "Your visits with them are over.

You hear me? Over. After this, you're never going to see these kids again."

I step forward, phone still behind my back. "No one is taking the kids anywhere. This is Fern's weekend with the kids. I'm telling you one more time. Please leave."

Robert shakes his head and focuses on me, now putting his face directly in front of mine, so close that I can smell his stale cigar breath.

"You're a child, a joke. My assistants' assistants have more experience than you. With all due respect," he snorts, "shut the fuck up and get out of the way."

"Let me just say generally, to the room, um, for the record, that anyone who interferes with Fern's time with her children is in violation of a judicial order."

Robert Walker barks a laugh. "Oh, okay, Ms. Grant. Thank you for clarifying the record." He looks around the room, his voice laced with disdain. "Did everyone note that for the record? My kids are not safe with your client. Period. I am taking them now. Period." He looks at me and at Fern, and folds his arms across his chest. "You're welcome to try and stop me, though."

I look over at Fern, who is frozen in place, her eyes downcast. What am I going to do? Physically grab the children? Punch Robert Walker? I feel weak and superfluous and I know Fern feels worse, as Claire and Robert sweep up the crying kids and storm out, leaving the door to our room hanging open for nurses, doctors and other patients to gawk at us.

I look at the phone. The time meter is still running. I hear a shocked, tinny voice saying, "Fern? Are you there? Fern? Hello?"

Fern doesn't respond. She's expressionless, standing still in the center of the room, her hands opening and closing quickly in a futile motion, fists with no grasp. A peppery, jagged burn ignites in my jaw and courses to my stomach. This must be what hatred feels like. Pure, concentrated hatred, leaving no room for

nuance or any other weaker, gentler emotions; all I want is to
eviscerate him, to stun Robert Walker the way he's stunned her.
The one tiny, minuscule piece of good news is that I might be
closer to doing just that: Emily Freed has been there, listening at
the other end of the line, for the entire time.

brownie bites are heaven

S pending twenty-four consecutive hours at Bacon Payne is not
as bad as it sounds. Sure, there's an underbelly to every all-
nighter, a moment, usually in the wee hours right before sunrise,
when the fatigue and stress win out and I wind up crying in the
bathroom. But before that, there's a long stretch of quiet during
which I can focus on my work without disruption, and the time
flies. In the matrimonial department, when one of the other associates has to stay late too, a glorious slap-happiness can emerge,
the camaraderie springing us through the night like ricocheting
pinballs.

I don't know when they hit me, my brilliant plans for tonight,
but I am almost trembling with anticipation. For weeks, each
time I've ducked into Jodi's Deli, I've bought a handful of
brownie bites—those processed, individually wrapped blobs of
chocolate dough that could probably survive a nuclear holocaust
but are somehow moist and tasty. Last week, Henry was out of
the office for an afternoon meeting and it occurred to me that a
good use for the brownie bites would be to sneak one in the
pocket of the spare suit jacket hanging on the back of his door.

Hilarious as I knew it was, that didn't get a response, so I kept
it up, one per day: the bottom drawer of his desk, on top of his file
cabinet, on his printer.

Nothing.

So late this afternoon, when Henry was stuck in the conference room, I went all out, boldly littering twenty-five brownie bites around his office: perched on the frame of his diploma, on top of his computer monitor, three sitting innocently in his chair.

That was a few hours ago and Henry has not given any indication that he's noticed, but just the thought of him walking back into his office, straight-faced, and discovering it is enough to make me—alone at my desk—erupt into maniacal giggles.

At eight thirty, I go down to the lobby to pick up the food for the late-night crew, which tonight is me, Henry and Liz. On the way back, I walk by Henry's office and stick my head in, scanning the room. The brownie bite that I stuck on the diploma has vanished. "Food's here."

"Okay."

I stand in his doorway. Wait for a beat.

"You looking for something?" He's expressionless.

"No." I try to match his poker face.

"Meet you in the conference room, then."

Liz, Henry and I sit around the marble table in the small room, peeling open the steamed lids of our plastic containers and talking about our work. Liz is preparing for a trial; I'm drafting a prenuptial agreement for a wedding taking place next weekend and working on a client's affidavit. Henry, who has pulled more all-nighters than anyone in this critical year, is doing catch-up work, just trying to manage his substantial caseload.

I keep searching Henry's face and finding nothing.

"What?" he says. "What?"

Finally, we're gathering up the trash, stuffing it back into the brown bag the delivery came in, and Henry, expressionless, reaches into the front pocket of his shirt. He holds a wrapped brownie bite in the palm of his hand. "Anyone want dessert?"

"Sure," says Liz. "But do you only have the one?"

"Oh no," says Henry, looking me squarely in the eye. "I have several." He reaches into his pants pocket and takes out two more.

I try to look surprised. "What's with all the"—I press my lips together to keep from laughing, but I know my eyes give me away—"brownie bites?"

"You identified these so easily, Molly. I'm impressed with your snack acumen." He raises his shoulders and eases them back down in a carefree shrug. "Apparently, I won some sort of contest."

"These are heaven," Liz says.

"Take another." Henry slides the second brownie bite toward her without even so much as a glance toward me.

By three thirty in the morning, I am not seeing the humor in anything; my punch-drunkenness has sobered. I'm tired and nowhere near done drafting the prenup's provisions, one of which is a complicated contingency scenario that reduces my client's share of the marital property if she has an affair with a younger man.

I go down to the word processing department on the twenty-fourth floor and almost fall asleep waiting to talk to Wendy, the night shift processor. On my way back to my office, I pass Henry's office, then Liz's. In the hour I've spent downstairs, they've both called it a night and now their office lights are off; the floor is quiet. I picture them at home, asleep, curled up in bed, and feel empty in a sorry-for-myself kind of way, like that one fall break at college, when I opted against flying home for the long weekend, and wound up wandering the deserted halls like some sort of sole survivor. Fatigued tears stab at the back of my eyes, which are bleary from staring at my computer screen. I slouch back into my office—my lights have been turned off too, to my annoyance—and flip the switch back on.

All I can see are Twinkies: in my pen cup; between the jaws of my stapler; framing the picture of me and Duck that sits on my desk; propped between my parents in the snapshot of them in the backyard, like it's another member of the family; lying at the base of my lamp. There must be fifty of them.

I start giggling, at first quietly and then it's more of an eruption, and soon, I'm laughing out loud, tears streaming down my face, a burst of pure joy, as golden as a Twinkie, releasing from within me and bubbling up to the surface.

newkirk's report

To access Dr. Newkirk's forensic report, I need the state government equivalent of a retinal scan. With an apologetic smile that acknowledges the ridiculousness, Mike asks for my ID. He examines it carefully, holding my license in his rough inky hands and squinting, eventually nodding. He thanks me and lumbers away, returning with a tattered manila file folder with "Newkirk" scrawled on the front in sloppy black-inked block letters.

He holds the folder just out of my reach. "This is your only copy," he says in a monotone-rehearsed voice reminiscent of a bored cop reading Miranda rights to a petty criminal. "It can't leave your possession or your office. No faxing, scanning, copying, sending through the mail or taking it home with you. If you want to share it with the client, she can read it at your office and take notes. Okay?"

"Got it." I nod, knowing that Mike and I could have a circular "Who's on First?"-esque conversation for days about the fact that the office of Molly Grant, PC, is my home. "I'm going to hang around here and review it first, okay?"

"Fine," Mike says, gesturing to the empty benches in the courtroom. "Take your pick."

I feel a shot of nervous adrenaline as I open the report.

It's been four weeks since the horrible scene at the hospital.

Right after Robert Walker stormed out with the kids, I led Fern to a taxi. She was silent and passive, slumping closed-eyed against the door after I leaned across her in the backseat to shut it. I nervously considered buckling her seat belt, but instead gripped her arm the whole way to her apartment, as if that could protect her. Her sister, Lolly, who had rushed back from Pennsylvania to Fern's apartment, later reported to me that Fern spent the next two days in the clothes from the hospital, curled on top of her bedspread.

It had been almost as bad as before, Lolly had said on the phone, before lowering her voice and whispering exactly what I had been thinking: *What the fuck's gonna happen if we lose?*

I had realized something then: I see only the tip of the iceberg for my clients, a mere marker for the whole submerged mountain of pain that lurks beneath them. I let Lolly's question hang in the air, stopping myself from some sort of glib, cheerleader's "go team!" answer. Because the truth is, I do not know what the fuck's gonna happen if we lose.

That Monday, there had been a flurry of letters between all the lawyers and experts, causing me to run back and forth between my two offices five times, mad dashes across the pavement that I would feel in my splintered shins over the next four days. That was followed by a conference call with the court—I had ducked into an empty conference room ten floors down for that one, murmuring into the phone as though Strand was my illicit lover. Everyone played their parts—Risa and I were nattering macaws, each trying to outdo the other's accusations. Roland, the calm voice of reason, was annoyingly neutral and noncommittal. Justice Strand was perplexed and disappointed that things were not going smoothly: yes, Fern should have visitation, but it was troubling that Connor had gotten hurt. Perhaps Fern could do something a little safer next time.

I bit my tongue before asking him whether having them stay

indoors and watching television for twelve hours would be safer than the playground, and as usual when I shut my mouth, things went okay, with Fern's visitation schedule resumed that evening. She, having somehow accessed the strength of hope, pulled herself together before the visit. The kids had been shaky, refusing to talk about the scene at the hospital, but in the weeks since, they had all been getting back into the new normal.

But frankly, I am worried that at this late point Strand still thinks there's any merit in Risa's accusations that Fern is dangerous. And I'm very anxious about what's in the report. I flip through the initial few pages, outlining the history of the case and noting that over the past several months, Newkirk met with all of the Walkers multiple times. He's also met with Claire, the kids' teachers, their sitters—Hannah and someone named Bobbi—their grandparents and their aunts and uncles.

I skim through the meetings with Fern: he calls her flexible, reasonable, self-sustaining, high-functioning. Good.

I read the Claire and Robert stuff more carefully. Apparently, they started dating about two years ago. She moved in after three months together and has lived with them since, stopping her work at Options to be a full-time caregiver about one month after that. According to Newkirk, Robert's hours are intense, and both Claire and Robert maintain that Claire has been responsible for the day-to-day parenting: hiring the nannies, coordinating the activities and their daily schedule, going to parent-teacher conferences with Robert. And to use Robert's words, as quoted by Newkirk, "Thank God those kids have her. She is a mother to them."

Robert is an involved "hands-on" father. He possesses a fine command of their activities (ballet and karate for Anna, piano and the unsafe-sounding ice-skating for Connor), medical history (Anna's history of ear infections, Connor's allergy to soy), personalities, likes and dislikes and friends.

Control freak.

Robert and Claire both bad-mouth Fern to Newkirk, which he puts in the report. They call her depressed, unhealthy and unhinged, and say that the children are scared of her. They report that before each and every visit with Fern, both kids, particularly Anna, have prolonged meltdowns for approximately one to two hours, trouble eating and sleeping. Connor has regressed from potty training.

There are several more pages about the kids and reports on the calls with Emily Freed. I flip past them and skip to his recommendation at the end.

Conclusion

Upon the various meetings and interviews conducted I conclude that while the Father is an involved parent, he has systematically and unrelentingly alienated the children from their Mother.

In layman's terms, the Father has undermined the Mother at every turn, maligning the Mother in front of the children and doing his best to completely shut out the Mother from their lives.

Especially notable is that the Father, the Father's girlfriend and the children spoke about the Mother's irresponsibility, mental illness and desertion with the same exact terminology. In both of my meetings with the Father and his girlfriend, they independently said that the Mother was "mentally unstable and could not be trusted."

In an independent interview, Anna, the six-year-old child, also said she was concerned that Fern was "unstable and not to be trusted," repeating the Father's concerns awkwardly and almost verbatim, with language highly unusual for a six-year-old. Additionally, Anna seemed preoccupied with whether I had talked to her Father and when I was going to tell him about what she said during the meetings and whether Claire was going to sit in on our meeting. When I asked Connor, her three-year-old brother, about his Mother during their joint interview and he clapped and smiled, Anna looked nervous, squeezed his hand and told him to be quiet. There is no doubt that Anna is attempting to stay "on message" for her Father's approval.

In contrast, the Mother, who expresses being haunted by the loss of a relationship with her children, acknowledges that their Father is important to them.

There is no alternative conclusion to draw but that the Father has been, in essence, training his children against their Mother.

Recommendation

My recommendation to the court: transfer of legal and physical custody to the Mother under the supervision of a treating team of therapists and subject to the Father's reduced and supervised visitation.

Postscript

Post the date of completion of the formal report, I had an additional conversation with Emily Freed that requires mention. According to Ms. Freed, after a playground mishap during her weekend with him, the Mother took Connor to the emergency room and notified the Father of same. The Father arrived at the emergency room, interrupted the visitation and, in front of the children, questioned the Mother's judgment, physically threatened her and left with the children. In my professional opinion, this exemplifies behavior that is harmful to the children and cannot continue without serious damage to their relationship with their Mother, and fundamental harm to them.

I put down the folder, my heart leaping. This is good. This is very good. It doesn't seem overly optimistic to say that the trial is the only thing between Team Fern and a victory. I pick up the phone to call Fern, to share the best bit of news we've had in the case. But then I think that perhaps I should temper my excitement when I talk to her: getting through the trial successfully might not be the foregone conclusion she would expect, given that I've never actually done one before.

hiding out in the sierra nevadas

Although Caleb's office suite primarily seems a place to play video games, this has not stopped him from throwing one heck of a company holiday party, complete with a swarm of butlers passing puffed hors d'oeuvres and a string quartet playing Shostakovich. Sadly for me, my enthusiasm for the food has scared off the waiter responsible for the sushi tray. It's out of this world, the sushi—thin little buttery, melt-in-your-mouth slices of salmon and yellowtail dotted with miniature salmon roe.

I scope the room, trying to find him among all the people in dark-toned skinny pants and draped tops, standing in clusters discussing things like Art Basel and social media iconography and the efficacy of property managers for third homes in tiny mountain towns. Duck, who would normally be my partner in assessing the culinary offerings, is gesturing to a white-haired man in mirrored sunglasses and a woman with a diamond-encrusted cuff extending from her wrist to her elbow.

Duck is networking, which is exactly what she should be doing. She finished her designing job just in time for tonight, and the place looks amazing. I watch her nod at something the man says as she pets the back of a gray chaise lounge.

I've lost sight of Caleb, who is presumably busy networking as well. And then I spot him: the flash of a white jacket, the warmth of golden bamboo. Is he trying to take the long way around the room to avoid me? Not so fast. I plant myself in his path.

"Oooh, uni," I say. "Yes, please." I select two and meet the gaze of the waiter, whose name tag says ERIC. "Are you getting anything new after this or will there be more yellowtail?"

His eyes dart around the room. "I don't know, miss. Please, I just carry the tray."

"Okay, Eric." He winces when I use his name. "Well, if you do, come find me. You know what? Never you mind, Eric. I'll find you."

He skitters away.

"Great night for you, huh?" I say to Duck as she walks over to me.

She nods, her eyes shining. "Do you know who just asked me to make an appointment with their people?"

"Someone really rich with a lot of properties in need of decoration?"

"Way to boil things down nice and crude." She grabs my second uni off my napkin and pops it in her mouth.

"You deserve it. This place looks unreal."

She smiles. "You can keep telling me that. I won't pretend it's not awesome to hear."

I look at my watch. "If you're supposed to be in Midtown in twenty minutes, you should probably head out."

"I should—but let's focus on you for just a second."

"What about me?"

"You seem to be doing an awfully good job of staying on the periphery of this event."

I hold up my napkin. "I'm captivated by the appetizers. Plus, all these people remind me of my clients. The thought of making small talk is painful."

She nods at Caleb, who's deep in conversation with a very large bearded man in a tuxedo. "Is he introducing you around?"

"He's too busy hosting."

"But he invited you here as his date, right?"

"His date?" I don an exaggerated drawl. "I can't believe your lil' antiquated Southern self decorated this modern monstrosity. You know what we need here? Some tea cozies. Maybe right there, on top of that resin sculpture."

She shakes her head, smiling. "I'm not crazy."

"I know you're being protective. But you don't need to worry. Things are good, totally different from college. We even have a little routine down."

"Right, booty calls and late-night dinners like clockwork."

"It's not like that. We're in tandem, I promise you."

"All I'm saying is he should be showing you off. You look amazing. I'm still in shock from the amount of grooming you endured. Unprecedented."

"Well, thank you. Beauty is a marathon, not a sprint."

"Is that an actual expression?"

"I don't know. It's a direct quote from Christy, the makeup lady at the Bobbi Brown counter at Saks. She did my face."

Duck peers at me. "She seems to know what she's talking about. You are poreless." She pats my shoulder. "I'm off. Later."

"Okay." I look back at Caleb. He and the bearded man are now talking to two women. I'm impressed by Caleb's hosting skills; he's smiling and laughing and going out of his way to make his guests feel welcome. It's endearing to see him all excited, his inner seven-year-old muzzling his usual veneer of cool.

Despite Duck's concern, I do not want to play the part of Caleb's cohost tonight. What I want is exactly what I'm getting: to sit back and watch him, enjoying the anticipation of what will happen later this evening. I recognize this feeling—patiently holding my breath for him to free up so we'll be able to focus on each other—and I should, because, really, it's exactly the same as it was in college. The only difference is that this time I get our arrangement. And it's all I want too.

Caleb is pointing at one of the centerpieces of the room, a huge wall-sized painting with interlocking fluorescent circles, and the bearded man and the two women turn to look at it. For a split second, before she turns back, I recognize one of the women he's talking to. It's freaking Claire Dennis. She looks different tonight. Her Upper East Side wardrobe must have been unsuitable for this downtown address, so she's put on sky-high heels, tight black pants with zippers all over them and a sparkly top that hangs off one shoulder.

I stare, immobilized.

I'm snapped out of it when I notice a shift in the group: the bearded man and the other woman are drifting off to the bar, while Caleb and Claire stay in the same spot, deep in conversation. Caleb is no longer laughing; he's nodding seriously. Claire looks upset, as if she's sharing something really upsetting, as if they're talking about——

Caleb says something and puts a hand on her arm. She nods, he looks around wildly and I can imagine, even without being able to read their lips, the transcript corresponding to their gestures:

CALEB: What an outrageous custody story! I am shocked and horrified!

CLAIRE: I know. It's proof that bad things *do* happen to even good people like me. And this mess *is* about me. It affects me more than anyone! All I can do is try to live my life. Donning six-inch heels and rubbing elbows with the downtown billionaires? This party is *just* what I needed.

CALEB: You are so brave. You know, one of my buddies is a divorce lawyer at a big and fancy firm. She finds me very persuasive and is here tonight—want me to try and get you some top-notch advice for free?

CLAIRE: Hmmm. I have access to gobs and gobs of money, but I do so love free things. . . .

I flee, bolting down the nearest hallway, and slipping in the first door I see, to a room called the Sierra Nevada Conference Room. It's catering central: several trays of food, stacks of napkins and crates of glasses line the room. There are a few waiters preparing, but they ignore me. I sit down at the conference room table and look at the big round wall clock. The party ends at eight o'clock, which is an hour from now. To avoid Claire, I can sit here as long as it takes.

Worst case, Caleb told Claire my name. But it's not like he could have told her anything really incriminating. I don't think Caleb and I have even talked about the Walker case. Come to think of it, I don't think Caleb and I ever talked about my job at all. I try to remember the last time he and I had a substantive conversation, but, well, we haven't really. Ever. That's not what we do. I pick a piece of sushi off the tray in front of me. And another. By the third piece, I have self-soothed—there are worse fates than waiting out a party in the Sierra Nevadas.

The door opens. Eric, the waiter from earlier, walks in and, seeing me, backs against the wall.

"Miss." His voice is a little shaky. "I understand that you're a guest tonight and think you can do whatever you want, but you're really not supposed to be in here looking for me."

"I'm not, Eric. I promise. I just needed a little break from out there."

He nods, unconvinced, which isn't surprising. Most people have the stamina to handle a two-hour cocktail party.

"Please," I say, "I'll just sit here quietly. I won't bother you."

I can see him softening, but when he ventures closer, putting down his empty tray and reaching for the one in front of me, he spots the six gaping holes left over from my sampling. It's too much for him.

"I can't believe this. You couldn't just wait outside like everyone else?" He stares at the floor and then, after a courage-gathering breath, raises his voice. "Aaron," he says, "this lady, she's a guest, and she's in here eating my reserve sushi."

One of the other waiters stops stacking dirty glasses and appraises me, stroking his goatee. "I assume you told her she's not supposed to be in here?"

"I did, but she's not moving."

Aaron, clearly the font of cater-waiter wisdom, shrugs. "There are a lot of weirdos in New York. Sometimes it's better not to incite them."

Eric isn't happy with this response. "Even if she's been harassing me all night?"

Aaron considers this.

"All right, all right," I say, pushing out my chair. "For chrissakes, I'm leaving."

I slink out of the door and down the hall to the bathroom. I jiggle the door—locked—and then feel someone turning the knob from the inside. She emerges, an apologetic smile on her face. It's Claire. Recognizing me, her smile hardens and freezes off her face.

"Hello," I say.

She stalks away, slanting forward on the pitch of her heels, grabs her coat off the rack and then hurries out into the night, without, thank heavens, stopping to say good-bye to anyone.

Oh my God. I have got to tell Henry this. He hasn't been picking up his cell lately, so I dial his office line.

"Aha," I say, when he picks up after the second ring. "I finally reach you. What wonderful case are you working on?"

"Mercer."

"I won't keep you, I promise, but I have the craziest story."

"Where are you?"

"I'm at this holiday party with all these fancy people who I have nothing in common with. Guess who was here."

"I don't know."

"Come on, a guess, please."

"The British royals."

"What are you saying? You don't think I have anything in common with the British royal family?"

"I don't. Are you truly as surprised as you sound?"

I consider. "No, I'll concede that. Can I tell you my story?"

"Out with it already."

"Claire was here."

"Awkward. What happened?"

"She gave me the full-on stink-eye and stormed out of the party. But before that, it was even weirder because she was talking to Caleb and I could see that he wanted to introduce her to me, and—"

"What party are you at?"

"Caleb's office one."

"That all sounds really nuts, Molly. I have the Mercer hearing first thing Monday, so I better get cracking on it if I want to ever get home." Henry's tone is brusque, as it's been on and off for the past several weeks. I chalk his grouchiness up to stress: the Bacon Payne partnership committee meets this month.

"Henry?"

"What?"

"You don't need to stress so much. You're totally going to make it."

"Make what?"

"Partner, Henry. I know you've been nervous."

"Thanks. I've been the most worried about locking down the disgruntled-associate vote, so your support is very comforting." He hangs up without even waiting to hear my laugh.

When I return to my perch in the corner, the party, blessedly, has broken up. Even the waiters are leaving. Eric has his coat on and, with one wary backward glance, shoots out of the door.

"Hey," Caleb says, coming over and holding up my hand in his as though I'm a debutante and he's my escort, "did you have fun?"

"It was great."

"I was looking for you before."

"You were?"

"I wanted to introduce you to this woman I know. She's in the middle of this horrible custody thing. It sounds awful. Her boyfriend was married to some insane lunatic who keeps hurting her kids and trying to get them back. Is that the kind of case you work on?"

"It's exactly the kind of case I work on. Did you give her my name?"

He scrunches his face, trying to remember. "I don't think so."

Despite my relief, I can't help myself. "You know, she might not have been telling you the whole story. Custody is a very complex thing."

"Okay, but I doubt it. She's pretty down-to-earth. Always seems to have her shit together."

"How do you know her anyway?"

"We sat on a board together and have some mutual friends."

"Like how many?"

He puts his arm around me. "Why are we still talking about her? I've met her all of six times."

"There are a lot of weirdos in New York," I say. "It's entirely possible she's one of them."

"I will readily agree that she is the queen of all weirdos if it means that we can move on to another topic."

I nod. "Deal."

"Have you seen this room?" Caleb propels me toward good old Sierra Nevada. "There's a mountain range theme to all the meeting spaces."

"Neat."

"Neater still, there's some leftover champagne bottles in here that I thought we should open. You ready to have fun?"

"I am," I say.

We can always count on each other for that.

congratulationshenry

The large conference room on the thirty-seventh floor has been transformed into Bacon Payne's version of a party room. Paper-doily-topped black plastic circular trays cover the conference table, dotted with the usual corporate catered fare: little sandwiches, cookies, cheese cubes, textured crackers and plastic-looking fruit. The wooden cabinet against the wall is the makeshift bar, offering a choice of champagne, individual Poland Spring bottles or Pepsi cans. In the center of the table is a personalized cake that reads "CongratulationsHenry!" with no space between the words. Kim's work, obviously.

I raise my glass as instructed by Lillian and clink it against Rachel's.

"To Henry." Lillian beams as we all cheer and Warren Jacobs, a shaggy-haired litigation partner with an office on our floor, starts an off-tune version of "For He's a Jolly Good Fellow." Rachel, a former member of her college a cappella group and not shy about bursting into song, jumps in as the rest of us celebrants—too self-conscious and sober to be on singing terms with one another—gulp our champagne and clap along. They trail off after the first "which nobody can deny."

There are about twenty people here feting Henry—the entire matrimonial department, plus some "department friends"—i.e., people with offices on our floor. I can't help but compare it with

Caleb's office party. It's not as jazzed up, sure, but at least there are people I want to talk to. There's no need to run for the Sierra Nevadas.

I sip my drink, pick at raisin nut bread topped with Brie and watch as Henry is swarmed by Lillian, Warren Jacobs and Everett. There's a lot of hand shaking, back patting and knowing chuckles.

Kim opens the door to the conference room and pokes her head in. Once she spots Lillian, she race-walks over and whispers something in her ear. In an impressively believable display of phony affection, Lillian throws her arms around Henry, kisses him on the cheek and excuses herself, running out of the room. After Lillian leaves, Warren wanders away from the group and I walk over.

"So, can you believe our boy?" asks Everett.

I smile, mainly because a year ago I would've choked at hearing Everett refer to Henry that way. "Actually, yes. He's worked really hard for this." I raise my glass at Henry. "Official congratulations, though."

He smiles. "Thanks."

"Well, I'm just glad not to be the only male partner now," says Everett. "We needed a little testosterone in here. I mean, obviously you were here before, but at the partnership level."

I nod. "Oh, yes. That's just what Bacon Payne needs. Score one for diversity, Henry. You go bust through that white-male glass ceiling and shake up that boardroom."

Henry laughs and I point at the conference room table. "The cake is so good. Have you had it?"

"Really?" says Everett. "Okay, I'll go get a piece. Be right back."

"So, is this the only celebration?" I ask.

"Well, there are some dinners out, but it's all classified information. I really can't divulge details to a mere associate."

"Oh, I see. So that's how it is now. Seriously, though, Henry— are you going to disappear and go all antisocial on me again? Your door is always closed."

"Nah. Of course not. Just a particularly bad end of the year. And beginning."

Henry and I haven't really talked since last month. I had hoped he'd be less stressed after the partnership announcement, but I've felt something increasingly stilted and awkward between us. I heard that he made partner the way the rest of the department did, yesterday, through a group e-mail blast. And while we had exchanged text messages of congratulations and thanks, I hadn't seen him in person until today.

I had been a little hurt, actually, until I sat down and thought about it. He's now my boss. Just knowing what he does about *Walker v. Walker* must stress him out; his best bet is to keep his distance from the madness of my involvement with it. But still, I miss him.

"So, how have you been?" He looks as though he really does want to know.

"Fine. You?"

"Fine, overworked. I've basically been caught up in all this." He motions around the conference room.

I nod appraisingly. "Be proud. This is a great party. You have a great future in planning intimate corporate events."

He laughs. "You know what I mean. You have the pretrial coming up, right?"

I nod. "Next week."

"Hey, listen—," he says as I simultaneously say, "Aaand Everett's back with the cake."

He leans close and speaks in a low voice, directly in my ear. "I'm sorry I haven't been around. I promise things will normalize. Let's try to get together this weekend. I can help you prep."

"That would be great, but not if it's weird."

He knits his brows, puzzled. "Why would it be weird?"

"I understand, you know, if things are different now. If you can't get too close."

He still looks a little confused, but then he shakes his head.

Everett walks up to us, plate in hand, a spot of icing on his lip.

"So, man, is it good?" Henry asks him.

"Strong, dude." He nods. "Second piece."

I slip out of the conference room feeling hopeful and head back to my office.

tfe mythss of bleckk coffeey

Rachel leans her head in my office. "Lillian's left for her lunch, but there's leftover champagne."

My expression, I hope, reads, *What's your point?* As is the norm this time of year, I have Bacon Payne party fatigue. Henry's partnership fete in late January was the kick-off, followed by celebrations for Groundhog Day, President's Day, St. Patrick's Day and the Winter Equinox. Two weeks ago, Rachel declared it "Papercut Friday" and the floater secretary ran downstairs for cupcakes.

I was already done, stress-dreaming about exploding communal sheet cakes when, during a girls' coffee in Lillian's office yesterday, she had demurred that today would be her fortieth anniversary of being a matrimonial lawyer. We had squealed—not stopping to question the date's validity or her values in choosing to honor *this* anniversary as opposed to, say, her wedding anniversary—and Lillian then faux-bashfully let slip that a few of her attorney friends had planned a day of fun for her: a luncheon, cocktails and pampering.

Liz, Rachel and I looked at one another nervously—something in Lillian's tone let us know that we were not to let the day pass without a celebration of some sort. With the assistance of the dining staff, we scrambled together a "surprise" breakfast, decorated her office with balloons and streamers and chipped in on

244 L. Alison Heller

an expensive silk scarf and a gushing greeting card. Then we had arrived early, waiting in her office so that when she strolled in at eight o'clock, we could jump up, applauding. Lillian was touched, we could tell, but wondered out loud, innocently enough, whether clinking glasses with only orange juice counted as a legitimate toast.

Rachel said something about it being a workday morning and Lillian had winked. "I won't tell if you don't," she said. "If you can't drink up on your fortieth anniversary, when can you?"

Liz and I had looked at each other, panicked, and she had fled, returning somehow fifteen minutes later with four bottles of orange-labeled champagne.

Rachel, still in my doorway, has started to mime clinking imaginary glasses, smiling invitingly.

I groan. "Don't make me go back in there."

Rachel drums her fingers dramatically on her chin. "Do you have to be sober for anything today?"

I look at my calendar, even as I know the answer. "Nope." This is the silver lining to Lillian's anniversary: a full Friday, no court appearances, no conferences, no Lillian.

Rachel's eyebrows arch wickedly. "Me neither. Even Liz is still in there. And we've decided, after that fire drill this morning, we need our own fucking anniversary party."

It is an appealing thought, seizing the moment, this springtime hall pass of a day, to just let loose.

Rachel senses that I'm weakening. "We'll just finish up the bottles that are in there and then I'm cutting out early. Like"—she leans her head in the doorway, ready to shock me—"four o'clock. Because I can."

"I'm in." I follow her to Lillian's office.

I had four more. Four of those fancy, fancy drinks and I'm back in my office, my spinning, spinning, spinning office. It was fun, it was so much fun, and I didn't know that Rachel can do good impressions, like really good impressions, of that woman from that show with the nasal voice and, oh, also of that cartoon character with the skateboard. I love Rachel. She's so helpful and funny, she got the bathroom door closed for me because I couldn't figure it out, the lock thingy was all stuck, and now we're getting quiet time. Shhh. Everybody quiet for nap time. I'm gonna close my office door here, tiptoe over and close it and close my eyes and let things spin and the floor, this carpet, this gray is soft and nice.

I hear a loud buzz. And again. And again. And it's a noise I recognize. It means something. So I get up from the floor and go to my desk and it's my phone, my secret Fern batphone, and she's texted me, so I squint and peer closer and it says:

You know how long court will take today?

And I know I'm a little buzzed from before, but Fern must be more, because we don't have court today. My fingers, which are not hitting the keys easily—small keys! so very small! why have I ever texted on this thing?—manage to write back, though, because it's important for Fern to know this: *Cpurrt is 2norow!* I blank on the day and look at my calendar for tomorrow, where it says, there it is, "Wv.W compliance conference 2:30, March 27th."

Fern is right there and she buzzes the batphone again:

Ha! Ha!

Hs! Ga! I write back, and it's funny. It's so funny, her joke, but then I realize I don't know why it's funny. Why is it funny? I should know why. I'm getting a little sad because I don't understand the joke and I should, we're tight, me and Fern, and I should be in on the joke, so I squint at my calendar. Tomorrow is Saturday. I put the Walker conference down for Saturday and I'm not sure how this happened. I remember Mike the Clerk calling and changing the date because, what was it? Strand was having a procedure and I was worried about him, what if it's serious and something happened to Strand?—and I put it in my calendar and said, no problem, Mike, I have no conflicts, because of course it wasn't a problem, I wouldn't have any conflicts if I thought it was Saturday and fuck. Fuck. Fuck. Fuck. Fuck.

And now, focus, where's my watch or something—it's one o'clock, which means I need to be downtown soon, really soon. I have to figure out how much time I have, and my stuff is in my apartment and I'm still a little buzzed. But I can sober up in an hour, I'm sure. I know I can. I can do this. I can do this. I can do this.

Somehow, I'm walking down the hall toward the elevator. One step in front of the other. One step per foot. I am looking at my feet, focusing on my feet.

"Molly?" Henry's voice floats from somewhere by the printer. "Why are you tiptoeing?"

"Court. I have court," I whisper. "For Fern."

His face swims above me. Stern expression, stern face saying something about canceling.

I make the stern face back at him and he says, "You're not going to court like this."

How does he know something's wrong just by looking at me? I look down and don't see how he knows. "I can't. Wrong date, scheduling snafu, screwup, yadda yadda. So I should just get some black coffee and do. This. Thing." I hit his chest as I say this and it makes a really funny noise, hollow, like he's a drum. "Did you know you could make that noise?"

He ignores me. "You need more than black coffee. Black coffee is kind of a myth."

I make a gesture to show my competence—arms forward-marching—and start off toward the elevator.

"Slow down," he says, and catches my arm. "You might want to check your outfit."

My shirt is untucked from my pants and unbuttoned and holy crap, my belly button is visible. I try to cover it, but my shirt and my pants seem all twisted and stuck, and it's really, really, really hard. I don't get it, this thing with my shirt, but it's so weird, but funny too, so I laugh, and punch Henry on the arm.

Henry's head is in his hands and then he's pushing me back down the hall to my office. "Figure out what's going on with your shirt," he says. "I'll be back with coffee."

"See? It'll work," I say to him, but he is gone.

I manage to stuff my shirt ends into my pants and all of a sudden Henry's there with some coffee.

"Superfast," I say, reaching forward to take it. I snap my fingers for emphasis, but they don't make a good enough noise, so I say it too. "ZZZZip."

He takes a step back from me. "You're going to need some mints."

"I gottem, I gottem."

He sighs. "Come with me."

We're downstairs and in a cab and pulling up to my apartment building, stopping to get more coffee downstairs—I insist on paying as the host here, although, somehow, by the time we're at the door to my apartment, he's got the keys and is the one who opens the door. "Welcome, Henry!" I say. "To my home!"

"Do you know," he says, in a voice that's slow and loud, "where the file is?"

"Right here," I say, walking over to the file. "Super organized. Oh, right—you've been here." I had forgotten that. How he was wearing shorts and his legs looked really good. He really had nice legs.

He looks surprised and then down at his legs. "Um, thanks."

That's funny. "I said that out loud? I thought I was thinking it and I said it."

"Great." Henry rolls his eyes at the couch. "The inability to censor yourself bodes well for a court appearance." He hands me another coffee, from where, I don't know. "Drink."

I obey, taking four gulps in a row.

"Go clean up a little." He points to the bathroom.

"Bos-see." I get up.

When I come out, he takes a step back. "Molly," he says, his voice low as he turns his back to me. "Put on a goddamn shirt."

I look down. I'm wearing my pants, but on top, I just have on a purple bikini top and I tell him that it's sort of like that dream when you have no clothes on in front of a bunch of clothed people, but it's real, and that's so funny, because if this is my worst nightmare, it's happening and look how well I am handling it. I laugh, but he doesn't laugh and he still doesn't turn around. So I tell him, my voice as friendly as I can make it, that he can turn around, it's a goddamn bikini top for godsake, it's not even a bra because all my bras are in the hamper, so what is the problem? Wouldn't he go swimming with me, for crying out loud? If we went swimming, I'd be wearing even less, plus, I mean he's Henry, for chrissakes, I say, I know he's not looking at me that way. You have that Julie girl, plus, P.S., it's not like we don't know each other, we're the real deal, I know we are, even if you have been sort of hot and cold and distant for months.

"Are you dressed yet?" is his only response.

When he turns around, he mumbles something—all I hear are the words "weird" and "bikini top"—and tells me it's time for me to go.

"I think . . ." I nod. "Yeah, I'm a little less spinny."

"You seem to be a friendly drunk. I guess it could be worse." His gaze rakes over me in a skeptical once-over. "Your best tactic today? Mouth shut, clothes on. You understand?"

I salute. "Clear eyes, full heart, clothes on, sir."

He doesn't find this as funny as I do, I think, because he covers his eyes with his hands and shakes his head. When he looks up, he says, tiredly, "Maybe we should try another coffee, not that it's doing much."

When we're standing on line at the coffee shop, Henry reaches an arm out and tells me to stop wobbling. "What does that mean, the real deal?"

"That means, usually it means, when something's not fake." I smile, helpfully, not sure what he's getting at.

"Back there with the whole bikini thing. You said we were the real deal."

"I meant we're really friends. You're, like, my buddy, even if you are my boss."

"Like your buddy," he repeats.

"Even if you are technically my boss," I say, wrapping my arm around him to pat his back. His body tenses in response, but only a little.

I have two more coffees before the court appearance—making my total for the day several coffees! (which the coffee cart guy doesn't seem to think is funny)—and I manage to make it in and out of the court's ladies' room without assistance, so I know I can do this, because earlier I couldn't and it means I'm definitely functioning like my normal self.

Another sign that I'm functioning, and this is really, really smart of me, is that I time myself to get there right on time, so I waltz in and wave at Fern, who smiles back, and she looks normal, smiling and waving back, so I know that I look normal and so I go right over to Mike, who's standing there with Risa, who's looking at some papers with Graham. I feel a rush of warmth at her outfit—hair in two plaits down her back, wearing baggy brown knee-length pants, knee-high laced-up boots and a matching jacket, cropped at the waist. Bygones should be bygones. Maybe I should say something nice, right our wrongs, press restart. "Hi, Risa. Hi, Graham. Risa. Fan-tas-tic knickers."

She doesn't acknowledge me. Maybe she didn't hear.

I try a little louder. "Risa? Hello? FAN-TAS-TIC KNICKERS."

After a pause, she nods, looking down at her papers. "Ms. Grant."

Then Mike is ushering us into Justice Strand's office. There he is, good old Strand behind his desk. I got this, I know I do. I'm kicking ass, I know. No one has asked me if I'm drunk, or even mentioned alcohol!

"Good morning, Your Honor." I smile as big as I feel. "Great to see you today."

"Well, hello there, Ms. Grant." He beams back at me.

Risa interjects. "Justice Strand. We need to discuss our new motions."

Strand flinches and looks warily at me. I give him another smile, again as big as I can. Control. Everything is coming in speed bursts and delays, but I am controlling what I say.

"You mean the disqualification motions?" I pat Risa on the arm and feel her stiffen through her soft, soft jacket. "So many motions, you know what I mean?" I nod at Strand.

I touch my forehead and try to remember what exactly her papers said. It's hard to recall, but I vaguely remember that there are talking points in my folder. I open it and somehow, the papers spill out on the floor. Kneeling down to pick up the pages, I notice a paper clip under the desk.

"Counselor. Are you all right down there?"

I lift my head. It's Mike. I smile at him. "Yes, Mike. I just found something on the floor." I stare at the paper clip. It is so very pink and bright.

"What did you find, counselor?"

Control. Mouth shut. I tear my eyes away and force myself to stand up.

Risa starts talking fast. She is saying something about Newkirk and grave ethical issues and me and I guess I'm not as okay as I thought because I can't follow any of it, but I should say something or else everyone will know I'm not following. "Right," I say. All heads—except for Risa's—swivel toward me. I look around. Everyone is silent. "Sorry. You have the floor, Risa." I turn to her and give a little bow.

She stares straight ahead, refusing to acknowledge me.

"Listen, I know you're just doing what you feel you have to do, even if it's kind of ridiculous." I pat her arm again. So very soft! What is it? Velvet? Brushed cotton? Velour? Do they make whole suits out of velour?

Justice Strand nods at me. "I appreciate your civility, Ms. Grant. It's very refreshing."

I nod back. It feels good to be civil.

Justice Strand clears his throat. "Mr. Williams. Any thoughts on all of this?"

"I've submitted papers today. As they suggest, I am against the removal at this point of Dr. Newkirk, Ms. Freed and, um, Ms. Grant too."

I flash Roland a thumbs-up.

Strand shakes his head at Risa and he's disagreeing with her. I can tell that much because he's saying no and she looks pissed. Then he asks us for something. I look around and catch Mike's eye and he mouths something at me. Christmas something? What is it? And I shake my head and shrug and finally he says, "Witness lists," and now everyone is looking at him.

"Yes!" I say. "Witness lists!" but then I can't remember where mine are. I shuffle through papers until I see a file marked "Witnesses." I count out three pieces of paper, and eventually it's becoming clear that everyone is watching me again.

Risa purses her lips and makes a lot of noise and I know she's objecting to something and I see that and all I can think is it must take a lot of effort to just fight, fight, fight all the time. She must be tired after court, what with the fighting and the commute from upstate. This thought makes me very sleepy, so I stretch, just a little, just my arms behind my back, and now everyone's looking at me again and Risa's stopped talking.

"Excuse me, Ms. Grant. What was that?" says Risa.

"What was what?" I smile at Strand.

"You just rolled your eyes at the judge," says Risa. I wince. She's got an ear-piercing shriek.

"I did? No, I didn't. I don't think so. Did I roll my eyes?" I ask Strand, who doesn't answer. "No, I think I smiled."

"Well, whatever. It's inappropriate," says Risa.

"I'm sorry. Did I hurt your feelings? I was smiling because I've gotten to know you, Risa McDunn, over the past months and you really are, without fail, you are a tenacious advocate. I mean, maybe the most tenacious advocate I've seen. You just, you know, grab hold of the argument and . . . you must be exhausted, which just really makes it all the more impressive."

"Miss Grant?" says Justice Strand.

"Your Honor," Risa says to Justice Strand, her voice going up at the end as though she's asking a question. "I can't really proceed when she's acting like this."

"I'm just complimenting her, Your Honor." Strand nods, so I continue. "She is a great, tenacious attorney. And she also has a lovely jacket today, very soft."

Justice Strand nods. "Ms. McDunn, I think you should accept Ms. Grant's compliments, leave it at that, and let's get back to the Walkers."

Risa turns red, shakes her head and continues. She's saying something about having an expert examine Fern.

"Ms. Grant?"

"Huh?"

Risa talks loudly and slowly. "As I was saying, it's only fair that we have an expert examine Ms. Walker. I mean, Ms. Walker's mental state is obviously at issue, which you've been arguing the whole time it isn't, so which is it now, Ms. Grant?"

"Ms. Grant?" Strand is looking at me encouragingly.

I blink. I know what I want to say, but the words, the words won't come. I manage to hold up one finger.

Roland cuts in. "If I may? Those are medical professionals testifying to a past condition, so it's not the same as examining Fern's mental state. Current mental state, that is."

Strand nods slowly. "Good enough for me. And might I also add that it was lovely to see you all in such good spirits today and so kind to each other. Let's exchange our lists, wrap up our business, and I'll see you in early June for the first of our hearing dates. Sorry for the delay between today and the start date, but—"

"We understand, Your Honor," I say, nodding. "Your removal."

The rest of the conference is somewhat blurrier, but I manage to convey to Fern that it all went fine and make it outside without talking to anyone else. On my subway ride home, my happy buzz starts to evaporate until I am wincing in pain, a metallic taste in the back of my mouth that quickly travels to the pit of my stomach and ends in a sprint to the ladies' room.

When I am done retching in the Bacon Payne ladies' room, I splash some cold water on my face and slink to Henry's office. He's out, which is a relief, as humiliating little snippets of the morning start to return to me. I scrawl a note of everlasting thanks and tape it to his monitor.

Then I let it sink in that I just made a court appearance while drunk off my ass. And that somehow, it went far better than any court appearance before Strand that I've made sober.

two points for honesty

Despite the heat lamps and the torches around the wooden deck, it's as freezing as it always is at the Bacon Payne Beach Retreat. It's early April, not the balmiest time of year for the coast between Westchester and Fairfield counties, and I pull my pashmina tightly around me.

"Want my jacket?" Caleb puts a languid hand on my back.

"Thanks."

According to the firm's party line, nothing—not even Paris—is more beautiful than the Long Island Sound in early spring. More widely believed is that Dominic Pizaro, whose membership allows us to hold the event at the Sound Club, refuses to waste a summer Saturday on anything involving the associates.

It is gorgeous out here, though. The cocktail hour is held on a wooden deck with steps leading down to the beach. Now dusk, the light is low and the sky and the beach are the same color, a shade between purple, blue and gray that extends forever into the horizon.

Caleb picked me up in his Mercedes SUV, a far cry from my first year, when I was one of the groups of junior associates trekking out to the suburbs via subway to Metro-North to the Rye Cab Company taxi. Rachel and Liz, themselves renting a car, were on hold to pick me up if Caleb had canceled at the last minute. (Not that I would've blamed him for canceling. I was still surprised he wanted to go.) He had been at my apartment when I got the cream calligraphic invitation to the beach retreat. Knowing what it was, I had tossed the letter off to the side.

He laughed. "That was cold. You're just ignoring that wedding invitation?"

"What? Oh, no, it's a work thing."

"Really?"

"Yes." I did my best lockjaw and handed him the envelope. "The firm beach retreat."

"It's for you and a guest?"

"Technically, yeah."

"Technically?"

"People bring guests. I just never have."

"Why not?"

"Why? You want to come?"

"I do need to talk some deals with your people."

"Well, I don't think much business actually gets done there. My people will be distracted making mind-numbing small talk with each other's spouses."

"Ah, to be so naive." He patted my head. "Business gets done everywhere, you know."

"Okay, Stephen Covey."

"So, anyway"—he held up the invitation—"is it fun?"

"Not historically." I paused when I saw he looked a little disappointed. "I think we could make it fun, though."

The next day, walking to work, I concluded that I'd underestimated Caleb by balking at the idea of bringing him to a firm party. Maybe we were ready for the step up in labels—introducing him to people as my boyfriend, recalibrating the terms of our arrangement. Maybe I owed it to my college self—who I know would have been screaming in frustration had I not invited him—to run with it, to not be too scared to jump.

So, here we are. Lillian is only showing up to the dinner part this year, so Rachel, Liz and I joined forces in rebellion and skipped the day festivities: an extraordinarily painful stretch of time where lawyers and their families play awkward rounds of tennis, golf or croquet or sit shivering by the pool, wrapped in layers of sweaters.

Caleb and I take slow steps, following the crowd pushing through the opened glass doors to the dining room. Kevin is in a group of corporate associates to the right of the doors. I reach for Caleb's hand so he'll follow me, but somehow he's already spotted someone else he knows in the group and has beelined away.

Kevin looks back and forth from me to Caleb. Eyes bugging, he clutches his chest in mock shock. "You brought a date?"

I roll my eyes.

"How healthy and normal," he says. "Between the firm spirit and the evidence of a healthy relationship with an actual person, I hardly recognize you."

"You don't need to worry," I say. "I can still access deep pockets of resentment."

He laughs. "But, seriously? Life is as good as it looks?"

I nod, unable to tell him the truth.

"It's so funny."

"What?"

"We're only four months away from the five-year mark, but the closer we get, the happier you become."

I manage to maintain my pleasant expression as someone grabs a microphone and begs us to find our tables. The seating gods haven't been too cruel. We're with Henry, a junior litigation partner and a pair of Trusts and Estates associates, two bland-seeming women with identical honey blond straight hair, olive skin, pearl earrings and pink mouths set in straight lines.

Henry looks at me. "Nice jacket," he says. "You doing a Charlie Chaplin skit later?"

I forgot I have on Caleb's coat. I shrug out of it, drape it over my chair and spot Caleb still talking to one of the corporate associates, a seventh-year named Marissa. I wave at him and he smiles in return.

I slide into the seat next to Henry and pat his shoulder. "How are you?"

"Great." He flashes a huge fake smile. "This event is a fave."

"Me too. Which do you like the best? The stale laughter or the hypothermia?"

"I'm a hypothermia man myself."

I grab us each a warmed roll from the basket in the middle of the table. "So did you play golf?"

"Yep."

"Ah. How'd you do?"

"It was fine. How about you? Tennis again?"

I look around quickly before replying in a quiet voice. "Actually, printing out pictures of Claire at society functions. And making five copies of them."

"You're becoming a real slacker, Grant. Ditching the retreat? That's a new level of disregard."

Caleb comes back to the table. I push out the chair next to me. Still standing, he turns to Henry. "Oh, hey, man. I've seen you before."

Henry gives a small nod. "Yes, you have. Duck's Halloween party."

"Oh right."

I pat the empty chair, but instead of sitting down in it, he crouches next to me. "Hey, um, you know how I said I wanted to do some deals here?"

I nod.

He points across the room to a table in the middle. "Well, Marissa says there's an empty chair at her table."

"Marissa?"

"Yeah, she's an associate in the finance group, but she says she's doing a lot of new-media projects. My buddy has worked with her before, actually."

"Oh, yeah. I know Marissa."

"So, I was thinking I should sit at her table for dinner."

"You're going to sit over there?"

He gives me a strange look. "You're okay with this, right? It's why I came tonight."

"Yeah, of course." I can tell my tone is harsh.

He looks about to say something but doesn't and walks away. At my table, Henry and the litigation guy are talking about junior years abroad. I'm guessing this is because it's the last time either one of them left the office for more than three consecutive days.

Everett comes over to our table. His eyes light up when he sees the empty seat next to me. "Is this free?"

Henry looks at me.

"As free as it could possibly be," I say, gesturing to the chair with a flourish.

Henry gives me his own strange look and turns to Everett. "You making the rounds?"

"Exactly. I like to circulate at functions like this," says Everett. "So, how is everyone doing?"

"Great," Henry and I say in unison.

"Good," says Everett, not picking up on our flat tones. "Molly, did you see what the box office winner was last night? I know you're into those stats."

Everett proceeds to prattle on about the detective sequel that beat out the animated sequel, apparently to the shock of him and Factsination! screens everywhere. I turn my head slightly in order to watch Caleb and Marissa. They're absorbed in conversation, their foreheads leaned in together, laughing pretty hard for people discussing corporate structuring. I've never noticed just how curvy she is. Of course, she doesn't usually strut around the firm in a strapless emerald green cocktail dress.

One of the Trusts and Estates associates starts talking about her year in Cologne. Everett asks her about the beer, and Henry leans next to me and follows my gaze. "What's happening there?"

"He wanted to talk to her about a deal."

He gives a skeptical look just as Marissa throws back her head and laughs so loudly we can hear it over the din. "Is it serious between you guys?"

"Nope. A loose end from college."

"Then don't worry about it," he says, his tone brusque.

"Well, all right, then." I tear my eyes away from the Caleb-Marissa tête-à-tête. "Where's Julie?"

"Not here," he says in a way that stops me from asking any follow-up questions, and imagining Henry heartbroken, I feel a twinge of protectiveness.

I try again. "So, you did a semester in Spain? That's cool."

"*Verdad,*" he says, turning away from me and focusing his attention on the Trusts and Estates associates, who are talking with Everett about the headiness of the bouquet on a sparkling Shiraz.

A painful two hours later, Dominic Pizaro starts his welcome speech. He's so glad to be able to share his slice of paradise with us and so grateful for all the hard work we do every year. How nice to spend time together as a family, without the pressure of the office. Everett leans forward in rapt attention, but almost everyone else is hunched over a BlackBerry, ignoring Dominic's remarks in favor of dealing with some pressure from the office.

When the servers start bringing around dessert—the ubiquitous molten chocolate cake—I know it's finally safe to leave. Caleb and Marissa are nowhere to be seen, having disappeared somewhere prior to Dominic's remarks. At least those two are getting a release from the pressures of the office.

I nudge Henry. "I'm going," I whisper. Not that he'll care. He's basically been ignoring me all evening.

"Wait," he says, turning away from patio furniture or whatever mind-numbing thing he's been discussing with the litigation partner. "How are you getting home?"

"I'll try to get a ride with Liz and Rachel. Or I'll just take the train."

He looks at his watch. "It's past ten."

"Trains run past ten."

"I'll drive you."

"I don't want to make you leave early."

He gives me a look that says he'd be happy to leave. "You have everything? You need to say good-bye to anyone"—he glances at Caleb's jacket on the back of my chair—"or return anything?"

"Nope," I say. "You?"

"Nope."

He gets up.

As I start to rise out of my seat, Everett grabs my arm. "Where are you going?" he says, his voice urgent and low. "You can't leave before Lillian does."

"Do me a favor, man," says Henry, leaning down. "I'm leaving, but I'm worried about missing more remarks. Will you cover for me?"

Everett cocks his head. "You shouldn't miss anything. There's usually not remarks after Dominic."

"But if there are. Can you tell me what's said? You know, just because this is my first retreat as a partner and what if someone asks me about it? I'd be really grateful."

Everett nods solemnly.

Henry meets my eyes. "Okay, Molly. You hear that? Because I know you have to leave too. Everett'll tell us if we miss anything. You comfortable with that?"

"Thanks, Everett." Before he can answer, I bolt after Henry, leaving Caleb's jacket on the chair behind me.

Henry doesn't say much in the car, so I fiddle with the radio, landing on a top forty station. He winces and pushes a button, rejecting my selection.

Music fills the car. I listen for a moment, not recognizing it.

"Who is this?"

"Guster."

"It's good."

Henry nods. I imagine him browsing through albums and purchasing songs. I glance at the backseat and picture him lacing up the running shoes that are peeking out of the navy duffel bag there, or filling the stainless steel water bottle that's been rolling around on the floor under my seat, making repetitive clanks.

We drive down I-95 without talking, so I listen to the music.

You've dreamed a thousand dreams, none seem to stick in
your mind
Two points for honesty
It must make you sad to know that nobody cares at all

"Very uplifting," I say.

Henry gives a wry smile.

"What?"

"It's just a little ironic."

"How so?"

"Well. I've always thought this song is about having the guts and effort to go for it."

"Like a Gatorade commercial?"

"Whatever, Molly."

"No, seriously. And your point is?"

"Nothing. No point at all."

"So, what are your plans for tomorrow?" I say as he downshifts off the FDR.

"Um, work," he says, an edge to his voice to let me know it's a stupid question.

"Okay. So, can I ask you some Walker questions or is it off-limits now?"

"Why would it be off-limits?"

"You haven't seemed that interested, you know, since you made partner."

He snorts.

I drop it. The rest of the car ride passes in silence.

As he finally turns onto my block, I unclick my seat belt and open the car door. "Okay," I say, one foot out of the door, "what's with the attitude?"

"Me?" He takes his eyes off the road and looks at me. "What's with my attitude?"

"Yeah. You. What's with your attitude? You've been hostile all night."

He whistles. "That's quite an accusation, coming from you, Molly."

"What does that even mean? I've been fine tonight."

He snorts again.

"Oh my God. Did you just snort at me? I don't even know what you're talking about. I haven't been the slightest bit hostile to you."

"Molly, take a look at yourself. You show up late to the retreat. You can't stand being there——"

"Neither can you, Henry. We were both saying how miserable it is. You said——"

"Yes, Molly, I know what I said. But I was joking. I was making the best of it. You just mope around, so caught up in your own complications, you don't even see it. You bring that——"

Henry stops midrant and clenches his teeth, his jaw tendon pulsing through his skin. "I just don't know if I can deal with all of this anymore."

"All of this?" My voice sounds far away. "What's all of this? You mean you can't deal with me."

Henry doesn't correct me and I sit stunned for a second, unable to think of anything biting or sophisticated to say. "Jesus, Henry. That's really mean."

He opens his mouth like he's about to say something else. Whatever it is, I don't want to hear it. I close the door with a slam.

where everybody knows my name

I'm in Fern's apartment, command central for *Walker v. Walker*, and increasingly the only place I feel remotely effective as a human being. In the weeks since the beach retreat, Henry and I have avoided each other so successfully it's as though we're motivated by a restraining order. Home has become a depressing mountain of paper, each pile a reprimand.

Being at Fern's feels like living that sitcom theme song, where I push open the door into a room where everybody knows my name and is glad I came. There's snacking and camaraderie, support and shared interests. Our first meeting, way back over a year ago, had been late at night in one of the conference rooms at my rented office suites. Fern had looked around at the mismatched gray and blue chairs, threadbare red carpet and artless white walls and offered up her place for the next meeting.

It's a definite step up. Since her divorce from Robert, Fern has lived in a two-bedroom in an old building in Beekman Place, a jewel of a neighborhood with charming town houses dotting quiet streets. The trees have started to leaf out this week, and the explosion of green makes me feel as though I've stumbled outside of Manhattan, into a cottage with Indian rugs in vibrant colors covering the knotty-planked wood floor, and an actual fireplace anchoring the sitting room. The couch design must have been certified by a therapist: its arms curl around its heavily cushioned back so that sitting there is like being hugged.

Right now Fern's boss, Brian Flannery, and I are perched there, where I've been prepping him for his testimony as a character witness for Fern for the past couple of hours. I can tell Brian's not feeling lulled by the couch's affirmations. He leans forward, his elbows on his khaki-clad knees, swaying his back in a side-to-side fidget until I look up from my legal pad. "So, that's it. Your testimony will probably be on Wednesday, so keep the time free."

"Freaking finally," Brian says, getting up and reaching his arms over his head until there's an audible pop somewhere on his body. He nods, satisfied, and looks at his watch. "Not much of my Sunday left." I know it's an act. Fern has required flexible hours for court dates, visits and meetings, and Brian hasn't missed a beat. I wonder what Bacon Payne would look like if Brian were in charge of corporate culture.

"Sorry, and thanks." I rip out my notes and bring them over to the dining room table where Jenny, Brian's daughter, is sitting on the floor, papers all around her.

"These go at the front," I say as Jenny nods, her ponytail bobbing against the hood of her yellow terry sweatshirt.

Every day, I thank the heavens for Jenny. A junior at Baruch College, she is interested in law school—poor soul—and wants some extra pocket money for a trip to France this summer. For thirty dollars an hour, she has become our document queen; since she started, our files have been tucked away in Bankers Boxes in proper-looking rows with uniformly typed labels, grouped in anticipated order of presentation. Jenny is neat and clean down to her gestures: folded hands, brisk nods, small, quick steps. I imagine her whole life is organized; her countertops probably have no evidence of daily preparation; deodorant, hairbrush, jewelry, are all probably returned to their place in a clutter-free drawer immediately after use.

Brian chucks Jenny's shoulder in farewell. Then he lopes over to Fern, who is exiting through the swinging kitchen door, carrying a container of hummus and a bowl of baby carrots, to give her a quick cheek-peck good-bye.

"Is this a good breaking point? Sandwiches?" Fern says.

Fern is a big believer in constant feeding. This, at one o'clock, is her third food offering of the day.

"Yeah, let's take twenty minutes and eat. Then"—I point to Fern's sister, Lolly—"you're up."

"About time. I have been so looking forward to this." Lolly rubs her hands together in mock anticipation. "I assume that I'll get to testify about my plans to superglue that bastard's nuts to cable wires."

Fern winces and Lolly and I exchange smirks, both committed to zealously hating Robert Walker on her behalf. We've speculated in front of Fern about her lack of venom toward Robert, our theories ranging from abused-spouse syndrome to her being blessed with a saintlike compassion, to her simply being too tired and broken by him to muster hatred. Last month at Fern's, I'd been reviewing the motion papers and Lolly, who'd been sitting quietly on the couch leafing through them after me, threw one—Risa's motion to disqualify Emily Freed—across the room.

Fern had stuck her head in from the kitchen. "Everything okay in here?"

"This gets me insane, you know that? Why are you so ... placid?"

Fern sat down on the coffee table. "What do you want me to do?"

"Tell us something. Something mean and nasty about Robert."

"That's not going to help anything."

They both looked at me and I shrugged. "It might."

"Okay," said Fern. "Okay. This would kill him and I don't know if he still does it, but"—she pointed delicately to her crotch—"down there. He dyes his hair."

"To match his?" Lolly clapped loudly. "That same beach boy wanna-be brown?"

"Yep."

We giggled, the three of us, for about five minutes, until Lolly stopped and sat straight up. "That was good, Fern. That was a start, but it wasn't really *mad*."

"Please, you two make me sound like some sort of martyr. I've gotten mad."

Lolly eyed her. "Name once in your life."

"How about when you forgot to put gas in the car and we got stuck on Carson Street and missed curfew?"

"Seriously?" Lolly had said. "That was high school. Your last example of being angry is from twenty-five years ago."

"Maybe I don't get angry," Fern said. "I get sad. And that makes anger seem, I don't know, too hard."

Lolly and I had both shut up.

Now we examine the sandwich offerings and I've reached out to grab some turkey and cranberry relish on rustic-looking bread when Fern's buzzer sounds. "It's Marie," Fern says. "She has something this afternoon, so she needs to prep with Molly now."

Lolly shrugs. "I'm here all day. What do I care?"

Marie Washington opens the door, wheeling a black hard-shelled bag behind her along with a hurried, formal air that alters the mood of the room, as though a teacher just walked in on the rest of us lip-synching Britney Spears songs in the girls' bathroom. A corporate lawyer by training, Marie met both Fern and Robert when all three of them worked in the executive offices at CBS. Now she's the vice president of marketing at Bakers Brands, a conglomerate with fancy offices on Park Avenue, and the only mutual friend of the Walkers who chose Fern. As she shrugs out of her camel trench coat, I drop the cranberry-spread sandwich and introduce myself. She looks a bit surprised as she adjusts the sleeves of her black suit. Then she recovers, her even features breaking into a warm smile.

"Can we do this now?" She pushes her cropped bangs off her forehead. "I have to fly out to Minneapolis in a few hours. Sorry for the rush."

"Of course." We sink into the huggy couch to walk through the points of Marie's testimony. She's the most engaged witness I've prepped, nodding, offering suggestions and asking questions about the case. After about an hour, we're alone, Fern having disappeared into the bedroom to take a phone call and Lolly having gone outside for a smoke break.

Marie has obviously been waiting for this moment. As soon as the door clicks behind Lolly, she leans in and lowers her voice. "So, Molly. I think it's great you're doing this. Fern loves you and is so grateful. Meeting you, I'm just a little surprised at how"— she pauses—"young you are, especially for a case this big. How long have you practiced law?"

I feel my cheeks start to color. "Almost five years."

"Wow, that's all? Um, where did you go to law school?"

I tell her.

"Oh, okay, okay. Excellent school." I can see Marie relax a little, relieved that I didn't announce that I got a correspondence degree from Our Lady of Jurisprudence in Virgin Gorda. "And you're out on your own?"

I nod. Technically true.

"So, where did you work before that?"

"Bacon Payne."

Marie gives a knowing smirk. "Break in Pain. Great firm. I started at Crowder Withersby myself. So, what made you leave? The hours? The lack of humanity?"

I nod vigorously. "Tell me about it. So, how was Crowder? I have some friends there now."

"No, really. When did you leave?"

I pause. "I still work there, actually."

"Wait. I don't understand. I thought you were out on your own."

"I am. I started my own firm and I'm associated with Bacon Payne."

"How is that even possible? You work both places? What does Bacon Payne think about that?"

"They don't know, actually."

She inhales sharply and looks down. I can tell she's trying not to raise her voice, which now sounds a little as though she's been strangled.

"Okay. And how many other cases do you have, as you work full-time for Bacon Payne and part-time for my best friend?"

"Oh, no other cases. Really, I—there's just this arrangement with Fern."

Marie stares in disbelief as I tell her the story: how hard it was for Fern to find an attorney, how Lillian refused to take the case. I leave out the part about the Payne-ment. I already feel fool enough.

Marie fiddles with the ends of an orange and black scarf around her neck. "Well, you do seem to really care. And that's something, Molly. I respect that. I know you're trying to fight for her." She catches my eye. "Fern is the best, you know?"

"Oh, I know. Fern is great."

"Not just great. She's the best. And she's been through hell. When did you meet her?"

"About a year and a half ago."

"She was a total mess before that. It was utterly painful to watch, especially if you knew her before. She needs her kids back. And I know your heart is in it. But do you really think you're the best person for the job?"

"I think so. I think I can do it. It's been going okay—"

"You think you can do it? It's been going okay?" She shudders. "No offense, Molly, but that's not exactly confidence-inspiring."

I feel a flash of anger. Where has Marie Washington been the past year as I've been pulling all-nighters and risking my job?

"Marie, with all due respect, you can question me all you want. It's really Fern's opinion that I care about and we've been doing great, actually. Her visitation is increased. The forensic report was in her favor. Everything is lined up perfectly."

"But we're talking about a trial, Molly. Have you ever done one by yourself?"

I shrug, way more nonchalantly than I feel.

"Oh, Molly, you've been practicing for all of a minute. And I'm sure you're bright and decent and will go on to have a storied career. But this all just doesn't sit right." She leans forward, meeting my eyes. Her voice is quiet but stern. "And if you make a mistake because you don't know what the hell you're doing, I'm sure you'll recover, but what will that mean for Fern? Have you ever in your life been this directly responsible for someone's well-being? I mean, not just how much money they get to keep, but their lifeblood?"

A sudden lump in my throat forms. Once, I think. Once, and it didn't go so well at all.

Lolly comes back in, bringing with her a waft of stale tobacco. She takes off her coat, watching the staring contest between me and Marie with raised eyebrows. "Whoa. Someone die while I was gone?"

I wince at the question and Marie leans back into the couch with a studied casualness and a tinkling, phony-sounding laugh. "No one died. We were just going over some strategy."

I agree with a nod, smiling in what I hope is a casual manner, but Marie's words, right as they are, hang in the air.

ditching the cricket

I am genuinely surprised at how it goes down, the phone call
with my dad.

"So you don't think it's a good idea for me to come up?" He
repeats my words, in the same order that I just said them, substi-
tuting "me" for "you."

I lean my forehead against the window, cell phone pressed to
my ear. "It's not that I don't *want* you to. But I'll be stuck. On trial."

"Couldn't I come up anyway? We could grab a few meals together. Beyond that, I promise I can be responsible for entertain-
ing myself."

"There's just too much going on. Hey, you know what would
be great? If I came to you guys for a change. How about the first
weekend after my trial? Maybe September?"

"But it's my year to visit you. And I always come up in the
summer. You know I don't have as much time any other season."

He sounds sad, which makes me annoyed and ashamed. Isn't
he always telling me to put my nose to the grindstone? Not to get
distracted? Work comes first? He's acting like he's forgotten the
Grant Family fundamentals, our family skeleton that has pro-
vided the underlying structure for every choice I've ever made:
fulfill your obligations; be a professional; stay on the path.
Obliquely, I remind him of this. "I'm worried about getting in
trouble, Dad. With work."

Although it's a phone call, I feel the effect of my words, which cause him to stand at attention. Danger! Red alert! He swallows. "Did something happen?"

"No. Nothing happened. There's just a lot riding on this. I can't have any distractions." And I can't.

Maybe, just maybe I can make it through this summer juggling the Walker trial and Lillian and Bacon Payne. But I don't stand a chance of doing it with my well-meaning dad coming up in the middle of it, proudly looking over my shoulder like Jiminy Cricket, trusting that I'm doing the right thing, sleeping on an air mattress surrounded by boxes and boxes of Fern's documents as I lie about what I'm doing each day. I know I can't.

He sighs and asks me for details about the trial, and I know I've won. He will not try to convince me further or surprise me with a visit.

"I'm just doing what I'm supposed to," I want to scream at the phone. "This is for you." But as I hang up the phone, it doesn't feel like I'm doing him a favor. It feels like the opposite.

part three

a civilian in my office

I have three days until the trial starts and all I want to do is work on my cross-examination of Robert Walker. Instead, I am stuck at the office, revising a separation agreement for one of Lillian's clients. My thoughts keep drifting over to Robert's testimony. I've started and crumpled up four drafts trying to figure out what to ask him. How do you trick the devil into exposing himself?

I look at the clock on my wall. It's almost seven, but if I get this done by nine, I can get home in time to start draft number five. Someone knocks at my door and I don't look up to send the message that I am Very Busy and should be Left Alone. But the knocking only gets louder and then, in a decidedly un–Bacon Payne move, morphs into the rhythm for "Shave and a Haircut."

When I finally glance up, Caleb stands in the doorway, his hands in his pocket, head down. Seeing him, I realize that— except for immediately deleting his text, sent the day after the beach retreat, in which he wondered, quite poetically, *where did u go?*—I haven't thought of him once. When I finally got home that night, it was what Henry said that kept playing in my mind, keeping me awake. And even though I know he was way out of line, I have to admit that I can see it, why he would want to distance himself from the train wreck of drama I've become.

"Can I come in?" Caleb shuffles in my doorway.

"How did you get past security?"

He points to the photo ID stuck to his suede jacket. "This got me in the elevator and then I just stood in reception on thirty-seven until someone took pity on me and buzzed me in."

"You know what floor I work on?"

"Of course I do. The matrimonial group and the thirty-seventh floor. It's like peanut butter and jelly, football and beer. . . ." His voice trails.

I refuse to smile, but I'm strangely touched. This must be the Bacon Payne associate's version of someone remembering your birthday.

He looks around at the stacks of paper. "So, what are you working on?"

"A big trial."

"Sounds intense."

"Is this bring-your-fling-to-work night, Caleb? You came over to find out what it's like to be a divorce lawyer?"

He sighs and looks down at his lace-free oxfords.

"Really. Out with it. I'm a little pushed here."

"I need to tell you something."

"Caleb, it's fine you hooked up with Marissa."

"Marissa?"

"Don't play stupid."

"Marissa? Marissa the lawyer?" He laughs. "I didn't hook up with her."

"Why not?"

"I don't even know how to answer that. How much of a slut do you think I am?"

"Well, you definitely like lots of . . . women," I say.

"Dude." He holds up both hands: *Slow down with the accusations.* "We were talking about my business. Seriously. She's helping me structure financing."

"Oh. Well, what is it?"

He shifts, hands in pockets. "I was seeing someone pretty seriously. Before you and I started things up again. She was out of the country for a bit. But she's back and now we're sort of . . . reconnecting."

Aha, the return of Anastasia Peppercorn. I nod. "Are you happy?"

He looks at me warily.

"Not a trick question. You and I were—well, certainly nothing exclusive. It's okay if you're happy."

"I'm, you know, we're taking it slowly, but it's good news."

"That's great. I hope it works out."

"Thanks." Caleb looks a little insecure. I wonder if Anastasia plays the kinds of games with his heart that he has played with mine.

There's a sound, like something slamming into the wall, and we both turn our heads. Henry—who has not been in my office in weeks—stands in my doorway, one palm against the doorframe, the other in his pocket. I sit up, at attention. He still looks mad, his eyes moving from me to Caleb.

Caleb lifts his eyebrows and looks at me.

"Henry, you know Caleb," I say, as tentatively as I can.

"Good to see you, man," says Caleb.

Henry stares at him, unsmiling. "You're fucking kidding me," he says, shaking his head as though someone's doused him with cold water. After a very long few seconds, he turns and walks away.

I look at Caleb. "Hold on."

Caleb nods and gestures to the door.

I stalk down the hall, catching up with Henry just as he's rounding the corner.

"Hey," I say. He doesn't stop, so, without thinking, I grab the back of his blue shirt and yank it toward me. "What the hell?" My pull doesn't even register, except to make his shirt parachute out.

He whips his head around to look at me. "Just forget it."

"No, tell me. What is your problem?"

He inhales slowly, and closes his eyes for a moment. When he opens them, he doesn't even look at me, instead fixing them on a spot on the wall above my head.

"Fine, don't tell me," I continue. "Let me guess. You're pissed because there's a civilian in my office."

"A civilian?" He looks as though I've lapsed into Kurdish.

"He can't even see any documents in there. Nothing is visible."

His eyes gleam with something and I think for a second that I'm off base, but then he nods. "Yes, Molly. The civilian. That's what I'm upset about."

"Seriously?"

"Yep. You understand me so well." His voice is devoid of any emotion, a regression to the wooden Henry of two years ago.

Now that he's confirmed it, I'm stunned. We're supposed to be vigilant about guarding access to the firm's case files, but no one takes it seriously. "Seriously? Not even Everett enforces the rule against outside guests. You've turned into a fucking cyborg since making partner."

"I'm sorry. Did you just call me a fucking cyborg?"

"Yes, I did. But I know it didn't hurt, because you're a cyborg, and neither will this: I can't deal with you anymore either."

He crosses his arms and leans against the wall, as though he's settling in.

I stare at him for a minute, unable to think of anything else to say.

"What else you got? Let it out, Molly."

Something about his tone—is there a hint of a smile behind it?—makes me so angry that I want to kick the wall. Or cry. I actually feel the prickly pain of tears pooling behind my eyes. So, like a three-year-old, I cross my own arms over my chest and jut my hip. "I'm sick of this, Henry. Just leave me the hell alone."

I storm back to my office, forgetting that Caleb's still in there, but there he is, sitting in my guest chair, palms on his knees.

My expression must recall the Furies, because he whistles. "You all right?"

"Fine," I say.

"That looked kind of like a lovers' spat," he says.

I stare at him, not amused. "I assure you, it was not."

"Good," he says, "then I don't have to be jealous."

"That makes sense," I say, my voice letting him know it makes no sense at all.

"It doesn't. It makes no sense at all."

He laughs and I feel my mood shift as my lips twitch in a smile. "We've evolved, Caleb."

"How you figure?"

"I can't picture us having this conversation several years ago. You just would have slunk away."

"Maybe, but I can't believe how calm you are. It's pretty cool."

I nod. I am awfully calm.

"I mean, we were seeing each other pretty regularly. And it was really fun," he says, as though now he's offended that I'm not more offended.

"I promise, I really—it's okay."

I realize as I'm saying it that I'm not just putting on a brave face. If Caleb and Anastasia had sent me a postcard of them getting hitched in Vegas on Valentine's Day, I would feel not a twinge of possession. I've never thought of myself as particularly low maintenance, but maybe he's right. Maybe I have matured.

As I give Caleb a friendly hug good-bye, my brain slams right into it. No, I am still high maintenance, still capable of jealousy, still incredibly uncool. And that anger I just felt? That rush of crazy that made me run after Henry and accost his shirt? It's like those separating couples who won't let go of the fight, picking and drawing out minor arguments until the very bitter end. Ask any divorce lawyer and she'll tell you that the bickering is the simplest defense mechanism there is—a rush of anger to mask the pain of love.

I'm definitely uncool. It's just that I don't have any feelings for Caleb. I have feelings for Henry, who, unfortunately, can't stand me.

i scream for edamame

When my cell phone rings at seven o'clock the night before the trial starts, I assume it's Fern—we've talked about twenty times today—and pick it up without looking.

"How are you?" says Duck, her tone cheerfully sympathetic.

"The same."

I had told Duck about the fight with Henry the morning after it happened. Initially, she pushed me to confront him with my feelings, a sign, I told her, that she had been watching too many romantic comedies and needed to read T. S. Eliot or something for balance. After I ticked off my reasons for not coming clean to him—his coldness, the distance between us since his promotion, his heartbroken reaction when I asked about Julie—even she agreed that I should just suck it up and suffer silently.

"Do you have any ice cream at least? Aren't you supposed to be in your sweats and tube socks right about now, spooning rocky road straight from the tub?"

"The only thing in my freezer is edamame."

"You're a piss-poor excuse for a heartbroken girl."

"I know."

"Did you see him today?"

"Briefly. He was walking out of his office as I was passing and he gave me an amnesia look."

"Like he didn't remember the fight?"

"No, like he didn't remember me."

"Cold." Duck pauses. "But you know what makes me happy?"

"Glitter nail polish and salted margaritas."

"Yes, true, but really, I'm just happy that you have feelings for an actual grown-up. That you didn't fall for it this time."

"Fall for what?"

"For Caleb's whole act. His whole"—she lowers her voice to a gruff mumble—"*this is what it is* thing. I mean, you were intrigued there for a while, but not like before."

"I'll say one thing for Caleb, at least he says what he means."

"Puh-leez. You two were like the perfect little supply and demand case study. The more he acted like there was something real between you, the less he would admit it, and the more you thought you wanted something between you. No way you would've been so hooked without the headfake."

It's a well-exercised reflex for me to silently erase whatever Duck says about Caleb as soon as she says it—select, highlight, delete—but I have to consider: maybe she's seen things more clearly than I've given her credit for.

"This time, you went for the real connection. Not the bait and switch, not something you conjured in your head."

"Except that there's no real connection between me and Henry."

"I don't know. My guess is it's just bad timing."

"Whatever. It sucks."

"Yeah."

We sit in silence for a minute. I get up from the couch, shifting forward my right shoulder and then my left in a stretch-shrug. "Thanks for calling, Duck. I've got to prep for tomorrow."

"Right, good luck. I meant to ask about that. Your thing is tomorrow, right?"

"Right."

"Well, I'm invested now, even though I still don't entirely understand what you're doing and why. So please let me know how it goes, whatever it is."

"I will."

"So, go get 'em. Whoever they are."

you don't look sick

This is my sophisticated and elaborate plan for covering my tracks on *Walker v. Walker* trial days, which are scattered like thunderstorms throughout the end of summer: as soon as I wake up, when my voice is still scratchy with sleep, I call the office and leave a voice mail for Kim, hoping it sounds like a sore throat. I'm not sure that the excuse will hold up, but so far so good.

Yesterday, day one, went by in a blur of nerves. Fern did well on her direct testimony and came across as I had hoped: responsible, loving, likable. But it's time for Risa's cross-examination, and I can tell that Fern, clenching her jaw in the witness booth, is nervous as she waits for Risa to begin.

Strand tries for the second time to move things along. "Ms. McDunn, your witness."

Risa doesn't acknowledge him.

"Ms. McDunn"—Strand coughs deliberately—"whenever you're ready."

Risa sits motionless, staring into space, red coils of hair atop her head in a regal bun. Her eyes are narrowed—they might be closed entirely—and her lips move ever so slightly. I can't tell what she's saying—perhaps she's visualizing a perfect cross-examination, perhaps remembering her grocery list, perhaps summoning the dark arts. Graham is standing up at the table, a flurry of activity, stacking and restacking files, bunching, grouping, clipping.

After a few seconds of silent chanting, Risa stands up quickly, as if clapped awake by a hypnotist. She briskly wipes her hands together and tilts her head to the side.

"Ms. Walker."

"Yes." Fern's shoulders bunch together as she slants her torso toward the microphone.

"You testified yesterday you had postpartum depression."

"Yes, after Connor. Yes. It was rough."

"Postpartum can be serious. Usually suicidal thoughts accompany it."

"Objection," I say.

"Withdrawn." Risa continues. "So, you were depressed, clinically depressed, for a period of over a year only two years ago?"

"I had postpartum depression years ago." There's an edge to Fern's voice.

"And in the two years since then, have you ever been depressed?"

"Depressed? No," says Fern.

"Humph. You're sure?"

Graham hands Risa a paper and she looks at it, nodding.

"You're saying you never e-mailed anyone in the last few months to say, quote—I don't know how I can keep going—end quote?"

"Objection." Both Roland and I shout, standing, at the same time.

Roland speaks first. "Your Honor, inadmissible on two grounds, no pretrial discovery under Rule Four Hundred and Eight, and it's hearsay."

Risa stands there with a small smile. "I'm not admitting this into evidence, Your Honor. I'm just asking Ms. Walker whether she wrote a statement like that over the last few months."

Strand nods. "Okay, you can answer."

Fern looks nervously at me. "I don't remember," she says.

"You don't remember whether you made such a dramatic declaration?"

"I might have, but I was probably talking about not seeing—"

"Just yes or no. Is that a statement you could have made?"

"Yes."

Risa keeps Fern for hours, interrogating her about one blind date she went on with a deadbeat dad; how Connor and Anna reacted to the first visit with her; the history of mental illness in her family. Risa asks each question in a tone designed to make Fern feel like a criminal. I want to scream.

Strand lets us take a brief recess during the second hour and I stagger to the ladies' room. Despite the grossness of the sink and the fact that I had applied mascara—not waterproof—this morning, I bend over the cracked porcelain sink, splashing cold water on my face until my fingertips are numb. I'm in the hallway, girding myself to walk back into the courtroom, when someone taps my arm and I turn.

"Hey, Roland."

"That got a little crazy in there," he says.

"Indeed." At this point, I know better than to try and talk shop with him.

He waits for a few beats. "Thing is, it's kind of like she's fighting a different case than the one I've been on."

"A different case?"

"Exactly."

"What do you mean?"

He tugs his ear. "Just an impression."

I notice it as soon as Risa resumes her questioning about the day Connor went to the emergency room—she's still playing her own game, hammering away that Fern is an unfit parent. But things have changed, because we've made them change; Fern has proven herself over the course of the year. I'm not sure why Risa isn't acknowledging this shift, but perhaps her rigidity is stagnation, not strength.

I know exactly what I have to do with my cross-examination of Robert.

Our team—me, Fern and Jenny—spends our lunch break at the diner across the street from the court. After picking at a turkey club, I leave the rest of the group to prepare for the afternoon. The hall outside Strand's part is empty, so I grab my usual bench and start reviewing my notes.

"Mols? Molly?"

There, wearing a monochromatic black suit and turtleneck, is Liz.

"Hi." I quickly clamp shut my manila folder with *Marie Washington Direct, Walker v. Walker* typed across the top, and then, trying to look casual, open my bag and shove it in.

"What are you doing here? I thought you were out sick."

I cough. "I am sick. I took a lot of meds."

"You don't look sick. You look great, actually."

"Makeup. Lots of makeup."

"But what case do you have in Brooklyn?"

"Oh, it's a new one. I'm filing an Order to Show Cause."

"You get it signed already?"

"I just have to pick it up at the clerk's office. I'm early."

"What case?"

"Walk—Walken."

"Like the actor?"

"What?"

"The actor, you know, Christopher Walken?"

"Um. Yes, like him, but not him."

"Any relation?"

"I don't think so, no."

"Really? I've never heard the name anywhere else. And he is from New York, you know."

"No, I'm pretty sure. No relation."

"Well, I love him. You have to tell me if you get to meet him."

"Um, okay. Listen, Liz, I'm still kind of out of it. Don't tell anyone you saw me, please. I don't want them to think I can function. So why are you here?"

She nods and rolls her eyes. "It's new. The parties live in Brooklyn Heights and wanted us to file here. It should settle, but there've been some discovery issues, so I had to come down today and talk to the clerk. Pain in the ass."

"So inconvenient. What discovery issues?"

Liz sits down and starts filling me in, just happy to commiserate on the ins and outs of work. She is probably five minutes away from offering to wait for me while I get my papers signed so that we can grab frozen yogurt together after court.

And here I am, willing her to keep talking as I half listen, lying about everything from my health to my reasons for being here. All I want to do is lose her so I can go back to focusing on *Walker v. Walker.* I feel like an asshole, and for a split second, I am tempted to tell Liz what's really going on. But I know I can't—it's too long of a story, she'd have too many questions and couldn't just knowing what I'm doing get her in trouble?

I glance at my watch. Fifteen minutes before our trial resumes, and while I am pretty sure Risa and Robert will waltz in late, Roland is consistently prompt. I want to avoid seeing him— he has taken to greeting me somewhat warmly—lest it inspire a new round of questions from Liz.

I stand up quickly and Liz follows suit, using her palms to smooth the wrinkles out of her pants.

"Let me walk you out on my way to the clerk's office," I say. "I want to check on the papers again. So, you were saying, Strand is appointing a discovery master? What's he like anyway?"

Liz smiles and continues her story as I lead her down the hall and toward the elevators.

At five o'clock, Strand breaks for the day. Risa finally released Fern and we've started her redirect examination. As we file out, I notice a man on the benches outside, waiting for Strand, whose day apparently isn't done. Perhaps judges do work harder than I realized, I think, taking in the guy's scruffy beard, wire-rimmed glasses and long shaggy brown hair. Typical bewildered divorcé, I think, giving him a sympathetic smile. He smiles back.

seriously, what's not to like?

Looking at the new girl trapped in Everett's office is so familiar it's like watching an old home movie. Her at-the-ready posture: legs crossed, leaning forward, pen in hand, legal pad on knee, stuck, as Everett yammers on about Atlantic beaches versus Pacific beaches or something equally relevant. Jane joined the matrimonial group at Bacon Payne a full week ago and I have yet to even invite her to lunch. But I can do one better. I lean my face in Everett's doorway.

"Hey," I say.

"Hey, Molly. What's up?" Everett swivels his chair around. "We were just talking about all of the Jewish holidays."

"Really?" I say. "For what case?"

"It's never too early to learn." Jane nods her head solemnly. "Everett was explaining everything. I had no idea there were so many." She gazes at him, her eyes pools of appreciation. Man, she's good.

"Yeah. Um, Everett? I could be wrong, but I think I heard Lillian on the phone talking about Goldburg or Greenburg?"

"Goldburg?" He sits upright and grabs a pen. "Um, what was she—well, okay." He turns to Jane. "Stay here. I'll be back in fifteen."

I feel almost bad as he hurries out of the door but lean my head in farther and speak in a stage whisper. "Just go, you're free."

Jane looks at me, brow furrowed. "But Everett said I should—"

"It doesn't matter. You'll be fine—just go and hide. Thank me later."

"Oh, that's okay. I'll wait here." She gives me a look that implies I am a crazy person.

"You don't need rescuing?"

She shakes her head.

"Everything's going well?"

Jane nods vigorously.

"You like working with Everett?"

She beams. "That's the best part. I love Everett. He's totally taken me under his wing. He is such a good teacher and so detail-oriented. No partner at my old firm ever spent this much time with me."

"Okay, then. Glad to hear you're liking it so far."

Jane gives a simple, genuine nod, as if to say, *Of course I do. What on earth would I not like about this place?*

Sure, I think, rolling my eyes as soon as my back is to her, *what's not to like about the matrimonial group at Bacon Payne?*

I walk by Henry's office, avoiding looking in, of course, but hearing him on the phone, doing his job. I pass one of the conference rooms. Liz is in there, meeting with a client, gesturing wildly, her curls bobbing. *No, really*, I think again, with slightly less sarcasm. *There's a lot not to like, but what's to be so bitter about?*

Henry, Liz and Rachel, and now Jane, are able to take it all in stride. Maybe the fact that I've struggled so much here—with the authority, the demands, the hours, the responsibility—says as much about me as it does about the firm. Sure, the bosses are crazy and phony, but let's face it: these days, so am I.

Five minutes later I'm back at my desk when Kim buzzes. "Linesevenforyou."

"Who is it?" I say, but she has already transferred the call.

"Liesel Billings here."

Her tone makes my skin freeze. "Hi, Liesel."

"Listen, Stewart is at it again. He's now claiming my art collection is marital property." She laughs without any musicality, three staccato syllables: *Ha. Ha. Ha.* "Apparently he met some appraiser and realized how much everything is worth."

I am speechless, a state that Liesel unsurprisingly interprets as an invitation to keep talking.

"I knew he was going to find every opportunity to drag me to court. Didn't I tell you this is exactly what he would do? Anyway, I'm not calling to chat. I need you to e-mail the cat motion papers."

I find my voice. "Sure. You don't have them?"

"I have the hard copies, but my new lawyers—I'm not quite sure about whether everything is screwed on straight there—should use them as a template. You know, the papers were pretty well done."

I nearly fall off my chair. "That's really nice to hear, Liesel. Thank you."

"It really was as much my doing as yours. And I will definitely need to change some of the things you put in, but they were a decent start."

"Right."

"Molly, one more thing."

"Yes?"

"I was thinking about you when I realized I needed these papers, and I wasn't sure you knew how difficult things were for me during that first year."

"I had an idea."

"You'll be heartened to know that I'm finally starting to realize I'm better off without him."

"I'm really glad to hear it."

"And," says Liesel, her rat-a-tat cadence not slowing down, "I wish that you had gotten to see me at my best."

I nod, knowing that for Liesel, this is an apology. "I understand, Liesel."

In the weeks after the Cat Hearing, a sense of guilt had motivated me to track down Liesel and Stewart's wedding announcement. I found it in that staple of newspapers everywhere, the section celebrating dewy-eyed newlyweds, neatly summarizing their lives in achievement-heavy blurbs. Especially heartbreaking was the photo of the two of them, their heads pressed eye to eye, shining with promises that I knew would be broken.

But there's a postscript to Liesel's heartbreak—it takes strength to figure out the way to move beyond a broken promise, and it makes me wonder, why isn't there a section devoted to those on the other side of the vows? "Betsy, teacher (42), who knew it was over when Mike forgot her birthday for the fifth consecutive year and hopes to keep the house," or "Peter, a computer programmer (40), who never saw it coming and whose primary concern is that the kids be raised Jewish." It will never happen—no one wants to linger on the sad truth that vows don't last forever. But still, it would be something to acknowledge the courage and tenacity and flexibility of those ready to start over.

after the allman brothers

By now, I have enough experience in Strand's courtroom to know whether he's paying attention when I'm examining a witness. He has not taken his eyes off forensic expert Gary Newkirk, PhD.

This fascination, I'm sure, has to do more with Newkirk's appearance than his testimony. The rest of the witnesses have been indistinguishable in their neutral suits and neat hair. Not Newkirk. From the neck down, he looks like a clerk at one of those office supply superstores: light blue button-down shirt tucked into precuffed generic khaki pants. From the neck up, however, it's another story. I'm not sure if the clumps in his gray and white hair are technically dreadlocks, but if not, they have serious potential. And though his hair is pulled back in a ponytail, not much of his face is visible, thanks to his substantial beard and large-framed glasses. It's as though Santa Claus became a huge fan of Phish and spent the off-season following them around the country, adopting the style of their fans.

Thankfully, Newkirk's appearance is the only surprising thing about him. Sure, his voice is a little surfer-inflected and he says "Mmmmm" too frequently in response to questions, confusing the record. His testimony, though, has been spot-on for Fern: this is a textbook case of alienation of affection caused by Robert Walker; Robert has not been acting in the children's best interest; Fern should have sole custody. Check, check, check.

When I rest, I look over at the defense table, although I already know what each one of them is doing. Graham hurriedly stacks and restacks papers; Risa, wrapped in some ridiculously heavy silvery fabric given the eighty-five-degree August day, channels her inner Wiccan; Robert scowls over his BlackBerry. Finally, Risa stands up quickly, as if poked by a pin.

"*Dr.* Newkirk," she says, her voice accenting his title just enough to indicate skepticism. Never mind that the guy's CV was read into the transcript earlier today and included three Ivy League universities.

"Mmmm."

"What did you do on the night of July fifteenth last year?"

"Objection." I stand up as Newkirk blinks and starts to scratch his beard. "I don't see how Dr. Newkirk's evenings are relevant here, Your Honor."

Strand nods agreeably. "Yes, yes. Counselor, where are you going with this?"

"Withdrawn, Your Honor. Dr. Newkirk. Please ignore that last question. On September sixteenth, you met with Robert Walker?"

"Um, yes. On September sixteenth and also another time the following month, I think. Can I look at my calendar? Mmmmm. October."

"Yes, well, thank you for answering beyond my question," says Risa, "but please stick to what I've asked you. What time did you meet with the father?"

"Um, hmmm. It must have been midmorning. Ten, ten thirty, something like that."

"And, did you—well, excuse me for asking this, hopefully this won't embarrass you and perhaps I'm wrong, hopefully I'm wrong—but did you partake in the use of any illegal substances on the evening of September fifteenth?"

"Objection, Your Honor." I stand as quickly as I can. "Dr. Newkirk should be advised to plead the Fifth."

Dr. Newkirk waves his hand. "It's only a matter of time before they legalize it," he says.

Strand shrugs. "Continue."

Newkirk raises his shoulders. "Hmmmm. I don't really remember." Is he grinning under that beard? It's hard to tell but Newkirk doesn't sound embarrassed. He sounds nostalgic.

"Let me help you out, *Dr.* Newkirk. On September fifteenth, you went to go see the Allman Brothers at the, um——" Risa pronounces it All-Man, as though she's describing a Navy Seals unit or a Chippendales show.

"At the Beacon. Go every year. But you're right, because usually it's in March, but not this year. I do remember that." He is smiling under his beard.

"Thank you, right. The Beacon Theatre, where you go to see the All-Man Brothers every year. And while at the All-Man Brothers concert, did you partake in using any illegal substances?"

"Objection." This time it's Roland.

Strand blinks. "I'll allow this."

"I don't really remember. That was many moons ago." Dr. Newkirk starts to chuckle.

"Is it possible?"

"Objection." I try again.

Risa presses her hands together and brings them to her lips. "Your Honor. It's entirely relevant to determine what kind of mind-set *Dr.* Newkirk was in. . . ."

"Let's just . . . see where this goes." Strand looks intrigued, like a kid who just discovered a stash of *Playboy*s in the attic and isn't ready to put them back under the mattress. Apparently the Allman Brothers never play Mayberry.

"Is it possible, Dr. Newkirk, that you used an illegal substance on September fifteenth?"

He nods. "It's pretty likely."

"And which substance was that?"

"Not sure entirely. Probably just a little marijuana."

"Okay, so within twenty-four hours of your meeting with Robert Walker, you used marijuana?"

"Hmmmm. Well, to be fair, I'd say I probably used marijuana."

"Okay. Let me rephrase. Within hours of a crucial interview with Robert Walker, you 'probably used marijuana'?"

"Hmmmm." Dr. Newkirk nods his head slowly. "I can agree with that."

"Is it possible you were still feeling the effects of those illegal substances during your meetings with Robert Walker?"

Finally, at this, Newkirk's mellow is harshed; he appears to be frowning, based on the creases that appear in his forehead. "Oh, no way. There's no way."

Risa arranges her features exaggeratedly, skepticism radiating off her raised eyebrows and twisted mouth. "Of course not," she says, all mock innocence. "No further questions, Your Honor."

I glance over expecting to see Robert looking smug as the proverbial canary-swallowing cat. Instead, his head is down and his jaw is clenched. And his forearms are moving almost imperceptibly, which any law firm associate would recognize as the mark of clandestine BlackBerry typing. Fern looks at me uncertainly and I try for a reassuring smile.

We both glance down at my feet, distracted, as we hear the barely perceptible buzz of my BlackBerry in the bottom of my bag, which I've stashed under the table.

She leans in. "It was buzzing like crazy during your questions."

I reach into my bag without looking down and feel around until I've pressed the off button.

Strand nods at Roland. "Your witness, Mr. Williams."

Roland walks over to a spot directly in front of the witness stand. "Dr. Newkirk. I must remind you again that you are free to plead the Fifth to any of these questions I'm about to ask you."

Dr. Newkirk looks at his fingers and nods.

"Were you high or under the influence of any drugs or substances when you met with Robert Walker?"

"No way."

"Were you high or under the influence when you met with Fern Walker?"

"Nope."

"Were you high or under the influence when you met with Anna or Connor Walker?"

"Nope."

"Were you high or under the influence when you wrote your report for this case?"

"No, for sure no."

"Okay. Thank you for clearing that up. Now I have a few questions about the parental alienation study that you were citing, the McLarnen report. What year was that done?"

Newkirk clears his throat and launches into a cogent explanation of how the study is applicable to the Walker case. I breathe a sigh of relief.

A little later, when Strand releases Newkirk and dismisses us for the day, Robert bolts up and out of the courtroom, his Black-Berry pressed to his ear. Claire says something to Risa and hurries after him.

I look at Fern. "Any clue what's going on there?"

She looks hopeful. "Maybe he's interviewing new lawyers."

I grimace. "At this point, even Risa would be preferable to starting fresh."

Fern looks like she can't imagine that would be true. "Should I worry about Newkirk's testimony?"

"I don't think so. Even our president has admitted to drug use. Just more lawyering by sensationalism."

"So, you still think we'll be done by next week?"

"I do." Strand has us booked for two days next week and Claire and Robert are the only witnesses left.

As I hold open the heavy courtroom door for Fern, I spot the same scruffy man who was there a few months ago. He's leaning against the wall and holding on to the strap of his courier bag. It's four thirty-five, but he's got a big smile, like he doesn't know what's about to hit him. I once again feel a surge of pity for this poor unrepresented soul.

"Hi again," he says.

"Hello."

"I'm Ari."

"Nice to meet you, Ari." I gesture back into the courtroom. "He's all yours."

He grins—wide and a little goofy—his eyes locking into mine. "You're a lawyer?"

"I am."

"What's your name?"

Fern pats my arm. "This is Molly Grant. She's WON-der-ful." She drags out the word, emphasizing each syllable and sounding like a Disney princess.

"Grant," he says. "Can you spell that?"

"G-R-A-N-T, like it sounds," says Fern.

"And you do custody trials?"

"Of course," says Fern. "She's doing one right now."

"Do you have a card?"

"No, sorry. Not on me, but good luck, Ari."

"Hi," he says to Fern, extending a hand. "I'm Ari."

"Yes, I heard." She smiles. "I'm Fern."

"See you later, Ari," I say, grabbing Fern's arm and pulling her past as Ari, apparently the friendliest divorce litigant in the world, stands and waves at us, still smiling.

"You should really have given him a card," she says. "He could be a potential client. Practice-building 101."

"Thanks, Fern. I appreciate the good word, but let me get my employment situation straight before I start adding clients."

"Oh, right."

She reaches into her bag and pulls out her phone. As always, watching another person check her messages makes me itchy to check my own phone, which starts ringing as I turn it on. It's Henry, calling me for the first time in months. I have no idea how to even talk to him anymore, so I press Ignore, at which point I see I have seventeen texts waiting in the wings. Seventeen texts!

I scroll through quickly. A few from Duck, a handful from Rachel and Liz. All of them are variations on *call me* and *where r u?*

Fern has her phone pressed to her ear, so she and I mime good-byes to each other as I dial Duck.

She picks up on the first ring. "Well, hello, wayyyy too yellow, and wayyyyy too clunky."

"Huh?"

"Oh, sorry. Checking out an end table. So, apparently there is big workplace drama round your parts."

"What? Wait, why are you the one telling me this?"

"Henry called me because he was having trouble reaching you. Are you guys talking again?"

"No."

"Well, here. Wait a sec. I took notes because I knew I wouldn't remember. Okay, so apparently Lillian was looking for you and had a mini-meltdown at the office."

"Oh, God. What did she do?"

"I don't really know details. There was something about her going into your office and yelling, slamming doors." She pauses as if actually imagining the scene. "I'm sorry. That sounds like a total tantrum. What will you do?"

"I don't know." I bite the side of my thumbnail. "Any thoughts?"

"Well, maybe it will all blow over by the time you're back.

Oh, and there's something else—I'm supposed to read you a blurb from that 'Nitty Gritty City' column." She clears her throat dramatically. " 'Robert Walker, reclusive head of Options Communications, has been battling it out in custody court with his ex. Word is things are getting nasty.' " She trills the last word to make it singsongy. "Okay, that's it."

"Oh, that's it? What a relief." I raise my voice. "Are you kidding me? What else could there be?"

"Eggplant meets violet. What is that, purple? No, the purple. Where did you find it?"

"Focus, Duck. Jesus."

"Sorry, Rico again. No, nothing else. This is your mystery case, I assume?"

"Yep."

"I wouldn't really worry about it. I've never heard of the guy and you're not even mentioned. And it's clearly a slow news day. The top blurb is about how some reality star was spotted at Home Depot in the faucet aisle. I mean, how desperate can you be? B&B Italia is blocks away." Duck snorts. "But you should call Henry. He sounded very shaken up—or is it shook up—shaken up? Anyway, he sounded very unsettled on your behalf."

"Okay, I'll let him know you got me," I say, knowing I'll do no such thing; I can't stomach pity from Henry right now. "Well, thanks. Really. So wonderful to hear that my career is in such dire straits."

"That place sucks. Getting fired would be the best thing to happen to you, I promise."

"So, you'll get your rich husband to pay off my student loans?"

Duck laughs as though I am joking. "Always keep that sense of humor, girl." She hangs up the phone.

I stand uncertainly for a moment in the hall of the courtroom with no momentum to go anywhere. For a split second, I contemplate just camping out here, in the Brooklyn courthouse. I wonder how long I could stay. After several moments, I force myself outside to one of the empty benches lining the plaza. It's a calm, beautiful summer day, the kind that would otherwise make me feel carefree and hopeful: sun, a warm breeze, happy little bird chirps.

Outside, people lazily circle the white tents of a farmers' market, canvas bags slung over their shoulders. I watch a man in army pants examining apricots like it's the most important thing in his world—pick up, discard, pick up, discard—and feel a stab of envy for the apparent simplicity of his life.

I press the third speed-dial button on my phone and pray that one of the boppy college kids doesn't answer. I can't handle making small talk about their fall break trip to New York.

"Cheddar and Better. How can we tantalize you?"

Ugh. They have to change that greeting. "Hi, Dad."

"What happened?"

"Nothing, why?"

"Oh, thank God. It's the middle of a workday, so I thought—"

"Well, actually. Something did sort of happen."

"Are you hurt?"

"No."

He exhales. "Okay." His tone is gentle as he waits a few seconds. "Can you help me out a little here?"

"No."

"Okay."

I hear the muffling of his hand on the mouthpiece and his whisper to someone named Bryce that he should handle something involving a delivery of heirloom ketchup.

Neither of us says anything for what feels like several minutes.

"Okay, so, the thing is I might need to come home, Dad."

He speaks quickly. "That's okay, Molly. Of course that's okay. Come on home."

"And I might need a job."

"That's fine, kid. We have jobs."

Pause.

"I'm sorry."

He makes his tone light, which must take a lot of effort. "Whatever happened, it's okay."

I scrunch my eyes shut, trying to cauterize the path of the warm tears I feel swarming my eyes. It's not okay. I have failed. I have gravely miscalculated, ignoring the pull of obligation that has defined me for as long as I can remember. And now everything is broken.

Worse, I know from my dad's light tone that he doesn't quite understand. So even though I'm not supposed to mention it out loud, I need him to know. Right now. "The thing is, I might not ever—" I swallow. "I might be somewhat of a lost investment for you guys. I might never help pay you back."

There is a long silence, during which I picture him examining his pride, seeing if he can suture together what I've just filleted. When he speaks, though, he doesn't sound embarrassed in the least. "Oh, don't worry about that."

My mom, who at some point must have picked up the extension in the storeroom, repeats the sentiment. "Not your job, Molly. You understand? That has never been your job." And then, softly apologetic, she says, "We should've told her that, Bill. We should've made sure to tell her that."

We sit in still silence, me on my bench, the two of them in different rooms, both having stopped the constant motion—the packing and unpacking, the greeting, the ordering, the filing— to talk to me. When Bryce's voice interrupts again, my dad tells him to shush and there's some whispered conversation about coffee bean grinders.

"Thanks. I'll call you guys later tonight."

I hang up and imagine moving back to Hillsborough until I'm debt free: twenty years of eating cheese straws and yogurt-covered pretzels. Snap out of the self-pity party, Molly. I clap and shrug my shoulders a few times. The little kid on the adjacent bench giggles and imitates me, sending his snack pack of Cheerios flying. "Jacksonnn, what are you doing?" says his nanny. "Stop that, Jackson. Naught-ee!"

The move kind of works, though. I find the energy to get up and take the few steps toward the subway.

surrender, molly

It's not as bad as it could be, I tell myself when I see my computer. The screen is black except for the familiar prompt for my log-in and password, meaning—thank frigging God—I logged off the computer early this morning before leaving for court. Meaning that Lillian was not privy to my personal e-mails.

Once I celebrate this little gift, though, it's hard to stay upbeat. Looking around, I can picture—as if in one of those shaky camera dramatizations—Lillian yanking open the file folders that had been neatly piled on my desk, toppling papers like a spread deck of cards. She's left some of my desk drawers open and overturned my Bacon Payne Summer Swing Cruise coffee mug so that there are gel pens and highlighters sprawled all over the desk. Several random sticky notes are on the floor, curled up defensively.

It feels no less invasive than that time in fourth grade when my mom and I came home from my softball game on a Saturday afternoon and found out we'd been robbed: broken window, drawers emptied of clothing, books strewn on the floor. I know part of the point behind Lillian's tirade, though, is that my office is her office; my case files are her case files.

Liz's office is empty; so is Henry's. Against my better judgment, I walk in to leave a note for him. Searching for a pad of paper on his desk, I see it, a yellow note stuck to his keyboard with the message "Julie called." There's a little heart over the *i*.

Great, true love for Henry.

I retreat quickly.

Jane is in her office. She looks up when she sees me walk by. "Oh, hi," she says, her voice bright, "good to see you! How are things?"

I want whatever that girl is on.

Rachel's door is closed, so I knock tentatively. She's on the phone, but when she sees me, she waves me in, motioning for me to shut the door. She wraps up her phone call with a series of brisk "Yeps," holding up her finger in the gesture for *Don't move.* Finally off the phone, she shakes her head slowly and looks at me with an exaggeratedly stunned expression on her face. "Where the hell have you been?" she whispers like she's talking to a fugitive, which I guess she is, in a sense.

"Down at court. In Brooklyn."

She inhales deeply and nods. "Oh, okay. I knew it. I told Liz you weren't dumb enough to just go AWOL like that. I can't believe Kim spaced a court date. Scary."

"Actually, it wasn't Kim's screwup."

She squints. "I don't understand."

"It's not one of the firm's cases."

Quick headshake. "Still don't understand."

"The case is mine. It's a very long story. No one knew."

"You've been secretively doing your own case on the side? Since when?"

"About a year and a half ago. I didn't tell because I thought I'd incriminate you."

Rachel rolls her eyes, visibly ticked. "Ummmm. O-kay. What is this, Langley? Is your client Jason Bourne?"

I half laugh.

"No, really, who's your client?"

I feel my face get red and I tell her the whole story.

W hen I'm done, she whistles. "Wow, what Lillian did today was mild compared to what she'd do if she knew that. She'd probably stroke out."

"Was it awful today?" I say.

"Um, a little intense. Liz and I were able to piece most of it together. Lillian was in one of those bored moods where she just wanted to play. She kept pacing the halls, buzzing us to come in, having little tea parties. She asked for you a couple times and then, at some point, she started to get angry about it. Kim said you had court all day and Lillian wanted to know which case. Kim didn't remember and looked on the calendar and they had a whole big thing in the hall." Rachel grimaces. "Anyway, then Lillian went into your office."

"What did she say?"

"Ah, well, you can imagine. Just where were you and this wasn't the type of shit any decent associate would do. And how you've been kind of absent lately, you're not a team player, you only care about yourself. Um, you know. . . . Just that kind of stuff." From her rushed tone, I can tell that this is a whitewashed version of events.

"And?"

Rachel's cheeks color a little. "She said some mumbo jumbo about you coming from nothing and not being able to hack it in the real world."

"Oh." For some reason—inexplicable, given my disdain for Lillian—this cuts to the gut.

"Then there was screaming, door slamming, the whole thing. Did you have anything incriminating in your office?"

"No, I don't think so."

"Good, because she was in there for a while."

"Yeah, I just saw it. Total tornado. I half expected to see 'Surrender, Dorothy' written on the ceiling."

We laugh, weakly and briefly.

"So, how long do you think I have?" We both know what I mean.

"Not sure."

"What should I do?"

"Grovel maybe? That didn't work for Hope, but . . ." She trails off. "You do have some time because, you know, she's out for bugville all next week."

"Oh, bugville, right." I had totally forgotten. Lillian is joining Roger in Australia this week for some sort of association-of-stick-insect bonanza. She made a big deal about how, for once, this trip she would just be Mrs. Fields. She was going to book tons of appointments at some posh spa and overload on their hibiscus facials. Or aromatherapy massages. Or something.

"You forgot about her vacation?" Rachel looks like I have just asked her whether you need fault grounds to get divorced in New York. "You really are in your own world."

"I know. I'm a mess."

I say good-bye to Rachel and go find Kim to ask for Lillian's travel plans. She makes fleeting eye contact with me, which is not a good sign of my shelf life. She pauses—the first time I've seen Kim do that—before answering in slow, measured tones that Lillian's flight doesn't leave until very late tonight, but it might not be the best idea for me to call right now.

I had been ready to throw in the towel a few hours ago, but now that I'm here, there's a tiny, idiotic ember of hope in my belly. I'm so close. Just three weeks until my fifth anniversary. Three more weeks in which I should be able to draw things out and put up with whatever Lillian throws at me. I have to give it a shot.

Lillian picks up on the second ring, obviously thinking it's Kim. "So, can she do Tuesday instead?" She's eating something, based on the smacks and crunches from her end of the phone.

"Lillian, it's Molly," I say quickly.

Silence. The chewing noises stop as abruptly as if she's spit out her fat-free bagel chips.

"Listen, I heard you were looking for me and I'm so sorry. I'm so sorry I wasn't here and I just wanted to apologize. Is there anything I can do?"

Silence.

"I know I let you down. I promise to keep Kim in the loop in the future."

Silence.

I know that she's waiting for an explanation. I wish I had the balls to blithely hang up, but I don't. "Yeah, I, um, I had a personal matter and I was actually down at court for it, and I'm so sorry. I know it was very unprofessional of me—"

"A. Personal. Matter?" She spits the words as if I had just told her I had spent the day down at the Hustler Club, snorting blow and catcalling at the strippers.

"Yes, but—"

"Enough. You have interrupted enough of my vacation time. I will deal with this inanity when I get back. In the meantime, organize your office. It's an embarrassment."

She hangs up the phone. I need one of those arctic sleeping bags to recover from the chill of her voice. I know I just made things terribly worse.

robert walker's very bad week

It's five days after my phone call with Lillian, and when I don't have court appearances, I'm hiding at home, where I am now.

My Molly Grant, PC, cell phone buzzes for the second time with a number that I don't recognize. It's eight thirty at night—too late for the court, so I let it go to voice mail, pacing around the room until a message notification appears.

"Hi, Molly Grant. Ari Stern from the *Independent*. I'd love to chat again. We're running an article about Robert Walker's recent troubles, mostly the custody issues. Anyway, I'd love to talk to you again, get some quotes, see where you think things are headed. Give me a call, 347-555-2121, or I'll try again. Ciao."

His tone is breezy and familiar, as if he is confident that we've met before, which we haven't, because I'd remember it. Unless I met him the day of Lillian's anniversary party. I don't remember whole chunks of that day.

I play it a few more times.

Around the sixth time I hear the "Ciao," his voice registers and it clicks. Ari is scruffy man from the hall. Who apparently is not a downtrodden potential client but the reporter. And according to him, Robert Walker has "troubles," as in more than one.

I turn on my computer. *Wall Street Journal, Crain's, The Deal,* the *New York Times* business section, the *Financial Times*—they all have an article about some sort of coup at Options Communications.

I take the shortcut and pick up the phone to call the one person who I know will be up on the issue. Like any good corporate lackey, he picks up halfway through the first ring even though it's almost nine o'clock.

"Kevin, what's happening with Robert Walker and Options?"

"How do you not know this? It's the biggest deal."

"So I gather."

"And why aren't you in the office?"

"I'm working from home."

"Wow, matrimonial is cushy."

"So, the Robert Walker thing?"

"Total bloodbath," Kevin says with relish.

"Why?"

His voice shifts to an imitation of a nasal-sounding professor. "Classic activist shareholder coup. Classic."

I laugh, which is nice, because I haven't done so in days. Kevin and I have a running joke that the names of corporate subterfuge maneuvers sound like titles of spy novels. I infuse my voice with mock suspense. "Was the corporate veil pierced? Was there a poison pill? Does he at least have a golden parachute?"

"Oh, he'll be okay. He has a big golden parachute—he'll get oodles of millions when they oust him."

"Oh, thank goodness," I say in mock relief.

Kevin explains the situation like a sportscaster giving a play-by-play. Apparently, a rogue group of Options shareholders bonded together to overthrow the board of directors. They succeeded two weeks ago and elected a new board of directors. The new board is having an emergency meeting, the result of which will likely be the ouster of our own Robert Walker. Although Robert didn't do anything *wrong*, Kevin explains, apparently there has been a lot of speculation that his ridiculously high compensation just doesn't look right amid record low third-quarter numbers. Kevin is in the middle of describing Robert's eight-figure departure package when his other line buzzes. I shout thanks as he clicks over without a good-bye.

This explains Robert's distracted behavior. Today after every break, he rushed back into the courtroom seconds before Strand appeared back at the bench, like this annoying little trial we all insisted on having was keeping him from the important things in his life.

And Fern told me that he didn't even register a reaction to my cross-examination of Claire, not even when I brought out the society page photos. (We had copied and indexed 150 photos of Claire from different events and were amazed to discover that she donned entirely different outfits, but the same open-lipped smile and slight head tilt to the right in each of them.) Looking at Strand, I had asked Claire, in light of her long list of charitable engagements, did she want to reassess her earlier testimony that she rarely missed a meal with Anna and Connor? She shifted uncomfortably in her seat and reassessed. It was a good moment for Team Fern.

Tomorrow Robert will take the stand. My cross-examination is ready, although now that I know he's losing his job, perhaps I should change tacks. I imagine strutting up to the witness stand and starting my testimony. "Mr. Walker, I understand you're having some trouble at Options?"

"Yes."

"Your new board is having an emergency meeting this week, the result of which will be that you're out of a job."

He hangs his head in shame. "Yes."

I lean in close for the kill. "Well, if you're free on Wednesday, want to meet up for an unemployed support group at the library? I know we've had our differences, but it's résumé workshopping day."

Then Robert and I could join hands and sing "Bobby Mc-Gee": "Freedom's just another word for nothin' left to lose." Or maybe Robert would prefer a Jimmy Buffett tune, like, say, "Wasting away again in Margaritaville." I'd let him choose.

One winter evening during my junior year, Duck and I were at a karaoke bar and "Bobby McGee" came on. We cracked ourselves up exaggerating those la-la-la-la-la-la-las. I mean come on, already. So over the top. Tonight, though, I recognize it as the truest song ever. I must hear it, and soon my laptop speakers are blaring Janis Joplin. Midway through the second verse, I realize it's been an hour since I checked my Bacon Payne voice mail. There is a certain irony to having my new anthem blare in the background as I scramble to check in with Big Brother.

"Freedom's just another word for——," I half shout with Janis as the Bacon Payne voice mail narrator intones, "You have three new messages."

I stop singing. New voice mail messages are rarely good.

Janis ignores the voice mail and keeps going. "——nothing left to lose," continues Janis. "Nothing, I mean nothing, honey, if it ain't free——"

"Liesel Billings here. I received the papers that you sent me over e-mail. Something is wrong with the margins——they're very wide, and I need you to fix them and resend. ASAP because my papers are due next week."

I stare dumbly at the phone.

Beep.

"Hi, this message is for Molly Grant. Molly, my name is Ari Stern. We might have already met. I'm wondering if you're the same Molly representing Fern Walker in the custody dispute with her husband. I can't find a picture of you on the Web site, but it would be a weird coincidence if there are two matrimonial lawyers around the same vintage, both named Molly Grant, one at Bacon Payne, one out on her own. Right? Ha, ha, ha. Anyway, call me soon or I'll try back. Ciao."

Crap.

Beep. "Molly, It's Kim." Uh-oh. She's talking slowly. "So, um, Lillian is back on Thursday morning and she wants to see you in her office. First thing. If I were you, I'd get there around eight thirty. Definitely no later than nine. Okay?" Her voice quiets to a whisper. "Sorry about this."

"Nothing, nothing, nothing YAAAAA," screams Janis, failing to read the moment.

Oh shut up, Janis.

the heart over the *i*

I have to think of Robert Walker as subhuman, incapable of vulnerability, as he stares through me from twenty feet away. No matter that this morning's *Independent* had a blurry picture of him frowning and pacing under the headline WORST WEEK EVER. He's still an arrogant bully. I hadn't had time to read the article, but Duck had texted me *U r in the paper!* Her enthusiasm indicates that she still does not get the gravity of my situation.

I leave my notes on the table and walk over to the witness stand, trying to keep my tone light, conversational. "Mr. Walker, you think that you are a better parent than Ms. Walker?"

He exhales loudly. "Yes."

"You think that Ms. Walker is dangerous?"

He nods slowly, as though I'm an idiot. "Yes, I think she needs help."

"Do you think that Anna and Connor's spending time with their mother is in their best interest?"

"Not currently, no."

"You think your children would be better off if they didn't see Ms. Walker at all?"

"Yes."

"No further questions, Your Honor."

Robert Walker looks a little surprised and there's a moment of silence in the courtroom, during which Strand wears a happy, blank smile. He finally blinks, nods and looks at Roland. "Your witness, counselor."

About two hours later, the defense rests.

Before letting us go, Strand reminds us that he needs post-trial briefs in a week and that he'll decide on our counsel fee motion then as well. And with that, we're done with the Walker trial with more of a whimper than a bang.

I am helping Jenny pack up the remaining Bankers Boxes when Roland approaches, his hand outstretched. "Pleasure doing business with you, Ms. Grant."

"You too, Mr. Williams. Thanks for your examinations."

He salutes. "Just trying to do right by my clients. You know, you're much more savvy than you look."

"Um, thanks?"

"Good move on the cross-examination, using the defendant's own words to prove your case. Efficient, smart and, most important, got us out of here early. Thanks for that."

"Anytime."

I gesture at Fern to signal I'm ready to go when Risa approaches with a wide smile, her arm outstretched. Stunned, I take it and am treated to a vigorous shake. Graham is at her shoulder, and when she drops my shocked-into-bonelessness hand, he grabs it and pumps.

"Great case, Molly. Pleasure trying it against you. Hope we bump into each other again soon," says Risa during Graham's shake. "If you're ever upstate, swing by. We can go hiking, or out to this little coffee shop on the river. It's beautiful up there. You'd love it." Graham finally releases me, nods and then, apparently unable to bear the loss of physical contact, pats my arm.

"Sure, sounds great," I manage to stammer as they walk away.

I turn to Fern. "Was her whole thing an act?"

She pats her temple with her index finger in mock rumination. "Maybe she has an evil twin."

As soon as the elevator opens in the lobby, I hear the noise, the low hum of a crowd. I can't locate the source until the revolving door spits me outside onto the courthouse steps and I see it: flashbulbs, people, microphones, cameras. Obviously someone newsworthy is in the courthouse today and I wonder—illogically and with a slice of fear—if it's one of Lillian's celebrity clients.

Then someone shouts, "Any comments, Ms. Grant?"

I look behind me for Fern and grab her arm as the flashbulbs continue to pop.

"No comment," I say, realizing that Liesel was correct—I am a rube when it comes to press strategy. I keep repeating "No comment" as Fern and I push through the crowd and somehow we duck to the side of the building, under some scaffolding.

Fern peeks around the other side. "I guess they're still waiting for Robert."

"Thank God. I didn't think to order a car. Can you imagine if they tried to follow us on the train?"

We walk around to the back of the municipal building and cross the street to a farther station, not opening our mouths again until we're safely through the turnstiles.

"Come out with us tonight," says Fern. "Brian, Jenny and I are going for something indulgent."

"How about we celebrate next week?" I say, not adding that I should be plenty free then.

"Deal."

As Fern's train pulls into the station, she throws her arms around me in a tight embrace. "Molly, thank you. You've changed . . . everything."

"Let's wait until we get a decision before claiming that."

"No, you have. You really have." She holds up her phone in a flash like she's showing me her ID, and I guess the picture on her home screen is a hallmark of her transformation. It shows Fern with her arms around Connor's and Anna's shoulders as they lean against her legs on the steps of the Natural History

Museum; Fern's looking down at Connor, saying something, and Connor smile-grimaces into the camera in the mugging way of preschoolers. Anna, flashing a peace sign, has her eyebrows raised and is sucking in her cheeks, pretending to be a model or maybe a fish. The whole scene is remarkable for its ordinariness, referencing the casualness and simple comfort—the *family*—that the three of them have forged over the past year.

Fern gets on the train, yelling through the closing doors, "Tally your bills and let me know what it is."

I nod, hold up my bag and point. "They're all in here." Fern's been asking me for the bills for weeks and I'm just humoring her. The total would take a huge chunk out of her savings and it just doesn't seem right to demand that, even if I do actually need the money now. The only way I'm getting paid for this case is if Strand orders Robert Walker to cover Fern's attorney fees, and I have no sense that that is going to happen.

"Okay. Good." She waves and blows a kiss as she steps onto the train, grinning.

I wind up at an Irish pub around the block from my building. It's dark and quiet, no surprise given that it's five o'clock on a Wednesday. I grab a corner table and spread out my time sheets, punching the calculator, adding and scribbling. Later, I will have to type it up all nicely and neatly and deliver it to the court along with my posttrial motion, but now, tonight, this is just for me.

It's probably just an obnoxious lawyer quirk—especially because I don't expect to see a dime—but I feel the need to quantify the time I spent on this case. *Walker v. Walker* went beyond seeping into my personal life; it caused irreversible tectonic shifts and I am curious—how many hours did it ultimately take to get to where I am now? And while where I am now—almost jobless, on the verge of losing my bonus and lovesick—is not anything

I'd volunteer for my alumni magazine's class notes, somehow it feels like an improvement from where I was.

It takes me four hours to total my time—apparently law firms have administrative support for a good reason. But finally, there it is, all my effort boiled down to one number. I have spent 630 hours of my time on *Walker v. Walker.* Which calculates to $315,000 in legal fees.

I would do it all again, given the choice.

As I walk into my apartment building, Marco gives me a big nod from behind the desk. "There she is," he says, singing out enthusiastically. He gives me a subtle wink.

"What?" I come home almost every night, but have never received such a reception from Marco.

"You have a guest. I've seen him before, so I let him go upstairs."

Class A security. I search my brain to remember whom Marco has seen before: certainly Caleb.

Marco shakes his head, it dawning on him that granting access to my apartment might have been a lapse in judgment. "I shoulda remembered his name, but I didn't. I'm sorry. He did ask me to give you this, though." He reaches down behind the desk and pulls up a white bag with a big bow on it. I peek inside. There are two Twinkies at the bottom.

I run into the elevator where there's a Twinkie resting on the railing, and I put it in the bag with the others. When the elevator opens on my floor, there's a median line of Twinkies leading to my apartment like the world's tastiest highway passing zone indicator. Henry sits on the floor, leaning against my door, his briefcase beside him.

"I won the contest?" I say, grinning, bending down to pick them up.

"Congratulations," he says, getting up and patting his bag.

He leans against the wall while I twist my key in the lock. Then we're inside my apartment and we stare at each other for a second. "Well——," I say at the same time he says, "Molly."

"Let me start," he says. "I'm sorry."

"You don't have to be, Henry."

He gives me a skeptical look. "Yes I do. I've been awful." He looks embarrassed. "I've been trying to call you about the article."

"The article?"

He sighs, opens the flap of his messenger bag and takes out a folded-up copy of the *Independent*, but I shake my head. I don't want to talk about the newspaper right now.

"I know you've been busy, but why haven't you returned my calls?" Henry stares right at me. "Are you that mad?"

"No."

He scrunches his eyebrows together. "No?"

I pick at a loose thread on the chair's upholstery. "Not mad, no. It's a little more complicated than that."

I have barely spoken the words and he's in front of me, grabbing my hand, pulling me down next to him so that we're sitting next to each other, eye level on the rug.

"Complicated?"

"Yes. Complicated."

He shifts his fingers so that our fingers are clasped. He squeezes them together, and then looks up, so our eyes are locked together.

"Complicated, as in difficult and confusing?"

I nod. "Difficult, confusing. Painful."

He winces, shakes his head and takes my other hand. "Painful."

"But somehow," I say as he leans closer, "things seem a little more hopeful now."

"More hopeful," he repeats.

"Yes, I'm getting the sense things will be, well, less complicated."

"Less . . . yes," he says.

"Henry, you're not even really listening anymore, are you?" I say.

He shakes his head. "Not at all." He pulls my hands toward him until we're entwined, and there's no space between us. And then we're kissing in a way that makes my stomach feel like the insides of the world's most crowded butterfly net.

The next morning, I wake up at six thirty, before the alarm goes off.

"Everything all right?"

I look over at Henry. It's still dark, but in the breaking dawn light I can make out that his hair is sticking up in front and that he's wearing boxers.

"You're in my bed and you're wearing only boxers."

He smiles and looks around in mock surprise. "So I am, so I am. I got the distinct feeling there was an invitation, though. What time is it?"

"It's six thirty."

"Oh, shit. I have to go home. Court today." He lies back down on the bed, pulls me down along with him and puts his head on me as though I'm his pillow.

His home. There's something I'm afraid to ask.

"Hey, Henry?"

"Mmmm."

"What about Julie?"

He sits, palms up. "Um, I don't know, Molly. What about Julie?" His voice is slow, like I'm not right in the head.

"I mean, you guys are still—"

"Together? No. No, no. We've been broken up for a while."

"But she called you."

He does the same helpless shrug. "Um, okay. She called me."

"In your office. Last week. There was a note, with a heart over the *i*."

"Oh, yeah. Her cousin needs a prenup." He gets out of bed and starts buttoning up his shirt. I get a little thrill from seeing the dressing process in reverse; it feels just as intimate. "But I didn't notice the heart over the *i*. Maybe that temp in reception loves her." He stops buttoning his shirt and sits down on the bed next to me. "You know when I broke up with Julie?"

"I don't actually."

"Last winter. You know why I broke up with Julie?"

I shake my head.

"I broke up with her because I finally got honest with myself about how I felt about you. Even though you were idiotically distracted by that Pretty Boy Floyd character, for some reason being with her still just wasn't right." He gives me a sidelong glance. "I assume this means you're all done with Pretty Boy Floyd, right?"

I clap my hands together and wipe once up and once down, in the universal motion for disposed. "You thought I was with him this whole time?"

"I wasn't sure, but I convinced myself it didn't matter. I had to come clean regardless." He lowers his voice. "I came by that night that he was there to apologize for that night in the car. But then, seeing him, just hanging out in your office, looking all smug, I sort of snapped."

"We were breaking up."

"Oh." He turns around, his smile abashed. "I might have been a tad better behaved if I had known that. The only thing worse than seeing him parked in your office that night has been not talking to you these past months."

"You weren't keeping your distance because of the Walker case?"

"No." He wrinkles his forehead. "Why would I do that?"

"Wouldn't it be bad for a partner to sanction such malfeasance?"

"I suppose it's not ideal." He brushes my hair off my face. "But I was already involved and frankly, I didn't want not to be."

I half smile. "So much for keeping work here and life here." My hands partition the phantom boxes.

"So much for it."

"Well, you might still be able to keep things separate. I will likely be out of a job by lunchtime."

He grimaces. "I'm sorry. Do you want me to stay and go in with you?" He gives the power salute, fist raised. "For, you know, moral support?"

"Nah. Thanks, though."

He kisses me and walks over to his shoes, stepping into them and grabbing his jacket from the back of the couch where he had draped it last night. "Okay. Good luck. I'll see you tonight whatever happens."

"Henry," I call after him as he opens the door.

He turns around. "Yeah?"

"How'd you know I was taking the middle elevator?"

"What are you talking about?"

"Last night. When I came home. There was a Twinkie in the middle elevator."

He snaps and points at me. "I put one in all three," he says, patting his briefcase. "Lifetime supply."

front-page news

I get to Bacon Payne at eight in the morning, so there's time to pick up a copy of the *Independent*. The guy at the news counter in the lobby starts to hand me the paper and then stops, looking at the cover and then back to me and then back to the cover.

"It's you! It's you," he says, very pleased at this turn of events. He holds up the picture. "Oooooooh, you look scared. Someone stole your lunch money?"

I grab the paper from him. The *Independent* has apparently shifted its tagline for the Walker mess. WALKIN' THROUGH HECK-UVA WEEK, the headline blares, and underneath it is a split image. The left side is a picture of Claire's dainty leg, retreating into a town car as Robert turns around, glaring at the photographers. He's hunched over Nixon-style, minus the victory arms.

The right side is an image of Fern and me, emerging from court. Hardly the composed face of professionalism, I'm clutching Fern's arm and looking straight through the camera, my eyes wide and stunned, my mouth slightly agape. The effect is twelve-year-old caught making prank calls. Fern fares slightly better; she's behind me, head down.

Once upstairs, I cruise by Lillian's office. She's not there yet, so I skim the paper. Robert Walker is out of a job as of yesterday's emergency vote of the board of directors. There's a quote from one of the board members about how Options needed a "new face and new leadership," and how Robert Walker's "personal drama and decisions" were distracting him from the mission of Options. I have a feeling that the last bit is a tacked-on reason, but I'm happy to have played a small part in his discomfort.

There's not much about the trial, just some quotes from an anonymous source that Robert is being accused of monstrous treatment of his children and ex-wife. Oh, and there's that tiny little line on page 3 about Fern being represented by Molly Grant, who works at the premier law firm Bacon Payne.

Duck calls at nine, to inform me I'm in the paper, front page! Hers is the first call heralding texts and e-mails from nearly everyone I know: Holt's fraternity buddies, law school friends, Kevin, Caleb. Apparently, most of the people in my life only claim to read the *New York Times*.

I walk by Lillian's empty office a few more times and when I see that her light's been turned on, I pace by Kim's desk. She shakes her head. "In a meeting. Not back yet."

Oh, to not care. To wrap myself in the romantic cloud from last night and, impervious to the nerves, glide to the guillotine with a smile. It's a job, a stupid, horrible, overly demanding job. But no matter how I slice it, I do care. I don't want to become a laughingstock in this field. I don't want to be fired; I don't want to fail on my student loan payments and have to move out of my lovely little studio apartment to go sponge off my parents instead of finally giving back to them. And of all these things, at this moment, I am most terrified of facing the music with Lillian, knowing that whatever she says when she publicly eviscerates me will be accurate.

Gliding around the circumference of the thirty-seventh floor like a deranged shark, one cogent thought forms in my mind. I have spent the majority of the last five years contorting myself, trying to stick to a plan despite the increasing complexity and discomfort of doing so. No wonder I recognized the inflexiblity of Risa's trial strategy; I'd used the same idée fixe for my life. How have I worked here and not gotten it—this is what people do: we obligate ourselves, we make vows, and then we second-guess, things shift, the landscape changes. Some promises cannot withstand forever, and the most we can do when they break is to recognize that and figure out how to regroup and what we want instead. What I want, I finally realize, has nothing to do with Lillian. Whatever she doles out will have no real consequences to my big picture.

At nine forty-five, my phone rings.

"Molly Grant."

A clipped female voice responds. "Molly, Dominic Pizaro would like to see you in his office."

"Now?"

"Yes, now."

I swallow hard. Standing up to Lillian is one thing. Dominic Pizaro is a whole other sport.

like the louvre, if the guards were assassins

This is my first time in Dominic Pizaro's office. Unsurprisingly, he's got the whole King of the Hill setup: dramatic views, a huge desk that acts as a barrier from the riffraff and, mounted directly behind his desk, an oil painting whose proportions, if I'm honest, are a bit too small for the space.

Odd choice, I think, but then, staring at it, I remember some vague grumblings from around the time that Dominic became chairman and realize that it's the Miró. Dominic had pissed off some of the partners by removing the firm's prize possession from the communal hallway and mounting it on the wall in his personal office.

I stare, hoping to find something big in the painting, something that makes my current predicament seem petty in comparison. Alas, when I squint at the spiny abstract black figures against a red and blue background, all I can think of are spiders and blood. This could, of course, have less to do with the Miró than the mood of the room.

Lillian and Everett are here, in the guest chairs to the left. This makes sense. I am being notified that, thanks to the article, my screwup affects the entire matrimonial group, as well as the firm. I am momentarily grateful that Henry is in court this morning. Firing someone you just slept with must be an irreversible Miss Manners "Don't": "Hey, last night was magic, but please remove yourself from the premises. Don't let this get in the way of the new us!"

In addition to Lillian and Everett, there's a man I vaguely recognize sitting on the couch across the room. He is wearing a plaid shirt and glasses and I assume he's some sort of HR person, here to make sure this is done according to the book. Hopefully this means Lillian won't stab me.

I work up the courage to glance around the room. Lillian's face is fairly neutral, but her eyes blaze with disgust. Everett smiles at me and then looks down quickly, as though he had briefly forgotten that I am now an untouchable. Dominic nods to a chair to the right of Lillian, and I perch on the edge of it.

"So, you're quite the little front-page story," he says.

I nod. No disagreeing with that.

"Look, Molly. You've been a good employee. Good billables, good reviews, obviously loyal to the firm." He looks down at a sheet on the desk in front of him that I assume confirms all of this. It must have been rushed to him early this morning after he barked at someone to find out who the fuck is this Molly Grant twerp. He looks me dead in the eye. "So, I gotta ask. What the hell was this move?"

I open my mouth, but he continues talking.

"It's a total mess. You could've really cost the firm a lot in PR, maybe even legal fees, business. It could've been miserable."

Wait. Did he say "could have"?

"You're lucky it worked out." He gives a little chuckle.

What? I look confusedly at Lillian, who is sporting the same expression that she had after Liesel's cross-examination: tight, fake smile and violent eyes.

Dominic takes a swig of coffee from one of those small blue cardboard cups, selected, I'm sure, to make his hands look bigger. "So, listen. Walker is looking like a total ass in this. You know he was voted off the board yesterday?"

"Yes."

"And you know what that means, right?"

I smile uncertainly.

"He's tainted goods. Options is washing their hands. What better than to have the same law firm that represented his poor, victimized ex-wife represent their business interests? We're like the anti-Walker firm. And that's a great place to be this week. You know Bart Luce?" Dominic doesn't wait for me to answer. "New CEO there. He used to date my sister, long story—anyway, he suggested I meet with the general counsel over there to pitch. We're set up for today. And honestly, this is all thanks to your little stunt."

I smile faintly and nod. Um, you're welcome?

"So, listen. You know Frank?" He gestures to the man on the couch.

"No."

"Oh. Hmph. Frank, guess we need to up your profile with the associates."

Frank nods in earnest.

"Frank does press."

I give Frank a tentative wave and he leans forward on the couch. "Molly, we really want to capitalize on the news cycle here. You'll do some interviews this week, figure out your talking points, you know. Your bosses have generously agreed to let us monopolize your afternoon for prep."

Dominic holds up my newspaper cover and gives me the once-over. "You could present well, but this picture of you is crap. Frank, make sure you get her comfortable in front of the camera."

Frank gives the thumbs-up and I have a flash of the Julia Roberts shopping scene from *Pretty Woman*. Maybe if I sit here long enough, Dominic will hand me an American Express Black Card and tell me to go treat myself to an Armani suit and some highlights.

"Oh, and there's one more thing. Your bosses told me that this isn't technically a Bacon Payne case?"

"No, I sort—I took it on myself. I—"

He holds up one hand. "Just sign a consent to change attorney and get retainers to Ms. Walker today. Last day of trial was?"

"Yesterday."

"Okay. You doing posttrial papers?"

"Yes, a brief."

"Okay, we should be counsel of record for that and going forward. We'll win this thing, right?"

"We should."

"All right. Well, better if we do, but I guess it doesn't matter in the scheme of things. Oh, tell me what you've collected so far."

"Um, it's sort of been pro bono—"

He holds up his hands and gapes for a second, looking around the room exaggeratedly. "You did pro bono on a case involving Robert Walker? Your balls are so big they're crowding out your business sense, I guess." He sighs, obviously disappointed in me. "Well, talk to Cecilia in accounting and we'll get everything collected. Don't worry, don't worry. You'll see some of it in your year-end bonus, right, Lillian?"

"Of course," Lillian says quickly, ever the team player.

"Yeah. Molly, your bosses are very relieved that this worked out so they can keep you on. You know if it hadn't worked out so well . . ." He trails off and draws one hand across his neck and laughs.

We all pretend to laugh along with him.

"Well, thank you for the second chance," I say to the room.

Lillian is nodding emphatically, but I can tell that one thing she is absolutely not is relieved to keep me on.

wait

Henry grabs a tuna roll with his chopsticks. "So. Do you want to talk about it?"

I nod to the empty third chair. "You mean that elephant chilling out right there?"

It's Sunday night, and my posttrial brief is due in Walker tomorrow. I can't avoid it any longer.

"Yep, I mean the elephant. You've been uncharacteristically silent."

"I have no clue what I should do."

"Okay. On the one hand . . . you stay."

"Which means I get the Payne-ment, no debt, guaranteed income, a big bonus. I get to work with you—"

"Right. A potential ethical quagmire, but a good time regardless."

"—but on the flip side, I'd still be at the firm, which means I would have to work with Lillian."

"You're kind of in the safety zone. What could she do to you now?"

"That's probably true."

"And if you don't sign, your option is what?"

"Going home while I figure out what I want to do."

"Sure, that's one option." He pauses. "Did you like trying the case for Fern?"

"Yeah, I loved it, actually. You know I loved it."

"Well, why stop? Have you ever thought about just running with Molly Grant, PC?"

"Of course I have. I've thought about it a ton, but what I keep coming back to is that I have no money and no clients."

"You have one client."

"But her case is over tomorrow, so yeah, after that, I'd just be out there, swinging in the wind." The thought terrifies me. I put down my chopsticks, which I've been fruitlessly dipping into my soy sauce tin. "Which means no income, which means I default on my loan payments, which means I have to file for bankruptcy—"

"Which means being thrown out on the street. Which means being homeless. Which means becoming a mole person. Yeah, I think I see where you're going with this. You could always just stay with me, you know."

"That's sweet, Henry. It warms my heart that you would interfere before I became a mole person, but I have real bills. I can't just dump them on you."

I go over to my bag to fish out the manila folder holding Bacon Payne's consent-to-change-attorney form and the retainer. I had asked Fern to sign both the day that I met with Dominic. She looked at me like I was crazy, but said she'd do whatever I wanted. They've been in my bag since then, safe in a manila file folder, traveling everywhere I go.

I put the folder on the table and hand Henry a pen.

Henry looks at me. "You really want me to sign these? Okay, here goes." He gives the pen a dramatic click. "Fern Walker is about to become a client of Bacon Payne."

"Wait," I say.

four months later

Four months later, I get out of the elevator along with some standard inhabitants of the third floor of the Manhattan Supreme Court: a puffy-eyed female client and her suited forty-something lawyer. I pull back the sleeve of my winter coat and check my watch as I round the hall to the benches outside Judge Traynor's courtroom. Fifteen minutes until my client shows up. Jason Manolo is the vice president of global product marketing at Bakers Brands, improbably referred by his former colleague, Marie Washington, Fern's friend. I sit down, BlackBerry in hand, and dial the office.

Phone pressed to my cheek, I look around. It's a little after nine and the hallway is filling up with Judge Traynor's morning audience: lawyers, clients, witnesses.

I swear, I sense her before I even see her: a steely block of cold to my left that makes the hair on my neck snap to attention.

I hang up the phone before anyone picks up and turn my head. Sure enough, Lillian is standing in the middle of the hall, her eyes darting around the room. I haven't seen her since August, in that meeting in Dominic Pizaro's office. Her eyes meet mine and she freezes, utter revulsion storming across her face. I look away quickly, but then channel Lot's wife and glance back again. Lillian is beaming at me, her smile wide, her arms outstretched.

Walking toward her, I wonder if I imagined the whole thing. "Hi, Lillian."

She puts the tips of her fingernails on my shoulders and leans a millimeter closer. "Mwah." There's a lot more air than kiss in the greeting.

"Hi, Molly." Jane, her hair up in a twist, her eyes as bright as ever, stands a step behind Lillian, her left hand wrapped around a rolling litigation bag.

"Hey, Jane. Great to see you."

Lillian puts her arm around Jane and gives a little squeeze. "This girl, let me tell you. I have never had an associate as sharp as this one. She is one to watch." A hint of concern shades her voice. "So, how are you? Is everything okay, dear? I haven't heard of you in ages. What on earth have you been doing with yourself?" There's a smile pasted on her face, but Lillian's gaze is bouncing around the hall, at Jane, at the wall.

Jane looks confused and opens her mouth to say something. I stare at her, silently urging her to play silent and dumb.

"I went out on my own," I say. "About three months ago."

"Oh, you hung out your own shingle. What fun. You getting some nice little cases?" Her tone of voice would be perfect if I were a Maltese who had just rolled over to have my belly scratched.

I smile. "I'm doing okay. I've got a few already."

"Okay? You're doing great," Jane says. She looks at Lillian. "You didn't hear about Molly's parental alienation case for Fern Walker? She won everything for her client: full custody, a huge amount of child support, counsel fees." She nods, impressed. "I read the article in the *Law Journal*. I can get you a copy, Lillian. How is Fern Walker doing?"

I received a text from Fern yesterday. *Swingers!* was the title, and it contained a picture of the kids, bundled up in winter coats, on the new swing set in their backyard. Anna was high off the ground, her legs pumping, her hair flying out behind her, a gap-toothed smile illuminating her features, and Connor was belly down on the swing, his arms stretched out like Superman.

"Oh, she's great. She moved to Putnam County with her kids. It's a transition but—"

Lillian's smile gets tighter and she cuts me off. "Oh, I didn't hear about that. So, what brings you here this morning? Dropping off some uncontested papers?"

"No, I'm meeting a client for a preliminary conference."

"Us too!" says Jane, like we're fourth-graders wearing the same unicorn T-shirt. "Wait. You're not the other side on Pickering, are you?"

Is that a flash of fear in Lillian's eyes?

I smile. "Not this time, but I'm sure we'll get a case together at some point soon."

"Now, wouldn't *that* be fun." Lillian's voice rings high and loud. She looks around again, somewhat frantically. "There's Selena. I've got to run. I'm trying to settle something with her. Darling, it was wonderful to see you. I hope we catch up soon, yes?" She waves an arm in my direction and starts walking away.

"Oh, I'll see you at the holiday party in a few weeks. We can catch up more then." At that, Lillian spins back around.

"The Bacon Payne holiday party? And why would you go to the holiday party, dear? You're no longer a Bacon Payne lawyer." She blinks pityingly, as though it kills her to break this news to me.

Jane looks at Lillian, surprised. I can tell she's wondering how such an impressive woman is so out of the loop. "She's probably going with Henry."

If she's processing for the first time that Henry and I are together, Lillian barely lets on. The only hint that her brain is imploding from the thought of having to see me on a regular basis is the rapidity with which she's blinking.

I nod. "So, I'll see you there? Oh, there's my client. Gotta run."

I can't help blowing Lillian a kiss. I wave and wink at Jane as I walk over to Jason, who is leaning against the wall, looking a bit paler than usual. "Was that Betsy's lawyer?"

"Nope. Just someone I used to work with."

Jason is trying to get out of a nine-month marriage to Betsy, while Betsy is desperately trying to stay in it. I put my hand on his shoulder. "How're you doing, Jason?"

"Never better," he says with an eye roll. "This is exactly how I want to spend my Tuesday. So, chief." Jason has taken to calling me chief, which I assume is his way of making peace with the fact that I am fifteen years his junior. "You're ready for today? You got it all figured out?" He is trying to sound light and breezy, but he swallows hard after he says it.

I know it's a rhetorical question and I know he's talking more to himself than to me, but seeing Lillian triggers me to seriously consider his inquiry. Do I have it figured out? Judging by my old standards—the ones I clung to so fiercely over the past five years—I'm empty-handed: no safe institutional clients, no fancy law firm job, no pot-of-gold Payne-ment making all my hard work worth it. And yet.

Jason is client number six at Molly Grant, PC, and I have generated enough fees from clients one through five to meet my personal expenses, lease a respectable Midtown office and hire an assistant—no loans required. All three members of the Grant family are loan-free, thanks to the counsel fees in *Walker v. Walker.* There will be an ebb and flow to my income, but it's happening. I'm making it happen. Tonight, after work, I'll go over to Henry's. We'll order in, crack each other up and curl up with our laptops for a little while until it's time to throw them aside. It might not be everyone's fantasy, but it works for me.

Do I have it all figured out?

"I'm ready, Jason," I say, getting up and motioning for him to follow me. "Don't worry. I got this."

Photo by Anne Joyce

L. Alison Heller is a divorce lawyer and mediator who started her own practice after working for several years in Manhattan law firms. She lives in Brooklyn with her husband and young daughters. *The Love Wars* is her first novel.

the love wars

L. Alison Heller

A CONVERSATION WITH
L. ALISON HELLER

Q. What made you choose the world of divorce law as the setting for your book? Do you hope readers walk away with an understanding of something specific about the world?

A. My years working at a big firm and as a divorce litigator in New York City were chock-full of surreal *How did I get here?* moments. I thought—many times—that someone should write a book about this unique world and its extremes. Eventually, that thought turned into *my* wanting to take a crack at writing such a book.

It's wonderful if readers walk away with an appreciation of how difficult and emotional the work is for both the lawyers and the litigants. That said, my goal was purely to entertain and *The Love Wars* is fiction. I am a strong believer in the power of the escapist novel, so I set out to write something that was fun, that hopefully makes people laugh and connect with the characters.

Q. How is being an author different from working in the legal field?

A. There are more similarities than one might think. The most talented lawyers that I've worked with have been great storytellers. From the beginning of a case, they start thinking in terms of constructing a narrative, weaving together a story to present to the judge and the other side. It's not lying; it's synthesizing—collecting the facts and organizing them around a salient, persuasive nugget.

In law school, I learned to obsess rather unhealthily over mountains of work. (This might have been a latent tendency of mine regardless, but going to law school was like rolling out the red carpet for that tendency and shining klieg lights on it.) I think my writing has benefited from my expectation to happily spend my days indoors staring at the computer, obsessively going over and over and over drafts. So, as you can see, both fields encourage balance. Balance and fresh air and exercise.

The big difference, of course, is that my characters are usually much more compliant than are flesh-and-blood client types—at least when I first meet them.

Q. In your work as a divorce lawyer, you've probably had the opportunity to meet a lot of different clients. Liesel stands out as a piece of work, though—brittle, demanding, cutting, miserable. Have you represented any clients like her, so difficult they made you as crazy as Liesel makes Molly?

A. I should probably equivocate here, but the short answer is yes. I have absolutely represented clients who have made me, er, frustrated, although Liesel is certainly not modeled on anyone specific. None of the characters in the book is based on any of my former clients—I couldn't write about them even if

I had wanted to (which I didn't), and Liesel's behaviors are the product of my imagination let loose.

What I did try to capture is how fraught the lawyer/client relationship can be in divorce litigation. In some ways, it's a no-win situation. Clients can be at their worst, understandably so—they are financially and emotionally stressed; many of them didn't initiate the divorce proceedings—and against that backdrop, suddenly decisions about the most intimate part of their family life are out of their control. It can be incredibly disorienting not to be able to do basic things—like pick up a child or choose a doctor or switch jobs—without judicial permission or consulting with their lawyer to see how those decisions dovetail with strategy.

As a younger lawyer, I didn't always understand that. When a client screamed at me or acted in a way that seemed unreasonable, I didn't always take the time to stop and understand the genesis of his or her strong emotion. I wanted to show that Molly found her clients annoying sometimes, but I also wanted to track her growth as a character in realizing what's at stake—even for someone as abrasive as Liesel—and what might be driving a client's actions beneath the surface.

Q. Where did you get the inspiration for Molly? The Love Wars *is a work of fiction, but is there some of you in her?*

A. Meaning have I ever taken on a secret second job because of my principles? Not even close! We're pretty different, Molly and I. Not only does she need less sleep—she's far tougher and braver than I am. When I was dreaming up the story, I kept wondering how it would evolve if the protagonist was a born fighter, which is really what Fern needs. Molly is human, though. She has faltering confidence; she questions herself, makes some bad decisions and is too eager to please (these are the parts of her I relate to the most, of course), but she is, at heart, a fierce advocate. She's totally got the eye of the tiger where Robert Walker is concerned. When I was writing all of the courtroom and confrontation scenes, I was so glad Molly had to do them instead of me. If I were in her shoes, I would have been hiding in the bathroom, hyperventilating into a paper bag.

Q. *What does it take to survive at a cutthroat law firm? Did your experiences inform Molly's personality when you started to write* The Love Wars?

A. I knew that Molly needed a sense of humor. There is so much that is serious and heartbreaking in matrimonial law, but there is so much that's comical in the world of big law firms. I wanted Molly to be able to comment on and bring the reader into that ridiculousness a little, and hopefully readers will respond to her enough to let her do that.

Q. *Did you find it challenging to strike a balanced tone for the reader in* The Love Wars? *How did you strive to contrast the seriousness of Molly's responsibilities with the comic relief her friends and colleagues provide?*

A. Finding that balance was very important to me, and I spent a lot of time thinking about how to do it effectively. I was striving for the book to have a light, humorous tone, but in a way that didn't undermine the pain of divorce. One way to do that was infusing the plot with comedy through the law firm culture and the character's quirks, especially Liesel and Molly's fellow associates.

Also, Molly and Henry like to joke with each other, and they both appreciate a certain gallows humor, which is not as rare in a law firm as you might think. Seriously, some lawyers do make jokes at work. I've personally borne witness.

Q. Molly has some wonderful love interests. Did you know as soon as you met Henry that he was the right guy for her? And with marriages dissolving all around her, how did Molly find the optimism and courage to deal with the dating scene?

A. Caleb has his moments, but he really can't compete. Molly and Henry are a team. They make each other better: He helps her focus and achieve and she broadens his horizons, which is good because while I am very fond of Henry, he can get a bit myopic and needs some shaking up.

That's a great question about Molly's ability to delve into the dating scene while working as a divorce lawyer. I've told people (only when asked, not, like, strangers on the street) that I am so grateful I was already married when I became a divorce lawyer. I've always thought it would be difficult to date and plan your wedding with arcane knowledge of what comprises marital property jutting into your cloud of romantic bliss.

Molly is a romantic, though. Seeing all the people in pain around her because of love derailed isn't enough to scare her.

Eventually, she's mature enough to say—I get it, things change, people change, and I've got to just grab happiness when I can.

Q. Speaking of the world of big law firms, was Bacon Payne modeled after places you've actually been employed?

A. Bacon Payne is a bit of an exaggeration, but really, not as much as you might think. There's a lot of silliness in big law firms, and I've speculated that this might be because lawyers are not trained to be managers—a lot of them, dare I say it, are not what one would call "people persons"—and yet they manage these huge businesses with tons of employees and hierarchy. Bacon Payne culture is based on what I've personally observed or what I've heard from friends who worked at other big firms. Some universal big firm truths: Expect a surfeit of alcohol and forced socializing at events, a combination that encourages embarrassing behavior. Expect to put in a lot of face time—i.e., sitting available at your desk with a ready smile, even when there's nothing to do. Expect beautiful onsite amenities—gyms and dining rooms and dry cleaning and snacks and sodas—so you never, ever have to leave. It's kind of like the Hotel California but with an annual billing requirement.

My one disclaimer is that I didn't practice matrimonial law at a big firm. I started working as a divorce lawyer at a small boutique firm where my colleagues had the expectation of working hard all day and then going home and maintaining some semblance of a life as well. There was no shortage of characters and strong personalities in that firm, to be sure, but the culture was different.

Q. You continued to practice family law while writing The Love Wars. *What's next for you in terms of balancing the law and writing?*

A. I still practice law, but I had, literally, the time of my life writing Molly's story. I have two little kids, love spending time with my family and am not the world's most efficient person, so the fact that I keep writing is testament only to my passion for it. There's nothing like the process of creating these characters and getting ridiculously and unnaturally attached to them. I've completed my second novel, which was even more fun and challenging to write than the first, and that will be out next year, and right now, I'm working on my third.

I'm also gearing up to talk to book clubs and groups about *The Love Wars* and would love to speak to yours. If you have any interest, you can contact me through my Web site at www .lalisonheller.com